WITHDRAWN
FROM
COLLECTION

THE GATE
TO FUTURES
PAST

The Finest in DAW Science Fiction and Fantasy
by JULIE E. CZERNEDA:

THE CLAN CHRONICLES:

Stratification:
REAP THE WILD WIND (#1)
RIDERS OF THE STORM (#2)
RIFT IN THE SKY (#3)

The Trade Pact:
A THOUSAND WORDS FOR STRANGER (#1)
TIES OF POWER (#2)
TO TRADE THE STARS (#3)

Reunification:
THIS GULF OF TIME AND STARS (#1)
THE GATE TO FUTURES PAST (#2)
TO GUARD AGAINST THE DARK (#3)*

* ✳ *

NIGHT'S EDGE:
A TURN OF LIGHT (#1)
A PLAY OF SHADOW (#2)

* ✳ *

SPECIES IMPERATIVE:
SURVIVAL (#1)
MIGRATION (#2)
REGENERATION (#3)

* ✳ *

WEB SHIFTERS:
BEHOLDER'S EYE (#1)
CHANGING VISION (#2)
HIDDEN IN SIGHT (#3)

* ✳ *

IN THE COMPANY OF OTHERS

*Coming soon from DAW Books

THE GATE TO FUTURES PAST

Reunification #2

Julie E. Czerneda

DAW BOOKS, INC.
DONALD A. WOLLHEIM, FOUNDER
375 Hudson Street, New York, NY 10014

ELIZABETH R. WOLLHEIM
SHEILA E. GILBERT
PUBLISHERS
www.dawbooks.com

Copyright © 2016 by Julie E. Czerneda.

All Rights Reserved.

Jacket art by Matt Stawicki.

Jacket designed by G-Force Design.

Jacket photograph by Roger Czerneda.

DAW Book Collectors No. 1732.

Published by DAW Books, Inc.
375 Hudson Street, New York, NY 10014.

All characters and events in this book are fictitious.
Any resemblance to persons living or dead is strictly coincidental.

The scanning, uploading, and distribution of this book via the Internet or via any other means without the permission of the publisher is illegal, and punishable by law. Please purchase only authorized electronic editions, and do not participate in or encourage the electronic piracy of copyrighted materials. Your support of the author's rights is appreciated.

First Printing, September 2016
1 2 3 4 5 6 7 8 9

DAW TRADEMARK REGISTERED
U.S. PAT. AND TM. OFF. AND FOREIGN COUNTRIES
—MARCA REGISTRADA
HECHO EN U.S.A.

PRINTED IN THE U.S.A.

**To Lili Pasternak, Mentor, Friend, and Colleague, and to the
Biology Department of the University of Waterloo.**

Looking back, my career's been shaped most by tiny dynamos. While I'm hardly tall, and may have been compared to a power generator myself, each time I've been with any of these three women? In the company of giants, plain and simple. I've talked about my fiction editor-dear and publisher, Sheila Gilbert of DAW. In the final book of this trilogy, I'll introduce you to my non-fiction editor and publisher. Today?

It's time you learned of Lili Pasternak. (Unless you attended the University of Waterloo in the almost thirty years she was there.) To me, Lili was the face and voice of biology. Literally. I walked into my first lab, breathless with excitement and some trepidation—after all, this was UNIVERSITY—to be confronted by rows of television screens, each filled the image of a dapper, dark-haired woman in an immaculate lab coat.

Busy staring, I tripped over a stool. Understand, this was 1973. Not even science fiction had prepared me for a virtual teacher.

Lili was far more than that. Yes, her videos introduced every lab, from procedure to her expectations, but I grew convinced she lived in the hall where the labs were taking place, ever-available, ever-ready to help. I'd spot her approaching—didn't matter that her students were taller—and feel awe. That glorious white lab coat. That efficient calm.

Here was Science.

As Lili's husband Jack will tell you (Dr. Jack Pasternak, Professor Emeritus), of course Lili didn't live in Biology II; she simply was there when her students needed her. Later, when I came back to U. of W. as staff (stepping into Lili's shoes, in fact, though I never dared the videos), we became great friends. Lili hosted a baby shower for our first child. She even helped arrange the Octoberfest reunion with staff for our "Bunch" of graduates.

As for my career? Lili showed me the joy that is teaching science and was responsible for my first work as a non-fiction author: I revised and updated the lab manuals. The ones from which she'd originally taught me, a privilege indeed.

I'd like to thank the University of Waterloo and all who've shared and share their love of science and learning there. You let me romp in what I love best, under the guidance of extraordinary professors such as Drs. Hynes, Morton, Thompson, and Hawthorn, to name but a few. Bonus? You've given me friends for life, including that chemistry partner I married, Roger.

And you gave me, and so many, Lili Pasternak.

Missed, but never forgotten.

Acknowledgments

How about that cover? Matt Stawicki, you are a genius! Thank you. My thanks also to the fine folks at DAW. Josh, you never cease to amaze with your dedication to quality and how you find ways to answer my authorly whims. Sheila, we'll be down to celebrate.

Drumroll, please, dear readers. It worked!

I refer to *This Gulf of Time and Stars,* my return to the story of Sira and Morgan begun so long ago, I've decided to call it "then." Then, I'd no idea where it would go or that anyone else would read it. Now? Oh now, I do know, and you've come along with me. Thank you.

Especially those who dared be first to blurb, for this was a great deal to ask. Hey, read my novel, it's about stuff you haven't seen before or if you have, it was . . . "then!" My heartfelt gratitude to these fantastic authors whose work I love, for reading mine for me: Doranna Durgin, Kari Sperring, Violette Malan, Vonda McIntyre (who read *Gulf* while packing to be the Worldcon GOH!), Stephen Leigh, Marie Bilodeau, Ursula Pflug, Kristi Charish, Catherine Asaro, Tobias Buckell, and Rhondi Salsitz (as Jenna Rhodes). And, because time travel works in here, I'm able to thank Karina Sumner-Smith for crying (twice) over *Gate.* When you can do that to your friends? Life is good.

When a blog tour works, why not triple it? (Ask me one day.) I was hosted around the world online for the 21 days of my #Time-AndStarsTour and, while I've no room to name all of my wonderful blog hosts here, please know how very much I appreciate your hard work, enthusiasm, and skill. We rocked the internet! I'm grateful to DAW Books, particularly Katie Hoffman, Sarah Guan, and Nita Basu, for prizes and support, as well as Audible books for theirs. Allyson Johnson? Fun, wasn't it? Thanks!

There's one host I must acknowledge. For years, SF Signal has been The Place to celebrate—and think—about genre work. You've been a mainstay for myself and so many. John, Kristin, and Paul, thank you from the bottom of my heart. It's been a honor. And Paul? What you've said about my work has inspired me and I won't forget.

There've been adventures in the real world too. Thanks, Coldwater Steampunk, for hosting me, and to Nicola and Saskatoon's Word on the Street for making me part of your excellent festival. The University of Saskatchewan Biology Department welcomed me back with open arms, giving me memories to treasure. Thank you all, especially Interim Dean Peta Bonham-Smith, Professor Jeanette Lynes, and Biology Department Head Ken Wilson. Thanks also to Betsy Rosenwald for publicity and Dot Clemens-Brown, who took excellent care of me. When I dedicated *Gulf* to Jan, I never imagined returning to USask or that we'd sit together at Timmies to talk about him again. My deepest thanks to Jean Smith and her family for their welcome.

As if 2015 wasn't great enough, (and it was, trust me) I'd SF-Contario and Canvention. Thank you, readers, for surprising me so utterly with the Prix Aurora Award for Best Novel (for *A Play of Shadow*) that I cried out, "WHaaaAT?!" Eloquent, that. (Thanks, Chris, for the after party and all else.)

The winner of the DUFF (Down Under Fan Fund) auction, Alex Lindsay, generously gave me his family to tuck into this book as characters. Hi Family! Surprise! Alison (*Alisi Di*), Paul the navy guy (*Pauvan Di*), and Emily (*Milly Su*). I hope you enjoy what I've done to you. Other character-namers continued into this book and I'd like to acknowledge them as well: Holly (*Holl*) and Lee (*Leesems*), as well as Ruth and Tim (*Ruti*). It's been a ride and I'm thrilled you were part of it. Those who know me will guess the brothers-three now become planets (*Yont, Hilip,* and *Oger*). Welcome, Susan Bound and Lee Datzell (*Susibou Di/ Susi di Annk* and *Lee di Annk*). Susan, thank you for so generously sharing your memories of Andre Norton with me. And my hearty congratulations to Agatha and Brad, fans of Sira and Morgan. Clear skies!

To our beloved Kate, Kevin, Josh, and Alfie. Here's to summer barbeques, gardens, wildlife, and the Bills. The path between's a bit longer now; it'll always be open.

To my family, wherever you may be when reading this. Stop and pinch yourselves every so often, because isn't life amazing? (By all means, say "WHaaaAT?" too.)

Last and never least, thank you, dear readers.

To quote Roger?

"Let the adventure begin!"

Previously, in the Clan Chronicles

Sira di Sarc could pass for Human. She isn't. She's one of the humanoid Clan, aliens who live, scattered, on Human worlds. The Clan have an innate ability to move their thoughts—and bodies—through the dimensionless M'hir, an ability they use to manipulate Humans vulnerable to mental suggestion and to keep their true nature secret.

Sira is the most powerful of her kind yet born, and a Chooser, a female ready to Join for life and Commence, her body becoming reproductively mature. To the dismay of her kind, no unChosen is a match for her strength in the M'hir; should they try, she can't help but kill them. Deliberate breeding for greater strength has brought the Clan to this, and Sira knows she's only the first. Within a generation no Joinings will be possible. The Clan faces extinction.

Desperate for a solution, willing to experiment only on herself, Sira blocks all memory of who and what she is, adding compulsions to seek out a Human telepath and attempt to Join with him. Clan find Humans repugnant, their vast numbers terrifying. Sira's hope, however faint, is that being near one with a similar Power will trigger her body to Commence.

Instead, she meets Jason Morgan, captain of the *Silver Fox* and learns how to love.

Together, her mind and memory restored, Sira and Morgan fend off attempts by the Clan and others to seize Sira's Power for themselves. In so doing, they learn the M'hir isn't simply a dangerous void, but filled with its own version of life, including the Rugherans, who exist there and here. Sira assumes leadership of her people and, with the help of Enforcer Lydis Bowman, brings the Clan into the Trade Pact.

Surely, with the expertise of thousands of other species, her own can be saved.

But the Clan didn't evolve in Human space. They arrived there, through the M'hir, having fled their original home. Their memories were left behind and most Clan believed their kind went through a stratification, into those able to use the M'hir and those who could not. All they have is a handful of tattered belongings and family names. To most Clan, including Sira, their past is unimportant.

They are wrong.

The Clan have forgotten they were once the Om'ray, sharing the planet Cersi with the sluglike Oud and the agile Tikitik. Oud and Tikitik managed separate Clans of Om'ray, each in their place, providing each the necessities of life.

And ending that life when they chose.

One of Sira's ancestors was Aryl Sarc, also powerful. Aryl was the first Om'ray to detect the M'hir and to move through it. She was the first to meet and befriend a totally new sort of being, a Human named Marcus Bowman. For Cersi was a world of interest to those who traveled the stars, rumored to be possessed of singular treasure: relics of the Hoveny Concentrix, the greatest interstellar civilization ever known. Marcus and his people arrived first, to conduct research and observe.

Others came to pillage.

Already strained by the rise of new abilities in the Om'ray, the pirate incursion disrupted the Balance, the agreement between Cersi's races. The Oud and Tikitik lashed out, Om'ray caught between. Marcus was captured by pirates and tortured. Aryl gathered her people, the M'hiray, to do the only thing they could:

run. They believed without them, the Balance would be restored and the rest of the Om'ray be saved. Using a device to strip away their connection and memories of Cersi, Aryl and her people used Marcus' final memory to decide where to go, for the M'hir has no markers or guide, only remembered places.

Their great Passage brought the M'hiray into a part of the universe teeming with Humans and other strange aliens, adrift on a world full of technology they didn't understand and faced with dangers they couldn't have imagined. Desperate, Aryl and the others hunted for help only to find the wrong kind. Criminals tried to kill them for the Hoveny artifacts they'd brought, and they were forced to use their Power against Humans to survive. Afraid of the consequences, the M'hiray used their new wealth to buy seclusion and privacy. Calling themselves the Clan, they made secrecy their new way of life, protecting it with their abilities.

But choices made generations ago create consequences of their own. When Sira exposes her people in order to find them a future, she also exposes them to their waiting enemies. The Clan of the Trade Pact are decimated by attacks coordinated by those they'd once manipulated, carried out by the alien Assemblers. They flee back to Cersi. Sira, their leader still, carries new life within her, life created by parthenogenesis and filled with the stored consciousness of her ancestor Aryl. They find themselves in the Cloisters of Sona, but there's no welcome waiting.

Cersi's Om'ray are on the brink of annihilation, for the Balance was never restored between Tikitik and Oud. The Oud are now in ascendance, their new Minded caste hunting Om'ray who can awaken the Hoveny technology they covet. The Om'ray are trapped where they live, dying as the Oud reshape their world. Only the Vyna Clan are safe, able to travel through the M'hir, but they use their ability to dreadful purpose: stealing children and resources from other clans.

Morgan and the newly arrived M'hiray scientists uncover the truth: that Cersi was an experiment designed to test if Om'ray could become capable of using the M'hir. The giant Cloisters are starships, not buildings, built to maintain and monitor the participants. Although begun as a cooperative venture between Om'ray, Oud, and Tikitik, the experiment faltered, imprisoning them all until even the memory of why they'd come and who they'd been was lost.

Until now. Sira is the culmination of those long-ago hopes, as are the other M'hiray, returned at last. Sona's starship reveals they are the descendants of the Hoveny and heirs to that civilization's technology. Guided by the starship's memory, Sira and the others activate its great engines using the power of the M'hir. They lift from Cersi in time to escape the Oud. Trying to do the same, the Vyna are caught by the Rugherans.

Sona's starship travels through subspace, carrying the M'hiray who survived the Trade Pact, the Om'ray who survived Cersi, and one Human. Its course was set before the Trade Pact existed and its hapless passengers must wait to learn their destination.

And if it is, at last, their home.

Subspace

Prelude

DAMAGE . . .
   Though infinitesimal, the gashes *bleed*, drawing the ever-hungry.

Though shallow, the wounds do not heal, being between reality and *something* other.

Damage . . .

Those who hunt Power gather. Mindless, they extend what aren't mouths and begin to feed. They fight for position, greedy and never-full.

Scattering when attacked, for their frenzy attracts those larger and more deadly to the feast.

Damage . . .

Feast . . .

In AllThereIs, a matter of perspective.

* **✳** *

The starship cut through subspace with the ease of a knife through soft flesh, systems dormant since their construction at last awake, carrying the answer to a desperate hope, not that it knew.

An answer late in coming, not that it cared.

For its builders were dust and their sacrifice for the future?

Scars upon the past.

Chapter 1

"THIS IS NEW." If glaring could melt metal, the innocuous green wall in front of me would be a puddle. Of course, if anything about our present situation paid attention to what I wanted—I glared harder. Take a walk, I'd suggested. Have a precious moment alone, I'd thought. Was that asking too much?

Apparently so, hence the new wall. My hair, the ever-expressive feature of a Chosen Clanswoman, writhed against my back and shoulders. Even if I could control it, there was no keeping my aggravation from my Chosen, the barrier between our thoughts and emotions thinned when we were alone, as now.

Chuckling, Jason Morgan lowered his scanner. "New to us," he concurred. "But according to these readings, this bulkhead could have been in place as long as anything on the ship. Impressive tech."

Inconvenient, annoying—I'd a list. "Impressive" wasn't on it.

When Sona Clan's Cloisters had been a building with its foundation properly in the ground—half submerged in a swamp, to be exact—this wide corridor had spiraled up the levels used by the Om'ray. The corridor, like the rest of the building, was illuminated by strips of light where walls met the ceiling, walls featuring tall arched windows interspersed with framed panels on the outermost side, with a series of doors to small rooms on the inner.

When the Cloisters became a starship, more changed than its location. Along this corridor the lighting remained the same, but windows had disappeared behind green metal plates. The panels glowed in varied colors, linked by pulsating blue lines across walls and ceiling, lines that converged to wrap the frames of those now-sealed doors.

While behind those doors, filling what we'd believed spare, empty rooms, was seething *darkness*. The starship, built by the Hoveny, had been designed to draw power from the M'hir, something it could only do once we, their descendants, followed its instructions and *brought* the M'hir here to be harnessed.

All of which was quite reassuring in a building that roared its way into the sky and beyond so we could escape certain death.

What wasn't? The starship, *Sona,* hadn't stopped its self-modification. Once moving through subspace, walls like the one in our way began to appear, severing some rooms or, as now, sealing off stretches of corridor.

These paled beside other changes. Doors once locked now opened, with others sealed. Lifts stopped at levels previously unknown to any of the Om'ray Adepts on board.

The same lifts bypassed levels once in use; according to Morgan's scanner, they'd been collapsed, as though the ship folded sheets for storage.

At least it waited until those spaces were empty—leading to a brief experiment where we left belongings everywhere, but the ship knew the difference between living and stuff and we only had so many socks—which wasn't the point.

From early childhood, the Clan moved by *pushing* our bodies through the M'hir. So long as the distance, translated by the M'hir into subjective time, was within an individual's strength, all we needed was a remembered place, called a locate.

Locates *Sona* kept removing.

Another reason, I thought grimly, we couldn't trust the ship. Hadn't its programming proved fallible already? When we—the M'hiray—first arrived, it had used a device called a Maker to forcibly alter our minds. It blocked our memories, giving us false ones to suit our new lives on Cersi, complete with skills and the local language. Being able to converse with our cousins, the Om'ray, had been vital; being transformed into eager farmers prepared to live near the Oud, when the land outside was Tikitik and a water-ruled jungle?

The error came close to costing our lives.

Fortunately, before it did, Morgan had saved us all. The Maker had no effect on his Human mind, and he'd helped us return to our former selves, though we retained the implanted information. With one exception. Me.

For some reason comprehensible only to the shipbrain, I remained its Keeper: the ancient ship's sole conduit to those aboard. Another mistake, for the person who should be Keeper stood beside me, diligently running his scanner along the seam between new wall and old.

The supple brown vest Morgan wore, with its useful array of hidden pockets, was old, though still new to me. The beginning beard, dark brown with a trace of red in certain light was new to me as well, the why of it another mystery. Clan didn't grow such facial hair; my Chosen may have sported a bristled chin on occasion, but never for long. As I'd grown to like the feel of it, I asked no questions.

Jason Morgan, however, would have a reason. He was careful and methodical by nature, leaving nothing to chance, traits that had made him a superb starship captain. More than anyone here, he understood space travel—and machines.

I'd a history of breaking them, especially any with plumbing, and suspected *Sona* had figured that out for itself. The ship had lifted on my command; it hadn't obeyed me about anything more important than lighting since.

That didn't stop me trying. I glared at the new wall. *Sona,* I sent, gaining the ship's instant attention.

>*Keeper, what is your will?*< The reply wasn't in mindspeech, not the sort we used. This was unsettlingly more as if the ship had stuck something in my head to allow me to receive a transmission.

Stop doing this!

The ship's voice remained placid. *>I require specifics, Keeper. What is it you wish stopped?<*

Servo brain. I gave up. *Nothing. Everything's fine. Wonderful.* Nine shipdays since leaving Cersi. Nine shipdays, I'd tried to argue with it. Tried commanding it to restore a level. Tried ordering the ship to shut itself down which, in hindsight, might not have been the right approach. It didn't help having Morgan caution me, several times, to not ask it anything at all.

In case it finally decided to obey, that was.

"Tell me how this makes sense," I muttered. "Why close off a perfectly useful corridor?" Except to be a nuisance, which by now wouldn't surprise me.

Morgan tucked away his scanner and patted the wall approvingly. "My take? *Sona*'s conserving resources. It was built to carry more."

The *Fox* had been "she," but nothing about *Sona* was like our former home.

Nothing was.

"How many more?" I'd led one hundred and ten M'hiray to Cersi, fleeing Trade Pact space. Eight had died within days, for Cersi proved no safer; worse, our coming led to disaster. The Oud decided to end their part of the Agreement and violently reshaped the world.

Of our cousins, the Om'ray, seventy-seven survived our arrival. Not our doing.

Our fault—my fault—all the same.

Two more had slipped away our first night in subspace, but they'd been Lost and already gone from us: Cha sud Kessa'at, once Chosen of Deni, and Ures di Yode, once Chosen of Tekla, the Sona scout who'd given her life in a futile attempt to save Deni from a clawed nightmare. That the final remnants of their minds stayed behind with their Chosen, in the M'hir around Cersi, was to me, a mercy.

None of us said it, but I knew the rest believed as I did, that we, the one hundred and seventy-eight now on board, were all that remained of the Clan.

Plus one Human.

Presently shaking his head, blue eyes somber. "Sira. Don't." We both knew, even if *Sona* could have transported thousands, it made no difference now.

I wrinkled my nose at him, but left the matter. "Have you marked our new wall on the map?" Anyone who discovered part of the ship reconfigured did so; even the Om'ray, who otherwise relied on their inner sense to navigate, understood the value of such warnings.

Morgan pulled the flat black disk of the placer from his vest pocket. "Already done." Deni's legacy, the Trade Pact device recorded spatial information. My Human used it to keep up with *Sona*'s modifications.

Modifications we didn't control and couldn't anticipate. "I hate losing more of the ship."

He grinned. "Just because you can't go 'poof' where you used to doesn't mean *Sona*'s shrinking. There are lifts. Doors. Remember doors? Walking?"

"We don't go 'poof,'" I protested, but my lips twitched. As Hindmost on the *Silver Fox,* I'd learned 'porting inside a working starship had its risks, chief among them startling my captain when he was busy welding. He was right. The Om'ray wouldn't care; most still preferred Morgan's 'walking.' The M'hiray, though accustomed since childhood to going 'poof,' had resigned themselves to what couldn't be changed.

I eyed the wall I couldn't change, resolved to be sensible. "So, air on the other side?" We hadn't found anything resembling a space-ready suit, nor tools to make one. We did have an abundance of knives and rope, not to mention seven fabric coats well-oiled against rain, but our technical resources consisted of the placer, Morgan's scanners and assorted lethal equipment, plus some packs of archaeological equipment.

Next time I ran for my life, I'd grab a wrench.

"Temp's dropping fast, but there's air. *Sona*'s doors can't open while in subspace," he reminded me, that having been the only reassurance we'd gleaned from the ship. "So, Witchling." Morgan took my chin between his finger and thumb. "What's this about?"

A lock of my hair wrapped around his bare wrist and I felt myself sink into the uncanny warmth of his blue eyes, reactions he knew full well I couldn't control. My Human wasn't above cheating when he thought it in my best interest.

Two could play that game. I leaned forward, hair sliding around his shoulders and neck, pulling us together. Our lips were a breath apart, my own breathing deeper than an instant ago, when Morgan suddenly chuckled. "You're mad at the ship again."

I pulled back. My hair, disappointed, stroked his cheek as it withdrew, diluting the impact of my scowl. "I am not. It's a machine."

One you talk to, came another voice. *I'd be angry at it, too.*

Great-grandmother, I greeted, surprised to find her *listening.* Aryl di Sarc respected the rare moments I could be alone with my Chosen, fading to little more than a second, smaller heartbeat.

Her consciousness inhabited my unborn, a baby I shouldn't have been able to conceive in the first place. Among other species, when a female reproduced on her own it was called parthenogenesis. For the M'hiray, the term was Perversion.

The Om'ray Adepts, however, considered such unborn to be Vessels, waiting to be filled. The Vyna Clan had taken that to the extreme of bottling themselves up before death, then installing such Glorious Dead into new Vessels, to be born again.

It was enough to want to be Human.

An opinion I didn't share with Aryl. If she'd not *tasted* change in our future, a change dire enough to destroy worlds; if she'd not had the daunting courage to sacrifice her own future to prevent it, storing her consciousness; if she'd not entered what grew within me? We would not have found Cersi and saved as many as we had.

While I did my best not to think of the future, I also owed mine to Aryl. An empty Vessel wouldn't leave the mother's body; her presence meant I'd survive this pregnancy.

That Aryl spoke up now meant I'd been a bit too fervent in expressing my feelings and disturbed her. I owed her an apology. Instead, I tightened my shields.

"I am not mad at the ship," I informed them both.

"Right." Morgan's grin broadened. He nodded the way we'd come. "Walk or poof?" fluttering his hands in the air.

Incorrigible, impossible . . . My temper hadn't a chance. I held out my hand. "Walk," I decided, laughing. I felt Aryl's *satisfaction* before my sense of her faded.

After all, walking gave us more time alone.

* ✳ *

Where large arched doors once opened on a world, with a wide pillared antechamber for those ready to greet new arrivals, or refuse them, *Sona* had left behind a cubby half the size of our cabin on the *Fox,* its floor become another mysterious panel of glowing shapes connected by streaks of blue to the walls.

A floor upon which I was not about to set foot or anything else. "On that?"

My Chosen, ever prepared, whipped out a blanket from the pack he carried on every excursion, spread it out gallantly, and bowed with a smile that held as much mischief as charm.

The bow was another message. It had to hurt; Morgan insisted time would heal the ribs cracked by an explosion, but there hadn't been enough of it. The truth was, we'd not enough Healers either, nor should their Talent be, as he put it, "wasted on minor injuries" when there were those who'd lost limbs or had internal injuries, crushed in the Oud attacks.

While I'd no such gift, I sent him my strength whenever he was too preoccupied to notice, to speed things along.

"Well, then," I said, answering his smile with my own, and stepped on the blanket, arms open. Time to be preoccupied.

My hair rose in a cloud of gold, fully in agreement.

* ✳ *

An uncounted while or so later, at the delicious point of no longer caring where we were and well on our way to somewhere else entirely, a voice intruded like a shower of cold, slimy eggs.

"Your pardon."

Normally, I was happy to see my cousin and heart-kin, Barac di Bowart, as was Morgan.

Normally, seeing what he was seeing in return, Barac would have made himself unseen as quickly as possible. That he didn't?

Meant a problem. I growled under my breath as Morgan's arms tightened and then let go. He whispered "Later" in my ear, finishing with the press of his lips. Beneath, *heat.*

With laudable, if ominous, composure, I detached from my Chosen and stood. Locks of hair, still aroused, whipped my shoulders, then sulked down my back.

No need to ask how Barac found us—he'd skills of his own, and was First Scout for good reason—only why. More exactly, why me? We had a Council. "What is it?" I grumbled, not hurrying to pull my clothing together.

"Who. Luek and Nyso."

I knew the pair. The di Kessa'ats were from Camos, the Inner System world where the Clan had had such concentrated Power and wealth, they'd built our Council Chamber inside the Human capital building with no one the wiser. It hadn't saved them from the Assemblers.

Like many who'd survived, the di Kessa'ats struggled to comprehend the drastic change in their fortunes, let alone find their place in a shipful of strangers. Nyso'd been having a harder time than most.

He'd the Power to be a problem, one well beyond my cousin. Tle di Parth had the strength to overrule him and would relish using it, but Barac, like others, prudently kept his distance from the unpredictable Chooser.

Making this, I sighed inwardly, my job. "What have they done?"

"They've moved back to their room. I couldn't stop them." Gesturing apology, Barac kept his gaze pointedly over my shoulder.

"Why?" I paused, my arm half inside its sleeve. "It's almost shipnight." After liftoff, we'd been relieved to find *Sona* provided an alternating cycle of light and dark; the need for a diurnal rhythm being common to Human and Clan. We'd spread ourselves out to satisfy another need, for privacy, *Sona* having more than sufficient unused rooms.

Only to discover that *Sona* stopped heating any area outside the Dream Chamber during shipnight.

I may have lost my temper with it then, too.

"They can't stay there." Morgan tucked away our blanket, unconcerned by the alien circuitry blinking under his boots. "They'll freeze."

"I told them." Barac gave a small shrug. "They claim they can't stay in the Core." My Human's term for the Dream Chamber; we all used it.

Just as we accepted his reasoning, for Morgan viewed *Sona's* bullying tactic as for our benefit, to ensure we stayed as much as possible in the center of the ship, which offered the greatest protection from radiation.

The Om'ray were reasonably content, appeased by their sense of one another; the M'hiray, who'd lived worlds apart, were far less so. Morgan had silenced complaints, including mine, with a too-casual comment that the ship could as easily confine us to the Core for the duration of the journey and there was no telling what might trigger that decision.

A reminder we dealt with a preexisting set of instructions, with consequences we couldn't predict. Only a fool would stir that pot, especially for something as minor as this. I gave in to the inevitable. "Leave Nyso and Luek to me, cousin."

Barac gestured gratitude and disappeared, leaving a hint of *relief* behind.

Later it is, I sent to my Chosen as I finished dressing.

When Morgan didn't respond, I glanced up in time to catch a frown. "What is it?"

He gave a dissatisfied shrug, as though unsure himself. "Treat them gently, Sira. Moving out of the Core doesn't make sense."

It made sense to me, I thought, keeping my bitterness from our link. They didn't deserve Morgan's compassion. The di Kessa'ats were among those who believed me unaware how assiduously they avoided my Human's presence, how they turned from him as though breathing the same air held contamination. So long as they kept their xenophobia to themselves, I could force myself to ignore it.

If it became overt, the Clan would become fewer; a loss I wouldn't mourn.

Morgan waited. There was palpable weight to his patience when it involved me and a point he wanted made. Feeling it, I eyed him askance. What was he after this time? I set my face to innocence.

"Gently," he repeated.

"Nyso," I said stiffly, "was a thoughtless, selfish child, even for Clan." A Choice delayed by over seventy standard years made me, despite my appearance, the eldest here, a detail I'd happily refresh should Nyso prove obstinate. "I see no signs of improvement."

A brow lifted.

"I promise to resist the urge to knock their stubborn heads together. Will that do?"

Hefting his pack into place, Morgan smiled at me. "I ask no more." He gave me a quick kiss, beard soft, lips cool and dry.

Good-bye, that was. My turn to look a question. "You aren't coming."

Tossing the placer up, my Human caught it with a flourish. "Time to stretch my legs. There's mapmaking to do, Witchling."

Something he enjoyed. I kissed him back, adding a flash of *affection*. "Happy hunting."

I concentrated, forming the locate of the Core, and *pushed* . . .

. . . to find myself surrounded by busy Clan who paused to gesture a polite greeting before going back to whatever they'd been doing: making beds, soothing children, talking, carrying burdens, finding clever ways to store belongings and keep Choosers apart from unChosen, doing what they must to share a limited space.

However much the di Kessa'ats disliked being here, I thought sadly, edging through the crowd, I knew someone who could hardly bear it.

Morgan.

Interlude

WASN'T RUNNING, Morgan assured himself. A brisk walk stretched legs in need of exercise, a fact of shiplife he enjoyed pointing out to the Clan. Just as well *Sona*'s levels were a maze of corridors. Most still open. Most still to explore. Why, he could walk like this for hours. Had done, pulling the coat from his pack come shipnight's chill.

He wasn't running from the powerful Nyso di Kessa'at and those like him, despite their being the sort of Clan who'd thought nothing of ripping apart Human minds to make pliable servants and pawns.

They couldn't touch his and knew it.

He kept his alien nose clear of Clan business, that was all. With him there, Nyso might dig in and force a confrontation. One the Clansman would lose, yes, but Sira would be miserable. She disliked exercising her authority at the best of times.

He wasn't, he told himself, running from the decent among the M'hiray, either, even if they—unconsciously or not—saw in him all they'd lost.

And who'd taken it.

The Om'ray? Well, they'd accepted he was *real*, but he suspected most lumped him with the ship and other incomprehensible technology now ruling their daily lives. Something to respect—from a safe distance.

Not running. To prove it, Morgan stopped and lifted his scanner instead of the placer, aiming it at another of what appeared a door but was, in effect, the outer casing of a power cell.

As usual, the scanner insisted there was nothing to scan behind the door, a small red flashing light its objection to squandering what remained of its own power.

Still a result, the Human thought, switching the device off and tucking it back in his vest. A significant one. The scanner might be old tech, but it would have given a reading for solid metal or vacuum. Nothing was—interesting. Evocative.

Or incredibly disturbing.

Morgan rubbed his beard. He'd shaved last onboard the *Fox* and hadn't found the inclination to do so since. The result entertained the Clan youngsters and if it reminded the rest what he was? Well enough. "Too late to change course." The words echoed down the curved hall, losing themselves in distance.

Not that he was flying this one. Not that he could pilot the ship or even talk to it or, so far, been able to do anything productive except map where the Clan couldn't go.

He'd hoped to find something better.

Trade Pact starships—proper starships—had controls. Controls related to internal systems, standardized across species by physics and common sense, systems accessible for maintenance.

Oh, he'd searched for them. Searched with growing desperation for the first, what, five shipdays—and some nights. Kept searching till he'd been forced to an unsettling conclusion, one he'd yet to share with Sira. *Sona* might not be a starship, not in the true sense. It might be nothing more than a gigantic lifepod: a well-supplied box programmed to ferry its naïve cargo to their destination.

If so, he hadn't found controls or system accesses because there were none to find. Galling, yes, but didn't that lock into the pattern he'd seen on Cersi? The Clan were pieces in a game, property, unable to act on their own until free again.

Putting away the placer, for this area he didn't want on any map, Morgan walked until he came to a junction, then took the right-hand corridor.

Free again. He'd known freedom once, had relished the life of an independent trader, however often he'd survived by his wits and luck. A luck aided by a Talent for *tasting* change, to be sure, but everyone had their tricks for dodging danger. Avoiding traps. Making the trades no one else could.

When Sira stumbled aboard the *Fox,* when she'd touched his heart and filled the emptiness inside, his life—their lives—had been perfect.

He should have known. Should have turned the *Fox* and run the instant he'd *tasted* that overwhelming warning. Stayed free.

Morgan snorted. "Had to find a partner with a conscience." Not that he'd have done differently. It helped to grumble in private.

The lift doors split on diagonals, four sections pulling apart in silence. He'd have preferred doors that made a proper *whoosh* of effort, a clue to the sort of mechanism he'd need to maintain or repair in future.

At least, he thought wryly, there were lifts. He stepped inside, the sections meeting behind him. The Om'ray Adepts, familiar with their Cloisters, had been shocked when the conveniences appeared overnight in various walls. Before, they'd moved from level to level using the ramplike corridor that spiraled around the outermost wall of the building, or taken the smaller, more discreet internal ramp that became, in some areas, a ladder. When *Sona* morphed into a starship, well, lifts were effective time- and space savers. The Human approved.

Once he'd figured out how they worked. The Makers—the Hoveny, Morgan corrected to himself, still feeling the thrill of that discovery—had been humanoid, meaning a design suited to hands like his as well as a placement of sensory organs like his. Eye level readouts. Finger-ready panels.

Even better, once they left the planet, he'd discovered the lifts accepted verbal commands. In the right language, but he had that now. "Thirty-four," he ordered, feeling the mechanism engage.

Sleepteach, reinforced by daily use, had made him fluent to the point where the Human caught himself thinking in the Hoveny tongue every so often. He'd begun to acquire the written language. Nockal di Mendolar had been his first teacher; while bedridden, she'd been glad to trade lessons for stories of other worlds. The elder Adept from Amna had an unClan-like curiosity about aliens; that she'd lost an arm to the Oud might have been part of it.

There was a fierce courage in all the Om'ray Morgan enjoyed.

The readout flashed symbols too quickly to read. No matter. He'd made this trip often enough to step forward before the door fully opened.

Shifting his pack to one shoulder, the Human strode down the bright corridor. A narrower hall, this, lacking the cushioned flooring and touches of art of the main living areas. When he'd discovered it, he'd felt at home. Closer, anyway. What did that say about him?

Morgan grinned. "Once a spacer, always a spacer." The walls, here true bulkheads, returned hollow echoes. Alone, at last.

Never lonely, not with Sira's warm, if presently distracted, presence along their link. Before her company, he'd had the *Silver Fox,* hard as that was to explain to grounders, the finicky old ship the ideal companion for a telepath who'd struggled to keep out the noise of other minds.

Not a problem around Clan, taught from childhood to shield their innermost thoughts and emotions. Anything they *leaked* was deliberate. By invitation.

To make a point.

Not a problem, regardless; with Sira's training, he'd added Clan shields to his own cobbled-together training. Morgan's lips twitched. Besides. Other Human minds?

No longer a problem.

He passed two doors, stopping in front of the third. The corridor curved right, with an upward slope. It led to a section of more and larger portals, widely spaced and locked.

Morgan chuckled and rapped his knuckles on the door in front of him. Once, twice.

It turned open, just as it had when he'd banged a fist against it in frustration. He hadn't found another door which would— likely wouldn't, as *Sona* continued to collapse unused levels.

Besides, he'd enough to explore right here, with no guarantee of time in which to do it.

Morgan walked through, the door turning closed behind him. From inside, it opened to the same knocking. He suspected he'd have liked the original user of this room.

Say, rather, workshop.

He'd recognized it instantly, despite the alien shapes. Counter-tops lined three walls, crowded with objects in various stages of assembly. A workbench filled the middle of the room, shaped like an X, with four outstretched arms, each brightly lit. A stool stood waiting beside one such arm. On top Morgan had found what had to be tools, laid as if put down mid-use, and a tipped-over glass mug. Someone had left in a hurry.

A mattress shoved underneath suggested a reluctance to leave some task. Or a task too important to leave.

Like his. Setting his pack on the nearest empty arm of the bench, the Human perched on the stool before an array of small objects, including the tools from that first day of discovery, sorted by shape and size, with the larger to the left.

"Which of you today?" The Comspeak sounded quaint, almost foreign to his ears.

All the more reason to use it. He'd another. The Hoveny lan-guage might be replete with scientific and technological terms, but he wanted to think as himself, for himself.

He had to. Morgan picked up a tool. The handle fit his hand, with indentations for four fingers and a thumb. Some Om'ray— including those Vyna Clan he'd seen—had a second thumblike digit. There was a dimple to accommodate it; for comfort, he decided, not function. The tool resembled a torch. The Human waved it experimentally, the business end aimed away, pressing various combinations of the indentations. It warmed; no more than explained by the heat of his skin.

"Hmm." He'd found this tool next to one very like a wrench or clamp, with nothing nearby to be held.

Shouldn't make assumptions. Still, the gap was the right size for the end of the torchlike tool.

Morgan eased the two together.

clickclick

Startled, he looked for the source of the tiny sound. It came from a small object toward the end of the array, a plain cylinder that rattled in place, *clicking* until he pulled the pair of tools apart.

His scans had pegged the age of the cylinder and its companion objects as older than what he took for tools. Older than the ship. Implying this room contained a treasure trove to make the syndicates of the Trade Pact wet themselves, or whatever they did, with greed.

Hoveny tech. His, for now, and worth more than wealth.

"Interesting." Putting aside those tools, Morgan picked up the cylinder and gave it a little shake. *clickclick*. Fainter, but still clear. Broken? Maybe. He didn't think so. A sensor, perhaps, or gauge.

For what? Holding his breath, the Human gripped the cylinder in both hands and *concentrated*, letting his consciousness touch the M'hir.

Nothing. And it no longer *clicked*.

Morgan refused to be disappointed. Hoveny tech was activated using the M'hir. As far as he'd been able to determine, *Sona* moved as any Trade Pact starship through subspace, the only difference being this ship drew its power from the M'hir. There were rooms connected to that other dimension.

A connection made by the Clan, descendants of the Hoveny. By something inside them. Something Humans weren't supposed to have, not being Clan.

"Sorry to disappoint." Morgan drew on his inner Power and *pushed*. The cylinder disappeared from his hands, to reappear on his pack. Sending objects through the M'hir he'd mastered. Moved the *Fox*, hadn't he?

"I can do this." Tech. Tangible. He'd figure it out.

Before *Sona*'s ports opened on whatever world would be home. Before they learned the price of their freedom there.

There was always a price.

Chapter 2

IN TRADE PACT SPACE, we'd had our Prime Laws, set by the ruling Council of the Clan. They'd nothing to do with notions of justice held by other species, including Humans. Over my long life, I'd obeyed most, found some irrelevant, and broken, lately, more than a few.

The Om'ray had their own, by the sound of them a mix of the disturbingly familiar guidelines the Maker had imposed on our memories—and so on those who'd first come to Cersi—and those related to the practicalities of life with alien neighbors.

While we'd yet to sit down together and compare specifics, I expected all would agree to keep those laws meant to guard us from each other. Courtesies to permit the testing of Power without giving offense. Protocols to protect the unChosen and oversee the meeting of Chooser and potential Candidate, mutual safety as important as a successful Choice. Rules to limit the depth within another's weaker mind to be touched, unless invited.

Then there was the one about not 'porting into a room unannounced—

Much as it pained me, flaunting that particular rule would offend the di Kessa'ats, and Morgan wanted them treated gently.

I hadn't been entirely fair in my description of Nyso. Yes, he'd been what my Human would call a brat, but as an unChosen, Nyso had shown a gift and love of music I'd nurtured. I'd started him with the keffleflute, delighted to see him quickly soar far beyond my skill to become a remarkable composer. That had been the start of the trouble. Most Clan only dabbled in the arts, more consumers than creators. Few could read his music, let alone play it. His Chosen, Luek, was tone deaf. Worse, she doted on small birds, claiming they required quiet surroundings, not that she and Nyso shared the same home. Or planet, for that matter.

Infuriated by his own species, Nyso dared the unthinkable.

He became Human.

As best he could, anyway. A new name, a rented apartment, and Gersle Nape the composer burst upon the stage like a shooting star, with an unnamed benefactor (himself) luring the finest musicians of Camos with fabulous salaries and the promise they would be the first to play Nape's work.

Whoever he was.

The mystery created quite the stir, as I recalled. Not only among Humans. The Council, notified by a justly alarmed Luek, sent First Scouts to make sure Nyso wasn't exposed as Clan. They needn't have worried.

Nyso, blinded by the chance to hear his music played, took up his shiny new conductor's wand and walked into the first rehearsal, completely unprepared to face professional musicians, let alone aliens.

Within minutes they'd tossed him out, as the Human expression goes, on his ear.

His music, they kept. They called it pure genius, and it was. Sold-out performances went on for years, proceeds sent to Nape's account, and for years the public clamored for more. Nyso ignored it all. If the Clan had one trait in common, it was pride. His own kind considered him a dangerous fool; his beloved music had been taken by Humans; and he couldn't even claim credit without resorting to a now-hateful disguise as one of them.

When his studio and instruments went up in flames, no one was surprised.

In hindsight, knowing Humans as I now did, the orchestra had treated "Gersle Nape" exactly as they would any Human amateur who'd presumed to lead them. If there was fault, it was in how little any of my kind understood normal Human interactions. We hadn't cared or needed to, was the truth.

My job, to make sure they understood Morgan.

Putting me outside this closed door. I let out a tendril of Power, enough to confirm those on the other side without alerting them, then knocked.

I counted to five, slowly.

Knocked again, though they'd surely heard me the first time. *Sona*'s interior doors transmitted the rap of knuckle.

But didn't, I thought all at once, transmit voices. If Nyso and Luek were unaware, they could have bid me enter and be wondering why I hadn't.

Or, I glowered, have told me to go away and leave them be.

Erring on the side of manners, I sent a calm, tactful *May I enter?* No need to name myself, as a Human might—the feel of my Power identified me to them beyond any doubt.

Silence.

Abruptly uneasy, I pressed the door control.

The tall panel turned open. The space beyond was dark, and I paused to let my eyes adjust, waiting to be acknowledged.

Like the others on this level, the room was rectangular, being deeper than wide. On Cersi, the Om'ray had used such rooms within a Clan's Cloisters to house their Adepts.

And the Lost, Aryl supplied.

Another difference between Om'ray and M'hiray. When one of our Chosen died, the other's mind was *pulled* into the M'hir, dissolving to nothing, the body a dead and empty husk.

That happens to some Om'ray, she sent, following the thought. *And has to less powerful M'hiray.* She referred to Deni, whose death had left Cha living—if you called it that. The Om'ray had insisted on tending her walking corpse.

We hadn't known how to refuse, and the memory rankled. *I don't forget,* I snapped back. In Om'ray, less connected to the M'hir, a remnant of a Chosen's mind was left behind: enough to keep the body alive, sometimes for years. They called such the Lost, for such individuals had no personality or will, and they became wards of the Adepts.

And useful servants.

Reminders of our vulnerability. Aryl's sending was sharp. *Useful now, Sira, when you deal with two acting strangely, not just one.*

Good advice. Unfortunately, I didn't know Luek di Kessa'at, other than her rumored fondness for pet birds. On second thought, they might not have been pets; after all, she'd answered my summons to the M'hiray wearing a coat of feathers. Though Luek hadn't been with Nyso when the Assemblers attacked, they'd been inseparable since coming to *Sona.*

The same could be said for most of the M'hiray Chosen, the instinct for self-preservation overriding mutual dislike. In the Trade Pact, Clan Joinings had been dictated by Council, determined to breed for greater Power in the M'hir; while instinct drove the reproductive urge, very few such pairings involved affection. Some, like my parents, had actively loathed one another and met in person only when ordered to produce offspring.

We'd done it to ourselves. Before Morgan entered my life and heart, I'd thought my mother, Mirim sud Teerac, and her group of M'hir Denouncers foolish in their belief our ancestors had Joined for love. She hadn't lived to know she'd been right. For those who'd never left Cersi, the Om'ray, had Chosen who shared a deep, fond connection, often passionate. Their overt affection for one another was all the more startling to us for being so commonplace to them.

As Aryl reminded me, I wasn't dealing with Om'ray. I was dealing with M'hiray Chosen who hadn't behaved normally since leaving the Trade Pact and now hid in a dark room like something wild.

Or something afraid.

Wishing for Morgan's handlamp, I took a cautious step forward. The room shouldn't have furniture, but they could have 'ported in some of the few loose pieces on the ship. "Nyso. Luek. I'm here." I kept my voice calm and steady. "Are you all right?"

Where were they?

I couldn't fumble around in the dark. Sona, I ordered. *Lights but only a—*I squinted in full simulated daylight. Stupid, annoying metal brain—

There.

Morgan's instincts had been right. The pair huddled side-by-side on the floor, their backs pressed into the far corner of their little room as if to face some threat, eyes closed. They were dressed as they'd been when they'd run for their lives from the Assemblers, Nyso in a laced shirt and embroidered pants, Luek in her evening wrap of brilliant bird feathers. His shirt was torn and her wrap was soiled, feathers broken or missing. Neither wore shoes.

Neither reacted to the light.

Drool glistened at the corners of their mouths. The ends of Luek's thick black hair twitched fitfully; otherwise, they might have been frozen in place.

Terrified, I wouldn't—couldn't—*reach* for their minds. The M'hir linked us, one to the rest; at its deepest level, beneath consciousness, below self, lay neither control nor defense. Not against what I suspected here.

Madness.

Even with my Power, even with shields stronger than any, I knew better than to touch either with my bare hands. Such a physical bridge brought Clan minds close: an ease for those weaker, a polite means of private exchange, an enhancement to intimacy.

Only a Healer trained to deal with ills of the mind, and with the Talent to do so, could dare help them.

We'd two on *Sona*. An Om'ray Adept, Ruis di Nemat, once of Rayna.

And Jason Morgan.

Who'd insist on helping—and whom I wouldn't risk, given another choice. I sent an urgent summons to Ruis. No point sending a locate; she was among the few Om'ray so far unable to 'port, which meant waiting while she ran here.

I looked down at the di Kessa'ats. *Ruis, is there anything I can do?*

Let them hear your voice, came the quick, confident reply. *Let them know they aren't alone.*

I took a deep breath, then squatted near the pair, out of reach. "I'm here. You aren't alone." As if that sounded convincing. I firmed my tone. "Nyso, it's Sira." Did an eyelid flicker? "You're safe, both of you. Nothing can hurt us on the ship."

Nyso's eyelids shot open, too wide, revealing pupils dilated despite the bright lights. "A ship? What ship? Where are you taking us?" The Clansman thrust himself to his knees, his lean face haggard, and I scrambled back. "You've no right!"

Luek covered her eyes and shuddered. "This isn't real. I'm at home. I'm at home."

"No right!"

"I'm at home. Home. Home!"

Their voices overlapped, protest and denial a chorus of misery I couldn't help or stop, their emotions *stirring* the M'hir. I moved away, going to the door in a nonsensical instinct to block it, fearing where they'd try to go.

Not that they'd use the door.

I could stop their 'port, if I must. But should I? Did I have that right, if dissolving in the M'hir was their choice?

Sira!? Morgan, feeling my agitation. *I'm coming!*

The pounding of running feet made me sag against the doorframe. *It's all right,* I sent quickly. *Help's here.*

I waved the urgent trio of Om'ray into the room, sharing with them my *relief* and *concern.*

Ruis went straight to her patients, gesturing back the rest.

I might have guessed Destin di Anel, Sona Clan's First Scout, would answer a call that could mean trouble. She'd been the first Om'ray we'd encountered on Cersi and steadfast through our adventures there. The formidable Clanswoman continued to wear the leather jerkin and gauze leg and arm wrappings of her former life. Paired knives hung from her belt: one long, with a wicked hooked tip, the other short; both incredibly sharp, by Morgan's account. How he'd convinced her to let him handle her prized weapons was beyond me.

Why Destin expected to need them, shipboard, was the greater mystery and disturbing to contemplate, but I wasn't about to argue. She'd helped save her people and mine.

By her quick dismissive glance at the di Kessa'ats, the First Scout rued making the effort for them, but I knew better. The athletic Om'ray of the jungle canopy might view the rest of us as soft and overfed, but above all they valued life.

"Sira." Destin gestured a respectful greeting as she came to me, one I returned. She was taller, her black hair confined by a metal net, her pale skin dappled with rich brown markings; a di Licor trait reduced among the M'hiray to freckling. Her comely face also bore the scars of a stitler attack, a creature I'd no doubt she'd killed for its presumption; a face that lost expression as the third Om'ray joined us.

The former Speaker for Sona, Odon di Rihma'at had changed his garb for that found in the ship's stores: a soft, light brown, pocket-rich garment so like the spacer coveralls Morgan and I had worn on the *Fox* I'd been astonished. My Human had merely shrugged, saying when a design worked, it worked. He'd cut the sleeves from his, saying he found the ship's temperature, set for Om'ray, too warm. If he'd go without his vest, it wouldn't be, a thought I kept to myself.

No matter what he wore, Odon was handsome, even for a Clan Chosen, with elegant lines to the bones of cheek and jaw, and thick black hair above a high brow. A brow now creased, his lips thinned. *What is this?* he sent with a *snap*.

I chose not to be offended. Honesty was more useful than manners, especially in someone I trusted as part of the ship's governing Council. "I don't know," I replied with matching bluntness but quietly. "I found them like this."

"Some malady of your people, no doubt." Odon had lowered his voice, but Ruis sent him a sharp look over her shoulder. He subsided, a six-fingered hand reaching to his breast, then dropping.

He hadn't lost the habit, to handle the pendant that hung there when he'd acted as Speaker for his Clan, the only one permitted to negotiate with their Tikitik neighbors. I'd worn one, too, briefly, a heavy bit of metal that had proved to be more than a simple badge of office. Not only could the Tikitik sense some material used in its construction and locate them—and thus their wearers—but the pendant itself was a transmitter. Oud, Tikitik, or Om'ray: every Speaker had had a pendant. Meaning every conversation had been overheard.

Who'd eavesdropped on the doings of Cersi's three species? Among the possibilities, an installation on one or both of Cersi's moons; there were Tikitik who believed the Makers "watched" their world from that vantage, ready to pass judgment. Morgan and our scientists felt there was another, not mutually exclusive. They suspected the Cloisters within each Clan might have used the transmissions to share and record data on the Hoveny experiment.

A puzzle of no concern to me. Who or what had gobbled up the pendants' data was a moot point, in my opinion, the experiment being over. To be sure, I'd ordered the revolting devices left behind on Cersi.

They had been, except for mine, snapped up by Morgan in case of some unforeseen eventuality. It sat deep in his pack, wrapped, he'd assured me, to mute any detection. I hadn't tried to dissuade him; my Human's curiosity was boundless.

I forced my mind to the present, watching Ruis. Lightly, with the tip of her smallest finger, the Healer-of-minds stroked Nyso's forehead, then Luek's. Each closed their eyes and slumped in one another's arms. I eased the part of my Power I'd held ready to stop a futile 'port, relieved.

"They're no danger to anyone but themselves," the Rayna Adept pronounced, getting to her feet. "They should be brought to the Core and kept as they are. From what I sensed, they haven't slept for too long. Such confusion can be the result." Calm. Convincing.

Liar, I thought with some admiration.

Destin and I concur. Aryl's sending was subdued. *A scout posted too many nights in a row might give a false alarm—we've never known one to forget where she was or fall.*

"I can take them," I told Ruis. Two could play at confidence.

The First Scout's eyes flashed to me, but she offered no other objection. Odon's frown deepened. "I don't like the idea of having them close to anyone else."

Ruis drew herself up. "Are you a Healer-of-minds?" She didn't wait for an answer. "Sira. If you could take me as well? Remarkable," she murmured at my nod.

I'll meet you there, Morgan offered.

No need, I replied. *Ruis plans to keep them asleep for some time. She thinks that may be all they need.*

The Om'ray Healer could be right, I told myself as I concentrated . . . gathering Nyso and Luek with Ruis . . .

I wasn't inclined to bet on it.

Interlude

BETWEEN, it was called, the *darkness* that separated Nothing-Real from the living vastness of AllThereIs. *Touching* it, ever aware, were Those Who Watched. Theirs was willing sacrifice, for to dip into Between brought memory, with its attendant confusion. Some went mad rather than bear it. Others, overwhelmed, became lost, Between. A few, more powerful, held intact; could be *heard* at need or by desire by those able.

All Watched for what didn't belong, for *instability*. Vigilance had failed once, long ago. Through the resulting breach had come such destruction, AllThereIs had reeled.

Never again.

One such Watcher *stirred*. Not alarmed, not yet. Watchers were beings of patience and caution, when there was no need to act. This one *reached* outward, seeking what had caught her attention. Was it here? A hint of *changespice*, perhaps, escaped its bed. A forgotten song, or new one, let roam free. Such things and any could happen, in AllThereIs.

Such things and any, here, weren't the worry.

Between, was. To be certain, she'd need to be closer. To move within AllThereIs required *purpose* as well as *direction,* and claim the attention of others in turn. Unkind.

Unwise.

She would wait, here.

And Watch.

Chapter 3

I WASN'T SURE what caught my attention. This wasn't the *Silver Fox,* prone to mechanical muttering just when I'd settled to sleep.

The *Fox* was gone, reduced to a mound of slag in a shipcity an unfathomable distance away from here and now, and the great starship we'd continued to call *Sona* for lack of a better name made no perceptible sound as it traveled.

Maybe that was it, I told myself, closing my eyes. The silence.

If I didn't count the deep, slow breathing of the multitude sharing the Core, the loudest of which was right beside my ear. Normally, I quite liked to hear my Chosen, not to mention feel the beat of his pulse against my skin; depending on the moment, such sensations were as apt to arouse as soothe or, as now, reassure me he was here and no longer roaming the ship.

From the current pace of his breaths, and to my inner sense, Morgan slept soundly. If he hadn't wakened me, I thought with a smidge of disappointment, what had? I resisted the impulse to sit up and look around. The faintest possible glow outlined the bases of the beds, to prevent stubbed toes during visits to the accommodation, and I was unwilling to disturb Morgan or anyone else. It was, after all, the middle of shipnight.

Were lights on in the rest of the ship?

Morgan, who'd again missed the evening meal in order to continue exploring, thought it likely the ship reacted to his presence, illuminating wherever he wandered, corridors going dark behind his back. There were lights on, I'd checked, whenever a door opened. Except if that door opened into here, during ship-imposed night.

I could ask *Sona,* I supposed, but then it made the whole question of lights seem overly important. I refused to guess what the ship might do then.

Our tenth shipnight, lying here together, speeding through subspace. Already a challenge to tell one shipday from the next. How many more before they blurred into a sameness? Until more of my people lost themselves like Nyso and Luek?

Not thoughts to help me fall back to sleep, I scolded myself, pushing them aside. We'd get there—all of us, including the di Kessa'ats, who'd be back to being a nuisance—when we did.

Wherever "there" was.

That did it. Like an itch impossible to scratch, thinking about our destination. I'd ordered the ship to take us home. In hindsight, that may have been—

. . . what was that?

My right hand rested on my belly, not yet round with the life inside. *I'm sorry I woke you, Aryl.*

It wasn't you. With a hint of *consternation. Something's not right—look here.*

She'd felt it, too, whatever had wakened me. *Where?*

Come.

I let her *draw* my mind after hers, into the M'hir. With no outward sign, Morgan came awake, instantly alert. Just as well, I thought, glad of his warm golden presence as I entered the dark.

The M'hir. Aryl had named it after the violent mountain winds that swept across her home on Cersi each year. The wind brought the Harvest.

The M'hir I knew was nothing so benign.

Its darkness *moved,* to Clan senses. Sometimes with a *snap* of pressure or unpredictable and crushing weight; sometimes, as now, a *heave* as if it sought to rid itself of me and mine. I didn't take it personally. Not a good place to linger, the M'hir; it was, however, part of us.

For a portion of each Clan mind was rooted in that darkness; it claimed the rest upon death, consciousness become ghost, to dissolve and disappear.

Enough of us, surely, to fill it, those past terrible days.

I let myself *reach* for the living. Their resting minds showed as fragile, distant lights; I took great care not to draw them deeper.

I felt— Aryl's mindvoice trailed away. *But where?*

Morgan's, strong and familiar, *Here.* As if he'd taken my hand to guide me, I found myself near one light in particular as it *sputtered,* about to fail. Nyso? Luek?

Heedless where I was, I cried out in furious protest, *NO!*

The M'hir reacted to my emotion, as of course it would, darkness whipping to maelstrom. Before it could get worse, I *yanked* the three of us to safety.

Morgan rolled to his feet, snapping on the tiny handlight he'd packed in anticipation of an uncertain future. Practical, my Human. I freed myself from blankets to pad after him between the beds.

The Core was more a village than dormitory. Yes, everyone slept together, finishing their day by changing into the sleeveless white shifts the ship provided, but where there'd been simple rows of beds, enough for twice our number, now stood organized clusters, with space between.

To create that space, about a third of the beds had been removed and stored. Others, stripped of their padding, became low tables. The modest reorganization helped us deal with the reality of our forced confinement here. If there was a hint of getting back at *Sona,* I was the last to argue.

Family groups took up the middle, male unChosen and the Choosers who might find them irresistible on opposite ends of the long chamber. Although there'd been no incidents, no one wanted a repeat of Ermu sud Friesnen's blatant ambush of her Candidate in the shower; the success of their Joining had owed more to blissful ignorance on both sides than sense. Since, to the simmering disgust of at least one M'hiray Chooser, I'd put Eand di Yode and her Chosen, Moyla—Om'ray Adepts and former Councilors of Sona—in charge of future matches. Tle could rail at them until exhausted, but she wouldn't. The elderly pair were among the few she respected.

Most importantly, Eand, however minimal her Talents as Sona Clan's remaining Healer, had the strength to help Tle, should we ever have a Candidate who could survive her. Time was on Tle's side, a Chooser's physiological age unchanging until Choice, or not. It depended on how frustrated she became.

I followed Morgan between the M'hiray families to the section housing the various Om'ray Clans. They kept themselves apart; I suspected they found us, though kin, at times as alien as Morgan.

His dot of light came to rest on a lump of blankets, a lump shivering as if cold. I hesitated, filled with new dismay; this wasn't where Ruis had left her patients.

Morgan moved forward, passing me the light as he knelt by the bed. "Easy—"

Blankets flew off. The figure beneath scrambled back, limbs flailing, to crouch against the wall at the head of the bed. Eloe di Serona, once of Tuana Clan. I lowered the beam to avoid the young Om'ray's face. She lunged forward, snatching the light. Holding it close, she rocked back and forth.

Her arms were striped in deep angry gashes; similar wounds marred the smooth skin of her cheeks and neck. Her hands were stained, nails dark with blood. Shields tight, sick to my stomach, I whispered. "I'll get a Healer."

A second incident in mere hours couldn't be coincidence. What was happening?

"Leave me alone." The Om'ray bent her head, hair sticking to the blood, and drew the blanket to her chin. The light bleached her skin, emphasized the damage. "Go 'way."

Instinct kept me from *reaching* for her mind. I bit back my protest when Morgan laid his open hand on the bed, inviting her to touch his. He knew what he was doing.

Hopefully.

A sullen shrug. "Wouldn't if I were you. It's dark. Always dark. That's what they do. Drag you under. Bury you deep. Till there's nothing but dark."

As the Oud had done to Tuana. To the multitude of Om'ray we hadn't reached in time. The flat calm of her voice chilled me more than any scream.

Morgan didn't move. "Sira, brighten us a bit, please."

The control for this bed's light was behind Eloe. *Sona,* I sent, *minimal light,* having learned that lesson. I was answered by a gentle glow where the wall met the bed.

With a relieved shudder, Eloe curled into a ball around the handlight.

I'll stay with her as long as it takes, my Chosen sent, not hiding his *concern.* I felt a *stir* as others, beginning to wake around us, expressed their own.

Morgan's here, I assured them. With the Talent to heal damaged minds. With the risk inherent in its use.

Not, I'd noticed, that my Human cared about risk when a life hung in the balance.

Heart heavy, I gazed down at the young unChosen. The Clan way, to consider the unChosen, lacking a bond to mother or mate, expendable.

It was no longer mine.

"How can I help?"

* ✳ *

My help, it turned out, involved granting Morgan and his patient privacy, easier asked than accomplished in a chamber full of disturbed and worried Clan. More and more sat up in bed, beginning to rise to their feet despite the lack of light.

Sona, I sent.

>What is your wish, Keeper?<

Start the daycycle now. While I didn't hold my breath, I felt a certain relief when light flooded the Core. I'd feel more when I could be sure the ship's compliance extended to warming the areas without. *And I want to make an announcement.*

>*At your convenience, Keeper.*<

"Good morning," I said cheerfully, the ship carrying my voice to every corner of the immense room. Adults blinked, startled, but looked to me as I'd hoped, not Morgan. "Sorry to cut the night short, but we need an early start today."

Dozens spoke at once. "Are we there?" "Have we arrived?" "Is it the Homeworld?" Frustrated, they fell outwardly silent, sendings darting through the M'hir. *Is it true? Sira, are we home?* Until that space began to roil and I realized my mistake.

I'd distracted them, all right. Swallowing a curse I'd learned from another species, I raised my arms, asking for peace. They subsided, waiting for answers.

So was I. Morgan, the only one of us capable of interpreting a starship's controls, had yet to find any. A preset course implied a destination, yes, but to what? No guarantee "home" meant the world where we'd evolved. Many starfaring species, Humans among them, had left their birth systems so far behind they couldn't retrace their steps.

Even if *Sona* took us to that world, what then? Morgan refused to say too much time might have passed, leaving us with a destination surely changed and possibly gone. Wouldn't say our belief Cersi had been an experiment, succeeding with the return of the M'hiray, was built from supposition and the slimmest of evidence, that if we were wrong, the Om'ray might have been abandoned or exiled or fled from worse—

Not kindness, that forbearance, to keep us full of hope. Morgan knew what this voyage could become if we had none.

Tell them the ship's asked for maintenance, chit. With familiar wry humor.

I latched on the idea as if drowning. "Maintenance," I blurted. "Don't forget, nine—ten days ago, this ship was Sona's Cloisters." There'd been one, housing Adepts and sheltering survivors through changes in their neighbors, per Om'ray Clan. We didn't know if any others had lifted from the planet. If they had, only the Vyna's would have had life inside.

The Om'ray didn't care for the reminder; the M'hiray exchanged glum looks.

>*I do not require maintenance, Keeper.*<

I need to keep them busy, I replied, perhaps a little too honestly.

>*Understood, Keeper.*<

I had an instant to appreciate how unlikely that was before the lights pulsed an alarming orange and something below went *BANGBANGBANG!* The vibration reverberated through the floor.

Those Clan who hadn't looked frightened before, looked terrified now.

Oh, dear.

* ✳ *

Luck, or the Makers responsible for the ship and its programming, was on our side, something I doubted I'd dare count on again, though it was hard not to grin as Holl di Licor made her report. The Healer and scientist, having guessed the likeliest source of *Sona*'s alarming "bang," had 'ported there herself to confirm it.

For someone who'd been a M'hir Denouncer, she'd come a long way in a very short time.

"A glitch in the storage system," Holl announced. "There are food packets strewn everywhere. Nothing appeared damaged," as *alarm* spread through the room. That *Sona* had preserved food suited to all of us, most of which Morgan safely could eat, too, had been the best news of all. To lose it? I shuddered inwardly. "We'll need to deal with the mess," she continued with reassuring confidence. "Move the packets to the galley for storage."

Lucky, Morgan concurred. I chose to ignore the hint of *incredulity.*

Faced with a clearly defined problem, my people wasted no time. In moments, they'd dressed and organized themselves into working groups, the first 'porting away with Holl to assess the task ahead, those charged with obtaining breakfast going out the door.

Those left tried not to stare at Morgan and Eloe, or look where Nyso and Luek still lay as though dead, their imposed sleep unaffected by the ruckus of moments ago.

Will there be more? Aryl, asking the hard question.

I don't know. The Clan I could see appeared the same as they had yesterday. If anything, they looked better: those who'd starved gaining flesh from a now-ample diet, our wounded able to stand and walk. Most showed reminders of their hurts, if only fading bruises. Our Healers couldn't regenerate limbs or prevent scars, but thanks to them—and Morgan's med-kit—we hadn't lost any to their injuries.

What was I missing?

Eloe had seemed fine yesterday, cheerful and busily occupied with Merr di Ulse, an Om'ray weaver, and others; the youngster had skill with needle and thread and Merr's group sought to salvage what clothing had come on board. The Om'ray regarded every scrap of value; M'hiray were happy to relinquish theirs, much of it in rags or ill-suited to daily wear, in favor of the ship's coveralls.

It wasn't as if most Om'ray hadn't adopted the new clothes as well, favoring grays and browns over more vivid choices, but in common with Morgan, they retained some small item of their own, be it vest, jacket, or a white gauze hood around their necks. In comparison, the M'hiray looked like shoppers on Plexis, bedecked in blues, reds, and swirls of yellow.

A dozen other Om'ray followed Destin's example and kept their former garb, complete with the knives of the canopy. Barac, only to me, expressed the opinion they couldn't fathom there was vacuum outside; as he kept his force blade on or near his person at all times, he was hardly one to talk.

The truth was, I knew Barac worried what might be inside the ship, well aware we couldn't open all of *Sona*'s doors or scan deeper levels. He wasn't alone.

To assuage such fears, I'd asked Morgan if he thought there could be something dangerous on the ship, something in hiding. What he'd said—

Aryl had followed the thought. *I remember, too. He said, "It won't be hiding."*

I'd taken it as a joke, to reassure me. Hearing it again, I felt chilled to the bone. A Chosen pair who'd lost touch with reality, now an unChosen no longer in her right mind. What had my Human seen that I hadn't?

He'd have warned me about a threat or if he'd *tasted* change coming, that warning having saved us both times without count.

Something more nebulous, though. A suspicion without facts. Oh, that I was quite sure Morgan would keep to himself until he'd proof.

He knows something, I replied at last, looking at my Chosen.

Nothing in his expression suggested it was anything good.

Interlude

BAD ENOUGH the ship only took orders from someone qualified to pop in a course disk and cycle air locks, Morgan thought grimly. While he loved and respected Sira with all his being, that wasn't the point. The wrong command could kill them.

Sira knew it, too. She'd promised not to give another operational command without consulting him first. She'd—

Gotten away with it again. The result appeared harmless, and it was keeping most of the Clan busy elsewhere.

Those still here gave him space, but he didn't need to lower his shields to feel the Clan's attention. Gazes slid his way. Mouths were downturned and shoulders hunched, ever so slightly. Worry and dread. A species able to share emotion and thoughts appeared uniformly terrible at concealing them.

Sira had picked up that Human skill. She'd taken charge, erect and graceful, her lovely face serene. For a wonder her hair held to the ruse, its usually opinionated red-gold a calm waterfall down her back, its ends moving no more than living hair should.

There was nothing serene to his inner sense of her. The Clan, reliant on their minds and will, had a horror of either failing. The connection between their minds, as the Human understood it, meant such illness could spread, one to the next. Sira was right to worry.

Just wrong about why.

An ache started in his hip, the one that had taken the brunt of an aircar mishap years ago, and his sore ribs protested in harmony, but Morgan didn't move. He hadn't since putting his hand on the bed. The distraught young Om'ray needed quiet and consistency. Time. To relax, if she could. He'd wait as long as it took.

As he'd waited for this: the moment the frenzy of survival reverted to the ordinary routines of life, a life different from any they'd known, and minds subjected to fear and overwhelming loss—

—broke.

This illness didn't need to spread. To some extent, everyone on this ship already suffered, whether they showed it overtly or not. He'd been through his own version of their hell, after the war on Karolus. Only the understanding of a friend had kept him from self-destruction; even then, he'd needed time and lots of it.

Time they didn't have, not with close to two hundred potential Eloes onboard ready to explode, not with their destination minutes—or possibly years—away.

Oh, and didn't that uncertainty add a knife twist to what seethed inside the Clan?

Lips moved. Shaped words without sound. "Go 'way."

Morgan couldn't obey; she'd only harm herself further. He had to act, but how?

Memory was pliable. He could remove the worst of hers.

No. Memories were all they had.

Dull the worst, make them bearable. That he could try to do, but it was the more delicate work. In the contrary way of things involving the M'hir and the Clan, delicacy required significantly more Power.

Sira's was his for the asking—and even when he didn't. There was something adorable about her belief he hadn't noticed her little gifts. Each flood of *strength* she sent surged through him like a stim, and it was just as well he'd had other reasons for gasping.

Morgan frowned. Whether they'd admit it or not, the Clan came close to worshipping Sira these days, especially the younger ones. Maybe it was his Human thinking, but he'd prefer to salvage this unChosen's pride. Ruis di Nemat? Was needed where she was.

Let alone the folly of risking both Healers-of-minds at once.

Morgan made up his mind. *Barac.*

The M'hiray First Scout excused himself from a discussion and walked over. His eyes, dark and expressive, filled with pity as he took in Eloe's woeful state, then fixed on Morgan. *What can I do?*

I'll need to borrow strength to help her. Not yours, before the other could offer. *It should be someone she knows. I'm strange enough.*

A fleeting smile acknowledged the truth of that. Barac and his brother Kurr had been among the few Clan to work freely near Humans. *Eloe lost her family when Tuana was buried, but Ruti will know if she has heart-kin here.*

Heart-kin being those closer than blood, as Barac di Bowart had become, to him as well as Sira. Morgan moved his free hand in the gesture of gratitude, hoping Eloe would see he wasn't totally alien. *Make it quick.*

* ✳ *

Grim-looking Clan surrounded the bed. The Chosen pair, faces lined with grief, were what remained of Tuana's Council: Nockal and Kunthea di Mendolar. Both were Adepts, learned and powerful; Nockal nodded a greeting to Morgan, her stump of an arm tucked into a pocket. With them came two slight unChosen, a male and female, alike enough to be sibs. They gripped Ruti di Bowart's hands, or she held theirs. Likely both. Before *Sona* had lifted from Cersi, Barac's Chosen had taken the young of Om'ray and M'hiray into her care and woe betide any who might harm them.

Being pregnant with new life herself.

Sira might seem absent. She wasn't. Morgan *felt* her presence tight along their link. *Give the word and I'll 'port the lot to the farthest part of the ship.*

She could. Where a similar group of Humans would object strenuously to being forcibly removed, the Om'ray would not. Sira's right to lead was based on her greater Power and unquestioned.

No need to exert it. The familiar faces had brought up Eloe's head, started a flow of unheeded tears. All to the good. *I'll let you know, Witchling.*

"Who's done this?" Ruti bristled. "Who's harmed this child?"

"Are you blind?" Nockal kept her voice low. "She's done it to herself."

Ruti, shorter by a head and a quarter the age, didn't back down. "Who made her? Can you tell, Morgan?" Her look at him was pleading. "Who it was?"

Behind her, Barac gave an oddly Human shrug. Morgan understood. Before they'd fled to Cersi, Ruti's mind had been taken over by the will of another's. She feared her attacker or an ally might have come with them, to bide his or her time before acting again. She could be right.

Just not now. "Eloe hasn't been *influenced,* Ruti," Morgan assured her. He looked at the sibs. "Which of you is Eloe's heart-kin?" The male unChosen swallowed and went pale. Ah.

"Both of us, Hom Morgan," the female asserted. "Well, we are," at something her brother must have *sent.* Rude that was, a private sending in front of other Clan; dangerous, in front of those more Powerful.

Brave, that above all.

"Let me introduce Dama and Tal di Lorimar." Kunthea reached over and rubbed Tal's head, the younger male blushing. "They're a set, these three. Always have been."

Eloe's eyelids flickered.

She gave a tiny nod.

Now, Morgan judged. He rose, gesturing to the bed. "Sit with Eloe, please."

Tugging their hands, gently, from Ruti's grasp, Dama and Tal took their places, careful to stay clear of Eloe. Even heart-kin had that instinct.

"I need the rest of you to leave."

A flash of dark eyes. *Is that a good idea?*

If it worked, yes. The Human wasn't about to open a discussion. "Please."

Ruti took her Chosen's arm. "If anyone can help her," she said firmly, "it's Morgan." With that, she led Barac and the other Chosen aside.

Leaving him with what were children.

The Human went to his knees, offered his open hands, and waited.

Dama touched two fingers to his right palm. Not to be outdone, Tal did the same to his left. If those fingers trembled, it merely spoke to their courage. He'd been right to ask for them.

As for risking them? If he was right, Morgan thought grimly, these two might need his help as much as Eloe. No time like the present.

He lowered his shields, inviting them in on their terms, not his. Their exploration was tentative at first, then grew bold. A little too bold, finding a moment of *heat* between Chosen.

Far enough, the Human sent, adding *amusement.*

Two pairs of eyes widened. *You sound normal.* A protest.

Of course he does, Tal! The sister gestured apology with her free hand. *Excuse my brother, Chosen of Sira. Take what you need from us.* The pair took firm hold of Morgan's hands, dropping their own shields with shattering trust.

He stayed clear of their thoughts. All he need draw upon was their Power, bonded to their love of Eloe, heart-kin to both.

If only it had been that simple.

Chapter 4

"YOU SHOULDN'T ALLOW THIS. It's too dangerous, Sira." Barac rubbed a hand over his face, uncharacteristically flushed. "I don't doubt Morgan's skill—"

"Nor do I," I interrupted, stung by the reminder. That skill had repaired damage I'd done to my cousin's mind and would always regret. "Stop fussing."

Offense wiped the worry from his handsome features. "I report a potential risk to you, Keeper," he said stiffly. "As is my duty."

Because Chosen followed each other into death. Since his Joining to Ruti di Bowart, Barac had acquired an annoying air of superiority on the subject, apparently convinced Morgan and I treated our lives as casually as any unChosen.

Far from it, but that wasn't for anyone else to know. "Noted." Relenting, I gestured apology. *We mustn't lose any more.*

He nodded. M'hiray shared the gesture; the Om'ray Clans adopted it, slowly. What we did share was Choice and Joining, with its perilous permanence.

Until my own, I'd known only the hunger. Like any—all—unChosen, I'd been incomplete. When my bond to my mother had snapped, strained by distance and overuse, something inside me, innate and wordless, longed to be filled. That mutual need brought Chooser and unChosen together.

Since, I'd learned more than was comfortable about Clan Joinings. The Drapsk, a species who roamed the stars in ships crewed
by vast tribes, studied the M'hir, which they called the Scented Way.
They'd proved to me the existence of *things* in the M'hir able to
cling to Choosers, *things* drawn to the Power-of-Choice used to test
unChosen candidates—to kill them, if their own Power failed. The
things consumed the energy released within that contest.

Making us food, plain and simple.

Or not so simple. My Human had taught me to look deeper, to
assume anything alien could surprise, and what could be more
alien than M'hir-life? The Rugherans were, yet weren't at whim,
plunging like giant fish into the M'hir, only to squeeze inside a
starship corridor and bargain for what they wanted. Or what their
world, White, wanted, for that was another disturbing truth about
the M'hir. Some planets existed there as well. The Drapsk settled
on them to fulfill their own desire to be complete; the planets
themselves seemed to Join, one to another.

The entire business being ridiculously erotic, discussing the
topic with my Chosen most often ended in an enlightening lack
of words. My hair twitched. Human and Clan were conveniently
similar but we'd such intriguing differences—

A thought to save for later, Witchling, if you don't mind?

I felt myself blush in earnest and couldn't help glancing at my
Chosen.

Morgan knelt by Eloe's bed, holding hands with Tal and Dama.
His head was bowed in concentration, the muscles of shoulders
and upper arms tensed. Eloe remained curled around the handlight, her eyes closed.

Tempting, to *reach* toward him, and them, to see for myself what
Morgan attempted. As that could be worse than distracting, I shifted
my attention back to my cousin. "Morgan knows what he's—"

Disorientation . . .

I lurched, grabbing Barac, feeling him steady me, his *alarm*—
Darkness!

Wasn't the M'hir, but suddenly, I couldn't see. Wasn't the ship,
but I couldn't breathe. I smothered, choked, couldn't scream—

NOT REAL! Aryl's mindvoice, like a blow. *Sira. This is their memory of Tuana and the Oud, not yours. What they felt.* Sensed *from others. You can breathe. You can see.*

I heaved for air, blinked for a stunned second at Barac, seeing my horror mirrored in his expression. Tearing free of his hold, I ran for Morgan, staggering as if the flat deck beneath me was loose soil and treacherous.

Too late. The three on the bed had tumbled together into a still heap. My Chosen, trapped in memory, convulsed on the floor.

Throwing myself atop him, I *plunged* along our link, seeking his consciousness. There. Faint, strained, but aware. *HERE! I AM REAL!* I sent with everything in me, *awareness* plus *strength*, knowing I'd one chance.

He *reached* as someone drowning. *Sira . . .*

YES!

I felt Morgan's chest shudder, then expand and fall in great gasps. His eyes opened, their blue at first dazed, then grim. "The others—"

Abandoning my Human, I went to the bed. The three unChosen had stretched out, Eloe sandwiched between the sibs, now sound asleep. Their faces were peaceful, arms overlapped. I let out a trace of Power, finding nothing unusual.

Morgan leaned on my shoulder. "Good," he whispered, gazing down. "It was just me."

And me.

That being a point to make later, once certain he'd recovered—and after I'd listened to Barac's "I warned you" and apologized—I eased my arm around my Chosen's waist. "What say we get you dressed?"

* ✳ *

To my dismay, Morgan dressed in record time, determined to consult with his fellow Healer-of-minds while, as he put it, everything was fresh.

Fresh was one way to put it. I still felt the urge to gasp, as if being smothered. "Are you sure about this?"

"No time like the present, Witchling," he said. The tone might be cheerful, but I knew that look.

He'd made a discovery while healing Eloe's mind, something important—

It was, I feared, nothing good.

He won't burden you until he's sure, Aryl sent, sounding more distant than usual. *My Enris was the same. We were Chosen, but our opinions and decisions were ever our own. I remember he once—* My awareness of her abruptly faded.

I understood—how could I not? Aryl and her beloved Chosen Enris had done the unthinkable, severing their Joining so Aryl could leave herself, mind and Power, in that crystal.

They'd done it because she'd feared what the M'hiray would become within the Trade Pact, and sought to save us from ourselves. They'd paid the ultimate price, she and her Chosen, without any surety of success.

I couldn't imagine such courage. If, every so often, Aryl needed to draw aside and renew it, or simply mourn, I thought fiercely, she'd more than earned the right. Without her, the M'hiray would have ended.

Without her, the life growing inside me would be empty and its birth—was much too distant to worry about now, having sufficient on my plate at the moment.

Morgan grabbed his pack with one hand, easing that concern; what he'd brought on board shouldn't be left unguarded, although having that pack at all opened a host of new and uncomfortable possibilities.

"You're not going to tell me, are you?" I asked my Chosen as we headed for the Rayna section of the Core.

The corner of his mouth I could see went down and *tension* sang along our link.

"Only if I'm right, chit."

* ✳ *

The distinct appearance of Om'ray Clans was, we now believed, no accident of nature. The original population would have been selected for the greatest variation. Since, each Clan had been subjected to different environmental stresses, with individual maturation speeded by additives to their diet to create new generations in a quarter the M'hiray norm. Clans were, in a real sense, pools of breeders, isolated other than the passage allowed unChosen who were themselves selected, we suspected, at least in part by ruthless shepherds. For the Tikitik had the knowledge to guide the evolution of living things, and the Oud—

Were partners in that endeavor, subjects themselves of the experiment, or somehow both. Those on *Sona* trying to piece together the whys and hows of Cersi remained undecided on that and other key points. I won't say it kept me from sleeping, but if *Sona* was taking us back to where all this started, those gaps could become serious problems. As Morgan would say, the cost of ignorance only went up.

The experiment conducted by the Hoveny had produced more than the M'hiray, with our ability to reattach the M'hir to waiting tech. Faces, voices, shapes, and sizes. Genealogy had been my passion, once, and walking through the Om'ray section of the Core was to experience the wild and wonderful diversity once inherent in the Clan. A diversity that would fold back together and blend, as it had in the M'hiray of the Trade Pact.

Giving us a fresh start. For most of my life, I'd known the Clan were doomed to extinction and sought a solution. The Om'ray, with their lesser Power and successful Joinings, offered one I'd never thought to find.

Survive first, I reminded myself. Repopulate later.

The Core remained empty of all but a handful, I hoped due to the natural Clan caution around faltering minds and not because of a worrisome number of food packets to tidy.

The Tuana watched over Eloe and her heart-kin; Ruis di Nemat tended the di Kessa'ats and she stood at our approach, relief written on her face. If I could judge a Clan by common features, like Ruis the few Rayna who'd survived were shorter than other Om'ray, with brown curly hair streaked with white from a young age. Their noses were blunter than those of Amna or Sona, cheekbones higher, and all had oblong eyes of pale yellow.

"My fellow Healer-of-minds. Keeper." Ruis made the gesture of respect we echoed. "I'm glad you've come. I'd like to try waking them simultaneously." A wave to her patients. "For that, I'll need your help, Morgan."

Nyso and Luek lay together on the same bed, their bodies wrapped as one would a newborn, arms snugged to their sides. While their expressions were those of any sleeper, slack and peaceful, their eyelids twitched without pause. Dreaming, I thought.

Nightmares, more likely.

"Of course." Morgan gazed down at Nyso and Luek, eyes filled with compassion, then up at Ruis. "My experience with Eloe may be relevant."

"Show me." Without hesitation, Ruis held out her hand, palm up.

I warmed to her at once.

Just as quickly, my hair took offense. Touch my Chosen? Locks writhed out, intent on slapping her palm away. I caught them just in time, gesturing apology with full hands as the stuff squirmed. The Om'ray Healer looked intrigued. "How—exuberant," she said tactfully. "A family trait, I assume?"

"So I'm told," I replied. An annoying one. "I'll get out of the way." Should I stand at the end of one bed or the others or—

Morgan raised an expressive eyebrow.

Meaning I—and my hair—belonged elsewhere. I resisted the impulse to stick out my tongue. *Be careful.*

Always. With *warmth.*

"I'll leave you to your work, then," I said aloud. Catching a flicker of *concern* from Ruis, I added with a smile, "My Birth Watcher's expecting me at breakfast."

* ✳ *

I 'ported to what had been the Council Chamber and was now *Sona*'s galley, not bothering to look for my Birth Watcher. Little Andi sud Prendolat had made friends on the ship and had more interesting things to do with her time than check my eating habits. When Aryl and I needed her, she'd be there to help. Let her be a child till then.

My hair, having expressed its opinion, settled politely down my back. *Put you in a net,* I warned it, rewarded by the *feel* of Aryl's smile.

Powerful Chosen females had hair that could be a nuisance—none, in my experience, as much a nuisance as mine. A di Sarc trait.

I'd left the name behind, Sira Morgan having a happier ring. Strange to think it was unknown, now, among the Om'ray. The M'hiray of Cersi had swept the name from the planet, along with its Power.

To be reborn, Aryl commented dryly.

As an infant. To me, Aryl di Sarc stood strong and proud, a black-haired Clanswoman of vast Power and shockingly new Talents—for her time. A natural leader. My confidante. "Reborn?" I couldn't imagine it. How could she be as she'd been?

She'd followed the thought. *Being born will do, Sira. Trust me.*

Aryl had walled away her *grief* at losing her Chosen; the blood red of that inner barrier ample warning to stay clear. Behind it lay, I suspected, her desperate need for freedom, too. She'd traded a stone prison for one of flesh. Could hear, after a fashion; see through my eyes when I helped, though that made her dizzy.

My fingers would turn the wide bracelet on my wrist without my intent. Carved and hammered to resemble water curling over stone, it had been Aryl's once, made by Enris from the Oud's green metal.

None of it a replacement for a body of her own. None of it what she deserved.

You're welcome to hurry things along in there, I sent, keeping it light.

Amusement. *It will help if you feed us both. Where's our breakfast?*

Working on it.

The ship's other modifications either mystified or inconvenienced. Not this. Gone from the former Council Chamber were the tall arched windows that had looked out on the grove, replaced or covered by a featureless wall of pale blue. Tables of gleaming green metal sprouted from the chamber floor, complete with benches. The benches themselves were topped with a yielding material patterned in swirls of the same varied hues as the floor. Our ancestors had relished color.

Or known its importance to those born under a sky.

Unchanged was the raised dais. When we'd arrived here, there'd been a solitary, innocuous-looking pillar set into it. Called a Maker, it was a machine allowing a Cloisters to manipulate the minds of its Clan. Not that Om'ray thought of it that way. Generations of Om'ray Keepers had used theirs to provide teaching dreams, or to break the connection between Om'ray—a last resort to protect healthy minds from a damaged one. Aryl and the first M'hiray had used this very same Maker not only to sever themselves from all other Om'ray, but to erase their memories of Cersi, allowing them to take Passage to Stonerim III and the Trade Pact.

Aryl's mother, Taisal di Sarc, had remained behind, sacrificing herself to operate the machine. We'd found her clothing and Speaker pendant by the pillar's base.

Our arrival, and my touching the pendant, had awakened the machine. Without Morgan and Aryl, our true selves would have been lost in the new personas it forced on us, and all likely would have died trying to fit into a Sona that didn't exist. For the Maker's real function was to prepare volunteers for their part in an appalling experiment: to see if isolated groups of Om'ray, put under different stresses, might develop the ability to access and control the M'hir.

The meddling in our reproduction had started early.

The Maker no longer stood alone. The ship had instructed me where to find two more such machines, these shorter and wide. Once told what they were for—one to open and warm food packets from the ship's stores as necessary, the other to produce a supply of hot or cold water—we'd rushed to put them in place, watching eagerly as they sank into waiting depressions on the dais and came to life. Here was technology we all could appreciate.

And desperately needed.

I hadn't looked for my Birth Watcher, but she found me. A fair-haired child appeared steps away, eyes of gray-green sparkling with delight, and Andi sud Prendolat ran into my open arms with a glad, "Sira!" *Aryl!*

I bent to press my cheek against her soft round one and to smell the sweetness of her hair.

Greetings, Birth Watcher, Aryl sent *warmly.*

"It's been the best morning ever," Andi said happily, dancing away again. "See?" She spun in a circle, holding out the ends of the filmy white gauze she wore as a scarf over her yellow ship coveralls. Her sleeves were carefully rolled up and fastened with thread, exposing her small arms from elbow to wrist. The sight always made me smile. Andi'd wanted her sleeves cut off like Morgan's; with so few child-sized garments in the ship's stores, he'd persuaded her this was the way young spacers wore them.

It hadn't taken long for the rest of the children to demand the same.

Knowing Aryl's interest, I let her *see* through my eyes. *You've received a fine gift, little one,* she remarked.

"Gricel gave it to me. She's happy I'm teaching Dre to 'port."

Even happier, it wasn't hard to imagine, to have her active son occupied until her baby decided to be born. Any time now, according to Jacqui.

Still, Andi teaching? She'd learned to 'port only recently.

She has the Power as well as Talent, Aryl reminded me, privately. *And I believe our Andi is very fond of Dre.*

A Candidate? How automatic, that assessment. How inappropriate, I scolded myself. These were children. More importantly, we weren't the Clan of old.

I let Aryl feel my *embarrassment.*

Our Birth Watcher will be a potent Chooser, when her time comes, came the steady reply. *If you're looking to the future, Rasa di Annk has become our Andi's heart-kin. Not an infallible prediction, in my experience, but a welcome start.*

Let's leave her a child a while. "Dre's lucky to have you for a teacher," I praised, rewarded by a smile that lit Andi's gray-green eyes. Gloom hadn't a chance around this joyful child. "Join me for breakfast? I'd like to hear about Dre's lessons."

"I'd like to, but oh—I can't, Sira. I promised Rasa I'd find his grandmother." Andi spun again and stopped, the gauze settling around her like closing wings.

My heart thudded in my chest. "Andi." I crouched to meet her eyes. "Rasa's grandmother is dead. She's gone."

"The dead aren't gone, Sira." With sympathy, as if I were confused. Her gaze was guileless and bright. "I *hear* them."

We've told you not to listen. Aryl, carefully not sharing the alarm I knew we both felt. Alone among the M'hiray, Andi had the Om'ray Talent to *sense* where others were in space. I'd suspected hers extended to finding them through the M'hir, a gift my sister Rael had had. But this?

The M'hir contained voices—none were safe to *hear*, the Watchers first among them.

The child's smile faltered. "But I promised Rasa."

I put my hands on Andi's little shoulders, sending *reassurance.* "Rasa can't have his grandmother back, no matter what you *hear*." The Clanswoman was lost, as Rael was lost to me—

As so many were lost. I fought to keep the tide of *grief* from the child; sent a plea for help. *Aryl—*

An instant response, patient yet firm. *Your friends are sad and you want to help, Andi. This won't, trust me. You'll hurt yourself and them.*

A lower lip quivered. *I don't know what else to do. I promised.*

Ask Rasa and your other friends to share good memories of those who are gone. Write down the names they share. The most important help you can give them is to be happy. Play together. That most of all.

Then, with a little *snap. And teach them some manners when they 'port before you startle your poor elders.*

Dimples returned. *Yes, Aryl.* Her head tilted. "Dre's calling me, Sira. May I go now?"

As if I'd a choice. "Have fun."

My hands dropped through empty air.

We did what we could. Children must leap to learn to safely fall.

In the canopy, I countered as I stood, uneasy at having let Andi go without a sterner warning. Vines and giant fronds could be grabbed by small hands; only strength of will and personal Power mattered in the M'hir.

I opened my sense to that other space, sought a particular mind. There. *Ruti.*

Sira. Power in abundance here. Along with an air of *distraction* the young Clanswoman put aside at once to focus on me. *What is it?*

I shared the memory of our conversation with Andi, finishing with, *what do you think?*

That I should keep an eye on her, came the prompt reply, *and will. What about her parents?* An afterthought, but Ruti was right. Nik and Josa should be made aware.

Presenting its own difficulty. Like Holl and her Chosen, Leesems, the pair had been M'hir Denouncers, convinced its use would lead to the downfall of the Clan. Unlike them, Nik and Josa clung to my mother's teachings. To have a daughter ready and eager to leap, as Aryl put it, into the M'hir couldn't be easy on them.

Did they even understand the risks? There'd been a time I'd had to relearn everything, from the existence of the M'hir to its dangers—

To what I was.

Pointless, to regret any of it. I couldn't have stayed half of myself. Couldn't have loved Morgan as I did—or helped my people. Still, the part of me that empathized with Nik and Josa and the rest of my mother's people knew what I'd given up in return. Had I stayed that person—been, as I'd believed, Human—I felt the M'hir *churn* and slapped it down. *I'll talk to Nik and Josa.*

Let me, Ruti sent, adding matter-of-factly, *You'd scare them.*

Amused agreement from Aryl.

Go ahead, I conceded. *Keep me informed.*

I will, Sira. I could almost see Ruti's grin. *Now go eat.*

The answering growl from my stomach prevented a more dignified response.

* ✳ *

Food packets were stored on a lower deck, dispensed twice daily through a wide opening from rotating racks, to be collected and brought to those waiting in the galley.

Sona's helpful distraction had been to send those racks spinning out of control, littering the storeroom floor. A little too helpful, I decided, wincing at the growing stacks on the tables in front of me. Two Clan, arms full, appeared, left their burden, and disappeared. More to come, then.

The galley had seating for our number and no more, *Sona* somehow aware how many it carried. Most of those seats were empty. During shipday, with warmth restored, the Clan spread out. There were tasks to be done: some essential, such as moving packets and refuse or caring for children; some, in my opinion, less so, but they helped pass time. Our lack of records inspired several. Those mapping out potential matches between unChosen were doing their best to create a genealogy, and a trio of Om'ray scholars had begun a history of the Clan. This group's approach being to question at tedious length anyone who'd sit still, I made myself busy elsewhere.

I'd no idea how the rest spent their days.

They couldn't all still be picking up in the storeroom.

"Sira!" Holl di Licor beckoned me to the table where she and four others were sorting the flat silver packets. As I came up to her, she pressed one into my hands. "Here."

With so many to choose from, I'd looked forward to a guilt-free indulgence. Certain packets contained something very like nicnics; this wasn't one of them. "Thank you," I said, swallowing my disappointment. "What are you doing?" They weren't sorting, as I'd first thought, but inspecting each packet closely before putting it into one of two groups.

"Look at this." Holl indicated a hair-thin crack along the side with every evidence of disgust. "Striking the floor damaged the wrapping."

"So don't eat it," I ventured hopefully, starting to hand the offending packet back.

Frowns from all five. "Yes, eat it. A compromised packet must be consumed as soon as possible," the scientist informed me. "We've no means to return them to stasis or even keep them cold. In my judgment, the contents won't last more than a few hours at best."

Most of what was here could spoil, then. I lowered my voice. "How serious is it?"

She blinked. "I wouldn't call it serious. The Om'ray think it shameful to waste what could be used. Rather than waste these, we should use them. That's all."

Save me from the planetborn, I thought. The food we had was what the ship doled out each day, rationed from a supply that would inevitably—even if enough for more than were on board—end. The below-freezing nights precluded any attempt to produce our own food. Coincidence? Unlikely, according to Morgan.

Morgan, who was little more than *distant preoccupation*, being focused on his immediate concern.

Don't invent more, I warned myself, forcing a smile. "Of course, Holl. You're right. Thanks for this," I lifted the packet.

Planetborn, but not slow by any means. "Are you concerned over the food, Sira?" Holl asked in a low voice. "What does the ship say? If there are repairs needed—"

>*I do not require repair, Keeper.*<

Was that a tinge of *annoyance*?

My own, certainly, having the ship interrupt. "*Sona* claims to be fine," I replied, preferring truth to accuracy.

"Good to hear." Holl's guarded expression told me she understood the difference. "I'll have someone do a final sweep through the storage area once we're done." Her lips sounded out "Morgan."

No one better, but I'd no idea how long my Human would need. "Ask Barac." I grinned. "Give him something to do."

Other than help his Chosen with the ship's children.

* ✳ *

I took my meal to an empty table, eating with slow care. There were green biscuits that tasted fishy—or like pepper, depending on how long they sat on the tongue—as well as shiny purple globes reminiscent of spiced tea. The sum was nutritious, without the metabolic accelerants of the Om'ray diet.

Along our link, I knew the moment Morgan laid his palm, space-tanned and callused, over Ruis'.

Deliberately, I took another bite.

She'd be surprised. My Chosen, especially in the M'hir, was unlike any Clan. Warm, *real*, and reassuring, his presence was steady and sure, as if nothing there could disturb him, a steadiness that revealed astonishing Power. That didn't make him invulnerable.

Not that I'd interfere.

Not, more grimly, that I'd leave him linked to another Clan mind without protection.

I chewed, ignoring taste, dismissing texture, my *awareness* of Jason Morgan strengthening until his heartbeat became a counterpoint to my own.

On guard.

Interlude

TO MORGAN, the M'hir flowed away, before and behind, as an endless beach, with firm yet yielding sand beneath his feet, the only sound the gentle lap of black waves to either side. Waves to watch, for they could become a tumultuous nightmare without warning, their foam like flame, able to sweep him away if he wasn't aware and braced.

Sira? If she were close, the light of her *presence* would burn away the dark and calm the sea to glass.

Ruis had no such *impact*. Her mind manifested in the M'hir as a faint indecisive shimmer, near, but not. They needn't be here to communicate—and wouldn't. But such introduction between adults was, according to Sira, important.

He'd the feeling his Chosen liked her kind to see him here, not that she'd ever told him why.

Introduction complete, by mutual agreement he and Ruis let go of the M'hir, their thoughts mingled only at their outermost layering. Wait. There. The *path* to the depths of her well-organized mind, unprotected.

A test, no doubt, of Human manners. Ruis had the Talent and skill to make him regret any intrusion.

Manners he had. As for his own mind—well, what he wouldn't share lay locked, shrouded, and beyond any possible reach. He let no one but Sira behind those shields. That there were some beyond which even she couldn't pass, not without damaging his mind?

Half the fun.

The tempting path vanished. *I am ready. Show me the child, Morgan.*

He guided Ruis through his memories of what had happened, protecting her, as much as possible, from those of the backlash that had consumed him and almost his Chosen.

She wasn't fooled. *Risky,* the Om'ray commented. *And for an unChosen?* Before he could react, she continued with overtones of respect. *Well done. But you've more to share, and worse, have you not?*

Perceptive, but a Healer-of-minds would be. Other Healers could remove a blockage or repair injury to the brain, but very few had the Talent to grasp and manipulate the workings of a mind.

Yes, he replied, letting her feel his *concern. I fear Eloe and these Chosen are only the beginning.*

You believe their madness has spread, despite our care? Doubt. *I've seen no evidence of it.*

Not spread. He readied another, much older memory. *I fear—* confined in this ship, with no escape? It wasn't fear. It was sickening terror. *I fear what's happened to the Clan has left wounds, wounds that will fester and become madness unless we heal them first. I know it can happen—*

Memories gushed forth as though from a reopened wound. Terrible, consuming. War. Loss. Rage born of grief twisting into self-destruction—

The agonizingly slow process to heal, to let go the past, to begin to live again. Hard, leaving that pain, even now. Hard—

Beloved. Sira, nearer than he'd expected, letting him *feel* her presence. He followed her *calm warmth* along their link.

As Morgan came back, Sira retreated, leaving him alone with Ruis.

To Om'ray, those who have gone before are no longer real, Ruis assured him, her mindvoice distant and proud. *We do not cling to our dead, as you or the M'hiray—*

Have you rung the bells? Aryl's mindvoice glanced by Morgan like a sharp and bitter wind, aimed at Ruis. *Have you spoken their names the final time? Om'ray may no longer feel the dead, but let us have truth here, Healer. You are the last of the Rayna Adepts—what of your fellows? You had children—a brother—his family—*

Ruis let out a cry, but Aryl, far stronger, had neither compunction nor pity. *Your dead haunt your memory, Healer.* The wind fell away, became like pealing bells. *As do mine. As do those of everyone aboard. We will be in pain until we have paid those respects and have time to mourn. Do not dare deny—*

The connection broke.

Morgan withdrew his hand, his eyes locked on Ruis'. Though hers were dry and met his with a surely justified anger in their depths, she caught her lower lip between her teeth and was silent.

Perhaps thinking better of a protest.

"No time." He used Aryl's word. "No certainty or comfort. Only this ship and where it might take us. Under such strain no wonder minds are crumbling. I'm amazed more haven't. We need to act before they do, Ruis. Heal their wounds."

"What you suggest is impossible." Almost bitter. "To pull a mind back from the brink, yes, that we can sometimes accomplish—if we catch that mind before it fails. But these wounds you speak of—" Ruis grimaced. "Grief and dark memories. Despair and unhappiness. Who doesn't struggle with those now? Morgan, you know as well as I do our Talent can't heal what isn't yet broken. Our only recourse is to watch for signs—"

"We're trapped in a can," he countered grimly. "Wait for madness to manifest, and it'll be too late."

Ruis gestured understanding. "The problem—and its answer. We must end this journey and get off the ship. Be under a sky—a proper roof. Feel some hope, Morgan. That above all."

Circling back to *Sona*, again. To a shipmind that wouldn't—or couldn't—answer the most basic questions about where and when and how. There had to be a way— "Which may never happen," he said, a warning to himself as much as the other Healer-of-minds. "What then?"

"One. Two and three." She made an unfamiliar gesture, brushing her palms across one another with each number to produce a soft susurration. "Eloe and her heart-kin took most of your strength. I value your skills and know my own, Jason Morgan, but if it is all of us, or even most? Four, five, six—" her hands moving faster and faster, more numbers tumbling forth, "—fifteen—" becoming a blur—

He trapped her hands midstrike. Held them. "There's too many," the Human agreed, his voice catching in his throat. "I know. We couldn't heal them all, not in time. But maybe we won't have to—not if we ease the strain within everyone's mind at once."

"I've told you—" She stopped, staring at him. "You would use the Maker. Morgan, no!"

"Yes. I've seen it in action. You were Rayna's Keeper. You know how to use it."

Ruis hesitated. When she spoke, it was as though the words were being pulled from her. "I've sent the dreams. Helped those Lost. But this—I wouldn't know how." She turned her hands in his, tightened her grip before letting go. "Even if I did, I'm not *Sona*'s Keeper." Softer. "Even if I were, Morgan, there's a greater problem." She nodded at the di Kessa'ats, still asleep—or unconscious—in their beds. "Everyone knows what the Maker did to the M'hiray, how it changed them into different people. No one will allow its use again."

"We don't tell them."

Her head rose sharply, hair twitching at the ends. "Dreaming to learn what's needed by a Clan is one thing. What you're suggesting—it's Forbidden."

"So is letting people suffer when we could have helped." The mind he'd touched cared more for her patients than her own life. "So is risking the lives of everyone on this ship, because it could come to that, Ruis, if any go mad and strike out, instead of in."

The Rayna closed her eyes. He waited without moving, watched her hair slowly settle over her shoulders.

When her eyes opened, their expression was bleak. "We need proof of all this. We Heal these two." Ruis indicated the di

Kessa'ats. "If you're right and their illness is like Eloe's, we search for similarities that could be warning signs. If—if, Morgan, we find such signs, we look for them in others. If we prove more are at risk, that we can identify them, then—" with *conviction,* "—we take what we've found to Council. They must decide what to do. It's not up to us."

"Agreed," he said. "But if we find those signs, the trick's who to test first." Of course, the Human nodded to himself. "Council. Decent sample of our population, none more discreet, and—as you say—it's their decision. What better way to show them the urgency of making one?"

Her lips had parted in a half-gasp. Very slowly, they curved into the first full smile he'd seen on her face. "You are different. I keep forgetting that."

Morgan gave a small bow. "Some never will," he replied honestly.

"'You can't make an Oud swim.'" Ruis' smile faded. "We need new sayings. As far as I'm concerned, you're the finest Healer-of-minds I've ever met, Morgan. You'd have made an exceptional Keeper." She gestured apology. "By so saying, I mean no slight to your Chosen. Though untrained for the position, Sira's done well."

By not doing anything—despite being unsaid, the qualification came through, loud and clear. Morgan grinned. "She'll appreciate that."

As for his being Keeper?

Oh, he'd been thinking about that, too, in his "different" way. Ruis was right about one thing—the sooner they'd a realistic hope of leaving this ship, the sooner most could start to heal on their own.

Which required answers *Sona* wasn't providing.

First things first. Heal these two, then—

Sira, he sent to his Chosen, *would you join us?*

Chapter 5

GIVE ME A MOMENT.
Morgan's unexpected invitation could mean they needed me. Just as likely, I grinned to myself, he'd decided having me there was better than my *listening* along our link, but I wasn't about to ask. Instead, I warmed four more of the damaged packets, reasoning they might be welcome—and it made Holl happy.

Then formed the locate and concentrated . . .

. . . I arrived, at a small distance, and quietly put the packets down on the nearest table.

Morgan and Ruis didn't notice, being busy doing whatever Healers-of-minds did for those in need.

I sat by the packets to watch. Not that there was much to see. Fingers on foreheads; looks of effort and concentration. Matching frowns that eased before I could start to worry.

And, in the end, eyelids opening on sane awareness. Ruis looked at Morgan. *Something* passed between them before she went back to Luek di Kessa'at, murmuring as she loosened the Clanswoman's wrappings.

Nyso, finding a Human leaning over him, twisted himself in a sheet-encumbered knot and fell off the bed, squawking like one of his Chosen's birds.

Why we'd saved the pair—

Prejudice, according to Morgan, was a greater problem for the one who harbored it. At the time, he'd been referring to my wearing a space helmet to our meeting with a roomful of Lemmicks, thus bringing the meeting to a swift, unprofitable end. There may have been insults, but as they were honked, loudly, I couldn't swear to it.

I suspected then, as now, that my captain hoped to convey a broader lesson than my regrettable lack of compassion for the odorous. Admittedly, I wasn't the best student.

Right now, I was in no mood for nonsense. I shared my *displeasure* with Nyso, pleased to see him gesturing an apology so frantically he tangled himself again.

Chit!

None too pleased, my Chosen.

Not a problem.

Neither was I. The tension between him and Ruis grated along my nerves.

"Tell me what's going on."

Morgan hesitated, so briefly I doubted anyone else would have noticed. Then, smoothly, "We need you to summon the ship's Council—"

Like that, was it? I concentrated . . .

. . . reappearing, with Morgan, under the stars.

* ✳ *

What we'd come to call the Star Chamber was the only place left on *Sona* to permit a look outside, courtesy of its partly transparent ceiling. Granted, in subspace, all we could see were the distorted smears that marked, Morgan assured us, stars, but it was worth it. Long trails of every imaginable color flowed overhead, punctuated at seeming random by sparks or pools of dazzling white, as if music could be seen.

Rows of elongated white benches curved along one side, facing an open space presumably for briefings or presentations. Add pillows and the benches would have been fine for sleeping, had *Sona* not sent the chamber below freezing each shipnight.

Hence its more euphemistic name: "Happy Place." Dim the ship lighting to free the ever-changing display, watch it flicker and dance around the chamber, and the Star Chamber became the most romantic spot on the ship.

No Chosen were immune; even those M'hiray who'd come together only at Council order eagerly sought this space and each other. Our kind, it turned out, was hard-wired to reproduce, an instinct avoidable when Chosen lived on different planets but not now, confined within the ship. Age was irrelevant: two thirds of our Chosen were beyond childbearing.

Why not seek comfort? As for the rest, we desperately needed to increase our number, no matter what the future held.

By unspoken protocol, Chosen weren't to sneak up here more than once a shipday and whomever 'ported first won sole right to the chamber, for a reasonable length of time. Rumor had it some of the Sona weren't overly concerned with privacy.

Though we'd the "Happy Place" to ourselves at the moment, there was nothing romantic about Morgan standing apart from me, arms crossed and a frown tight between his eyes. "What are we doing here, chit?" he snapped, in full "captain" mode. "Council must convene. We'll need someone to step in for Ruis with our patients, so she can attend as well. There's no time to waste—"

I arched an eyebrow. "I've time."

Silence. The sort that might imply I'd cycled the air lock backward—again—except I hadn't. This time, my Human, my esteemed captain, was in the wrong.

I watched the realization slowly dawn. "Sira, I—"

"Wait. I almost forgot." I concentrated . . .

. . . reappearing with his pack in both arms, it being heavier than I remembered.

Morgan took it without a word. He pretended to check a fastening, then swung the pack, one-handed, onto the nearest bench. Gathering thoughts, at a guess, behind shields I wouldn't challenge.

He looked up at last. The sober intensity of his gaze told me he wouldn't be tricked or cajoled.

Honesty, then. "Jason, you keep two kinds of secrets from me.

Where you've hidden a present—which is fine, by the way." I couldn't smile. "The other? The 'thing you suspect is so terrible you must prove it first' kind? That's not fine. Not here."

"You've—" my Chosen stopped, running fingers through his hair. "That obvious?"

"It's hardly the first time," I reminded him, glad as something *eased* between us. "I can guess some of it. You showed Ruis your past." The darkest part, a forge that had, in many ways, created the Morgan I loved with all my being. It could have destroyed him. "You think Eloe—Nyso and Luek—suffered as you did. That more Clan will unless—" of course, "—you fix it."

"Yes."

I narrowed my eyes. "Fix it how, exactly?"

Morgan sat, hands locked around a knee. "That is the question, isn't it?"

He'd a plan, or the start of one. A plan he knew I wouldn't like—or was it worse? Was it something "Forbidden," putting it squarely under the authority of— "Is that why you want a Council meeting?" I accused. "To trick them into letting you do what you want?"

"I wouldn't put it quite like that."

I would. Watching Morgan manipulate others, especially those Clan who underestimated the master trader's skills, was my favorite sport: warmer than hockey and often profitable. Not this time. Not when I suspected what he wanted to do was Forbidden because it should be.

I sat beside him, turned so our knees brushed. "Tell me," I said gently. "I could help." Or stop this first.

His hand cupped my cheek, eyes searching mine. "I'm counting on it."

Not good. That meant it wasn't only the ship's Council he intended to trick into whatever this was, but me as well. A ploy we'd used before: my ignorance of a move he planned made my reaction admittedly more convincing than any I could rehearse, but—

I pulled from his touch. "We're not bargaining for engine parts. This is—it's not a game."

Beneath the beard, muscle worked along his jaw. "That's where you're wrong, Sira. The stakes are higher, that's all." Our eyes locked for a moment, then he tipped his hand, palm-up. "You decide. I tell you what I have so far, which isn't much. Or you let me do this my way and we'll see where the sparks fly."

He asked me to trust him—trust Human instincts, which weren't mine and had, on notable occasions in the past, conflicted. To let him use me along with those leading the Clan.

To swallow my pride, I thought, all at once feeling the *rightness* of it. To be his partner and help those who trusted us.

"Your way, then. But watch those sparks," I advised primly. "We've a closed atmosphere."

"'Closed—'" The start of a relieved smile transformed to a grin. "Good one. Remind me to tell—"

The grin vanished. A flicker, no more, of pain; then, in the next instant, Morgan's face showed nothing at all.

He'd no one to tell I'd made my first spacer joke. No other spacers. Not Huido Maarmatoo'kk, the giant Carasian who was his closest friend. Not Russell Terk, the gruff enforcer, nor his boss, the redoubtable Lydis Bowman, who'd been part of Morgan's life—and the Clan's, I now knew, from the start. Everyone who'd have cared was gone from his life.

Left behind, for me. "Jason—"

"A good trade." *No regrets here, Witchling.* Shields fell away, and it was true and beyond wonderful that what coursed between us held only *love.*

A finger lifted in invitation. A lock of hair accepted, slipped around his hand and wrist, wove distractingly up his bare arm. I watched the blue of his eyes deepen, resisted the urge to lose myself in them. "What about the Council meeting?" I said, attempting to be responsible. "We—"

The rest was lost beneath his lips. *Later . . .* the kiss exquisitely tender and slow, as if he discovered the shape of my mouth for the first time.

Or wanted never to forget it.

Later, I agreed, with all my heart.

✳ ✶ ✳

How long it was before we lay still, bathed in starlight and sweat, cloaked in my now-sated hair, I didn't know and couldn't care. Our hearts slowed in harmony; our breaths matched, then didn't, then did again, like dancers; and the meaning of life itself could be found in the scent of him and the warmth of us and now.

Yet there was more. With us, between Chosen, always, there was more. Our thoughts mingled, heavy and comfortable, wrapped together like our legs and arms. The rush of heat and ecstasy that had exploded—or had it sung—between our minds eased into bliss.

Wife. Morgan stroked my hip.

I smiled. *Husband.* In the Trade Pact, lifemate was more common, or contract partner, but my Human had his own heritage and it wasn't only war.

As he had his own needs. We weren't the same. What gave me pleasure lay within my mind, cued by touch, but *felt* inside. Among Clan, only Chosen could satisfy one another. What fulfilled Morgan lay outside, conveniently accessible to any partner.

He'd not dared just any partner, nor let down his guard. The risk to a telepath—of exposure, of fatal vulnerability—was too great.

Until now. I found I could squeeze closer, and did.

I *felt* his smile. *Didn't know what I was missing. Witchling.*

No other partner would do for him either, I thought rather smugly. Not now. As a telepath, Morgan had discovered he also *felt.*

Making what we did together, for one another, work very well indeed.

Fingertips tenderly traced where scars had once crossed my abdomen, then his hand pressed warm over where Aryl slept—or didn't. Either way, she kept a discreet distance, allowing us this.

Odd. The memory of my scars had been a reminder of survival and pain. Now, Morgan's hand reminded me I held within me a treasure.

Family. With a certain *smugness* of his own.

I could, I thought, grow to like that word, too.

Interlude

FOOD STORAGE was two levels down from the former Council Chamber, reached by a lift that had appeared, first shipnight, behind a door that had also appeared.

Leading Barac, from that morning, to think twice before opening any door and be sure his Chosen did, too.

Down the lift, then a short walk along a plain corridor that ended in two doors, also "new," set side-by-side. The left door gave access to a seemingly bottomless chute, identified by *Sona*'s Keeper as for the disposal of emptied food packets.

Jason Morgan, who knew about such things, suggested they drop nothing other than food packets in the chute, the ship silent on how it dealt with waste and there being significant risk involved in messing up a system that might use heat and/or other form of disintegration. Apparently, it was impossible to toss garbage out into subspace. Another horrifying tidbit known only to the Human.

The right door led to food storage, a large room lined on one side with wheeled carts clipped to one another or the wall. Each cart was a metal box with slots for fifty packets, either full or ready for disposal.

Meaning every day, before anyone could eat, the ship expected someone—several someones—to walk here, load those carts, and wheel them up to the galley. The return trip, to waste disposal, was equally necessary, it being unwise—according to Jason Morgan, who knew about such things—to leave anything that could move during an unexpected maneuver loose and able to do so.

To no one's surprise, the Om'ray thought this an admirable arrangement, especially, Barac thought glumly, those still unable to 'port themselves, let alone a cart.

To the M'hiray who took shifts? Some were unpleasantly surprised when Council expected them to walk as well, in interests of fairness. And, as Jason Morgan suggested, to get at least some exercise.

Barbaric, the entire process. Practicing with his force blade was exercise. Making love with Ruti—definitely worthwhile exertion.

Give him a fine restaurant, servo-free, like Huido's *Claws & Jaws*. He'd even settle for full automation, assuming the ship's food replicator was up-to-date. But no, for the duration of the voyage, they'd this.

Hopefully, they had this.

"Well?" Gurutz di Ulse peered over his shoulder. "What do you think?"

"What I think doesn't matter." The business side of the room was opposite the carts. Barac straightened, causing the shorter Om'ray to step back. He wouldn't be rushed, particularly when faced with a mechanical maw large enough to swallow an aircar.

Machinery of any sort couldn't be trusted, in his experience. Especially this machinery, having spewed food packets like so much vomit and now gaping as though exhausted.

They'd cleaned its mess, for once eschewing the carts in favor of 'porting packets by the armload to the galley. The faster they could sort out damaged packets, the better. Luckily, most were still intact, now taking up useful table space. He supposed Morgan would insist they be secured, too. Maybe the Om'ray could make nets—

Gurutz scowled. Maybe it was his normal expression; Barac hadn't seen the Sona scout smile since the Cloisters turned into a starship. "We should have brought the Human."

"Holl sent us." A selection based, the First Scout suspected, on his cousin's whim. Sira might forgive the interruption of her stolen moment with her Chosen; that didn't put her beyond making the cause—him—pay. "If you can find Morgan, feel free to invite him along."

"Find that one? Easier to spot a red brofer under a blood bush."

No doubt an apt comparison, whatever a "brofer" might be. He'd known Morgan wandered. Where, being the question. Barac eyed the Om'ray with real curiosity. "You tried to follow him, didn't you?" Something he'd have advised against. The Human had—disquieting—skills.

Then again, so did the Sona. Gurutz lifted a hand, holding it out empty. "We've all tried," he admitted. "Do you know where he goes?"

Away from us, Barac guessed, with a certain sympathy. "Mapping," he said out loud. "Besides, we've the help we need right here." He glanced down to his left, where a silent presence quivered with desire to matter. "Ready, Arla?"

Dappled fingers touched the strip of cloth acting as a blindfold. "Whenever you say, First Scout." Young Arla di Licor was a Looker, his rare Talent reacting to any change from his last memory of a place.

It wasn't a comfortable gift, the sensation incurred ranging from mild awareness to nauseating disorientation. Which would be why Arla hadn't come alone. His older brother, Asdny, hovered nearby. His role, normally, was to keep Arla away from *Sona*'s modifications and safe.

Not today. That Talent should tell Barac what they needed to know.

Holl and Leesems hadn't objected when he'd included their son in this excursion—who would, seeing the delight on Arla's face—but they'd not been pleased. Holding him responsible, they were, for Arla's well-being.

As if he could guarantee the unknowable.

The younger M'hiray waited, fingers ready. Gurutz looked at Arla, frowned, then dared send *disapproval* at Barac. *He shouldn't be here.*

The First Scout didn't bother to reply. Gurutz grumbled because Om'ray were like Arla's eccentric family, keeping their unChosen close until ready for Choice and even after, the newly Chosen living with one set of parents or the other. More protective than Aryl remembered, but Cersi's Clans had been forced to change, isolated by the Oud, under attack by the Vyna.

They weren't on Cersi, Barac told himself. Arla's temporary discomfort could identify a serious problem. Besides, as a M'hiray, he should consider the male unChosen expendable, if he considered him at all.

Enora hadn't—why was he arguing with himself? Enora sud Sarc, his mother, was—had been—an empath and kind. Oh, he'd known his worth to the Clan; he'd been made a First Scout because his death wouldn't matter.

Gurutz and other Om'ray scouts were selected from Chosen who'd earned the right. They had skill, experience—

The best of reasons to be cautious. When his brother had been murdered, hadn't his Chosen, Dorsen, and their unborn died, too?

Different ways—he was M'hiray—

"Something wrong, First Scout?" Was the corner of Gurutz's lips turning up?

"We each have our strengths," Barac replied, uncaring if he made sense. Why keep comparing them? Why not—combine them?

Why stay M'hiray and Om'ray? Together, weren't they already something else? Something new?

Clan.

Sira's type of thinking. Contagious, heady stuff. Barac gave himself an inner shake. It was all too much for a simple scout. He couldn't change anything.

You just did, Ruti sent, her attention drawn by his troubled thoughts. He felt her *smile.*

Barac stiffened. *What do you mean?*

Yourself. Us. How our family will be. I see *the future you do, beloved, and I want it, too. We all do.* A tender *warmth.*

Daunting, her faith in him. *I don't suppose you can tell me how?*

You already know. His sense of her faded.

He knew enough to start small, Barac thought warily. Smiling at Asdny, he put his hand on Arla's thin shoulder, sent *reassurance.* "If anything bothers you, your brother's to 'port you both to the Core at once. Find your mother or any Healer. That's an order."

"But I—"

"Prepare your locate," Barac said sternly, receiving Asdny's nod of agreement. He ignored Gurutz's small but growing smile. "Or I send you both back now."

He felt the sigh. "Yes, First Scout."

Barac tensed as Arla lifted the blindfold from his eyes.

The Looker squinted at the machine, then around the empty, high-ceilinged room. His dappled face filled with relief. "It's the same as it was before. All of it." He pointed to the gaping machine. "That's just how the unit opens to deliver the packets, First Scout. Then it closes."

"Excellent." In every way. Barac coughed. "Let's hope it doesn't close now."

Hiding his reluctance, he put his hands on the rim of the mechanical mouth and leaned cautiously into the cavity, craning his neck to look up. There, well out of reach, he could see the wire racks that—until this morning—slid down to offer one hundred and seventy-nine packets with machine precision before each of the ship's two meals.

They looked empty. Didn't mean anything, he told himself. The cavity stretched beyond those moving racks, disappearing into the dark bowels of the ship. For all he knew, the racks weren't filled until ready to drop down—

—through the space presently occupied by his head and shoulders. The First Scout hastily pulled himself clear. "I imagine it will reset itself before breakfast, during shipnight." He waved his hands to imply that complex but surely normal process.

The youngsters smiled trustingly.

Gurutz looked skeptical but didn't argue. How could he? The Om'ray knew even less than he did about machines. What they needed down here was the Human.

Failing that? Well, he'd one more trick, as Morgan would say, up his sleeve. "Gurutz. You and the lads report to Holl." Barac gestured gratitude, finishing with a bow. "Well done."

They bowed back, Arla's eyes glistening with pride. His brother patted him on the shoulder.

"Will you make your own?" the Sona scout asked, no longer smiling.

"Only," Barac said honestly, "if I've one to make."

Once they'd disappeared, the Clansman sat on the floor, choosing a spot in the middle, his back to the maw. Wrapping his arms around his calves, he dropped his forehead to a knee.

Cleared his mind.

Waited.

Discipline, he had. It only felt as though the walls were as thin as issa-silk, the deadly twisted space outside as apt to consume him as the M'hir itself.

It only felt he could, for all he really knew, be buried beneath dirt instead, running out of air.

Barac waited. He'd the Talent to *taste* change. A flinch rather than insight, but a reliable warning nonetheless.

Even if, half the time, such *tastes* arrived too late for him to do more than pull his blade and duck.

CLANK!

"Seventeen Hells!" Barac scrambled to his feet and whirled to face the dispenser, heart pounding in his ears. His hand reached for his force blade—

—stopped short.

The machine looked the same. Was the same. He took a deep breath. Resetting, that was all. Not that he'd stick his head in again to see for himself. And what was that? Faint, steady— *grindgrindgrind*—barely louder than his pulse at first.

Getting louder.

A sound like that, Barac decided, came from a machine too busy to be bothered.

Time to leave.

Barac, could you come here? Ruti. *I've a situation—*

CHANGE! He staggered, the *taste* overwhelming.

Gone again.

—need your advice. Is everything all right?

Yes.

Nothing was. He'd his warning: a strong one. But was it about the noises, his Chosen's "situation" . . .

Or some trouble yet to reveal itself?

Barac laughed at himself. Not all was his concern. Morgan could take care of the machine; his powerful cousin, the unknown future.

He concentrated. *Coming, Ruti.*

* * *

The *taste* still rank in his mind, Barac picked his way through a maze of children. Given the freedom of the galley between meals, they whooped and laughed, some running between tables, the rest 'porting ahead to surprise them. Their mothers were gathered around a table of their own, outwardly unaware; bonds *sizzled*, connecting each with their child. The need to hold on to one another burned Power through the M'hir so long as their bond lasted, be it days or months—or Sira di Sarc's incredible years.

Only three of the eighteen so bonded were M'hiray: Andi sud Prendolat and two toddlers. All had been with their mothers, by chance safe during the Assemblers' first attack.

They'd lost the rest. M'hiray children were fostered, taken as far as possible from their mothers. The strain on their bond produced passages, those scars through the M'hir that made it easier for others to 'port between those points. The M'hiray, forever turning instinct to advantage.

It had put everyone at risk. Fosters died with their hosts, the bond dooming distant mothers; or mothers died first, dragging their children behind. Chosen died worlds apart and the M'hiray left were pursued—

To their deaths. Yes, the Om'ray had died as well, but not like this, Barac thought bitterly. When the Oud reshaped the ground beneath them, families rushed to the safety of each Cloisters and survived, together.

Unless the Vyna found them—

Don't think about them. Ruti hadn't turned; no need. *You'll scare the children.*

As if they're listening *to me,* he scoffed. They were too busy playing their new games, M'hiray games, like those he'd played as a child with his brother Kurr and their cousins. 'Port and seek while young and unaware; the more tantalizing Chooser/Loser once old enough to look ahead and wonder.

Outside games. Confined in a room, even a large one, the combination of laughs and squeals was close to deafening.

Could be worse. A mother stood, gesturing apology to her companions, shielding everyone else in range from the urgent inner *DEMAND* of her not-yet-verbal offspring.

"Risa." Barac stepped aside to give her room, bowing as their eyes met.

She inclined her graceful head. "First Scout." A weary but accepting smile. "Duty calls."

"Our turn's coming," he replied, earning a dimple. Risa hadn't known him before they'd met on Cersi, a lack of recognition for which Barac was grateful.

Council had arranged for him to be a Candidate for her Choice. By warning him of Risa's greater Power, Rael di Sarc had saved his life, however reluctantly he'd taken her advice.

After a Choice made elsewhere, Risa di Annk had Commenced into the fullness of her adult beauty. However, like too many M'hiray, her Joining with the Clan Healer, Jorn di Lorimar, now Jorn di Annk, was loveless. They'd met once more to do their Council-appointed duty, producing a son, and might never have occupied the same planet again if not for the Assemblers. Forced into proximity on the ship, they avoided one another—at least in public—civil in their mutual dislike. Jorn avoided their son, too, though Noson was a delight and favorite among the other children, with chubby cheeks and a sunny disposition.

His loss. Barac intended to spend every waking moment cuddling their daughter, once she was born. Except for those moments—

An elderly Om'ray shouted as two mischievous children

appeared in front of him, almost dropping his drink and packet. Before he could draw breath to scold them, they giggled and vanished. He gestured forgiveness to thin air, smiling himself.

Children's laughter. They'd come too close to never hearing it again. Anything joyous helped the mood on the ship. Gurutz wasn't the only one to stalk around with a grim face; each ship morning, Barac thought, more Clan, both M'hiray and Om'ray, shielded their emotions rather than share them. The weaker, like himself, could only be grateful.

For more than that. Lovelier than Risa, than the stars of any sky, Ruti di Bowart raised her eyes at his approach, her pleased smile finding his heart. *Love* soared between them, wiping away the *taste*, and Barac stepped forward eagerly.

Stopping short as his practical Chosen bent to lick her thumb, using the moistened digit to remove a smear from a small nose. "There you go." The nose, and the smiling face it belonged to, disappeared with a giggle.

Barac snuck a kiss, then grinned down at his Chosen. "I owe Holl a report," he reminded her. "What's this 'situation' requiring my always-sage advice?"

If about the children? The Sarcs had hired tutors; he'd be useless. Ruti had grown up on Acranam, where children were combined in a crèche until unChosen. With matter-of-fact competence, she'd taken charge of the children before anyone else thought to, and would, he was certain, have swept up the younger unChosen had they let her. Her determination they be happy and protected was a kindness to their parents and, he'd been told frequently, a credit to his Chosen.

Other than the part where they hadn't had their chance in the Happy Place since arriving on the ship. He'd felt no guilt whatsoever at interrupting Sira and Morgan's private moment.

"You're not arguing with Dre's grandparents again, are you?" he asked. There'd been a spectacular disagreement between Ruti and the Amna Om'ray, Ghos and Worra di Eathem, the pair far from ready to have their descendant "play" in the M'hir.

"Of course not." *Smug.* "They've come around."

Who could resist her? "So?"

Her sweet round face turned grave, dashing any hope he'd had this would be easy. "It's Andi. I promised Sira I'd talk to her parents."

Surely an easy conversation. Nik and Josa were friendly and kind, if absentminded; Nik tended to mutter numbers under her breath and when together, the pair would miss meals if not reminded, busy building unClan-like devices. As far as Barac could tell, they spent just as much time dismantling what they'd built.

"And?" he prodded patiently, knowing better than to rush his Chosen.

Unhappiness leaked through. "I tried. They wouldn't listen to me."

"Why not?"

"They didn't believe me. That something's wrong with Andi."

Was this what he'd *tasted,* a warning about the Birth Watcher? Which could only mean—Barac tensed. *Is something wrong with Sira's baby?*

Why would you think that? With sudden *alarm. What's WRONG?!*

Wincing, Barac held up his hands. "I asked you first."

Sorry. Ruti stooped to toss back a fabric bag being used as a plaything. She took a breath, then looked up at him, eyes moist. "You know how I am when I'm upset."

Ferocious.

Fragile. Those of Acranam had been more connected than other M'hiray. They'd died all at once, Ruti linked to that devastating loss. He'd almost lost her.

She'd pulled herself through it. Barac rested his chin atop Ruti's head, her hair winding around his neck, and folded her in his arms and Power. Let others underestimate her; in her way, his Chosen was as strong as Sira.

He let go, drawing her with him to sit on the nearest bench. "Start at the beginning, my love." When she glanced anxiously at the clusters of children, he refrained from mentioning the other dozen or so capable adults.

Ruti sat, the ends of her hair twitching. "Andi told Sira she promised Rasa she'd find his grandmother."

"His dead grandmother." He knew Andi had the Om'ray Talent, to sense the physical location of other Clan, but this? "A cruel trick."

Disapproval. "You know Andi wouldn't do that. She believes she hears the dead. Sira—and Aryl—were worried enough to ask her to stop *listening* in the M'hir. I'm not certain she has, or can." Ruti's lower lip trembled. "Barac, is it even possible?"

It wasn't.

He held in the words, thinking hard and fast. Kurr had read the works of Clan philosophers, the more obscure the better, and would, if provoked, happily quote passages at his lesser-read brother. Most had been over his head, but Barac tried to remember. Clan minds created the M'hir, or was it that the M'hir created part of the mind? Existence was mind more than flesh, or some weird blend of both. There'd been something about death being transformative—

But no less final. That was a point of rare agreement.

Because the dead became ghosts. Everyone knew it, because anyone could *hear* them. A ghost was the final trace of a mind before it dissolved in the M'hir. An incoherent ramble. A scream. A last cold *sense* of Power.

Ghosts were tied to a place, as much as the M'hir could be said to have location, and were uncomfortable to encounter at the best of times. The more powerful lingered; he'd met a few himself, serving as object lessons for those learning to 'port. This will be you, if you overestimate your strength.

They were a potentially fatal distraction, as if the M'hir needed more.

There'd have been hundreds of ghosts in Trade Pact space. Around Cersi. Reason enough to stay out of the M'hir in either location till they faded to nothing.

Nik and Josa traveled by starship, not the M'hir; they thought in terms of physical distance. They'd know *Sona* had left Clan-touched space behind.

No wonder they'd dismissed Ruti's concern. "It's not possible," Barac said heavily. "We've moved too far. It has to be Andi's imagination."

"That's what Josa said." Ruti's little chin lifted, firmed. "They've told me to stop talking about it, but I must—someone must. I've been with Andi since we lifted, Barac. She's a kind child and thoughtful. She isn't capable of making this up, not on purpose. I believe she *hears* something."

"Not ghosts. Not here," Barac began. "Not unless—" He stopped, mouth gone dry.

—unless they'd dragged the dead with them, hooked into the ship's engines with the M'hir—

Now whose imagination was out of control? He held in a shudder. "I'll take a look."

Barac opened himself to that other space, anchored by his link to Ruti. Darkness boiled and dropped and heaved. He sensed but couldn't see the lines of light that connected the Clan—the living Clan—one to another. That wasn't within his Power.

He had heard a ghost before. He *listened,* but all he *heard* was a low, rising growl. His agitation come to life, building, being echoed back even louder—

Time to leave. He pulled out, reassured. "No ghosts, Ruti."

She made a rude noise. "You think I didn't check right away? I don't *hear* them either." Taking his hand, she worked her fingers between his and squeezed, hard. When she spoke, her voice was low and troubled. "There's worse. Andi doesn't understand the meaning of death. Or doesn't want to. She insists everyone is still—out there."

Barac looked for the child, spotting her cross-legged on a table with her Om'ray friend Dre. They clapped a complicated rhythm, Andi laughing when she failed to keep up and their fingers tangled. Implausibly normal.

"I don't know what to say," he admitted. "Other than it may take time—"

He felt Ruti tremble. *What if Andi's mind is failing? Like those of Luek and Nyso—like poor Eloe.*

Could a child be stricken by madness—and no ordinary child, but Sira's Birth Watcher? He refused to think it.

Barac kissed his Chosen's cheek. "You asked for my advice."

She nodded, eyes wide.

If this was what the *taste* warned of, there was only one option, Barac decided. If it wasn't, well, he refused to take that chance. "Stay with Andi and the other children. Have Jacqui come and help you—" Jacqui was their Birth Watcher, who might sense what others couldn't, who at the very least would protect Ruti and her unborn. "I'll talk to Sira." With what *confidence* he could muster.

And find Morgan, who understood the workings of the mind, even a Clan one.

They'd need him, if the worst were true.

Chapter 6

S*ONA*'S COUNCIL GATHERED in the Star Chamber, members answering with a promptness that told me my mental *summons* had been expected.

The best shields couldn't stop rumor—or worry.

The day had started too soon and poorly, with Eloe's troubles. I'd a feeling it wouldn't end much better. Still, watching them arrive, gesturing respectful greetings Morgan and I returned, I allowed myself a moment's satisfaction. This group had come together our first shipday without me; met since, most often without me, although any one might have me *summon* the others. After all, I was the ship's Keeper, responsible for communication. They weren't the most powerful of select families—a couple of members could barely 'port—but I'd put this Council against any I remembered. Experience, compassion, skill. We'd do well, if these were the ones who guided us in our new home.

Five Om'ray represented the Clans of Cersi: Odon di Rihma'at and Teris di Uruus from Sona, by cruel fate now the most populous; Ghos di Eathem from Amna, a gifted Healer, though not of minds; from Tuana, Kunthea di Mendolar, and Rayna, Hap di Annk. All but Ghos had served on their respective Councils.

I'd heard Ruis di Nemat had been Rayna's first choice, as that

Clan's sole surviving Adept. She'd declined. Perhaps, like me, she'd been glad to relinquish authority.

As Morgan asked, I'd brought her to this meeting; she chose to sit down the curve, at some distance from the rest, her face set in tight lines. Hap went to her, offering a palm for private communion; Ruis refused with a Human shake of her head.

Being here for Morgan's purpose.

There were three M'hiray on Council: Degal di Sawnda'at, once Councilor in the Trade Pact, and Tle di Parth, the powerful Chooser who'd held the same post and was certain to show up, invited or not, plus one more.

Nik sud Prendolat, representing our four scientists, stood a little apart, not because the tall, brilliant Clanswoman was among the weaker here but because her nature was to observe, giving opinions when asked for them. I suspected she'd been Morgan's quiet suggestion, a good one.

Aryl di Sarc would have been mine—Om'ray as much as M'hiray, aware of our past and present—but I knew better than to suggest it. While she allowed these Clan to know of her, my great-grandmother refused to reveal herself to the ship's entire company. Her decision, but in this Aryl and I agreed. An adult consciousness within an unborn would affront the M'hiray and be a dark reminder, to the Om'ray, of the Vyna.

I trust I'll have your excellent advice, Great-grandmother, I sent to her at a level no one else would sense. A benefit to my unusual pregnancy.

I may have none to offer. We've left the worlds I know. A flash of anticipation. *I hope for wonders.*

I hoped to arrive in one piece, but that I kept to myself. *Do you wish to look through my eyes?*

A pause, then: *My thanks, but I prefer not.*

Was that *exhaustion?*

As to why—I felt my face grow hot. *Aryl—*

I promise you, I wasn't there, Sira. You had your privacy. A pause for which I was grateful, busy trying not to share my *relief* at that while keeping it from Morgan. The lives of Chosen could be complicated.

Then, the feel of her mindvoice oddly languid, *I dreamed.*

As if this was a problem. Aryl slept; I'd assumed she dreamed. A mistake, obviously. *Are you all right?*

Involuntarily, my fingers found the bracelet, traced a ripple like water along the metal, then stopped. *I will be.*

A less than reassuring answer. *Rest,* I sent. *If I need you, I'll wake you.*

Try not to need me.

My sense of her vanished, worrying me even more. I put my hand over my abdomen, pressed gently. We'd talk about this later, I promised myself, Aryl willing.

Meanwhile, *Sona's* Councilors were almost ready. I watched them take their seats. We'd brought with us a few robes of office, heavy with embroidery and tradition; by mutual consent, they'd been cleaned and packed away. Dressed to work, these Clan, arranging themselves along the first long bench.

I stayed on my feet at one end, facing what had been the entrance to the Star Chamber before *Sona* sealed the corridor beyond. Morgan stood before the blue panel as though guarding the nonexistent door. He'd tucked his pack out of sight after retrieving one item.

He wore it: his coat, the knee-length garment half armor and half armory, although those functions were well concealed. Today, I decided, the coat served a different purpose. Like the beard and vest, Morgan's coat reminded those here what he was and where he'd come from—that he'd knowledge the Clan did not.

I felt some anticipation of my own.

Two figures appeared: Destin di Anel, who gave her greeting before going to stand behind Teris di Uruus—answering who'd invited the Sona First Scout—and Barac.

Who'd no reason to be here as far as I knew, but such meetings were open to all, another difference from the past. After the courtesies, my cousin took a post beside Morgan, eyes ahead.

Human fingers flickered in a covert message, convenient in this place where sendings were, quite rightly, forbidden. <u>Trouble.</u>

Something the tension in every line of Barac's slender frame shouted to anyone who knew him. Or was it more? Morgan could

taste change, a Talent shared by my cousin and the now-sleeping
Aryl. I made the tiny motion that meant, depending on context,
End the party? or Run for it?

Stay.

He'd had no warning, then; a relief. Morgan made another
sign. This asked a question. Defer?

Leave his plan in favor of hearing from Barac. Under the ruse
of pushing back my hair, I bent a thumb. No. Whatever brought
my cousin would be important; it wasn't urgent. He'd have broadcast news of a crisis at once.

No, I thought, permitting myself a touch of self-pity, he'd have
told me first.

After a pause without further arrivals, Hap rose to her feet and
moved into the open space. "The meeting is convened," she announced in her hoarse whisper. Healers had restored her crushed
throat; her full voice had been left on Cersi. "First on our agenda
is the motion from Teris di Uruus, regarding the appropriate
naming of children." She returned to her seat.

Well aware this wasn't about children at all, I kept my tongue between my teeth. Teris and a couple of other Om'ray Adepts wanted
the to-them meaningless "sud" removed from M'hiray names. It had
been left behind in their history following the discovery that the "di"
in the name of Adepts was the key to opening a Cloisters' outer
door. Aryl, partly responsible for that discovery, had elected not to
remind *Sona*'s Council "sud" once simply denoted an Om'ray Chosen who'd assumed the last name of his or her partner.

I'd no objection to the change. The M'hiray'd used "sud" to
designate those family lines of lesser Power. Useful in a list of
dead ancestors—pointless among the living, for Clan instinctively
measured theirs against others.

Mine being the greatest. It meant, among other things, that my
dear cousin—and the rest—brought me bad news first, as if I'd
know any better what to do.

It'd be easier excusing myself from breathing than such reports. I eyed Barac. My deepest wish was for no more occasion to
lead. Ever. Not even to forestall what was bound to be a long and
heated debate about nothing.

Vy. Ray. So. Gro. Ne. Tua. Ye. Pa. Am. Nor. Xro. Fa. Hoveny numbers. Add the "-na" and you had the Om'ray Clans, past and present, neatly identified for the experiment on Cersi. For all we knew, our names were just as contrived. If there was an answer, it lay ahead, wherever this ship, *So-na*, took us.

In the meantime, Council was welcome to debate the "sud." Barac and Morgan best get comfortable.

Teris, about to rise, hesitated as Odon stood next, taking a step and then turning to face the rest. "Nomenclature can wait," he declared. "We were summoned. By whom? Why?"

My turn. I beckoned my Chosen, who strode forward to stand near Odon. "By me, Council," he said calmly. "I've a matter I believe warrants your attention. My thanks." He made a small, courteous bow.

Shields up, but my kind had never learned to control their faces. Most, including Odon as he granted Morgan the floor, showed honest concern; reasonable, considering Morgan's expertise with the ship and its workings.

Teris looked to have swallowed something sour and Degal shifted as though uncomfortable. Neither objected. Wise, I thought, staring at each in turn.

Ruis rose and went to put herself beside Morgan. She bowed. "By me as well."

Part of the plan. Change the equation, my Human would say, and I could see the result. Attention sharpened and not just the Councilors'. Barac leaned slightly forward, lips tight.

"Proceed, Healers," Hap instructed.

To make it clear I'd no part in this, I took the nearest seat, joining Tle di Parth. My hair slid to the opposite shoulder. Hers, though still lifeless, was caught up in a familiar metal net. She'd taken it from my mother's husk. I could hardly object; Tle had been more family to Mirim than any by blood.

On any other Chooser, the net would have been presumption, maybe pitied. In Tle, almost my equal, it was a warning. I will need this, the net proclaimed, more than any of you.

She leaned over, pitching her voice to my ears only. "You know what this is about."

The unChosen believed many things about Choice, including that those Joined had no secrets, that we somehow blended together, the more powerful mind ruling both.

Not for me to educate Tle di Parth, even if I'd been inclined. I gave a noncommittal shrug.

Point being, I didn't know. Morgan had seen to that. Though I found myself leaning toward an idea.

"We ask the Council's guidance and support." Confident yet respectful. Morgan paused to look at Ruis, who gestured him to continue. Establishing that they were of one mind. Clever, my Human. "My fellow Healer-of-minds and I have encountered a potentially serious problem."

Ghos stood to speak. "We're aware of the M'hiray Chosen and that they are doing well. And how you helped the Tuana child, Eloe. Our thanks."

Kunthea rose as well. "Thanks aren't enough. I was there. Morgan saved Eloe and eased the hearts of those closest to her." Voice husky, pale eyes moist, the elder gestured beholdenness. "We're few. So few."

Few indeed. We'd rescued twenty from Tuana and seventeen from Rayna. From Amna, Ghos' Clan, a pitiful nine, but the Healer echoed the gesture as he resumed his seat with the rest. "We owe you a great debt, Jason Morgan."

Degal's eyebrows drew together until they tangled. "Saved the child from what?" he snapped, not bothering to rise. "What was wrong with her?"

"An ill of the mind." Odon leaped up again. "That's why you're here, isn't it? It's spreading. I've heard. Did it start with those M'—?"

"Before you incite panic, Councilor," Ruis interrupted in a tone to make even my back stiffen, "let my colleague finish."

Odon's eyes narrowed, but he sketched a mute apology, sinking down.

"Nothing's spread," Morgan stated, to more than my relief. "Our three patients weren't in contact. They've been healed." He nodded to Ruis in acknowledgment. "But we have concerns. Their afflictions were similar enough we suspect they had the same cause. Not a contagion—" before the room could erupt at that terrifying possibility, "—but it could become as serious. With your help, we will be able to confirm, or put aside, our suspicion."

He'd confirmed mine. I kept my smile to myself. A test. It had to be. Of me as well as the rest. I admired his gall. To examine our ruling Council meant they'd see the results firsthand. If Morgan was right, and they showed the same inner stress, Council would want to act and, why then, he could present whatever he intended to do to "fix" the problem.

Too easy, I realized, the flicker of triumph gone. If I knew anything about Morgan, this was only the setup, the first offer on the table. The trick was yet to be played.

Hap rose, giving a small bow. "Our help is yours, of course. Whatever we can do. Which is?"

"Our thanks. Ruis?"

"We've identified what to look for in a mind." The Rayna Healer-of-minds walked over to Hap and lifted her hands. "Allow us to scan you."

She'd a decent amount of gall, too, I thought.

An instant's silence, then bedlam, everyone on their feet, more than one shouting.

My Human clasped his hands behind his back, his legs slightly apart. Ready to do this for hours, that told me.

Tle's laugh silenced the rest. "Ridiculous. No offense, Healers, but you would waste your effort and our time. I don't know about my fellows here, but I assure you I've no urge to rip my own skin or cower in a corner."

"Then you should have no objection," Nik di Prendolat stated.

"I do not. We make a reasonable sample of our population diversity, other than age." With a slide of her eyes to Morgan.

Who dipped his head, conceding the point.

The Chooser hesitated, then looked to me.

Of course she did. Before I could offer to go first, Ruis spoke up. "Sira's been scanned already, Tle." She smiled. "To confirm our method."

Play along, or object? Play, instinct told me. Morgan was too subtle for this to be my moment. I stood and moved a little distance, smiling at Ruis. "Painless," I said, confirming the lie.

If it was a lie. Could my Chosen have scanned me without my knowledge? Or Ruis, while I watched them work with the di Kessa'ats? I found myself oddly flustered and checked my shields to be sure none of it came through.

Shields or not, Morgan could read me like a vid. His fingers moved. <u>Steady.</u>

And knew my mind—who better? Relieved, I gave the tiniest of nods.

"Council, are we to permit this?" Hap rasped. "Your hands with mine if so." Hers lifted and Ruis bowed her head in appreciation.

Nik raised her hand, followed by Odon, Ghos, and Kunthea. Tle's rose, albeit slowly, and Degal's, ever one to wait for the rest.

"Wait." Teris frowned, the ends of her white hair coiled with tension. "How deep a scan?"

A person with a secret, or what she viewed as one. Trade Pact thinking, I chided myself. Who here wouldn't protect their private thoughts?

Again, it was Ruis who answered, Morgan who watched, his blue eyes intent. "Slight. We will look for effort where there should be none, the sign a mind unknowingly struggles with itself. This warns us the cause is present. We learned from the di Kessa'ats this effort leaves its mark upon the link between Chosen—a strain. By scanning one, we gauge the health of both." She shared a quiet, reassuring *confidence.* "Remember, only if that struggle is lost does the mind become afflicted. We've healed with success. Retain full shields if you wish; we will touch nothing of your active mind or memory."

"'We,'" echoed Degal, hand lowering as though pulled by a weight.

Hair, a thick twist of it, slithered over my shoulder and curled, the tip flicking back and forth. Fully in accord, I pretended not to see.

<u>No.</u>

I pretended not to see that, either. How dare the fool reject my—

"I'd hate to work on this old stick myself." Ghos smacked Degal on the knee, much to that worthy's shock. "Ruis, you take him, along with Hap, Teris, and our Chooser. Over by them," he ordered Degal, the formidable Clansman scrambling to obey before he'd the chance to realize he'd just been "dealt with" as if a child. Teris smoothed the moment by inviting him to stand by her side. Something about that pairing made me uneasy, but I shook it off. I wanted the Om'ray to accept us, didn't I? Ghos finished, "The rest of us acceptable to you, Jason?"

Morgan bowed. "At your service."

Destin stepped around the bench to join Teris, her face unreadable. No outward reaction from Odon, but I couldn't imagine he'd be pleased. Politics, history—I neither knew nor cared which had the First Scout align with one member of her former Council over the other.

But when Barac moved to sit beside Ghos, a deliberately charming smile on his handsome face, I didn't care who felt my *approval.*

"Let us begin," Ruis said, resting her palm over Destin's forehead, for the scout had put herself where she would be first. Destin's eyes closed.

Wisps of the Healer's hair drifted forward to be met—greeted?—by the First Scout's. The delicate, fleeting almost-touch was like nothing I'd seen or heard of before.

Certainly my hair did its painful best to avoid contact with any other Chosen Clanswoman's. I tucked away the sight to share with Aryl when she awoke.

Ruis straightened, looked at Morgan, then wordlessly moved to stand in front of Teris.

While my Chosen took his place in front of Odon.

Much as I'd have liked to see if Teris' hair responded in the same way to Ruis', I wasn't about to look away from Morgan. To my intense embarrassment, the instant my Human's palm covered Odon's high forehead, I was blinded by hair boiling around my head.

Outwardly, Morgan ignored me and my misbehaving hair, but I felt a touch of *amusement.* Done, he took away his hand, exchanging another look with Ruis. If they signaled one another, it was beyond me to know how—or what they communicated. Some

Healers-of-mind trick, I thought, slightly insulted. It was like being in a roomful of Drapsk, with their feathery antennae and drafts for coms.

Drapsk did teach patience, among many other lessons, especially when it came to caring for one's tribe. They might take that to an extreme—a ship's company able to clear a bar filled with other species simply by walking in the door—but I missed the little things.

Would we encounter other aliens? Find those who were like us or mysteriously not, those with complex life cycles or merely messy? The dangerous who nonetheless shared common interests—

My people hoped for the simplicity of a world of Clan and nothing more.

They'd get at least one alien.

This was what I'd drawn Jason Morgan into, I thought as I watched him move from Clan to Clan. To be utterly alone.

Will closed any distance along our link; my Chosen, as usual, deciding when and which rules applied. *Not so, Witchling. You owed me a new world, remember? I intend to collect.* Almost *fierce*, that, as if nothing mattered more than I believe him.

And I did. *We'll explore it together,* I promised.

While in the realm of what breathed air and flew within a starship, my Human stood away from Barac, saying, "And we're done."

Interlude

THE WATCHER WAITED, almost within *reach* of the Great Ones, where AllThereIs sank and rose along their elliptical dance, having form at times . . .

Or none.

The endless beauty of the dance could distract a Watcher from her duty, had not protecting that beauty been her duty.

And worth any sacrifice.

She hadn't moved. What had caught her attention had come closer, moving Between, if not yet close enough. The *substance* of it, if substance there was, remained unclear. Faint, that sense of *tearing*. A wound?

She couldn't be certain, not yet. Others, small flickers of *intention* and *hunger*, gathered around it, coming closer as well, adding their *taste* to what she felt. *Feeders.* Opportunists who'd scatter as soon as they sensed her *interest.*

Beautiful, in their own way. AllThereIs encompassed them as well, whether they understood such things or not. These had been less before the breach. More, she remembered, many more afterward.

Having *feasted.*

They were less again. Others, more. Such weavings enriched song and story, even as the dance moved with the Great Ones and AllThereIs changed with the journey.

While she would wait, here.

And Watch.

Chapter 7

WHILE RUIS AND MORGAN conversed, heads together and away from the rest, I pointedly watched a large white something-or-other plop its way among the colorful streaks of stars across the ceiling, making it clear I would not be part of any discussion before we heard their results.

A point lost on Tle di Parth. I saw her approach out of the corner of my eye, saw when she moved Barac—who'd had the same idea—from her path with an absent flick of her right hand.

Silencing my impulse to call my cousin over first.

Instinct and, in Tle's case, tedious practice kept a Chooser's right hand away from possible contact. Choice was offered with the right hand; a Joining could only be attempted with the physical connection between the right hands of Chooser and Candidate.

She might not have noticed doing it, but even if I hadn't once been a Chooser, I'd been taught to pay close attention to such involuntary acts—most memorably the time Morgan had me watch for purple excretions from some Nrusans who'd appeared uninterested, said excretions a sign of desperate longing for our goods—

What mattered here and now was Tle's state of mind. Nyso had hidden; I'd no hope Tle's break with reality would be so peaceful.

We'd five, soon to be seven, eligible unChosen aboard and nowhere to hide them if she lost control. I wasn't the only one
amazed she, Jacqui di Mendolar, and the Om'ray's sole Chooser,
Alet di Uruus, continued to exhibit such unusual restraint.

So far.

I offered my hand, palm up. With Council momentarily ad-
journed, and members busy communing in seeming silence, the
rules didn't apply.

Tle's dark eyes gleamed as she put her left hand overtop. Cool,
damp, with long elegant fingers. I braced, ready for her to test
her Power against mine, the preliminaries being important to
M'hiray, particularly this one.

Instead, words formed, soft and slow. *I have this madness.*

Ruis told you?

A dismissive curl of her lip. *The Om'ray didn't find it. Her scan
was pitifully shallow.* Tle held herself straight, well aware she was
an imposing figure, even unChosen, tall and with the striking
green eyes of her Parth heritage. *You could.*

Go deep into a mind that believed itself mad? Hardly worse
than going into a sane Tle, as far as I was concerned. *I'm no Healer—*

He is.

RAGE surged across our link before I could think to stop it. I
did, somehow.

Pain whitened lines at her eyes and mouth, but Tle's hand
didn't budge. *I don't ask for myself, Sira. If I am mad, Asdny's at risk.
I know no one believes we will Join—*

Because Asdny would die, but I couldn't interrupt. This wasn't
the Tle I knew.

—and that may be true. A staggering admission. *But he is ever in
my thoughts and heart. I fear if I succumb I won't be able to keep myself
from—from spreading this to him. No one should face such horrible things
in their dreams. No one.*

I sent *calm*, buying time. 'Horrible things?' I'd faced what
would fit that description in my dreams, as a Chooser.

They'd been real: monstrous forms in the M'hir that fed on
the unbalance caused by the Power-of-Choice. They'd found me

thanks to the dear little Drapsk. I'd survived them, in part, because of the Rugherans.

The M'hir, I sighed to myself, used to seem so simple.

I pulled forth a memory, careful to keep it small and quick, then *shared* it with Tle.

She gasped and stumbled back. "You're mad, too!"

HUSH! I snapped, hoping no one else had paid attention. I reached out and caught her hands, pulling her toward me. *Neither of us are, if that's what you've dreamed. Such creatures are real. They exist in the M'hir. You saw the images the Drapsk machine showed us.*

She frowned, but no longer resisted. *None like this memory—like my dream. None with such teeth.*

The dear little Drapsk had edited what they'd provided. *These are only attracted to Choosers of great Power.* It wasn't flattery; I needed her confidence to return. *Asdny's safe from them, and they can't hurt you unless you linger in the M'hir.*

If she did, they'd fasten what weren't mouths and drain her Power, leaving her to die there. A detail for another conversation. I trusted Tle's instinct for self-preservation.

She glanced toward Morgan and then back to me. *Are those things in the M'hir why I've lost the urge to Call?*

They hadn't stopped mine, another bit of information Tle didn't need at present. *It's just as well, isn't it?* I said to Tle, proud to keep a straight face when hers wrinkled first with confusion.

Then dismay. *What if they don't go away? What if I can never Call?*

I released her hands. "One problem at a time," I said brightly. A motto to live by, that was. "Let's hear what our Healers-of-minds have to say about us first."

It didn't satisfy her, but only Choice would at this stage in her life. I'd need to talk with Eand and Moyla about our other Choosers, not to mention monsters, the M'hir, and restraint.

To my surprise, Tle bowed. "Agreed, Sira. I look forward to the education of this Council—" a tight little smile, "—in the ways of a certain Human."

As did I, I thought, seeing Morgan and Ruis come toward the rest.

So long as there wasn't shouting.

✳ ✳ ✳

There wasn't shouting.

I hadn't realized stunned silence could be worse.

Nik slowly rose to her feet. "Half, you say."

"Yes." Ruis' face was as pale as Morgan's was grim. "Better than we'd feared."

"Better?! If that proportion carries across the ship's population, close to a hundred could be on the verge of this—this affliction!"

"Whom among us?" Odon looked around the room. "We should know."

"You do; you just haven't realized it." Morgan's gaze touched one after another. "Have you been afraid to fall asleep because of nightmares—or because you can't be sure you'll wake up again?" Calm, relentless, like a tide. "Do you believe you survived by mistake? That others judge you less worthy than those they lost? Is facing each day harder than imagining being buried alive by the Oud or attacked by Assemblers—"

STOP! From more than one.

My Chosen didn't flinch, but his voice softened. "These feelings are normal, however terrible and powerful, and they can leave wounds; I believe that's what we're seeing here. Most would heal on their own, with time. We don't have any. This—" he lifted one hand to our surroundings, encompassing the uncertainty of our lives, "—only makes it harder."

"There will be some," Ruis elaborated, "whose wounds go too deep for time alone. They'll need our help."

If I had to guess who wouldn't need any, I'd pick Sona's tough First Scout, busy assessing the rest, her eyes narrowed in speculation.

One who would? Hap. Despite her outward strength, something about her concerned me, not that I was a Healer-of-minds.

"You talk of wounds. A 'cause' inside us." Degal repeated Morgan's gesture. "What if that cause is here?"

Ruis frowned at him. "'Here?' What do you mean?"

"The ship." The M'hiray Councilor looked around for support. "It meddled with us once. Implanted memories. Altered us."

Had he not been listening?

Support came from the last person I'd expect. "A valid point, Degal," Morgan acknowledged with every evidence of sincerity. "Keeper?"

Another silence; all eyes turned to me.

It wasn't a "valid" point at all. What was he thinking? Why, I thought darkly, waste time on this?

"Give us a moment," I requested, trying not to glower. Sona, *have you been inside our heads again?*

>I am in your head, Keeper, and no other. That is what a Keeper is.<

Shipbrain. "The answer's no," I relayed.

Ruis gestured agreement. "Of course it's not the ship. To use the Maker," she said carefully, "a Keeper must Dream."

Meaning nothing so innocent as a nightmare. The Dream Chamber had been so-named because hidden within it was an apparatus to physically connect the Keeper's sleeping mind— mine—with the ship's.

A connection unlike any I'd experienced with a living mind: invasive, intrusive and, for all my supposed Power, disconcertingly more under the ship's control than mine.

"I haven't Dreamed," I confirmed. And had no intention of doing so again. Having *Sona* establish a comlink in my head? Enough for a lifetime, thank you.

"Thank you, Keeper." Ruis turned her attention to Council. "I assure you, what confronts us is not the Maker's doing."

"What matters is dealing with it," Ghos said. "Let me be the first to ask your aid, Healers-of-minds." His mouth twisted. "No need to name names, Morgan. I'm among those who cannot sleep, for fear of what awaits me there."

"As am I." Hap, barely a whisper.

Degal gave a short nod, before putting his face in his hands. The rest remained silent.

"We will heal everyone afflicted." Ruis' hair strained against its net. "But we ask your patience. Any of our Healers can scan for the cause, but only Morgan and I have the necessary Talent to deal with the damage. Healing Eloe and the di Kessa'ats drained us both. We must rest before we deal with any more."

"At that rate, it could take—" Nik stopped short, her expression grave. "Do we have that long?"

"No. If matters remain as they are, I fear most of our afflicted will fail before we can help them." Having pronounced what seemed our doom, Ruis lifted a hand toward my Human. "Which is why we have brought a proposal for Council. Morgan?"

Did anyone else remark how he adjusted his balance, ever-so-slightly, setting his body as if to prepare for—what?

Here it was, his endgame. I braced myself, too, for all the good it would do.

Morgan bowed to Ruis, then the Council. He rose, his face expressionless. "Let's use the Maker to repair everyone at once."

I shot to my feet, the others doing the same, and I'd no doubt the look on my face held the shock on theirs. *There has to be another way.* If there was a pain-dealing *SNAP* to it, I was in no mood to apologize.

Morgan met my disapproving glare, his blue eyes sober, shields lowered. *The backlash of their memories almost trapped us both.* His *dread* filled me until I could hardly breathe. *Memories and emotion can't affect a machine like the Maker. Its function, properly targeted, could be the answer.*

Aware we consulted—no doubt also well aware of my *outrage*—the others waited.

Consulted being the key, here. I wished for Aryl's council, then stopped before I disturbed her. Aryl wasn't who I needed.

I swallowed my abhorrence. I trusted Morgan. That didn't mean jumping right into a Dream, not if I could help it. *I can ask questions, for a start.*

A fleeting hint of *warmth. Good. Let's test a hypothetical, Witchling. The designers of the Maker should have installed a protocol for passengers distressed during the journey. Ask if it can help someone afraid of enclosed spaces. If yes, ask how.*

I swallowed, doing my utmost to sound as though about to

request new blankets and not the rebuilding of our minds, again. "Your pardon. Give me a moment to communicate with the ship."

They sat down without protest, though Barac looked as uneasy as I felt.

Sona, *can you help someone afraid of enclosed spaces?*

The answer was immediate: >*Yes.*<

How?

>*Such fear can be removed.*<

That sounded promising. Almost. I shared the ship's response with Morgan. *How would it help someone who has suffered a traumatic loss?*

I dutifully relayed the question.

Immediate. >*What is a "traumatic loss?"*<

Save me from servo brains. I thought hastily. *An event that leaves a disturbing memory.*

>*A memory can be removed.*<

As if our minds were full of bits and pieces to be discarded at random. We were made of our memories; something I knew better than most. Though I sensed Morgan ready to twitch, I couldn't let this pass. *What if the memory is important?*

For the first time, a delay. I looked at my Chosen, raised a brow. Lips tight, he nodded.

Finally, >*The disturbing quality of a memory can only be moderated. The disturbance cannot be eliminated while the memory itself remains. A memory can be removed.*<

As if trying to talk me out of an imperfect procedure.

Sira? Beneath my name, *caution.* Morgan, fussing.

Not fussing, I corrected. Reminding me I had a partner, one who understood such cold and logical minds. I shared what *Sona* had told me.

Well done, he sent. *State that the memory in question must be left intact. Ask for options.*

You can't take away memories, I told *Sona. We mustn't forget what's happened. Do you understand? To move forward, we need to remember without*—I faltered. Without pain? Without grief?

Without guilt?

>*Keeper, my understanding is this. Your initial request was "how would I help someone who has suffered a traumatic loss?" From your subsequent qualifications and their tone, I conclude this is of present, critical concern. Am I correct to rephrase your request as follows: "How can you make my memory of traumatic loss bearable?"*<

Nothing could. I knew it, in that moment. Felt hopelessness replace everything and reeled.

Hundreds lost . . .

. . . a sister.

A world decimated . . .

. . . our home, destroyed.

Morgan wanted to heal the impossible—we were shattered beyond repair.

I was—

Sira. Like arms around me, holding me upright. *Beloved.* Like the feel of a warm cheek against mine. My hair *lifted,* sweeping soft around me as other unseen but *felt* arms took hold. Morgan. Aryl, awake and with me. Putting themselves between me and the cliff beyond which plunged black, unending despair, somehow calming even the M'hir that connected us so we three seemed to float outside of time.

We aren't done, chit, with confidence. *Not even close.*

The support was theirs; the effort could only be mine.

With an act of will I didn't realize I had left, I made myself open my eyes to focus on those waiting nearby. To see them, as they really were. Odon and Degal, determined to succeed in a world new to both. Ruis and Ghos, committed to making us one Clan. Nik and Tle, refusing to consider defeat. Teris, ever-questioning. Destin, scarred and callused, ready for any battle. Kunthea, his face creased not from grief, but from a lifetime of smiles and laughter.

All but Tle had a Chosen, another life bound to theirs. Of the Chosen, three had children or unChosen or grandchildren, relying on them to make a future.

My eyes rested last on Barac, who'd lost as much as I or any.

Somehow, I'd known he'd smile at me. "Well, cousin?"

"We're not done," I told him, surprised to believe it.

Meeting Morgan's gaze with a smile of my own, I sent to the ship. *You are correct,* Sona. *We all need to bear our losses and remain strong. Can you help without tampering with our memories? Everyone is unique, as is their loss.*

>*Words are insufficient, Keeper, for me to respond in a meaningful manner. Will you Dream with me?*<

There it was, then. "*Sona* wants me to Dream," I announced. "But I don't see how that can help. I wouldn't know what to do or say," my voice shook. "I'm no Healer-of-minds."

"I am."

No. He couldn't think—

"I propose to Council that we Dream together, so I can show the ship how to help those in need if it becomes necessary."

He did.

"No." Morgan understood machines—but this wasn't the same, I thought, horrified. Dreaming with the ship, that mental invasion, was safe for me only because it had been designed for our species, not his. "No!" I said, and louder, in case anyone missed it the first time.

"The Keeper answers to Council, does she not?"

I turned my head, very slowly, to look at Ruis. Whatever she saw in my face made her blanch, but she didn't back down. "We ask a vote."

Eyes flashing, Barac stepped forward. "We won't be remade again. Not even for this."

"Agreed." Morgan, reasonable. Confident. "We'll only use the Maker if I'm convinced it can and will heal this particular trauma—and do nothing more."

Nothing more? They didn't know him as I did.

A starship we couldn't control; a captain intent on just that, asking to be put inside whatever passed for its mind—

My Human wanted to fix things. He always did. Starting with those afflicted, of course, but oh, he wouldn't stop there. We were at *Sona*'s mercy, and he trusted the ship's ancient programming no more than I did.

This wasn't the way. *Dreaming is guided by the ship, not the Keeper,*

I sent, with all the *urgency* I could. *Let me do this alone. It answers my questions. Tell me what to say.*

I can't tell you how to Heal, Witchling. The ship can take that information from me.

And what if it takes more?

He didn't answer. Likely couldn't.

Hap signaled the others to sit. "The Council votes. Raise your hand with mine, if you agree our Healer-of-minds should Dream with our Keeper."

"Wait!" Ghos stood and stepped forward, smiling. No, beaming, from ear-to-ear. "Worra's sent word. Gricel's baby's coming!" Their daughter's second. Ghos' joy and the news lightened spirits around in the room. "Sira, we have to go. Now. The vote can wait."

"Pardon?" If that had a shrill note, I was entitled. This discussion was far from over, and I intended to stay for every word. I was the Keeper—Morgan my—

SIRA!! Come Come Come! Andi, her sending *happy* enough to ring in my head, followed by Jacqui di Mendolar's calmer, but no less determined: *All those pregnant must be present. Hurry, Sira!*

The baby's coming? Aryl, with joy. *Sira, we mustn't be late.*

All around the chamber, heads bobbed in agreement. Hap's smile was almost as wide as Ghos' "Go. We'll receive our First Scout's report."

"Sira." Ghos held out his hand. "They're in the Core."

You'd best do as they say, Witchling. Oh, and didn't Morgan look properly contrite?

I glowered. *Did you plan this, too?*

He had the grace to blush. *No.*

SIRA!

Defeated by biology, outnumbered, I gave an irritated bow before taking Ghos' hand and preparing the locate for the Core.

I paused, looking at Morgan. He opened his mouth, then closed it, lips tight. Not done, that expression said.

Oh, but I was.

I let a fraction of my Power *swell* outward to press against the shields of *Sona's* Council, and one Human, providing a relevant comparison. The only authority they had over me was what I chose to give them, and in this?

I chose to give them none at all.

"Vote whenever you wish," I told Council. "I'll refuse."

Chit—

Excuse us. Baby being born—

Interlude

THEY'D DISAGREED BEFORE.

This had been—different. True, some on Council could use a reminder exactly whom they'd been ordering around these past days, but that flex of Power, with its underlying *ANGER*, had been aimed right at him. For, Morgan thought with disgust, the very same reason.

"I do believe I deserved that." He ran a rueful hand through his hair. Crossed the line, that's what he'd done. "What was I thinking?"

"I couldn't begin to guess, my friend." Barac grinned. "You'll be forgiven. Eventually."

The Human grimaced. Sira'd slammed a wall between them, leaving only the faintest thread of their link. "Or longer."

"Good thing we're down here, then." Where Council had sent them, unanimous in their concern over the First Scout's report.

Wisely so; anything amiss with their food supply posed an immediate threat. Morgan looked around the utilitarian space, free of the alien—to them all—swirls and patterns of color found in main living areas of the ship. The carts were secured and idle. The floor showed no sign it had been covered in food packets some hours before.

"Morgan." No smile now. "You're sure? About—" Barac pointed to his head.

"You're fine," he answered, firmly. "As is Ruti. And—" because the First Scout would be among those watching the others, "—Odon, Teris, Kunthea, and Destin. Tle, too." Ruis having assured him, despite the *distress* he'd sensed from the Chooser, she'd none of the telltale signs.

"Good to know." The Clansman shook his head. "But the rest. Ghos? Nik? Hap? Degal—" A twist of his lips. "He doesn't deserve this either."

"It'll help to know their symptoms have a cause." Even more, to have their Chosen warned and on guard. Morgan rubbed his forehead; Ruis was right, the resources he'd depleted were still too low to tap. "Need a night's sleep," he admitted ruefully. Till then, he'd continue scanning those around him, as would Ruis, who would instruct their other Healers how to do the same.

The question of using the Maker had not come up again. And wouldn't, Morgan resolved, unless from Sira. He owed her that.

"I'd be surprised if any of us sleep tonight." Barac chuckled at the Human's startled frown. "New baby, remember?"

"Ah." There was a happier subject, Morgan thought, and one of recent and deeply personal interest to them both—which in no way took priority over their food supply. "Where did the sound come from?" He swung off his pack, pulling free his scanner.

The Clansman walked to the center of the room, turned around once, then shrugged. "I can't say for sure. It seemed to come from everywhere at once."

"And you *tasted* change."

"For what it's worth." Exasperation. "About this, or Ruti. The business with Council—any of it or something we haven't seen yet. You?"

Shaking his head, Morgan aimed the scanner at the floor and took slow steps toward the still-open access port, moving the device back and forth. "'For what it's worth,'" he echoed.

Barac watched him, then went to the carts, giving one an idle tug. "Any other schemes to take over the ship? I'm on your side, by the way."

Seen through him, too, had he? Although "take over" required a system able to be controlled, something he'd yet to be convinced existed. No, his mutinous ambitions were much simpler—to discover what he could of where they were going and when they'd arrive, in order to prepare as best they could.

And to be sure *Sona* had no more surprises in store.

Morgan half smiled. "Nothing I'd discuss over live coms."

"'Live—?'" *The ship's listening?*

"I assume everything that can be recorded—" he waved the scanner "—is." Not that he'd located any records storage—any he recognized, Morgan corrected. Sira'd passed along the question, the ship replying it was "unaware." Just as it hadn't been aware of the Speaker pendants either, which they had caught transmitting. Implying secrecy—

Or such questions hadn't been anticipated by the ship's builders. Least cheerful prospect? Ignorance in its passengers served a purpose.

They'd no proof the experiment was over.

When Barac didn't respond, Morgan glanced up, grinning at the look on the other's face. "I wouldn't worry about it."

"I would." A faint smile in return. "But I'll add it to the list. Anything else, my friend?"

Morgan hesitated.

The Clansman stopped smiling. "Sorry I asked."

"Don't be." Sira preoccupied. Alone with the only other of her kind he trusted—who trusted him, that rare commodity. He made up his mind. "I'd like to show you something."

Going to his pack, Morgan reached in, fingers finding the smooth, cool curve of the Hoveny cylinder. He'd brought it from the workshop, hoping for such an opportunity.

Before he could doubt, he pulled it forth.

"So that's what you've been up to." Barac whistled, then gave a charming shrug. "The Om'ray were curious. What is it?"

"My chance to belong. Maybe." He met the Clansman's gaze, braced himself for any reaction, including ridicule. "I've been trying to make it work, whatever it is. See if my Power can affect their—your technology."

Giving him a purpose, a future, on a world that might run on nothing else.

Barac merely nodded. "Any luck?"

"Not yet. I'm only guessing it has a function." If not, he'd been doing the equivalent of trying to start a fire inside a brick. "Even if it does, it could be broken." Morgan held out the cylinder. "You can help me find out."

Barac took it, his nose wrinkled in distaste. "It's old. What do you want me to do?"

"I've no idea."

"Helpful." But the Clansman was doing *something*. Morgan could feel his concentration, if not what he did.

The cylinder went from dull white to pale blue—

—dropping from Barac's hand to bounce on the floor, dull white again.

"What happened?"

The Clansman made a face. "It *talked*." He stooped and picked it up between two fingers, gingerly offering it to Morgan. "Gibberish." Something flickered across his face. "No. Numbers."

Finally. Doing his best to stay calm, the Human took the cylinder back. He'd hunted for records; had he had one all along? Although numbers could mean a scanner readout. "How did you activate it?"

"I'm not sure. To fuel the ship—" with disgust, "—each of us *reached* into the M'hir while touching one of those hall panels. I tried with this, but nothing happened. So I—" Barac's cheeks turned an interesting color.

"Yes?"

"I was thinking I didn't want to fail. Ruti—she came on our link and—" His eyes widened. "Morgan, she sent me encouragement. The feeling. That's when the numbers started."

"Let me try." The Human lifted the cylinder, watching it, then *reached* for Sira. *Any sign of the baby?*

A not-unexpected: *Don't distract me.* With a blast of *ice.*

The cylinder turned vivid purple. Morgan poured everything he had into his inner sense. Concentrated.

"Hear anything?"

The pound of his heart. Barac's breathing and his. "No."

He refused to admit disappointment. Useful, learning the

device—for now he knew it was a device, without question—responded to what passed unsaid between Chosen. Both Ruti and Sira were stronger than their partners. Relevant or not, another bit of data. The numbers could be a measurement of that strength, or potential along the link.

As easily, a coded message unlocked only when in the hands of a Chosen.

"Interesting." Morgan concluded, turning the again-white cylinder over in his hands.

"Only to you. If you're done, put it away." Barac gave an exaggerated shudder. "Taking what's inside us—using it to power machines? It's unnatural."

The Human froze, caught by an incongruity. Barac was right. It was—and yet the ability to do just that had been bred into the *nature* of the Clan.

At great effort. With unimaginable sacrifice. They'd assumed it was to recover what the Hoveny had somehow lost from themselves.

What if they were wrong?

"I know that look." The First Scout narrowed his eyes. "You've thought of something. I'm not going to like it, am I."

"What we know of the Hoveny Concentrix comes from structures and artifacts locked in stone before there was a Trade Pact, but the creation of the M'hiray is almost contemporary."

"Your point?"

"What took them so long?"

Barac blinked. "An interstellar civilization collapsed."

"Without sign of destruction," Morgan countered. "It's as if the Hoveny abandoned their technology—beyond our understanding even now—and walked away, leaving the rest of the Concentrix to fend for themselves. The rest did. Most species kept the capacity for sublight travel; members of the First were back trading between systems well before Humans arrived in their space. Yet knowledge surrounding the Hoveny themselves disappeared with them. Deliberately or as a consequence?"

Morgan kept from pacing with an effort, ideas tumbling faster than he would sort them. "Now we know they didn't die off.

Instead, the Hoveny hid themselves so well other spacefaring species had no idea they still existed or where. And a thousand years later, a new generation sent ships like this to Cersi—and who knows where else—in what I assure you was a very costly attempt to wake technology ancient even to them. Why?"

"They could have tried before or since," argued Barac, "and succeeded. Nothing says we continue to matter," with abrupt bitterness.

Except to themselves, but the Clansman wasn't wrong. Still . . .

"A worry on my list." A keen look. "What's on yours?"

"A delay of a thousand years, Barac. Think about it." The Human pressed his palms together, blowing through his fingers as if to warm them. "What if it was long enough for the Hoveny themselves to forget why they turned off the lights and ran?"

Barac made as if to speak, stopped, then gave a short laugh. "You almost had me, Morgan," he said fondly. "The past is dead and gone. Whatever happened to the Hoveny is a mystery I don't need solved; we aren't them and weren't part of it. The future's what counts. Starting with making sure we have one." A nod at the access port.

"Fair enough." Speculation wasn't supper. Chuckling himself, the Human leaned into the opening, more than ready to get back to work. "Pass me my light, please. Outside left pocket." Barac put it in his outstretched hand and Morgan squirmed inside, bracing himself with an elbow and hip against the far wall.

"Must you do that?"

"We're here. May as well be thorough."

His voice echoed; hard surfaces. Good thing the headache was fading. His light danced along shiny metal racks, teethlike rows of them extending as far as the little beam reached. Empty.

Might be normal.

Might not. Until now the wide portal had opened on full racks, ready to be unloaded; he hadn't been able to crawl in like this to do a proper inspection. Morgan twisted to send light down, finding only space below. Rails along the walls implied the racks, once emptied, would move down, perhaps to cycle back around to be refilled.

"Seen enough?"

About to climb out, Morgan grunted something noncommittal, his attention caught. There. A spot on the wall with a different texture. "Now, what are you?" he murmured.

"Ready to leave."

Ignoring the Clansman's plaintive comment, he put the light between his teeth and stretched, brushing the tips of his fingers over the wall. Hard. Smooth—

The tips sank in.

Quickly, Morgan pulled back his hand. His fingers were coated in a liquid the same color as the wall. "That can't be good."

A head appeared. "What's wrong?" demanded the First Scout.

The next unpleasant surprise. Morgan held up his hand. "I'd say *Sona*'s about to change something."

"It can't," Barac protested. "We're here."

"Let hope it knows that." Staying where he was, the Human played the light over the wall. More spots with that revealing texture. More and larger, he noticed uneasily, the longer he looked. "Time to go—"

His elbow and hip were suddenly braced against nothing. Morgan contorted as he began to fall, reaching up—

—meeting a firm grip. "Got you!" The Clansman hung by his hips, half-inside the opening.

"Don't 'port!"

The Human could almost feel Barac's incredulous stare, but the other didn't argue, pulling until Morgan could bring his feet against something still-solid and push himself up and out.

As the other steadied him, their feet began to sink. "Can we leave now?" Barac pleaded.

The walls were, Morgan noted, noticeably sagging in— explaining much about the reshaping process. He lunged for his pack and pulled it free of the floor. "Definitely."

A hand clamped on his shoulder . . .

. . . and what had been food storage, now rapidly becoming something else, disappeared . . .

. . . The Human found himself standing in the deserted hallway outside the galley.

Barac gave him a shove before letting go. "Next time we're in a dissolving ship, I'm not waiting for your luggage."

"Agreed."

They looked at one another, neither moving.

"So that's it, then," Barac said at last, very quietly. "We don't go mad. We starve to death. That's what I *tasted*."

Curious he hadn't received any such warning. A first. Unless they hadn't been in real danger, other than being frightened to death. Made sense the ship would have some way to allow for passengers wandering where they shouldn't—

But why food storage—why now? "Starving's one possibility," the Human admitted, thoughts racing.

"What else is there?"

Morgan told him.

Chapter 8

M'HIRAY GAVE BIRTH in the presence of witnesses and their Birth Watcher. The father, if approved by the mother-to-be and her family, could attend if interested.

I tried not to step on toes, or be stepped on, in the very interested crowd surrounding the bed where Gricel di Eathem lay, sweating and smiling. According to the Om'ray, not only must the father and Birth Watcher attend, but every pregnant Clanswoman in range.

Having never planned to be pregnant, I found myself at the bedside with the rest, Ruti to one side and Andi to the other, wondering if anyone else was terrified.

The child and Jacqui di Mendolar, our other Birth Watcher, seemed confident they could share their duty to the unborn and mother. Far be it from me to point out neither had attended a birth before. The Om'ray had lost their Birth Watchers, a wrenching loss among the rest, and gratefully accepted the help offered.

Gricel made a face as another wave of contractions rippled along her abdomen. "Impatient, aren't you?" She sounded improbably calm. I supposed it helped that this wasn't her first.

What's happening? Morgan, no doubt full of curiosity. If there'd been any space at all around the bed, he'd have squeezed right in, scanner in hand.

In my present mood, as well he didn't try. *Don't distract me,* I sent and slammed down my shields.

Jacqui ran her fingers over bare, distended skin and nodded. "Time to get you on your feet, Gricel."

Others helped, taking hold of her arms. Once standing, Gricel's abdomen began to flex in and out, each powerful contraction driving air from her lungs. Andi dove to the floor, her arms full of pillows. As Gricel's hair lifted like an aura of dazzling red, the birth sac slipped free in a flood of clear liquid.

"Got you!" Andi exclaimed. She stood, juggling the sac to her chest with one of the pillows. *Welcome! Welcome!*

Those gathered made room as Andi carefully brought the birth sac to its little hammock, strung between two beds. I'd a clearer view than I'd hoped.

The sac was as black as the M'hir, flecked with starlike patches of pale, new-grown skin. Human babies didn't arrive like this; I'd found a vid on the *Fox* and watched with a certain skepticism. Clan newborn were locked within an impenetrable case, a case that opened from inside.

The first Choice: be born.

Or not.

If the unborn refused to come out, he or she would die, as would the mother, their bond sending both minds—and, among M'hiray, the father's—adrift in the M'hir. The Birth Watchers' role was to communicate with that new, nascent intelligence, to encourage and, most importantly, allay any fears—

Don't be afraid, Aryl sent gently, sensing mine.

She understood what was to happen, what must happen. Would make the Choice that preserved us both—and Morgan. I had to trust her.

I did. It was just—*I may not be right, inside.* There, what I hadn't told her. *A toad put me back together.*

What's a toad?

I shared the image of Baltir, the Retian who'd experimented on my flesh. *A Human med-tech supervised him*—and my Human, a blade at Baltir's loose-skinned throat—*but there are no guarantees he fixed the damage.*

You wanted to be sterile, then, Aryl observed with grim accuracy. *Now you have me, a gifted Birth Watcher, and Clan Healers with experience. Don't be afraid, Great-granddaughter.* With *warmth.* Then, *Hurry, show me the birth.*

Smiling to myself, I did just that.

Jacqui joined Andi, pressing her palm gently to the sac. The Birth Watchers smiled at one another. *NOW, little one,* they sent together, mindvoices full of *love* and *warmth.*

The sac quivered and shook, then split!

A chubby fist poked through first, then a foot.

Followed by *HUNGRYHUNGRY!!!*

I wasn't the only one to flinch; Clan offspring weren't quiet. Gricel smiled peacefully, her shields taking over, and opened her arms. "Welcome, daughter."

✳ ✳ ✳

"We can't know her name yet," Andi di Mendolar informed me, dignity quivering every bit of her little body. "It's revealed at her naming ceremony." The dignity dropped away, letting out the child. "A party, Sira! We're all to come!"

The Om'ray gathered around the bed smiled cheerfully and murmured. Gricel gave me a hopeful look. I was gaining a sense of their culture—the culture we'd lost—and it ran heavily to communal gatherings for any occasion, with feasting when there was food to spare. Explaining, I thought, amused, why the organizers of the ceremony had caught up to me before I'd made it out of the Core. "A party would be a welcome change," I replied, somehow keeping a straight face. "I look forward to it."

Gricel's mother, Worra di Eathem stood nearby. Her fingertips brushed Andi's, who nodded. Talking to me through my Birth Watcher, were they? Sure enough, "Everyone wants her to have the best naming ceremony, Sira," Andi told me. "Oluk can make the—" a tiny frown, "—I think it's a cake. As Keeper, you could grant permission for him take what he needs from the food in little packages."

Had to be a direct quote. Raising a brow, I looked over the bed at Gricel's Chosen, who had the grace to blush. Taking ingredients from the food packets—would it waste the remainder? "How many 'little packages' would you need?" I asked cautiously.

"Merely a day's worth, Keeper," Oluk replied, his courage restored by a touch from his Chosen. "It's the sweet, you see. To create the—"

"We'd use what's left," Ghos interjected, anticipating my concern. "Worra plans a stew."

I should have guessed Om'ray wouldn't be wasteful. A stew, though? The unlabeled packets, each a complete meal for an adult, came, so far, in twenty-one distinct varieties. While my cooking skills involved occasionally successful arguments with a kitchen replicator, even I could see combining such a range of ingredients might lead to an inedible disaster.

On the other hand, Holl wanted those "use first" packets consumed as quickly as possible. Letting any spoil would waste more.

Finally, a problem I could solve on my own, free of *Sona* or Council. "Go ahead," I told the family. "Take whatever you need." I grinned. The more I thought about it, the happier I was. What could be better for a ship full of weary grief than a celebration to welcome new life?

Morgan, something inside me whispered. What if he could use the Maker to mute that grief? What if I could keep him safe while he tried?

What if *Sona* damaged his mind beyond repair—that being far more likely?

I focused on the present. "So. When's the party?"

* ✳ *

Word of the birth, and the planned celebration, spread as quickly as thought, the news a tonic. As I walked back toward our little home within the Core, I imagined the mood throughout the ship lifting, imagined smiles and laughter—

Barac and Morgan appeared, close enough to reach out and touch, the look on their faces enough to freeze me mid-step. "What's happened?"

My cousin shook his head and disappeared.

"We've had a small adventure." Morgan put his pack on our bed. His hand was streaked with a dull, metallic fluid. Streaks of the stuff were on the elbow of his coat and down the back. Details I took in without thought, too busy trying to puzzle what I sensed from him. *Exhilaration* or was it *dread?* Was that *fear* or *relief?* All this and more muddled our link.

I watched him glance assessingly around us, notice who might be in earshot. Enough, I decided, taking hold of him . . .

. . . My Human leaned his shoulders against the wall, grinning down at me. "Best you could do, I take it?"

As we were standing, very close together, in what passed for a 'fresher stall on the ship, he had a point. I didn't care. "What's going on?"

A hand—his clean one—buried itself in my hair, pulling me close until we touched noses. I stared at him cross-eyed. "I think we're landing," in a low husky voice.

"Or—" with a quick kiss, "—we're in big trouble and about to die."

* ✱ *

Morgan told me—and Aryl—everything in a quick concise briefing, at the same time taking advantage of the shower to clean the remnants of ship from his hand and clothing.

Standing out of range, I found myself stuck on a word. A wonderful hopeful fabulous word. If a new baby raised spirits on the ship, the change from this? "'Landing.'"

We'd be saved.

He ran fingers through his hair to straighten it. "It's a possibility." With typical caution. "The ship's acted to conserve resources all along. Shutting down the food supply system makes sense if we won't need any more."

Implying *Sona*'s little stunt this morning when I'd asked for a distraction had served its purpose more than mine. This once, I didn't mind.

Morgan checked his coat, then folded it over his arm. "There remain other options. There could be a new food storage area waiting for us. Or—" he looked at me, "—this was a malfunction."

I frowned at what wasn't a wonderful word at all. "I like landing better."

"So would I, if—" His fist slammed into the wall. I jumped. Morgan regarded it, his face expressionless. "Sorry about that," he said after a too-long pause.

I took hold of his arm, tugged hard. It didn't move. "What's wrong with landing?"

"Nothing, if this was a new ship, with current information. Nothing—" his fist opened, hand pressing against metal. "—if where *Sona* is set to put down remains nice and flat—or hasn't grown a city full of innocents since." He stroked the wall, as I'd seen him do so many times on the *Silver Fox*. "Nothing at all, chit, if we had hands-on controls and could make last-minute corrections."

I felt Aryl's attention, her quiet *support.* "So we do that."

Blue eyes bored into mine. "I thought—"

"We're in a shower discussing if we're going to crash, kill people, or starve to death. I would rather be in a control room, watching you stop us from crashing or killing people. As well as not starving," I added, to be clear.

Witchling. I loved the little lines beside his eyes, how they deepened before a smile.

"Greatest profit for the least risk. Isn't that what you taught me? Well, Dreaming with the ship fits." There, I got the words out, with some authority, too.

Before fear could dry my mouth entirely.

* ✳ *

We came out of the accommodation into a buzz of activity. Everywhere I looked, people were doing what they could to dress for the occasion. Jewelry glinted, freed from wherever it had been tucked away. The M'hiray who'd arrived in formal wear were trading issa-silk wraps and gem-studded tops for colorful woven scarves or pieces of fine gauze from the Om'ray. Joy was blending us as I'd never expected.

We have to stop this, I sent to Morgan, my heart sinking. *We can't spare the food. They have to know.* No doubt Barac had told Ruti; this wasn't a secret to keep from one's Chosen. Or great-grandmother. Aryl, having been told, stayed *near,* like an island of calm. The rest?

Calm wasn't the reaction I expected.

On the contrary, this is just what we need. He took my hand as we walked through the crowds, exchanged smiles and nods. *Buys us time to find answers for them.* Aloud, "I'd say," with a curious lightness to his voice, "a celebration does us all good right now."

Those who heard him beamed their agreement.

I didn't. Postponing the inevitable wasn't my way of doing things. Cool-headed assessment, however, was Morgan's.

I resigned myself to patience. My hair, oblivious, rose in a cheerful cloud.

We hung back, waiting as everyone else began to leave the Core for the galley and the naming ceremony. I'd sent to Nik sud Prendolat, requesting she and her Chosen wait as well, as we'd a matter to discuss. If she'd thought it was about Andi—for Ruti had shared the situation with me at Gricel's bedside—she'd known better when I asked for our other two scientists as well.

Pretending to tidy a blanket, I turned my head to see Morgan, who wasn't pretending to shift the contents of his pack. "If it's answers we need, let me try asking the ship." It had, I thought optimistically, to work eventually.

He didn't look up. "I thought we'd agreed to wait to Dream until tonight, while everyone's asleep."

Well, yes, but tonight was so far away. "We could do something now."

"If it is a malfunction," my Human countered as he clipped the flap closed, "the wrong question could prompt an action we really don't want."

I grabbed a pillow and sat, wrapping my arms around it to keep myself still. Nothing could settle my hair. "You're right. I'd just like to know why." With perhaps too much emphasis.

>*Keeper. 'Why?' is insufficient. Please elaborate.*<

I spared a moment to think very unkindly of the

universe—especially one part of it—before admitting in a small voice. "*Sona* heard me."

Morgan gave me that look.

"I'll have to say something back to it," I retorted. "It's waiting."

"I've known Skenkrans with more patience."

The winged beings had an attention span measured in heart-beats. I lifted the pillow to throw at him.

He raised his hands in mock surrender. "Ask it this, then." After my nod. "What is the status of our food supply?"

But we knew that—reading his face, I pressed my lips together and repeated the question word for word.

>*Adequate nutrition has been provided, Keeper.*<

A reply—and nothing, as far as I could tell, had changed around us. I gave a sigh of relief. "It says it's provided 'adequate nutrition.'" I hugged the pillow again, this time to hold in hope. "Does that mean what I think it does?" That our journey was almost over, that we had "adequate nutrition" until we left the ship at last—

My Human shrugged, refusing to commit himself. "It means we need to talk to our scientists."

"I expect you to do the talking." They shared a common language, science and technology, as well as a similarly dim view of authority. Years doing forbidden research in a hidden lab did things to your trust. "You know how they are."

The corner of his mouth twitched. "I've a feeling what they'll have to say this time won't need any translation."

* ✳ *

Josa welcomed us to the portion of the Core I'd come to think of as the laboratory, the grouping of cluttered tables and beds he and his fellow scientists called home. It was well isolated from any others, having gained a reputation for strange smells and the occasional startling noise. Until I got a report of explosions, I wasn't worried.

I sat on a bed, easing between some disassembled equipment and a neatly folded lab coat; treasures, now. "Thanks for this."

Holl sat on another bed; Leesems, her Chosen, perched on a

table. Their sons were absent; just as well. Josa joined Nik on their bed, faces solemn.

Because Morgan was present.

My Human squatted, as comfortable on his heels as sitting. Not by accident. It put him where all of us could see him and, more importantly in my opinion, he could do the same.

"We need you to run some numbers," Morgan began without preamble. "Quick and quiet."

Eyes gleamed with interest. Hands reached for devices; others for noteplas. When they were settled, Nik nodded. "Go on."

"Two scenarios, based on the food packets in the galley. You did an inventory?"

"Of course." The four exchanged glances.

"Give us your scenarios," Leesems said, looking back at my Human. "We're ready."

Morgan almost smiled. "Good. The first: time remaining if we ration to keep as many alive as possible, as long as possible. The second: time with normal meals."

Holl set her noteplas aside. "This isn't hypothetical."

"No. We have what *Sona* dumped this morning. That's it."

Brutal, maybe, but facts, I reminded myself, were what these four preferred. "I tried a 'port," I said, ignoring Morgan's frown. What he hadn't known, he couldn't stop. "The locate didn't work. The food room is gone."

"Barac's checked the lift," added my Chosen. "It no longer recognizes that level."

"The ship." Leesems leaned forward. "But why? Removing unnecessary space makes sense, but this?" He looked at me.

I looked at Morgan.

"Something we plan to ask." He kept their focus, studying their faces; I saw the moment he came to some conclusion of his own. "We've very little time. By breakfast tomorrow, everyone on board will know our food supply is finite. It could be sooner."

"Understood." Holl drew her noteplas back on her lap, but didn't consult it. "Second scenario, maintaining normal rate of consumption, gives us one and a half shipdays of food."

There were packets stacked ceiling-high in the galley—

As if she heard my protest, she continued, "That's a total of three meals, for one hundred and seventy-nine of us. The ship's been meticulous in its math. I've assumed we'll use the compromised packets as tonight's meal, at the party, rather than any intact ones."

"Just as well," Leesems pointed out. "If we'd thrown them down the waste chute, we'd be in worse shape."

Assuming the "stew" was edible, I told myself. Then again, if it wasn't, we'd still need to eat it.

I'd just have to explain why.

"To continue." Holl's fingers brushed the back of Nik's hand.

The other scientist rapidly entered something into the device she held, then went still. "First scenario—rationing as best we can—" Nik faltered and Morgan reached out, put his hand on her knee. She stared down at him. "Being Human, you'd outlive us, except—" Her eyes went to me.

This kept getting better, I thought, waving her past the obvious.

"Seven shipdays before we run out. Two after that, we start to die."

Josa leaned forward. "You've assumed the ship doesn't turn off the water."

"Correct," Holl nodded. "And there's another factor beyond our control. We don't know how the packets were stored by the ship. If we ration those we have, some could spoil before we eat them."

Lovely.

"Thank you. I ask you keep this to yourselves as long as possible." Morgan stood, a signal bringing us all to our feet.

"That's it?" Leesems demanded, his eyes fierce.

"It can't be. What are we going to do?" Josa took Nik's hands in both of his, but her voice continued to tremble. "What do we tell— How do we—"

Holl shook her head. "That's not up to us." She raised her eyes to mine. "Is it."

"We have questions for the ship," Morgan reminded them. Nothing but calm in his tone, nothing but confidence in his bearing. "It's kept us fed this long. For all we know there's another area with supplies. Give us time to find out what's really happening."

An exchange of somber glances. They knew, likely better than I, how slim a hope this was, but Leesems gave a slow nod. "Agreed."

Somber on the outside; inside, their *despair* was a weight on my heart. *We have to tell them about the landing,* I sent in desperation. *We have to give them some hope, or everyone will feel this.*

And if I'm wrong? If I'd thought their emotions a burden, it was nothing to the appalling *dread* Morgan allowed me to feel. *If that hope's a lie?*

Peace, Morgan. From Aryl. Sira.

Guessing what she wanted, I held my hand, palm up, in the center of our group of six. One by one, they put their hands on mine, shields down.

Morgan last, his eyes still troubled.

Through that link poured Aryl, strong and vibrant; she might have stood with us.

Courage, heart-kin! Her mindvoice swept us along like the beat of a drum. *Put aside your fear. Put your trust in each other.* With a swell of *pride. We will survive this as we have survived all else, one day at a time, and together.*

For alone, we fall.

Interlude

*Y*OU'RE SURE THIS IS A GOOD IDEA?

Sira insisted. With Morgan's devious mind behind it, Barac thought as he surveyed the galley. Distraction. Delay. It seemed to be working. Om'ray mingled with M'hiray, voices rising and falling with the buzz of cheerful conversation; the occasional laugh rang out.

The di Eathems were the center of attention, their as-yet-unnamed daughter asleep in her mother's arms.

The only ones missing at the moment were his cousin, the Human, and the four M'hiray who might have answers.

He could use the distraction himself. Landing? Not his favorite aspect of space travel, plummeting down through an atmosphere, though it beat the alternatives. *Our job's to enjoy ourselves. Without leaking* anything we shouldn't.

Speak for yourself. Other than her sending, Ruti was virtually invisible to his inner sense.

Barac gave her a quick hug. "Speaking for myself," he said with a smile, "I'm impressed with what you've done to the place, and so quickly." The former Council Chamber, witness to the first mention of every name for its Clan, had been transformed.

She hugged him back. "Not alone."

Oluk and his helpers had managed to create a naming cake—a colorful concoction layering every variety of sweet found in the packets—along with their promised "stew," warmed by the addition of heated water. The aroma filled the air, surprisingly appetizing; it could have been they'd gone too long without smelling cooking at all, but the cooks themselves had tasted the result and appeared pleased.

While this was going on, Ruti, along with the parents of the youngest children and those among the small ones able to sit still, had made decorations. Gauze strips tied into surprisingly lovely bows hung at the ends of benches, held in place by, yes, those were the fabric bags used by the children in their games. Emptied food packets had been sliced into strips, twisted, then tied along threads. The ceiling being out of reach, the threads were supported above the tables by columns of intact packets at each end.

The strips danced with the slightest bit of air, reflecting sparks of light.

"I told the others about our balloons," Ruti said wistfully. "Only Risa knew what I meant—she said her foster sister could make them into animals. They were doing that together for Noson, before—" Her eyes filled with tears; she dashed them away impatiently with the back of her hand. "We could use some balloons."

"I remember ours," Barac answered, thinking of the round, floating balls of color, several proclaiming "Happy Anniversary." Morgan had bought the silly things for their baby shower at the *Claws & Jaws*.

Like Risa, he thought. Balloons to mark their last moment of peace and happiness.

A lifetime ago.

No so, his Chosen sent firmly, drawing him close to the new, growing *awareness* within her. *Our daughter-to-be's started to laugh, Beloved. It won't be much longer before we hear her first words. On a new world!*

His ever-practical Ruti knew the odds, knew their chances may have gone from slim to nonexistent, yet kept hope alive. More, she offered it to him.

Barac kissed the top of her head. *You're braver than I am.*

Her small hand found his, laced fingers between his, squeezed with improbable strength. *It's all right. I'll hope for all of us.*

Chapter 9

WE MADE IT to the naming ceremony before missing anything important or being missed, taking seats near the
back, on the only empty bench.

You were right, I told Morgan. They'd know soon enough, the
thought painful as I opened my *awareness,* feeling the hope and
joy flowing back and forth through my people. Even Tle looked,
if not happy, then entertained.

There were small knots of nameless *misery,* shielded, if not well
enough to prevent my sensing them if I tried. I could guess.
Barac. Ruti. Likely the scientists who'd come with us. Holl and
Leesems squeezed in to sit with their sons, Arla and Asdny. Nik
and Josa might have hoped to be near Andi, but the child was
with her friends.

We may not have been missed, but our arrival was noticed. Ruis
excused herself, coming over to sit beside Morgan. "We've had
no more incidents," she reported quietly. "That won't last."

I'd almost forgotten how this day'd started. Amazing how a
new crisis could shove an old one right out the air lock.

"We've finished scanning the Om'ray," Ruis continued. "Only
eleven show the signs and every Healer knows who they are. I'll
give you their names." She touched Morgan's forehead with
casual ease.

"You've told them," he said, when she was done.

The Rayna shrugged. "We aren't enough to watch them properly, let alone the M'hiray we identify. Their families know what to watch for—they'll alert us of any change. I didn't see any choice."

Morgan nodded. "You're right."

"Eleven. That's good news, isn't it?" I ventured, thinking of Nik's numbers.

"So long as they don't all fail at the same time. In that case, we'll need another option."

Morgan, who didn't forget a thing—or, for that matter, abandon a plan—still intended to see if the Maker could help. I looked over rows of heads toward the dais. The machine was a tall cylinder wider around than our arms could have reached together. It stood in its spot, sporting a large gauze bow. Its dull green surface no longer rippled with light, meaning it was quiescent. Harmless.

Nothing here was. *Don't make me regret this,* I sent dourly.

Odds are we won't live long enough for regret, chit. That's what makes this fun.

"Fun?" I tried not to smile, but it was hopeless. Morgan was, with his dare-anything approach to life. A life I was determined not to lose. In agreement, a lock of my hair looped around his wrist, tangled in his fingers.

"We Dream tonight, Ruis," I informed the Rayna Healer-of-minds. "If anyone can teach *Sona* how to help those who'll need it, it's Morgan." I leaned into his shoulder, cheerful for no sane reason beyond we were going into this, as we should, together. Find a cure for those mad with grief. Seize control of this capricious ship, once and for all.

Determine our own fate.

What, I dared think, could go wrong?

Besides, this was a party. When the moment came, we added our voices to the rest as Gricel and Oluk held up the newest member of the Clan, to name and welcome Yanti di Eathem.

A shriek cut through like a knife.

*　＊　✳　＊*

In horrified unison, we turned to stare at Dre.

While Morgan moved.

He ran to the child—no, children, for Dre, Andi, and their friends stood close together, all looking down. Threw himself to his knees, gently pushing them aside.

They parted, keeping hold of one another, to reveal what I took at first for a pile of discarded clothing.

Until Morgan scooped up a limp little body, rising to his feet. His dear face—the look on it—

I shut my eyes.

"Risa asked us to mind Noson," I heard Andi say in her clear, high voice. "Then she went away. She went too far. Why would she do that?"

* ✳ *

Risa di Annk and her Chosen, Jorn, were no longer on the ship. Neither M'hiray had the strength to 'port to any conceivable safety.

They'd gone anyway, whether one first or together didn't matter, leaving behind a baby too young to survive the tearing of his bond to his mother.

I'd thought I'd saved my people. Instead, I continued to fail them. No more, I vowed, watching Andi go to her parents. Others came, were comforting their children. Ruti arrived, taking the husk of our latest dead from Morgan despite his inchoate protest.

To send it into the M'hir, as was our way.

Morgan. If he could stop any more of this, I had to let him try. I closed my eyes, seeing him as if he stood before me, and concentrated . . .

. . . we arrived in the Core—no, the Dream Chamber.

Come to safety, I ordered my people. *Rest if you can.*

But do not disturb us as we Dream.

Turning, I opened my arms. Morgan stared at me, his eyes unfocused and swimming with tears.

I took the step to bring us together.

⁕

"The ship will put us to sleep," I told Morgan. "Temporarily. I could go first."

He gave me a look that needed no interpretation.

"Together, then." He'd witnessed what happened when *Sona* drew its Keeper into its embrace. Whatever bed I chose would be drawn up to the high ceiling. Wires would emerge from hiding to—it didn't matter.

Neither of us could bear another tragedy. None of us had time to waste.

I sat beside him, a lock of hair slipping up his arm to curl around his neck. "It may not work." *Aryl?*

This is your duty, Keeper, came the reply. *I plan to stay well clear.* With that, my sense of her faded . . .

As my sense of my Chosen increased, our link strengthening until I felt his heartbeat echo mine, the boundary between who we were less than that between our lips.

Now, I told *Sona.*

And fell asleep.

Interlude

>*WHAT ARE YOU . . .*<

Asleep, Morgan thought. Which was a surprise. He'd planned to pay close attention to the happening in the Dream Chamber. Catch the machinery at work. The last thing he remembered paying attention to was the comforting strength of Sira's mind within his, and the warm soft press of her lips.

Cheating, that was. She'd distracted him.

>*You are not the Right Kind. Only the Right Kind are able to access this portal. What are you?*<

Ah, a machine brain. Cheered, Morgan challenged the dream voice. *If only the "Right Kind" are able to access this portal, does it not follow I must be one of them?*

>*You are Chosen of the Keeper. As she is the Right Kind, you have taken advantage of her to access this portal.*<

Sly, for a starship. He'd best not underestimate it, even in a dream.

No one takes advantage of me. Sira's voice, endearingly grumpy. *What's going on here? Oh.* As she came awake, so to speak, her tone turned formal. *Captain Jason Morgan. Meet* Sona.

>*Hello.*<

Dream or not, the courtesy sent a chill down Morgan's spine. Yes, he'd imbued the *Silver Fox* with personality. Their

140 JULIE E. CZERNEDA

conversations—albeit one-sided—had helped pass many a lonely voyage, but he'd never lost his awareness of the dangerous line between imagination and real. Never dared add an AI to the ship and have that line blur in the depths of space.

Greetings, Sona.

>Keeper, have you come for my answer to your question about traumatic loss?<

Straight to the point. He'd thought to start with ship operations—

No. He couldn't hold another tiny body. He would not. *That is why I am here,* he told the ship. *I've been able to help afflicted minds.* No boast; he'd checked on Eloe and her heart-kin before going to the Council meeting, relieved to find them clear-eyed and sane; grieving, yes, but no longer fixated on the Oud attack. *My technique—*

>I see it.<

How? What? Morgan hurriedly checked his mental shields, relieved, then puzzled to find them exactly as they should be: impenetrable, other than by his Chosen. What this implied about the technology in play here—

The ship continued. *>Your abilities are impressive, Captain Jason Morgan, but not relevant. I cannot replicate them. I can neither merge nor connect with a living mind other than the Keeper.<* A pause. *>And you.<*

Sira entered the conversation. *What can you do?* Warily. She would have noticed *Sona* ignoring his shields.

>I can move a memory to storage. I can supply memories from those provided me.<

A bank of memories, cued to be "supplied" as necessary to the Clan on their new home? Those wouldn't help now. *If that's all you can do,* words Morgan aimed as much at his Chosen as the ship, *why did you request this Dream?*

>I can do this.<

And he was no longer dreaming.

And no longer on the ship.

✳ ✱ ✳

Terk grunted, slowed their rush through the air, then pushed a control to release the aircar's portlights, sending them soaring outward, their broad white beams slicing through the night. Water, water. Then a shoreline, reed grass burned in a long streak, wreckage—Morgan heard 'Whix muttering into a com—then the edge of a tiny forest, dwarf trees toppled this way and that, as though tossed by a giant before taking root.

"We'll land back at the wreckage," Terk began, slowing the aircar even more and beginning a banking turn.

Morgan didn't listen. His every sense insisted Sira was below them—and there was no time left. His hand was already on the latch to the emergency door. He heaved it open with one quick jerk.

Then threw himself out into the darkness.

But this wasn't real, it wasn't now. He'd left Russell Terk and P'tr wit 'Whix behind on Stonerim III, the enforcers, in their gray body armor, covering their escape from the Assemblers. This—this was the past, when they'd helped him search the swamps of Ret 7—search for Sira, who was near death—

Chapter 10

A loud splash brought me closer to consciousness again. I cracked open one eye, seeing light, and congratulated myself on lasting until dawn.

The splash had an echo: several echoes. Weight shifted off my legs as the orts abandoned their perch; I'd felt no discomfort with them there, but now my skin itched fiercely, as though inflamed.

What was coming? I fought waves of dizziness, quite sure I didn't want to die in the jaws of something slimy and large. If I wanted that kind of ending and still had the strength, I could *push* myself into the M'hir. There was, naturally, nothing I could do about either.

"Sira!"

Much better, I thought, relaxing and letting the darkness creep over me again. To fade away dreaming of Morgan's voice? My mind was kinder to me than I'd imagined.

"Sira!? Answer me!"

I smiled, sinking deeper. What a convincing dream.

Sira, wait for me. I'm here! His sending flooded my thoughts, pulling me away from that brink like a spray of cold water wakes a sleeper.

This, I told my subconscious, was going too far. How could I die peacefully with—

With someone dripping all over me? With urgent hands lifting me up?

I opened both eyes. The light was too harsh to be part of the afterlife I'd planned on and the face of my love, so close to mine, was too haggard, dirty, and scared to be anything but real.

But this wasn't real, it couldn't be, for this had already happened . . .

A voice came from the ground beneath, or was it in my bones? *>I can put those who have shared an experience back in that moment.<*

All at once, I was standing—on water—some distance away. Though it was dark—night—I'd no trouble seeing *me* within a filthy blanket, half-buried in mud and vegetation. I felt perfectly normal, no longer near death, watching *Morgan,* soaking wet and haggard, his light tossed aside, reach for *me*—

While Morgan stood beside me, watching *us,* too. *Interesting.*

I'd other words for it. Part of me wanted to stay and watch what was about to—no, what had happened next.

The rest wanted out of here, now. *END THIS!*

✳ ✱ ✳

I fell out of bed.

Well, that was annoying. As Morgan swung his legs over the side, I got up and sat beside him.

"Interesting indeed." With a tender smile.

Because next had been our Joining, at the edge of death and end of hope. Unspoken *warmth* flowed between us and my Chosen collected my hand in his, bringing the fingers to his lips. *Witchling.*

My hair coiled around his neck, teased an ear. Had we been truly alone—but no. In fact, the Core was full, some occupants already settled in their beds, lights dimmed, while the rest sat, studiously ignoring us. It was eerily quiet; what conversations were underway weren't being shared aloud.

Some had to be about what they'd seen, our bed rising to the ceiling, and what they hadn't, that ceiling mercifully in shadow. I would, I promised myself, explain later. First—

Sona, I sent, *what did you do to us?*

>*By accessing the null-grid across connected points, Keeper, I was able to select a powerful shared memory and lead you to experience it again, together.*<

"That made no sense," I whispered.

Morgan half-turned to face me. "What did it say?"

He hadn't *heard?* I relayed *Sona's* strange explanation.

"'Null-grid?'" His eyes gleamed.

"It makes sense to you?" I asked hopefully.

That earned me a noncommittal shrug, my Human rarely willing to leap to conclusions. I'd have been happy to, had I seen anywhere to leap. "We have to get back in the Dream."

I was afraid he'd say that—not surprised. I put my hand on his chest and pushed him back. Morgan settled on the bed, arms open in welcome.

Sona.

>*Keeper. What is your will?*<

To Dream.

∗ ✱ ∗

This time, I caught the moment when my mind awoke within my sleeping body. Practice, I supposed. Disturbing, to exist in the absence of anything but awareness. Even the M'hir provided more sensation. *Jason?*

Here. His mindvoice reassuringly normal.

>*The not-Right Kind continues to access this portal.*< I could have sworn that sounded aggrieved.

And happy to be here, old ship, Morgan replied. *Explain how your ability to share memories across the null-grid answers your Keeper's initial query.*

My decision to pull us out of the last Dream having been hasty.

Individual memory of an event is incomplete. Combining multiple sources provides more information and offers clarity.

How many can you combine at once?

>All who experienced the event.<

Mind-destroying horrors weren't "events." *How could that help anyone?* I protested.

>Incomplete information causes distress.<

Maybe to a machine mind—

It does. I could almost *feel* Morgan's worrying at the problem. *We fill in the gaps with what we imagined took place—and those imaginings can take hold and grow to be worse than the reality. This could help some of them see the difference. As could reliving the trauma from a safe distance, with someone else.*

Was my instinctive resistance because if I believed this, I had to believe my mind and memory fallible, too? Or because I didn't trust *Sona*'s motives?

Likely both. Fortunately, this wasn't my decision, and the one who'd make it I did believe in and trust.

What's the procedure? my Chosen asked.

>The Keeper requests use of the access portal interface and identifies those individuals and events to be connected across the null-grid. Those individuals are brought in proximity to the interface. The not-Right Kind need not be further involved.<

Oh, yes, he does, I ordered, before *Sona* could cut Morgan from the Dream. There'd been a distinct shift in the ship's inner voice, one my Human would have noticed, too. An Om'ray Keeper wouldn't communicate with it in such terms. Was it drawing them from Morgan—or using what it knew he understood?

Another reason to keep Morgan in the Dream.

>As you wish, Keeper. Do you request use of the access portal interface?<

Jason?

He answered not in words, but with a rush of emotion. *Hope. Confidence.*

Yes, I told the ship. Finally, some progress.

>Your request is denied, Keeper.<

Well, that hadn't lasted. I shouldn't have been surprised. *Why?* I asked it, with what I felt was commendable restraint. Learning, I was.

>*The access portal interface is in use.*<

It couldn't mean—

Sira.

If the ship was meddling with our minds again, I was more than happy to set Morgan against it. *Fix this,* I sent, uncaring if *Sona* could detect my rising fury.

Or the fear that came with it. Was it about to install more false memories, so we'd arrive believing ourselves in the past—or some other manipulation, to change who and what we were—

Or had we been altered already, and only the machine knew how?

>*I do not require repair, Keeper.*< Wary.

We require clarification, Sona, Morgan informed it. *To what current use is the access portal interface being put?*

>*It seeks a readiness confirmation from the Source access portal interface. Once confirmation has been received, I will transmit my records and receive final instruction.*<

Reveal nothing, I told myself, burying my emotions as deeply as possible, keeping silent. Was this a clue how to affect the ship's systems—how to perhaps take over control? It sounded promising.

Only Morgan knew if it was. *What is the procedure if you do not receive confirmation?*

Sona rarely delayed. Now, a pause long enough to make me wonder if I'd fallen truly asleep and wish I'd a way to pinch myself without being noticed. Then—

>*I will receive confirmation.*<

Unforeseen contingencies arise, Morgan pressed. *You will arrive later than anticipated. What is the procedure?*

>*The not-Right Kind is in error. Keeper, I will receive confirmation.*<

Seeking reassurance or making a promise? *Answer the question,* Sona. The ship was hardly less alien than any species we'd faced over a trade. Toss its own words back. *This is a present, critical concern.*

>*Failing confirmation, I am—I am—I am—*< Each "I am" was followed by a sharp pause, as if the ship were prevented from completing what it wanted to say. >*I am—I am—*<

I withdraw the question. Morgan, with a *grim* undertone.

>*I will receive confirmation. All will proceed as expected, Keeper. At your request, I will end this Dream.*<

Relief?

It wasn't what I felt, nor satisfaction. *Jason?*

Sona. *You have provided three more meals. Please confirm.*<

>*Confirmed. Adequate nutrition has been supplied.*<

>*Will you provide a fourth?*<

>*It will not be necessary. Upon arrival at our destination, further nutrition will be supplied by other means.*<

"Arrival." The question it hadn't acknowledged in any way until now. I'd have hugged Morgan if we'd been flesh and not Dream.

Glad to hear it. What is the precise time of arrival?

Hesitation. Then, >*Once confirmation has been received, I will transmit my records and receive final instruction, which will include the precise time of arrival.*<

A straight, comprehensible answer. I waited, knowing Morgan, having pried one loose, wouldn't leave it at that.

Understood. What can you tell us about our destination?

>*The Keeper requested to be taken home.*<

We knew that.

But *Sona* wasn't done. >*Home is the Source, not-Right Kind. It is from the Source I will receive confirmation.*<

And if not?

End the Dream.

* ✳ *

We curled together in the dark, under our blanket, outwardly peaceful.

Appearances were deceiving. *Self-destruct?!*

Morgan's arm tightened around me. *I'm guessing.*

Guesses that were right, I thought glumly, more often than not. *So if* Sona *doesn't hear from "home," you think it's going to blow itself up. And us.* Even a rational being could start believing in a cosmic conspiracy. *From a stutter?*

The shipmind tried to answer and was unable to do so. To me that suggests an internal setting to prevent alarming its Keeper and so its passengers.

I'm alarmed, I assured him. *What can we do?*

Not worry, Witchling. The Hoveny built this ship to last. The Source will be just as well-maintained. Sona *will receive its confirmation, and all will go as planned.*

Things never went according to plan. I started to roll over, to try and see his face. Morgan held me still and I felt him chuckle. His beard tickled my ear, followed by a barely audible whisper in Comspeak: "Time to stay off the record, chit." Louder, in the language of Cersi, "Time to sleep. It's been a very long day."

My resourceful Human had a plan. Something the ship— which did, I admit, seem to pay too much attention to whatever I said aloud or, chilling notion, sent by what should have been most private of means—shouldn't know about.

Liking the sound of that, I yawned and snuggled close.

Tomorrow was going to be, as Morgan would put it, "interesting."

Then I remembered what else tomorrow would bring: having to tell everyone about our food supply, as in lack of, ideally before anyone tried to go to the nonexistent food storage to collect the day's ration and started a panic.

On the bright side?

After ten shipdays hurtling through subspace—

I could tell them to pack.

* ✳ *

"Sira."

I cracked open an eye. Dark. With a firm, if incomprehensible, "Mummphf," I pulled the blanket over my head. There should be rules about facing the next day before it arrived.

The blanket disappeared. I squinted at Morgan, who was a looming more-dark standing over me, handlight aimed down. "Not morning," I pointed out.

A corner of the little beam illuminated the noteplas he pushed under my nose as I rose to an elbow.

A noteplas with a message written in Comspeak. I came fully awake as I read.

Can't trust the ship didn't pick up my sleepteach. Will brief Barac same way.

I put my hand in the light, gave the signal for agreement. He flipped the page, revealing more lines in his tidy script.

Today prep to disembark. As is, ship's not secured for landing, so warn them to watch for more modifications. No one to be alone. Everyone ready to 'port here. Be confident and keep telling them you trust the ship.

So *Sona* would believe it.

Next page. Ship refuses to land, we destroy the interface. Take a chance there's an emergency landing protocol. If we land and the ship refuses let us out, we blow the exit.

Forget trying to reason with it. Stop hunting for nonexistent controls. Prepare to act. To die on our own terms, if necessary. This was the Morgan who'd grown up in a war—and survived it.

I wished for half his courage. *Nik said seven days on rations.*

The noteplas and light moved away. I counted five heavy heartbeats before they came back for me to read:

We land or die in one.

He put away the noteplas, then Morgan's hand entered the light, found mine. *I'll be back to hear your breakfast speech. I could use company.*

He wore his coat; was dressed, I realized, to roam the still-cold halls before anyone else woke to notice.

I hated getting up in the cold even more than the dark, but so be it. I started to move.

I've someone else in mind, Witchling.

Gratefully snuggling back down, I *reached,* finding a mind I knew well, even asleep, and gave my cousin a sharp *nudge. Dress and meet Morgan at the door. Quietly.*

Barac came awake with a speed I envied. *Problem?*

Our hope to survive one.

Keep him safe.

As my Chosen's hand left mine, the light vanished. He stepped away like a ghost.

I tucked my nose under the blanket, warm. Cozy.

Then flung myself on my back.

As if I'd sleep now.

Interlude

THEIR BREATH left clouds in the air and Barac, coatless, shivered violently, but the lift continued to work and that hadn't been guaranteed. Morgan watched walls, floor, and ceiling for any sign of softening, knowing his companion did the same. All looked solid.

Nonetheless, when he saw the number marking their destination, he wasted no time getting through the doors as their sections split apart. "We're here."

The Clansman was right behind him. Lights were on in the narrow corridor, already or provided in timely fashion. "Wh-where-ss—her-re?"

Sona wouldn't heat outside the Core for another hour. "Hang on." Morgan swung off his pack and produced a blanket. "Put this around your shoulders. Don't," when Barac made a face, "argue."

The other wrapped himself without a word. Morgan led the way to the workshop door, knocking twice. It opened and he waited for Barac to go through before doing the same. The door closed behind them.

Barac gave a low whistle. "What's all this?" He wandered around the arms of the bench, examining but not offering to touch the objects along it.

"Some are tools, the same age as the ship." Morgan picked up a flattened disk with an inlay of crystal. "The rest, and the cylinder I showed you, date much older."

"Older as in Hoveny Concentrix?" At the Human's nod, Barac peered curiously at the disk, then straightened with a shrug, holding the blanket tighter. "I assume you've a reason for dragging us down here."

"We'll grab what we can." Morgan put his pack on a stool. "There are bags over there." Originally intended for waste, at a guess, but they'd nothing else.

And no time to hunt for more.

The Clansman looked incredulous. "Take these things with us? You don't even know what they are."

"Someone thought them worth bringing to Cersi. They've value, whether in what they are or what they represent. We may need that."

"Once a trader—" Barac shook his head, but went to the shelf, pulling out the green-colored bags. "At least we're landing soon." At Morgan's expression, he gave a wan smile. "We're down here before anyone's awake—Sira orders me to come along, no doubt to 'port us back without wasting time. Am I right?"

"After breakfast tomorrow, according to *Sona*."

"It's true, then." The Clansman let out a long slow breath. "I wasn't sure I believed there'd ever be an end to this."

A feeling, Morgan thought, he shared. He walked over to Barac, right hand smoothly taking a share of the bags, while his left, held low, slipped the noteplas into the other's free hand.

He returned to the bench, standing by the stool with his pack, and deftly began to fill one of the bags. "Learned something else interesting," the Human said conversationally, his tone light. "The ship refers to the M'hir as the 'null-grid.'" Finally, a name that offered something to work with. The M'hir. The Scented Way. Only the Rugherans knew what they called it. "Could be a clue." He glanced at Barac.

The First Scout's face was set and pale, jaw working. He used the blanket to shield his arm and hand as he wrote a reply, the precaution perhaps unnecessary.

Considering what he planned, and the demonstrated nature of *Sona*? Morgan preferred unnecessary to any mistakes now.

"You'll need this." Barac joined him at the bench, handing him the noteplas with another bag.

"Thanks. I've sorted the artifacts from the tools here. Leave anything too big to fit. I'll just check this." Morgan bent over as if to examine the disk, instead reading what Barac had written.

Must you always blow things up?

He almost smiled.

On your signal, I'll open the door. Hope you don't give it.

Raising his head, he met Barac's steady gaze and nodded, once. Morgan tied off the top of the bag in front of him on the bench, having surreptitiously switched its contents for a pair of small objects neither Hoveny nor Clan. He gave it to Barac. "These could be special. I'll let you take care of them."

Barac's eyes widened and if he took the bag with extra care, just as well. It contained two blastglobes: sufficient to obliterate the former main entrance—as well as crack the hull. He'd written instructions in their use. Twist top and bottom firmly in opposite directions, put on the floor near the target, then get back to the Core. Until twisted, they were harmless. Undetectable.

Expensive, though he hadn't paid in credits. Omacron III's telepaths had a useful curiosity about the Human variety. Playing along had been—instructive.

Another life. Morgan intended to preserve this one. "Two bags each, no more," he advised, not without regret. They were leaving ten times as much and he picked by instinct alone.

He felt the material of a bag: resilient, but tough. "Might be watertight," he mused and collecting the unused remainder to add to his pack. If so, they could prove of more value than any of these trinkets.

Barac shrugged off the blanket and folded it, offering it to Morgan. "Heat's back on."

So it was. Meaning lights would come on in the Core, with breakfast to soon follow. Sira would tell her people the truth. Morgan wondered what the Clan would make of it.

"Time's up."

Chapter 11

IGRABBED THE CLOTHES I hadn't put away yesterday and 'ported to the accommodation, seizing the chance to shower—and think. We'd till tomorrow, if Morgan interpreted *Sona* correctly; a shipday and night to prepare for the best possibility, arriving on our Homeworld.

No point preparing for anything else.

As my hair vibrated and squeezed itself dry, I dressed, pondering how to break the news. *I could wake Council first,* I suggested to Aryl, pleased with myself. *Let them make the announcement.*

I've briefed them. They voted to have you to do it.

That wasn't fair— I may have forgotten, temporarily, who rode inside my body: the Clanswoman who'd once led all M'hiray.

This isn't about fair, Keeper, with a tiny *snap.* Then, with characteristic bluntness, *They'll look first to you, Sira, whatever else. Trust yourself. You know what to say.*

And what to keep to myself, I thought grimly. Morgan's plan to sabotage the ship was pure desperation, more likely to buy us a quick end than freedom. He hadn't said it.

He hadn't had to. *We've run long enough,* I sent, oddly at peace.

Ready, I stepped outside, pleased to see the lights were up and people rousing.

I opened my mind to the ship. Sona, *are you there?*

>Keeper, what is your will?<
Let's get this day started.

* ✳ *

"Good morning." *Sona* carried my voice to the far corners of the Core; I stood on the nearest empty table to be seen—and see.

As I'd seen Morgan and Barac appear near our sleeping area, depositing unfamiliar green bags on our bed. I appreciated their timing; the sooner I did this, the sooner—well, it'd be done.

"This has been a journey none of us expected to make. Full of hardships we couldn't have predicted, as well as joy." I gestured to Gricel, standing with Yanti in her arms.

Nods, one or two hesitant smiles, but those who allowed me to sense their feelings were sharing an understandable *doubt,* this being how I'd started their day—

Was it only yesterday?

I'd be embarrassed some remote time in the future, when we could look back and laugh. "Our journey began when I asked our great starship, *Sona*—" a little flattery couldn't hurt, "—to take us home. I'm glad to tell you it's about to end. We arrive tomorrow." And if I put a flare of *hope* under the words, with the Power to reach each and every one?

It was no more than they deserved—and needed.

With a collective gasp, smiles blossomed and people turned to one another. Some hugged, others brushed fingers. There were no few tears. Sendings *sizzled* and voices rose, full of excited anticipation.

Well done. I let myself look at Morgan. He sat at seeming ease on our bed, hands locked around a knee. He wasn't smiling.

Waiting for the rest, I thought, steeling myself for the same reason. "We have a great deal to do." The Core fell silent; all eyes fixed on me. "Breakfast's waiting for us, as are packets for our final two meals before landing. The ship's begun to prepare for that, starting with what was the food storage room." A fine job of justification, if I did say so myself. "More changes could happen at any moment, in any area, so please stay with someone who can 'port you to safety."

They settled, growing serious. Change and peril was a connection we'd learned to make. Now what did I say?

Council's turn, Aryl said. *I've conversed with each. They're ready to
support you, Sira. We all are.*

I made the gesture of respect between equals. "Council will
detail what's needed and apportion tasks. We're almost home."

Jumping down, I headed straight for Morgan.

* ✷ *

People absorbed the news, unsure what it meant—for none knew
where *Sona* took us—but with relief. We'd existed since leaving
the Trade Pact and Cersi, nothing more. All would be glad to see
this journey's end.

Council kept us busy. Belongings were packed into rolls made
from extra blankets, secured with the last of the gauze brought
on board by the Sona and Tuana, including that from the party
bows. Groups scoured the ship—on foot and ready to 'port away
if spots appeared in the walls—looking for anything useful.

Not that anyone knew what useful would be, but we wouldn't
abandon what could be moved. Barring a welcome we knew better than to expect, *Sona* would have to shelter us. Would the
starship reshape itself again to our convenience? Be a building
again?

An outcome I knew Morgan would consider "interesting." For
myself, the sooner we moved out of these walls, the happier I'd be.

Morgan, of course, had completed his gleaning, his pack having gained a few new bulges, plus whatever was in the bags. He
wore the pack at all times now and others took notice; soon it was
common to see blanket rolls under an arm or slung across a
shoulder, rather than left behind.

Destin stayed by the water dispenser, supervising the filling of
whatever containers could be found that were clean and didn't
leak. Drought might be a novel concept to those familiar with
Cersi's rain-filled groves, but the former scout comprehended
the danger it posed. Morgan gave her bags like the ones he'd left
on our bed. Filled, they resembled bright green balloons.

And might, I reminded myself, save lives.

In case we faced a blizzard instead, Barac volunteered to sort what warm clothing we had, something that amused Morgan, if not the result. The Amna had brought seven heavy coats and there were a few decorative fur wraps. Moyla set Eloe and any who'd skill with a needle to making cloaklike covers from our extra blankets.

Sona filled with an atmosphere of purpose and urgency, refreshing as the showers everyone took care to have.

Our Healers had been busy, too. Like a cheerful tide, they'd eased through families, going from person to person, chatting and smiling as they checked for what they termed "readiness." While I'd no doubt they did exactly that, they also scanned for that perilous strain within minds. Our list of those to watch, and who could need help and soon, had grown.

The topic likely under discussion, I decided as I approached the table where Morgan sat, deep in conversation with Ruis and Ahur sud Vendan.

The oldest of the M'hiray to have survived, Ahur was renowned not for his Power, which was limited, but his Healer's Talent and breadth of knowledge. The great Cenebar di Teerac had studied under him; Jorn di Annk was—had been one of Ahur's most promising new students. I gestured respect as I sat.

"—joyful, yes, but with the uncertainty of how we land and what we find, some could tip over the edge," Morgan was saying. Blue eyes flicked up to acknowledge my arrival, then went back to Ruis. "We should keep a close watch on the Chosen at risk."

"Should, yet cannot," Ahur disagreed in his slow, soft voice. "Our patients are not only spread about but 'porting from place to place, or roaming the ship. Tonight, together in the Core, yes. Until then, we must rely on them to watch one another."

"I'm more concerned about what happens if several fail at once. Sixty-three M'hiray show signs." Ruis leaned forward, her gaze turning to me. "Morgan's told us that the Maker could help, but the ship won't let us use it. Is there anything you can do, Keeper?"

"Ask again," I told her. "That's all."

I could see the pillar past their shoulders. Machines should prove they were working, be it lights, bells, or annoying hums, as far as I was concerned. The Maker—the ship's vital "access portal interface"—might have been an inert chunk of stone.

Sona, I sent, as I had regularly since waking, *have you received confirmation from the Source?* Wording my Chosen and I had agreed upon: neutral and clear.

>*I will receive confirmation, Keeper.*<

Excellent, I replied, despite it being the same as every previous answer. Morgan sensibly warned not to ascribe emotion to the ship; it made me happier to believe I heard stubborn optimism. After all, the ship couldn't want to fail and die either. Could it?

A question I was not going to ask.

"The Maker remains unavailable." I put my hand on the table, turned it palm up. "My strength is yours, if ever you need it."

Morgan's eyes softened; Ahur and Ruis gestured gratitude. "A great comfort, Sira," the latter added. She eased back, lifting her hand upward. "Our people are full of hope and well-occupied. They're as safe from themselves as can be, for now."

Ahur raised a gnarled finger to the side of his head. "I suggest we offer a peaceful night to any who ask it."

Imposed sleep had its risk. Each person would have to be awakened as well, taking time. I saw that understanding cross my Human's face, waited for him to protest. Instead, "I concur. It would be a kindness."

Morgan, if there's an emergency—

An eyebrow lifted.

Nothing we could do, that meant, awake or asleep.

There were times, I sighed to myself with resignation, I'd have liked a less honest Chosen.

* ✳ *

Having no skill whatsoever with a needle and thread, I offered my help elsewhere, 'porting containers of water to the Core, joining the search through what remained accessible on the ship, and, likely most useful of all, stopping to listen. Everyone had a question or opinion or concern. I answered, nodded, and consoled as best I could.

Everyone, it seemed, but Aryl. She'd withdrawn after the morning's excitement to a distant brooding presence. We each prepared in our own way; if hers required solitude, I was the last to disturb her.

The day flew past, full of odd moments. I tried to explain landing on a planet to four Om'ray elders—not that we knew *Sona* would power its way down like the *Silver Fox,* but at least I'd that experience to share—only to then have to explain what a planet was. Signy di Sawnda'at, Degal's Chosen, drew me aside, offering her rings to help cover any parking fees, leading me to wonder how she'd known such things existed. Clan 'ported to stations like Plexis Supermarket; they didn't dock starships. I assured her, shamelessly, that such details were under control.

Morgan had laughed.

Odon's Chosen, Japel di Rihma'at, came with a more delicate concern: Noil, their son and our most likely Candidate for Choice, had expressed interest in Alet di Uruus, the Tuana Chooser. Understandable. While I'd hoped for Tle or Jacqui, Alet had lived in the canopy, training, like Noil, to harvest dresel with the astonishing-to-me skills of that life. When I said as much, Japel had looked distressed. Did I know if there were groves where we were going? Should they encourage him to look elsewhere, to someone with the skills needed on our new home? What could I tell her about it, please, to prepare him? And if the proud Om'ray begged, and if her eyes filled with tears?

She wasn't the only one. I told her, as I'd told the others, we'd find out together, tomorrow.

Then *reached* along our link to my Chosen, for the comfort of his understanding.

Given the number of such conversations I'd had by day's end, I'd firmly expected one would have been with Ruti, about Andi and the dead, but whenever I'd passed through the galley, Barac's Chosen was in the midst of sixteen excited children, plus a newborn, a marvel of calm behind a noisy, impenetrable barrier.

The same couldn't be said about Ruti's Birth Watcher, Jacqui di Mendolar. I spotted her sitting alone, eyes downcast, at the far end of the galley. Our second-last meal was underway, unChosen at the dais heating packets and handing them to those waiting. The shrinking stack of food was proof of Nik and Holl's calculations—and slightly terrifying.

Sona? *Have—*

>*I will receive confirmation, Keeper.*<

Learned to anticipate the question, had it? Well, that saved time. I refused to worry if it was a good thing.

Worry. The word, or something I was sensing, drew my attention back to Jacqui. Making up my mind, I took my food packet and walked to her table.

The Chooser made to stand and bow as I approached. I motioned her to sit. "May I join you?"

"Of course, Sira." She'd yet to touch her own supper.

I settled in, smiling comfortably. "All that packing—I'm exhausted!" The little joke was running through the room; like the rest of the M'hiray, I'd only what I wore and what I'd arrived on Cersi wearing—mended and more-or-less clean. Oh, and a night shift and blanket.

Jacqui di Mendolar didn't smile back. The Birth Watcher was slight, with upturned green eyes and fine black hair. Normally, she had an air of calm attentiveness, her eyes sparkling with intelligence. Now, though, her gaze fixed on her hands, long fingers toying restlessly with a strip of gauze; perhaps the remnant of a bow.

No need to *reach*; the Chooser broadcast *anxiety* like a beacon. About what? There were, regrettably, more than a few possibilities, beginning with Noil and Alet.

I ate in silence, having learned from Morgan the importance of eating when the chance arose. It also gave Jacqui time.

Finally, her eyes lifted. "I've meant to talk to you, Sira. About Andi."

Ah. I nodded encouragement. "Go on."

"It's—" The gauze knotted and she put it aside. "Not—just Andi." Jacqui hesitated, then offered her hand.

Odd. No one sat nearby. Or was this invited intimacy because she found it difficult to utter the words aloud?

I touched two fingers to her palm.

Worry. FEAR!

At once I responded with *reassurance* and *peace*, my shields protecting Aryl and Morgan, waiting while Jacqui reestablished control.

The flood of emotion shrank back to the trickle of *anxiety.* "I'm sorry, Sira," Jacqui whispered.

I hadn't moved my fingers. *Tell me what's wrong.*

Birth Watchers are closer to the M'hir than any others. It's our Talent, so we see *the bond between mother and child and form our own. Andi's ability to* find *other Clan could be an extension of the same gift, so I thought I might—I've tried, but I can't, Sira.*

This couldn't be what upset her. Mystified, I sent *encouragement.*

Andi doesn't just find *the living. She says she* hears *the dead.* Sees *them.* Jacqui stopped, fighting to remain calm.

The matter was worsening. Ghosts were *heard,* not *seen.* I should have dealt with the child. Instead of being swept up in the anticipation of landing, I should have found Andi and stopped her before her wild claims could cause harm. *Her imagination,* I sent gently. *It's not possible.*

Her eyes filled with horror. *Then why do I* see *them, too?*

Sira? My Chosen, feeling my echoing *dismay.*

It's all right, I reassured him, knowing it wasn't. *Show me,* I sent to Jacqui.

And me, suddenly, from Aryl.

Take it, the Birth Watcher sent. *Here.* Shields toppled, exposing her deepest thoughts.

As befitted someone who would have happily spent her life archiving old and rare bits of our past, Jacqui's mind was orderly, with strong, ingrained patterns and a fondness for connections. Had it been safe, she would have found a new home with Holl and the other scientists.

Spotting a distinct, breathless naïveté in how she viewed the outside world, especially the unChosen, I stayed carefully distant. *Where?*

I see it. Aryl drew me with her.

. . . *A Clansman stood at a counter in his workroom, busy with something I couldn't see. A salt-scented breeze came from my left, and I heard more distant sounds from the city that sprawled down the hill to the sea, just beyond the garden wall . . .*

I saw him only in profile, but I knew who it was. That hawk's beak of a nose and angular jaw—it was my father, Jarad di Sarc.

And he was, most certainly, dead.

. . . His head turned and he looked right at me . . .

"That was—" I pulled my hand back, fingers curling into a fist. "—not what I expected."

"Nor I. I mean, I didn't know what to expect. I'd never seen a ghost before," Jacqui explained hastily. "I didn't think they looked so—real."

They were screams. Echoes. Incoherent mutterings. Not this. Never this. It had to be a memory. "I didn't know you'd been to my father's home. On Garatis 17."

"His—?" Her hands began to tremble and Jacqui seized the knot of gauze as if drowning. "No. I never went there. I wanted to, to see his new collection, but the Watchers wouldn't allow any visitors."

The Watchers. I'd successfully avoided them since leaving Cersi. Among their more disturbing habits was to *howl* the names of the newly deceased through the M'hir, as though the *gibbering* of ghosts weren't enough.

Whatever the Watchers were, attracting their *attention* in the M'hir was the last thing I wanted to do again, yet this time, when Jacqui said their name—

What is it, Witchling?

—it was as though I'd heard my own.

"Sira. Am I going mad—like Risa?"

The whispered plea brought me back to the present, and poor Jacqui. I took her hands; they were cold and trembled. "Morgan scanned you. You're fine. Whatever this is, it doesn't appear dangerous. I think it's possible you and Andi are drawing from the memories of those around you—not deliberately—" as she looked even more upset, "—but we did Dream together while under the influence of the Hoveny machine. Who knows what that did to us?"

I watched the idea sink in, putting color back in her cheeks. Her hands warmed. "Yes. That makes much more sense than ghosts." Jacqui managed a timid smile. "Thank you."

You shouldn't lie to the child, Aryl scolded. *It wasn't the Maker.*

Do you know what it was?

Silence answered. Well enough. *Until we know what it was, Great-grandmother, I'd prefer to spare her nightmares.*

I'd hoped to have none myself. A fresh vision of my father didn't bode well for that ambition.

I can help with that, Morgan, oh so innocent.

You are not putting me to sleep, I told him.

Nor me!

I could *feel* him laugh.

"Sira." Jacqui, her equilibrium restored, nodded toward another table. "I'll explain to Andi what's happening, if you like. I'm sure she'll understand—she's very quick."

"That she is." Easy to see the child's head of tousled golden hair; less easy, I thought, to know what to say. "I'll talk to her, thank you. Aryl and I could use more time with our Birth Watcher."

Jacqui rose with me, bowed, gesturing gratitude. "Should I— would you like me to tell you—or someone—if this happens to me again?"

"Tell me— or Morgan," I added, seeing him come toward us. Good.

I could use his help with Andi. Ruti believed what the child didn't understand was death, something I'd envy—

If it wasn't now my duty to ensure she did.

* ✳ *

Brows furrowed in concentration, her eyes closed, Andi moved hands half the size of mine over my abdomen with adult assurance. "Good," she murmured. "Good." Her eyes shot open and she looked down at me, her entire face a silent laugh.

"Let me guess," I said wryly. "My great-grandmother's complaining I don't get enough sleep for her liking."

"And you eat too fast." Gray-green eyes rounded with curiosity. "She says you can swallow an entire packet in one gulp, like an esans. Can you?"

"Not quite." Admittedly, I could have picked up some bad habits on the *Silver Fox*. The number of times we'd grabbed tubes of e-rations and eaten while working?

Grumbling at the taste. Morgan smiled.

Then. Now? I'd give anything, I thought wistfully, to be back there.

Unhelpful. Aryl was being just that, engaging with the child, making her comfortable. I swung my legs over and sat up, patting the bed beside me. "Sit with us, Andi. I'd like to talk to you, too."

We were in her "home," not ours. Her parents were nearby, silently packing up their bits and pieces of gear. They had what Deni and Cha had brought from Stonerim III as well, but fortunately it had come in tall custom-made brown packs.

The color wasn't the only difference between their packs and Morgan's, on the floor by the Human's feet. His was larger, wider, a worn dark gray, and had padded straps, including one that rode his hips. Its capacity seemed endless, by the stream of previously unseen objects he produced from its depths. When I'd commented, my Chosen had given his quiet half-smile. Just practice, he'd assured me. More likely, I'd judged, there were clever hidden compartments; on my list, one day, was to have a thorough look inside.

In so small a way, I'd joined the rest and thought of a time outside the ship and safe. Ruis had been right in her assessment. The mood on the ship, tonight, held as much content as excitement. "At last" was the most common phrase to be heard.

A mood easily lost. I met Morgan's gaze and found the resolve I needed. This wouldn't be a happy conversation, but it would be spoken. Nik and Josa must hear what I said to their daughter; they'd have to reinforce it and be ready to offer comfort.

Andi leaned against me, tucking her little arm under mine. My hair swept around her small shoulders as if to protect her and she wove a lock of the stuff between and around her fingers as though we played a game. "What do you want to talk about, Sira?" she asked. "Is it the people I see?"

"Yes, it is." Morgan smiled at her. "I'd like to hear about them, too, if you don't mind."

"I don't mind, Hom Morgan. But—" Her fingers stilled. "I'm very sorry, but I don't see anyone like you. I think Humans go away when they die."

Something flickered across his dear face before it returned to its normal, pleasant attentiveness. "I think so, too," he replied softly.

Nik and Josa, leaking *concern,* no longer pretended to pack.

Their daughter, on the other hand, appeared more at ease than any of us. Fair enough. "When Clan die," I asked, "what happens to them?"

She resumed playing with my hair. "Oh, they go to their boxes. They like it there."

DENIAL! struck with such speed and fury I knew I couldn't protect Andi or Morgan, except—

Only I'd felt it. I reeled with *pain,* mutely grateful.

Witchling?!

Great-grandmother . . . took offense, I told Morgan, who looked ready to leap to his feet. He settled with a frown.

At what?

I'll ask her later. When my head finished pounding and Aryl di Sarc was in a safer mood and I wasn't so off balance—"*Boxes?*"

—something Morgan felt, too. *Could she mean the rooms on the ship? The ones containing the M'hir? Could you have swept ghosts up as well?*

I stared at him while the universe continued its thoroughly unpleasant tilt. *What?*

Something troubling our heart-kin lately. His eyes were somber. *Barac either wanted me to* hear *or couldn't help broadcasting when I would.*

"Andi. The boxes you say the Clan go to—that they like. Are the boxes here, on the ship?" My entire body tensed as I awaited the answer.

"No, Sira."

I relaxed.

"Or maybe." Andi squirmed away to look up at me, her eyes earnest. "The boxes are always near." She touched the side of her head, then moved her hand as far away as she could stretch her arm. "But they aren't always close. I think that's why I had trouble finding Rasa's grandmother." She lowered her head, looking up at me through her eyelashes. "Don't tell him, but I was glad you and Aryl told me to stop. There are a lot of boxes now and everyone is talking at the same time. I was getting tired."

Nik flinched. "You weren't to touch the Great Darkness—"

Josa took her hand, keeping them both still. "We knew nothing of this, Sira."

"Because she didn't tell us. Why, Andi?"

The child blinked with surprise. "I thought you saw them, too."

"Saw who? Who, child?" Nik demanded, growing frantic. "Deni and Cha. Mirim. Are they—"

Hush, I sent her urgently, as Josa put his arm around his Chosen. Andi looked uncertain, as if finally aware her elders were upset, or did enough of their bond remain that she could share her mother's pain? "I used to," the child said, very carefully. "Their boxes don't stay as close as the rest." She gestured apology.

This was a nightmare. I looked at Morgan. *Delusion?*

Could be. Without conviction, as if he'd decided otherwise. "Andi," my Human asked the child, "how long have you been able to see the dead—these boxes?"

"For always."

"And there are more now?"

"Oh, yes."

I hadn't thought it possible to grow so cold, when all around was warmth—

"When did that change?"

He spared no one, not this child, not me, never himself—not when it meant this much.

"When Sira came to visit," she said in her clear high voice. "And after we came to Cersi. There are a lot now."

I'd believed I'd known the shape of my grief, understood how it tried to slow my steps and steal all hope.

I'd been wrong. This child knew better. When I'd arrived in her life, I'd brought death with me—and it hadn't left.

Sira—Witchling—

A hand, small and cool, rested on my cheek. "You shouldn't be sad, Sira. It hurt to go, but they're happy now. Even Noson."

"Andi!" With a frantic rush of hands and arms, a tide of *concern* and *contrition,* she was whisked away from me.

My side grew cold. I may have heard her sweet voice reassuring her distraught parents, may have felt my Chosen, steady and strong, along our link, but my mind roamed elsewhere, relentless, chasing the truth.

Om'ray believed only the living and those they'd known in life existed . . .

M'hiray, that the living were the sum of those come before and gone . . .

In common, that the physical body was a husk, discarded once empty. The mind *was* the individual, inextricably connected to the living whole through the M'hir, at the end of life destined to dissolve and vanish into that *darkness . . .*

And become nothing . . .

Had we'd been wrong about that?

Morgan had stayed with me, followed my thoughts. *We live; we die, Witchling.* With a spacer's pragmatism. *Why does what happens after matter so much now?*

It's not that, I sent, suddenly sure what bothered me. *If we believe Andi—if what Jacqui saw wasn't a dream, but somehow real—the question isn't where we go when we die—*

But why, now, do we matter to the dead?

* ✳ *

Dream Chamber. Core. Home. Whatever we chose to call it, this was where everyone came after our meal was done. Unlike the previous shipnight, there was no desire to linger in the galley.

Nor any for sleep.

I was as restless as any. Sona?

>*I will receive confirmation, Keeper.*<

Nor, I thought, any surer answers than that. Which stopped no one from speculating.

I wasn't immune. "So," I said brightly, "after breakfast."

Morgan's lips quirked. "Before we'd need supper," he corrected. "Leaving a margin of a full shipday."

"Or not."

My persistence earned a smile. "Or not. We're ready as we can be." He touched the pocket that held his noteplas and stylo.

My Human and I, Barac and Ruti. While everyone else believed tomorrow would bring us the world about to be our home—while some might have reasonable concerns ranging from the ancient starship's ability to land to what awaited us on the ground—we four knew tomorrow could be our last.

Barac and Ruti stayed close together, politely refusing contact with anyone else, but weren't alone or strange in that. My people gathered in their natural units: families, Om'ray Clans, M'hiray, our cadre of scientists. Gurutz stood sentry on the door as he hadn't since we'd lifted. Perhaps he prepared for the changes to come away from the ship.

Just before the lights dimmed for shipnight, our Healers—Morgan as well—would walk the Core, offering a dreamless sleep to any who doubted their ability to rest.

Sona's Council might be among those who asked. They'd worked without pause throughout the day. Now they sat together, with Leesems and Destin, poring over lists for tomorrow. They planned for what came after our landing and how we'd start our future.

They'd asked Morgan to join them. I cheered up and smiled at him. "Ready for this?"

An eyebrow lifted. "There's no 'this.' I'm sure they just have questions."

I gave him a look back. "They'll want you in charge."

"Sira." Patiently. "Degal's behind it. He knows I've experience with new worlds, that's all."

"Hah! He doesn't want to go purple and die."

"Reasonable attitude, don't you think?"

"What I think?" I ran my hand along his bare arm, enjoying the feel of his skin. "I think you're the finest explorer in the universe and they've oort fungus for brains if they don't insist you be first out of the air lock—the door."

Muscle tensed like cables beneath my fingers. "It can't be me. You know why as well as I do. There could be a greeting party—and they'll be expecting the Clan."

"Which is why it has to be you." I took Morgan's face in my hands, tilted it to the light, other than the beard seeing features so similar to ours it was tempting to imagine a connection, some combination of long-lost lineages able to produce such a nose and mouth, those ears and forehead, the brilliant blue of those eyes. Tempting, but wrong.

Morgan wasn't Clan. He was who and what he was.

We desperately needed both.

"When you walk off this ship first," I told him, "you prove we aren't just the result of some experiment, wrapped up and sent home to be used or discarded. You, my dear Human, prove we've become so much more and they'd best pay attention."

The smile I loved, that started in his eyes and spread slowly to his mouth. "I'll make a trader out of you yet, chit."

So I wasn't the only one to think beyond tomorrow. "I've a good teacher," I replied, finishing the words with a kiss.

＊

It wasn't the *Silver Fox*, being too quiet, too large, and entirely too self-important, but I found myself sentimental when we curled up for our final rest within the ancient Hoveny starship. Once I knew Morgan slept, I sent, Sona.

>*Greetings, Keeper. What is your will?*<

To thank you.

A doubtless confused pause.

Gratitude is a feeling, I explained. *You've taken care of us and that's how I feel. That's how we all feel. Grateful for your help.*

>*It is pleasing to do one's duty, Keeper.*< Was that caution? >*I will receive confirmation and continue to do so.*<

I'm sure you will. What more could I say?

What would Morgan have said to the *Fox,* if he'd had the chance?

You've been a good ship.

Interlude

A FLARE OF *unease* pulsed through AllThereIs, disturbance in its wake. Some tumbled aside to safety. Some were drawn haplessly close and consumed. The Watcher saw the danger. She chose to remain where she was.

And accept.

The pulse slammed into her.

Through her.

For an instant, she was *unmade*.

The next, in sped all she'd been and known, reforming, gathering.

The next, in flooded all the *other* had been and known, reforming, gathering.

Enlightenment: a second Watcher, drawn with the *unease* or accompanying it.

Communion.

Concern.

The Watchers pulled apart, one to Watch.

One to summon.

No proof, not yet, the *unease* was the peril that must never come again.

No need. This time, AllThereIs would be protected.

* ✳ *

The starship squirted from subspace, gliding along the curve of gravity in a descent planned before it was built, bleeding velocity.

A signal preceded it, repeating, through the long, lonely dark.

Confirmation request. Identification: Cersi-So.

Alarms cried out.

Confirmation request. Identification: Cersi-So.

A sleeper woke.

Confirmation request. Identification: Cersi-So.

A cup fell, rattling—

—and its contents spread like blood.

Chapter 12

I FOUND myself staring into the dark. Why was I awake—too soon—this time? *Morgan*—

Noticed the drop, did you, chit? He nuzzled my neck. *Bet none of these grounders did.*

Which made no—then every possible sense. *We're back—back in normal space.* Meaning we were about to arrive—

That we are, with immense *satisfaction.*

No more blobs and streaks—real stars? I concentrated—

—and went nowhere.

Of all the— *We can't take a look,* I informed my Chosen, doing my best not to be disappointed. *The Star Chamber's gone.*

Who knows, Witchling. Maybe tonight, we'll walk outside beneath all the stars we'll ever need. A tender press of lips against my throat, then I felt him roll over and settle.

Unbelievable. *What are you doing?* I demanded.

Going back to sleep. We've a while yet. A hint of *amusement. I suggest you do the same. This should be an interesting day.*

Before I could respond, he was sound asleep. Whether a Human trait or simply Morgan's knack to rest at whim, I knew one thing for certain. I couldn't do it.

I stared at the ceiling.

Unless I cheated.

If I didn't, I'd lie here till morning, awake, struggling to keep the thoughts and emotions whirling through my head from bothering anyone else.

Let alone rein in my imagination, already fixating on a starry stroll, which could be disrupted by alien monsters, maybe cannibals—

Cheating was, I told myself hurriedly, acceptable under the circumstances.

Opening my *awareness* of the link between our minds, I let my consciousness *curl* around my Chosen's inner self, savoring the peace of his slumber.

Until that was all there was.

* ✱ *

As if to remove any doubt the Clan would leave the ship on this day, Om'ray and M'hiray stripped their beds and secured their belongings. Not by any recommendation from Council; Tle di Parth started it, the Chooser standing defiant and alone at her end of the Core, arms around her bundle of things.

The di Haons quietly did the same. The di Kessa'ats.

Then Ruti.

Blankets began flying from beds, unanimity spreading across the Core until everyone stood, arms full, among rows of bare mattresses and empty platforms, ready to go that instant.

Tle did an admirable job of appearing unaffected; I knew her well enough to guess she was touched—and discomfited by the feeling.

Morgan, having somehow squeezed our belongings into his pack when I wasn't looking, pulled off our blanket, rolled it, and handed it to me with a flourish. "I'd say we're done here."

His shields were impeccable, and no one else could read the grim resolve in his eyes. A chill feathered my skin, but I ignored it, giving a tiny nod.

Sona, I asked silently, *have you received confirmation?*

>*I will receive confirmation, Keeper.*<

Nothing had changed, then.

I smiled at my Chosen. "Breakfast first."

＊ ✳ ＊

Sira.

At last. My spoon paused on its way to my mouth. I made it finish the trip, this being my last bite. *Yes, Great-grandmother?*

Between us, alone.

Those sharing our table or walking nearby weren't who she meant.

Morgan.

I'd see him if I looked up; what I felt was *focus.* Having finished his breakfast, he walked through the galley, pausing to speak with this Healer or with one of the scientists. In reality he prowled, there was no other word for it, and most who saw his face gave him room.

Just as well. He'd tucked something round and undoubtedly dangerous into his coat pocket, and was slowly making his way to the dais and *Sona's* access portal interface, to be there and ready for whatever came.

Aryl wants a private conversation.

About time.

I smiled to myself. My Chosen valued Aryl as much as I did; what had happened yesterday, and her silence since, concerned us both.

My sense of Morgan faded as I firmed an inner wall between us. *Alone it is, Great-grandmother.*

My profound apologies, Sira, for the pain I caused you. I was overcome and shouldn't have been.

Already forgotten, I lied.

Not by your Chosen, with a *wry* touch that became something darker. *I trust Morgan to think of you first. For that reason, what I would say may need to remain between us. I don't ask you to promise, but to decide for yourself.*

Not good at all. *Go on.*

Before the Council meeting, I told you I'd dreamed—that wasn't the truth. It wasn't a dream at all. I would share it with you.

Of course. I put the spoon down and brought my elbows up on the table, leaning my chin in my hands. Inwardly, I braced.

. . . finding myself in a shack—no, it was nicer than that, a home

made of wide logs caulked with red clay, with a floor covered in thick woven rugs and a snug roof overhead. A door stood open on a wide green valley crossed by a sparkling river. There were tall, thin trees in the distance, framed by mountains that touched a purple-blue sky; nearer, rows of tidy crops. Flowers, pink and white, in a bowl sent forth a heady fragrance for which I'd no name.

My feet were bare and I dug my toes into the prickly pile of the rug. I wore nothing but the warm air playing across my skin and a cloak of heavy red-gold hair. A strand tickled my nose, trying to make me sneeze.

Hands gathered the stuff, guiding it into a smooth knot, as I couldn't do. "That better?"

Male, the voice, so rich and deep I felt it in my bones.

If I turned, I'd see who it belonged to—but I mustn't, for it couldn't be—

Arms, big and strong, went around my waist, drawing me back against a wide, warm chest. "Welcome home."

But I had none . . .

I found myself sitting at a table, staring at a spoon, both improbably less real than Aryl's sharing.

Giving myself a little shake, I looked up to see if anyone else had noticed, then pulled the band from my arm, tipping it to see the artist's delicate signature: a square no larger than my fingernail, open at a corner. Another, finer, inside. Within that, six tiny dots, of varied depth, representing a constellation seen from Tuana—when it had been Oud and not smothered in jungle.

Enris, I stated.

Yes. Although it cannot be. What I experienced—what you shared— cannot be. Her mindvoice was distant, almost cold. *None of that was from my memories, Sira. Yes, we'd started to make a home at Sona, but this—this is what we'd hoped to build, dreamed of, not what we had. And yes, that's his voice—his touch—but as if he hadn't aged.*

Tread carefully, I warned myself. This had to be why Aryl reacted as she had to Andi's declaration that our dead went to boxes. Boxes they liked. Enris, this place? *Dreams can take us—*

Did it feel like a dream to you?

No. No more than Jacqui's, of my father in his workshop: his box. Both had been so convincing, I might have 'ported there.

You heard him speak, like Jacqui. Cold settled into my bones. *Like Andi.*

Her wordless *agreement* held a grim foreboding. *And more. I* felt *him, Sira, for an instant. Not as the ragged ruin I carry inside me, but* him. *As if Enris were still alive and we were still—Joined. Only to have our link fail. Again.*

This wasn't a wish she'd made before falling asleep. This was a trial no one should have to bear once, let alone relive in their sleep. Part of me was astounded anew by Aryl di Sarc's strength, the rest pitifully grateful I'd never need it. *What does it mean?*

It means I now understand why the taste *of change has filled me since then. These visits by our dead have a purpose, Sira, one we should dread. What came to me was a trap, intended to lure me from reality into some-thing else. The link between Chosen pulls* the living after their dead into the M'hir, as is right and natural. This box, baited with everything I've lost, is neither. I fear to be exposed to it again. I fear a second time, I may not be able to resist, that what I am will abandon you.*

Leaving the Vessel within me empty; dooming us all. Little wonder Aryl hadn't wanted Morgan to *hear* this.

Risa and Jorn. Bile rose in my throat. Had they been lured by their dead?

I refused to think it. Refused to believe any of it. *We don't know these aren't somehow still dreams and harmless, however disturbing,* I insisted. *We need to learn more. Find out what's causing them.*

And if it's not what, but where?

What did she mean? *The "where" of ghosts is the place they died and last touched the M'hir,* I replied cautiously. *The few who linger at all.*

Yet here is where Andi sees them. Sira. The ship's taking us back where this started: Cersi, the Clan, you and I and M'hir—

What makes you think that's as simple as a world?

Interlude

THEY'D MADE A BRAVE START, but with breakfast done, however long they'd stretched out the meal and how many hot beverages they'd consumed afterward, the Clan grew restless. There were no tasks left, nothing to focus on but one another and it wouldn't, Morgan judged, be long until their eager hope cracked to admit worry. Dread and despondency would follow, and those at risk fail first.

Wouldn't happen, he told himself, the faint *taste* of change for once a reassurance. Barac felt it, too. They'd exchanged looks, but that was enough. The elegant Clansman—his friend and heart-kin—could be trusted to use what he carried.

In return, Barac and Ruti put their trust in him.

Good thing the rest remained unaware how fragile this ship—and their futures—were, and that they might die at the hands of a Human after all.

Morgan squatted beside the column, tracing—but not touching—the path of a dot of blue light with a fingertip. It moved along straight lines, turning at right angles, its glow intense enough to leave a pattern behind closed eyelids. "This is new."

Sira squatted nearby, carefully distant; she knew what rode in his lower left pocket. "Do we like 'new?'"

"Depends on what it means." He glanced at her. She'd been subdued since joining him on the dais. Whatever Aryl'd had to say, it hadn't been good. "Please," he said firmly, "don't ask if I know."

Her lips pressed together to prove her restraint, then curved. She continued to study the dot, most likely not seeing it at all. *Aryl* saw *Enris. In—in his box.*

Gods. No wonder Aryl had reacted as she had. *Is she all right?*

"She" is right here, Human. With a reassuring *snap.* Aryl's mind voice gentled. *Thank you for your concern.*

Sira, tight and private: *For a moment, she sensed* him*, as if their link was restored.*

Through the null-grid. The M'hir. Was that truly the Clan resting place, newly revealed, or was there a simpler, more concrete explanation?

Alien minds. He'd been so sure he'd known what he was doing. What if he'd missed a sign they were slipping—even Aryl?

Was he the only one aboard still sane?

Finished? From the mind forever part of his, with *incredulity.*

Under other circumstances, he'd have laughed.

"Definitely." The Human checked his scanner; no change from the last time. As plays went, this was extreme, even for him. Ridiculous to believe they'd get a warning the ship was activating its self-destruct—even more to think they'd get that warning in time to set a charge, 'port to safety, and blow up the interface, which, to tip the scales further toward hilarity, he'd no way to know could change the outcome one iota.

However satisfying.

Shrugging off his pack, Morgan turned to sit with his shoulders against the Maker, and stretched out his feet.

Sira stood, staring down at him. "That's—What are you doing?"

"Getting comfortable. Join me?" He offered his hand. Not that Sira, ever-graceful, needed his help—

But he loved the feel of her hand in his, treasured each moment and sensation, now more than ever, when they could be the last.

She accepted the invitation, studiously ignoring dismayed

looks from those who noticed—no others would willingly come close to the Maker, let alone touch it—and sat next to him. "Nothing new from *Sona*." Sira left her hand in his; through their link, she shared *warmth* with him, her *belief.*

Human poets could keep their versions of love and understanding. Since their Joining, he was whole as he'd never imagined being. How could he regret anything that had brought them together?

He couldn't, even if it ended, today.

A dimple appeared in one cheek and her glorious hair stirred over her shoulders, catching the light. "Such deep thoughts."

You inspire.

The smile he'd been waiting for lit her eyes as she reclaimed her fingers, then disappeared. Sira drew her knees to her chest and hugged them close. "Destin's asking what you're up to. In not very kind terms."

Morgan looked for the former First Scout. Her scarred face was set in hard lines and her stare was openly hostile. Not someone to fool. "Tell her the truth," he said, surprising himself.

Tasted change, stronger than before. Rising.

"I thought we were—" Sira gave the pocket where he kept his noteplas a meaningful tap.

Stronger still. He chose another pocket, the blastglobe filling the curve of palm and fingers, and stood.

Sira rose with him, rested her hand on his arm. Destin started to walk toward them. Heads turned. Silence spread.

"Tell them all—" Morgan tried to say.

CHANGE!

Chapter 13

I FLINCHED at the blaze of searing orange light—no, yellow—
—blood-red. It splashed over faces, mouths open as if shouting, but with the red came a shrieking pulse of SOUND louder
than any voice—

While *inside,* a scream of another kind: >*TO THE DREAM CHAM-
BER! TO THE DREAM CHAMBER! TO THE DREAM CHAMBER!*<

Some vanished. Most hesitated, startled or distrustful or simply
afraid.

GO!!! I sent, blasting through shields and hesitation. *TO THE
CORE AND SAFETY!* Not that I knew it was, but I'd lived on a
starship. You didn't ignore an alarm.

The Clan couldn't ignore mine. Within a heartbeat, Morgan
and I were alone in the galley. As though satisfied, the lights returned to normal and the shrieking pulse ended, leaving a loud
echo in my ears.

Morgan stood with the innocent-looking ball in both hands.

I saw his grip shift.

Knew the instant he began to twist.

I put my hand on top, held his gaze with mine. "One more try."
Sona, have you received confirmation?

> *KEEPER AND NOT-RIGHT KIND TO THE DREAM CHAMBER!*<

Which wasn't at all helpful, though I was touched it cared.

Morgan's remarkable blue eyes darkened with emotion. We have to do this, they said, as clearly as words.

And it has to be now.

Nodding, I removed my hand, ready to 'port us to the Core at his signal.

My Human spun on a heel, hands twisting—

Only to stop. "Look!"

The pillar glowed from within, its green overtaken by a network of glowing blue circuitry along which streaked a multitude of dots, faster than my eyes could follow.

Was the ship signaling?

The bright dots stopped moving, all of them at once, and the circuitry faded away, leaving an afterimage of yellow when I blinked.

The pillar was again dark green and lifeless.

"*Sona?*" I said it aloud, unashamed of the quiver in my voice. "What just happened? What's going on?" sending at the same time.

>*Keeper.*< Did I imagine something gentle in its tone? Something almost wistful? >*I have received my instructions. You and the not-Right Kind must go to the Dream Chamber now.*<

I sagged. "*Sona*'s received instructions, Morgan. It wants us in the Core."

His hands twisted—the other way, I noticed with relief, a relief lasting only until I saw the resignation in his face. "We won't make it," my Human said dryly and pointed.

The pillar was—it was melting! Not only the pillar, I saw in horror, but the walls were softening, oozing—

Drips began falling from the ceiling like obscene rain—

The dais softened beneath my feet—

Morgan, the ball nowhere in sight, opened his arms with an inexpressibly tender smile. *Ship's done, Witchling. So are we.*

I stepped forward, ready to die together, as we should—

COME!! Hurry! from Barac, from everyone! Sendings so full of *anticipation* I saw it light Morgan's face—

As I concentrated with desperate hope . . .

* ✳ *

. . . arriving in what had been the Dream Chamber, become the Core, and was now—I gasped—something else again.

"Ship's been busy," Morgan commented.

The walls, floor, and ceiling were solid—for how long was anyone's guess—but the beds had vanished, replaced by rows of large bowls of the same green metal as the Maker.

They had a pleasing resemblance to the bizarre vehicles of the Drapsk. Sona, *what are these?*

>*Conveyances. Keeper, please instruct there can be only one person per conveyance.*<

"Conveyance" was, I decided, my new favorite word. "Everyone," the ship picking up my voice "these are—"

Lifepods, my Chosen suggested helpfully.

An even better word! "—lifepods. One person each. Get in and hurry!" I added, hoping it was my imagination that my feet were beginning to sink.

Though *dismay* filled my inner sense, everyone moved, sorting themselves quickly. Perhaps the alarm *Sona* broadcast had been to this end as well: so its passengers act with urgency.

It wasn't only that, I thought. My people accepted this latest, possibly greatest, challenge with a courage no less profound for being quiet obedience. I sent *reassurance* to them all, and my *pride.*

I followed Morgan to the pair that would be ours. He looked inside. "Not much room. No padding. Wait. There," pointing to a series of grates on the burnished inner surface. "Could be an extrusion point. Maybe a gel—"

I went on tiptoe to kiss his nose. "Just get in."

"You first." He swept me up in his arms, depositing me gently inside the bowl, then leaned in. "Don't go exploring without me. Here."

His pack arrived.

I glowered; he grinned. "You've more room." Morgan's face softened and he reached in, his fingers meeting a curl of my hair. "See you planetside, chit."

He disappeared from sight, but not my inner sense.

Nor was I alone in my bowl. *Aryl?*

It seems we fall together, Great-granddaughter, with good humor. *Wish for a soft landing.*

I've done this before—once, and we'd landed upside-down in a jungle, but those were details she didn't need. *It's safe.*

Although landing under power, with a qualified pilot—ideally Morgan—at the controls, was by far my preference.

We get what we get, from my Chosen. *Watch the sides.*

I'd been trying not to watch the bowl's rim expand in a distressingly fluid manner as though to engulf me, thank you, but reminded, I squinted up in time to catch the sides meeting—merging—in the middle.

A middle that provided a soft illumination, similar to that of the ship's.

I hugged Morgan's lumpy pack, clung to my sense of him and Aryl, and waited.

And waited.

Just when I felt about to burst, *Sona* entered my thoughts.

>*Keeper, I connect the null-grid*—<

Silence.

No, I realized. Absence. "Good-bye, *Sona*," I whispered.

And was plunged into the *seething dark* of the M'hir.

Interlude

I N ALLTHEREIS, what had been *substance,* bleeding Power to feed those who'd discovered it, *vanished . . .*

While in normal space, what had been a starship became a moving cloud, momentum working with gravity to smear its droplets in a long, brilliant trail.

In AllThereIs, the Watcher who remained saw the feeders scatter, chased by odd, tiny streaks of *vitality.*

While on the surface of Brightfall, there were those who marveled at the brilliant trail arching across their sky.

And those who prepared.

Brightfall

Prelude

KEEPER EMELEN DIS pressed his palms together as he took a deep, centering breath, striving for calm. Outward appearance was everything this morning; worth the extra *slas* to smooth the tassels of his vestment and properly school his face. A flaw could betray him—betray them all—and there were those to be gathered in secrecy and haste. This was his sacred charge, passed down generations, given urgent reality with that first transmission from the Heavens: "Confirmation request. Identification: Cersi-So."

"'Cersi-So.'" Words to swell the heart of any believer, core of the Invocations to welcome each day and praise the night: Cersi-Vy. Cersi-Ray. Cersi-So. Cersi-Gro. Cersi-Ne. Cersi-Tua. Cersi-Ye. Cersi-Pa. Cersi-Am. Cersi-Nor. Cersi-Xro. Cersi-Fa. One for each digit the godly stretched toward the Heavens.

Once again, to finish with reverence, for in such were the Prime held: Cersi-Vy.

Being alone, Emelen indulged himself, saying aloud: "'Confirmation request. Identification: Cersi-So.'"

A mere *orlas* ago, his helper, bless the youngling, had run four flights of stairs to wake him, handing him what shone with its own inner light. Had stood watching, disheveled and panting, eyes bulging with wonder, as Emelen had taken the silken piece, stretched it out with trembling fingers, and read the holy script.

And if Emelen had leaped from bed, not bothering with clothes, to race back down to the Sanctum Access, feet hitting each familiar step in the dark, so that the youngling, reliant on her lamp, fell behind—

And if he'd cursed her diligent resealing of the door under his breath, she hadn't heard—

And if he'd entered the Sanctum, buried deep in rock smoothed by the grace of those before, and fallen to his knees so ardently the skin had torn and he'd bled on stone that rose from the heart of the world and wept—

Any would forgive him, for as foretold, as so long awaited and by so many disbelieved, the simple pillar that was the access portal had come to life, its glorious light bathing him, waves of shining silk tumbled at its base.

And if this were true, then so was it all, and he lifted his eyes to the walls, glittering with inset crystal, in awe. Could he not— surely he could—feel the benevolent regard of the Ancestors? Dusted by generations of apprentices, ignored by the rest, awaiting the Rebirth they'd promised.

When Gerasim Su caught up, she'd gone to her knees beside him, but there was, he'd realized, no time to waste in worship. Composing himself, he'd set her to removing her unseemly belongings and grass mat, reserving to himself the privilege of collecting the waves and curls of holy script.

At his summons, the Sect of the Rebirth would gather on the Sanctum roof.

Most had mouthed the words, their piety suspect, for they'd never truly believed.

Emelen allowed himself the smallest of smiles. "Cersi-So."

All would, today.

Lights were flashing. Yellow. Some blue. Requests from other ComPrimes: for updates, for permissions, for answers. Traffic blinked ceaselessly: orbital, interplanetary, busy clots of tiny mining ships within the asteroid fields, enormous freighters on their programmed courses. This was the Hub, where SysComPrime, Director Lemuel Dis, managed the information flow of the inhabited portions of System Cooperative and the lights were the stars in *nes* sky.

Whenever *ne* felt poetical.

Not how ne felt at the moment. Someone silenced the alarm. Lemuel raised nes left magboot from the path of the Cleaner Oud, ignoring the creature as it slurped the remnants of nes midmorning *cafen* from the deck. Regrettable, dropping nes cup.

It proved even ne had a pulse, something nes staff likely doubted. "Could it be a hoax?" Lemuel was relieved nes tone was properly calm and expression-free, less so when no one answered. Ne repeated the question.

Nes second-in-command started and turned, his face pale. "No, Director. We've confirmed. The signal originated outside the System."

Hence the alarm. Hence the unease of the most disciplined, capable staff in the system. Heads shifted, those with eyes staring at *ner*, not their boards. No one else appeared to breathe.

Predictably, the Tikitik stirred first, unfolding from its bored squat. Sexless, but so was Lemuel, neuter being commonplace among Hoveny. Nameless in any way that mattered to non-Tikitik. Among themselves, they used symbols for rank and, it was supposed, told one another apart using their exquisite chemoreception. A Tikitik's mouth cilia remained the foremost analytical "device" known. Relying on what a Tikitik claimed to taste/smell?

To someone in ner position, in charge of cross-species data flow, what couldn't be verified by equipment was, at best, slippery, at worst, fraught with potentially dangerous confusion. Ne'd rather interpret the babble of a Minded Oud.

Lemuel's eyes flicked back to the sprawling display that filled the Hub's longest wall, finding Tikitna, stained green. One world was all the Tikitik claimed, home to their Makers and mothers and young. No visitors were welcome closer than far orbit, lest they taint its atmosphere or some such cultural nonsense, though individual Tikitik, like the one presently staring at Lemuel with all four eyes, had no issue with leaving it to bother their neighbors.

It hadn't always been their world. Latecomers here, the Tikitik, arriving in the system just as the Hoveny were stretching their reach well beyond it. They'd been uninterested in contact or sharing technology, intent on treasure of another kind: the Oud. Barely sentient. An impediment to construction, with their tunnels and mounds, and had the Hoveny System not contained three other inhabitable worlds—Hilip, Yont, and ringed Oger— and had the galaxy beyond not been so full of wealth, the Oud world would have been urbanized and its "people" reduced, like other wild things, to a curiosity in a preserve.

Enter the Tikitik. They landed among the Oud and, admiring what they called the species' rare plasticity, their Makers offered the Oud another future.

Or ruined them, for no living Oud resembled their original kind, but Oud kept no history and Tikitik viewed things— differently. The Oud agreed, giving away their world and themselves. Or were overrun. A moot point. The Hoveny, preoccupied with the myriad worlds and species of its growing Concentrix, cared for neither so long as their home system remained at peace.

After the Fall, when the home system was all that remained, Tikitna and its modified inhabitants were waiting.

Today's civilization, Lemuel mused glumly, couldn't run without them. There were Oud on every station and space-capable vessel. Oud living throughout the five worlds and every civilized moon of the System Cooperative. The majority were mindless workers, like the Cleaners, engineered by the Tikitik Makers to fulfill specific tasks. There were Minded Oud, some quite brilliant, but they were rarely involved in the doings of their kin, other than to arrange a sufficiency of raw material for the Tikitiks' tinkering.

The Tikitik eying Lemuel wasn't a Maker. It was, as far as ne was concerned, worse, being a Thought Traveler and so officially charged with poking its cilia into the business of others. It gestured languidly with a claw-tipped hand, the jeweled bells depended from its wristlet set tinkling. No doubt its intention; the thing knew ne didn't care for ostentation. Or bells. "Why is this significant, Director?"

Lemuel tensed. Because signals didn't come from outside the System. Not anymore. Not since the Fall. The System Cooperative was all there was—

Ne composed nerself. A Thought Traveler qualified to be in the Hub would know, making its feigned ignorance a provocation, either to amuse or incite a reaction. Ne walked over to nes second to gaze calmly over his shoulder at the board. The Hub was more than traffic and information. Nes task, to protect those who shared this sun.

The incoming signal was narrow; credit to nes staff and quality of the Hub's sensor sweeps that they'd spotted it. Incoming—to where, ne wondered. "Target?" ne murmured.

The tech's arm lifted, finger pointing to the wall, indicating a pale blue dot near the bottom of the display. "Brightfall."

"Your place of origin," the Tikitik commented, having followed ner, and if it meant the Hoveny species or simply nerself, both were correct.

And neither mattered. Brightfall was nothing but empty ruins and dust, inhabited by those who cared for the past, and those stuck in it. "Fine-tune it," ordered Lemuel.

Another tech stood. "There's been a response, Director!"

"Isolate and prevent any more. I assume we now have the location."

"Yes, Director." Numbers appeared on the screen.

Lemuel raised a brow to summon nes personal aide. "I'm going down. Make the—what are you doing?"

The paired back eyes swiveled into their cones to meet nes stare. The front pair remained riveted on the Cleaner Oud the Tikitik had swept up in both hands. Its little black appendages flailed in midair, but there was no escape as Thought Traveler brought the Oud to its mouth, thick gray mouth cilia patting and probing. Done, it tossed the creature aside. Righting itself, the Oud scurried under the nearest stool.

All eyes fixed on Lemuel. "How disappointing," the Tikitik declared in its smooth, not-quite-but-so-close to patronizing tone. "You haven't used the supplements I brought you, Director. Given the high-stress position you hold here, they would be—"

"In my position," ne interrupted, matching its tone precisely, "I'm prohibited from unsolicited additions to my diet, however much I personally appreciate the gesture." Lemuel bowed nes head, slightly, then turned back to nes aide. "I want to leave at once."

"As do I," Thought Traveler Tikitik's head thrust forward. "Unless you don't appreciate my accompanying you, Director. Personally."

Being a nuisance was its right. Lemuel Dis allowed nerself a tight little smile. "Suit yourself."

Maybe the thing could be useful—if not, ne would have it shipped home.

Controlling information was the first and foremost goal. They'd approached swiftly, landing on the emergency platform even as nes staff shut down all access, in or out, including theoretically private feeds. Enough? Lemuel Dis doubted it. A bonded mind's *haisin* was the unknown and there were those heart-kin able to transcend distance. The only reliable measure of that mental connection was to bring in an Oud-Key and have it sniff, or whatever it did.

Ouds able to think for themselves refused work on airless moons, including this one, Brightfall's industrialized Raynthe. As for reliable? Ne'd be further ahead to toss purple *wirill* stems in the air like the choosing rhyme chanted by planet-born younglings. What would dismay ner staff most, ne thought with amusement: having the SysComPrime bring foreign plant material onstation, or that ne, so many cycles their elder, remembered the rhyme?

You left your world, ne could have told them. It never left you.

"How much longer will this take?" Sorina Din's only concession to being summoned below the surface had been to toss back the hood of her vacsuit and remove her gloves. She eyed the Tikitik, then ignored it. "I've crews in locked accesses, Director, and materials I need stuck in orbit. My schedule's behind *arns* already. Can't you just destroy the artifact?"

Lemuel gazed at Sorina Din until the other closed her thin lips, conceding authority. If up to ner, the engineer would have been locked in with her crews. By her designation, "din," the present Head of Reclamation topped nes list of those liable to spread rumors, sharing haisin with at least three heart-kin, not uncommon in someone who managed others and had no secrets.

Some days it felt nes head was stuffed with them. While neuters bonded to heart-kin, too—be they lovers, confidants or both— Lemuel had no regrets; choosing the "dis" of a life-long solitary mind protected the Cooperative: five worlds, twenty—soon to be twenty-one—settled moons, and the great stations orbiting each.

"You'll be notified when I'm done," Lemuel said, signaling. Techs festooned with gear and goggles hadn't been all ne'd brought to the moon.

The seniormost of nes security left nes post, coming to the engineer's elbow. "This way, honored official."

Sorina had no choice but to incline her head and leave without argument, though she shot the Tikitik a disturbed look when it barked its laugh. Most Hoveny wouldn't encounter an active Thought Traveler in their lifetime.

Lucky them.

"It's no artifact," Lemuel murmured, walking around what had been an inert pillar of ancient dark green metal, aware the Tikitik paced behind. "Not anymore." The object was disconcertingly familiar. Ne'd spent nes youth on a farm in the Ribbon Lands. Dig an *um* anywhere, and you'd find the same; farmers plowed around them, or used them for gate posts. The pillars were among the more useful of the empire's remains.

Familiar, yet nothing so ordinary. This pillar had been found, as had this curve-walled complex, beneath Raynthe's surface. Luck or fate. The moon was slated for a life-sustaining atmosphere and all the fittings to please Oud and Tikitik alike before they began establishing a working biosphere. Surveyors readying a crater for its new life as a lake had discovered this centuries-abandoned installation; more accurately, they'd rediscovered it, for the site proved to be listed in documents produced by a mid-rank historian.

Lemuel had been briefed on the flight here. Brought in to inspect the site, Koleor Su had claimed the entire complex to be a control facility, over three hundred cycles old, built in secret by a rebellious planetary government.

Over the generations, there'd been several so inclined. Bright-fall remained the thorn in more reasonable hides. Sentimental-ity, to allow it to be resettled, but it had been before nes time.

The pristine condition of the find, itself rare, meant postpon-ing demolition until the complex could be thoroughly studied, the start of Sorina Din's scheduling woes.

A form of demolition was presently underway, techs with no interest in history going through rooms and corridors, where necessary tearing open walls, while Koleor Su sat fuming on a stool, barefoot and in his nightshift, having been dragged from his bed at Lemuel's order. Seeing the pillar, he'd exclaimed once, then fallen stubbornly silent.

A "su" had no heart-kin—yet—and so no haisin to breach se-curity. He could wait.

The pillar, now surrounded with recording apparatus, contin-ued to flash a dizzying display as it cycled fruitlessly through what Lemuel's techs concluded was a preset sequence of reception and transmission. They'd thrown a frequency specific shutdown field over this side of the moon once the location had been verified.

Perhaps in time to keep this quiet. Nes staff were the best.

"Tech," Thought Traveler dismissed the object. "Old at that."

"Director." A tech offered Lemuel a curled sheet that, by rights, should be protected in a case; that it had been spat out by the pillar before the shutdown gave ner a profound sense of disloca-tion. The present mattered. Planning for the next cycle mattered. Offensive, to have the past assert itself.

There were marks on the sheet, none familiar. Lemuel tossed it at the historian. "Read this."

The stool toppled with a bang as Koleor scrambled for the sheet. Cradling it, he glared at ner, fury burning red on his cheeks. Like younglings, academics; to be forgiven their lack of social grace. Certain no emotion crossed nes features, Lemuel gestured for him to proceed.

His anger faded as he concentrated, lips moving silently. All at once, Koleor's hands trembled. "Received or sent?" he demanded, looking up. "Quickly! I must know!"

Nes staff were offended, the Tikitik bored, but the question was, Lemuel deemed, pertinent. "Received."

The historian let the sheet fall, his face gone sickly pale.

The techs paused to stare; at nes look, they resumed their activities, shoulders hunched. "What did it say?"

"It's impossible." He collected himself, lips twisting. "Exactly that. This is some trick to discredit—"

Lemuel Dis swept up the sheet and closed the distance between them, boots clicking on the colored metal floor. "My presence proves it is not."

He recoiled, dread flooding his appallingly expressive face.

Ne raised the sheet with the marks toward him. "Please." Quietly. "Tell me what it says."

Later, Lemuel would remember the moment and wish ne'd listened to Sorina Din, destroyed the pillar and everything here, then run, not walked away.

"Yes, Director." Koleor locked eyes with ner as if for strength. "'Confirmation request. Identification: Cersi-So.'"

Lemuel ignored the tech who gasped out loud, busy controlling shock of nes own.

"Let me explain the significance—"

"One of the Twelve," Thought Traveler broke in. "Is it not, Director?"

"It is." Children learned the names; the religious prayed with them. Twelve starships had been sent into the Heavens by Brightfall in 1030 AF, their mission to circumvent the System Government by establishing contact outside it. To recreate the Hoveny Concentrix with themselves once more in charge. "The Twelve disappeared without a trace," Lemuel responded, keeping nes eyes on the historian. "You're telling me this—" ne crumbled the sheet in a fist, "—is from a ship lost over three hundred cycles ago?"

Koleor pointed to the pillar, still flickering through its display. "That's telling you."

"I find your reaction inappropriate." The Tikitik prowled close, cilia tasting the air near the historian. "I read about your work. You've spent your life researching the Cersi Rebellion. Surely this is vindication. Why are you fearful?"

A grimace. "I didn't expect the past to just—show up. If this is Cersi-So—" The historian swallowed. "Director, how freely may I speak?" He tipped his head at those around them.

Ne didn't look. If nes personal staff couldn't be trusted with what he planned to reveal, no one in the System could. As for Thought Traveler?

Oh, there was curiosity aplenty twirling its eyecones now. "Say what you wish," Lemuel stated, "but do not waste my time."

"I won't." Though his skin remained paler than normal, Koleor steadied. "The Twelve weren't what we're taught, nor was their mission. I planned to release my findings—" he waved the rest away impatiently. "Director, those ships couldn't return, not on their own. They were built around pre-Fall technology and the only way back was to get it working again. Do you understand? Their real mission was to find and restore the null-grid. That's what Cersi and her followers believed would bring back the Concentrix."

Thought Traveler gestured abruptly, bells strident. "Fools and nonsense. That technology failed. It destroyed your Concentrix."

Technology the Tikitik had rejected, Pre-Fall. Afterward, they'd helped the rest of the System recover from its loss.

If by "helped" you meant traded for permanent and equal say in the new order. Fair enough. Thanks to the Tikitik, the surviving Hoveny hadn't lost their space capability.

Only their taste for it.

The null-grid, Lemuel thought, mind whirling, was like something out of a dream. Ne signaled and a tech hurried to bring ner a stool. In the brief pause, the historian retrieved his and sat, grim-faced, an improbable prophet in a nightshirt.

The null-grid had created the Concentrix, for that had been the Hoveny's lavish gift to any who joined: a pure and inexhaustible power source greater than any previously known. No physical fuel. No wires or broadcasts. No waste or stockpiles. The null-grid arrived in the marvelous technology the Hoveny offered, from buildings to machines to the tiniest devices; those who adopted them could be forgiven for believing the Hoveny had ushered in a new golden age, for such it seemed.

Until the Fall: the instant, without warning, the null-grid disconnected and vanished. Communication devices no longer worked, starships plunged from subspace, lost, and this remote system, birthplace of the Hoveny and heart of their empire, was cut off from all else.

At first, they hadn't understood the scope of the disaster. Civilization continued, technology predating the null-grid brought into play even as questions were asked. The capital world suffered most, having been completely rebuilt as a gleaming showcase for all that was new, all that was promised. The other worlds went from chagrined at being left behind to quietly grateful for their older buildings and tired infrastructure—

To horrified. Nothing remained of the billions who'd lived in the capital. The discovery of handfuls of survivors, clustered in remote regions, was scant comfort.

Still, surely this was temporary. Surely they'd be helped. The priority was to reestablish contact outside the system but before they could reach out, a flood of messages began to pour in.

Messages of anger, fear, and betrayal. The Hoveny had done this—the Hoveny had stolen back their power—the Hoveny had abandoned them.

The null-grid hadn't failed here, in this system; it had failed everywhere. The empire was gone, and more.

As they listened, the surviving Hoveny had cowered in silent despair. Where were the multitudes who'd made homes on other worlds?

For none of the voices were theirs.

Cycles passed, decades. The Hoveny no longer heard their name, truth be told, they no longer listened, and hoped to be forgotten. Centuries, and the Hoveny—sensible, ordinary Hoveny—no longer thought about the universe beyond their warm, yellow sun.

Until now, and another message: "Confirmation request. Identification: Cersi-So."

No wonder her predecessors had set alarms. Lemuel roused. "Our ancestors buried their dead cities. That's where the past belongs."

"Yet," the Tikitik lifted a hand, turned it over with the faintest chime of bells. "Are there not those who remember the name of your world? Might they not be—interested?"

In the deathly silence after the words, the faint *chirp* of a comm notification made them all start. A tech lifted her head. "Director," almost a whisper.

"What?" What could possibly matter at this moment, Lemuel thought, when the shape of the universe failed to hold and—

"Your pardon, Lemuel Dis, but Sar-lyn Station reports a ship on approach."

They hadn't been in time. Hadn't stopped whatever "confirmation" Cersi-So had demanded.

What would be next? Thought Traveler was right. Their world had had another name, long ago, before being renamed Brightfall to mark the end.

If the Twelve had found what they'd sought—could it have that name again?

Hoveny Prime.

Chapter 14

IT WAS *PASSAGE*, in that we rode within the M'hir, and I could feel its darkness *seethe* at our intrusion.

It was not, for I could feel my pulse hammering and the awkward press of Morgan's pack—which smelled comfortingly of the *Silver Fox* and him—

Yet was, for all around me crowded my *sense* of the Clan, my people, each dealing with the strangeness in their own way.

There! Morgan, for his part filled with curiosity and delight, as if being flung through space in a bubble was the height of normalcy and he couldn't wait to see what happened next.

Even as I tried to find my own anticipation, I reeled, hit by a flare of *loss*.

No! I refused. We were so close. No more. No more—

<<*Let them go.*>>

—wrong, that voice. Hollow. Reaching into my consciousness like burning fingers, leaving ash behind and grief.

I *pushed* it away with all my will even as *loss* after *loss* struck me, those torn from their understanding of the possible escaping the only way they could.

<<*Let them come.*>>

—I wouldn't listen, terrified those slipping away were *hearing* voices of their own.

Watchers began *howling* names—too many, so many. I despaired. *No!* I shouted in answer, in anger. *Stay!* I urged those left. *Trust me! Don't* LISTEN!

I felt others pick up my plea and send it forth.

Felt it *hold* us together.

Then everything . . .

Stopped.

Interlude

CESSATION OF—he wouldn't, Morgan thought grimly, have called *that* movement. More being shaken like the yolk in an egg.

Little wonder he'd felt stabs of panic through his link to Sira. They hadn't all arrived, of that he was certain. Nothing to be done about it, but care for those here.

The pod cracked like a shell, letting in—he took a deep daring breath—air.

Cool. Not so much fragrant as sharp. Fresh.

Moist.

Rain! The Human worked himself to his feet, shoving aside pieces of the now-brittle pod. Using a hand to shelter his eyes, he took an eager look around.

Daylight, luck or intention. Gloom rather than bright, but the rain was falling from scudding gray clouds. Darker and massed to his left; pale and broken, tinged with rose to the right.

If dawn? East. West.

Flat here, where they'd come down; again, luck or intention. A featureless plain as far as he could see, which would be farther once the sun—for now he assumed only one—broke the cloud layer. And they'd come down—or arrived—together. More than together. The pods formed a tight spiral, with his midway down the left arm.

Lowering his hand, Morgan tilted his face to the rain.

Going to turn purple and die? Sira's mindvoice was light, his *sense* of her muted but calm. She'd bury her grief as all the times before. Draw strength from it. Move forward.

Gods, he loved her.

"One way to find out, chit." He stuck out his tongue to collect drops and brought them back into his mouth. Cool, fleeting, tasteless. Sensual stuff, rain. Born of an open sky. A spacer thought, most likely. *So far, so good.*

The Human eased from what was left of his pod, wary of sharp points. Contact had shattered the pieces along regular planes; curious, he stepped on one.

Snap. Blue flickered along the newly made edges, like a tiny flame quickly burning itself out. If not for the gloom, he'd have missed it. Morgan put his boot to another shard, releasing more blue light.

A spark leaped to the ground. The ground, almost too quickly to see, flared blue in answer.

Sira, are you seeing this?

Now that he knew what to look for, the subtle discharge was taking place everywhere as people struggled free of their pods, cracking the material. The ground's fleeting response didn't echo the spiral; tempting, to discern a meaningful pattern in what could be random.

And was gone, most likely before anyone else noticed. Freed, the Clan were immediately preoccupied, standing without motion or sound, busy communing with those closest to their hearts. All but one. Morgan grinned, spotting that slender arm waving vigorously.

He waved back and headed toward Sira, then stopped, staring at a brightening horizon no longer flat, but rippling with movement.

Movement coming this way. He changed course, walking forward to intercept whatever it was. One pocket disgorged a distance lens he quickly pressed to his left eye. The lens had a targeting function as well, though the blaster now filling his right hand wasn't precise.

It could, however, make an impression.

Chapter 15

RAIN. A gray, drizzling what I hoped was dawn across a plain empty of form or shape save for us: a tidy spiral of people standing amid eggshells, belongings in their hands. Nothing I'd imagined incorporated those elements. Nothing.

Fair enough. I shrugged inwardly. The *Fox* had landed on less prepossessing planets; if I'd learned anything with Morgan, it was not to judge a world by its shipcity. Or lack of.

Home, I sent, before those who'd survived—most, I assured myself—could begin to doubt, making sure the words went to all of them. *Safe.* I'd no ship to project my voice and I wasn't about to shout.

Not until we knew what else might hear. Not until—but there was no certainty, not here, most of all, not in the M'hir.

What had I *heard?*

Or was the real question, who?

We were on solid ground. The air was breathable. Progress, I reminded myself. Hair shivering itself free of moisture, I grappled with Morgan's bulky pack and looked around for its owner, finding him near the end of an arm of the pattern we'd created. Even from here, I could tell he was already engaged in exploring this new world.

Lifting my face, I dared taste raindrops, too.

Sira, are you seeing this? An image.

I checked. *Yes.* Closer to the spiral's center, I found myself surrounded by ephemeral sparks of blue and stepped awkwardly free of the remains of my conveyance to see more, so distracted by the sight I forgot to notice my first step on this world.

A world, I saw as I crouched, pack balanced on my knees, busy absorbing the flickers of glowing blue we'd brought with us. Harmlessly, I hoped. Poisoning the landscape wasn't the best first impression.

Reassured, my people stilled, numb at a guess. Putting down the pack, I waved at Morgan then sent my own message. *Aryl? How are you?*

Not seeing this, my great-grandmother informed me with a hint of *impatience.*

My apologies. I gave Aryl access to whatever I could see and turned slowly, scanning our surroundings. The clouds had lifted along the horizon, letting through beams of sunlight that stroked pale pink along their gray undersides and sparkled the last of the raindrops. *Our new home,* I sent with growing satisfaction. *What do you think?*

It looks like Oud territory, grimly.

Not everything flat—I stopped, frowning as Morgan spun around, walking away from us with distance-eating strides. Where was he going?

More importantly, why had he pulled a weapon?

Sira! There!

I squinted at the horizon beyond my Human's silhouette, at first confused how the line between sky and land appeared to rise and fall, then afraid.

It wasn't land at all, but a mass of shadowy indistinct forms. Forms moving this way! *Jason, what are they?*

Checking on that. Calm. Absentminded, which only meant his focus was elsewhere. *Keep the others together.*

Come back.

Thought I was to go first, Witchling. He let me *feel* his smile.

Not like this. I'd envisioned him walking out of *Sona* to a civilized meeting with whomever greeted us, not this solitary march toward the unknown. *Morgan*—

He walled me out, sensibly reserving his full attention for whatever he faced.

Cursing under my breath at Humans, planets, and life in gen-
eral, I wrestled his pack over my shoulders, leaving the blanket
roll on the ground. If things went well, I'd be back for it. *This way!*
I sent urgently, pointing away from Morgan. What use the scattering of shards and belongings might be as a barrier I'd no idea,
but it put something between us.

The Om'ray moved, herding the M'hiray ahead. Children held
tight to their mothers; Barac and Destin, along with the Sona
Clan scouts, came last, their attention divided between their
charges and the distant horizon. Pod bits cracked and snapped
underfoot, there were voices, but another sound grew louder.

The heavy, low drumming was like rain on a roof, not that we'd
roof or rain, patches of purpled sky breaking through overhead.
I waited for the others, my eyes and inner sense locked on the
receding form of my Chosen, ready to 'port him back.

The rest of the Clan settled around me like a shroud. We'd no
option but to stand here and wait. The gradual increase in light
revealed nothing but ourselves, some far-off hills backed by still-
dark cloud, and the approaching line.

Before long, the drumming could be felt through our feet, silencing even the M'hir.

Barac came to stand beside me, tension rolling from him like
smoke. "It's not right. He shouldn't be alone out there."

"He's not," I reminded him, much as I agreed.

Low and angry. "You know what I mean."

I shook my head. "If Morgan wants company, he'll ask for it."
Poor choice of words. My Human was about to have an abundance
of company. What at first had appeared a line was now clearly
lumps, large ones; a daunting number of large, moving lumps.

"What are they?"

Gricel, Yanti snugged in a wrap across her breasts, overheard.
"Oud," the former Amna said quietly. "I've never seen so many
above ground."

The neighbors.

I supposed it was too much to ask for new ones.

Interlude

OUD. A wave of them coming this way, above ground. Through the lens, none were the varieties he'd met on Cersi. Oh, they'd the sluglike shape of worker Oud, but instead of pale flaccid skin, these had brown hides that flexed to allow them to hump forward.

Not to mention, by the lens' scale, these were easily three times the size.

Morgan chose an arbitrary tuft of sun-touched grass and stopped, tucking away lens and blaster. The blastglobes in his lower pockets were worse than useless. He'd barely escaped a Brexx stampede on Ret 7. Having seen a normal-sized Oud move with speed, he'd rather not see what the bigger version would do if panicked.

Barac's fussing.

Words to warm the heart. *Tell him he's better off where he is. They stink.* It was true; the freshening wind, still humid from the rain, brought the fetid aroma of Oud with it. The fastidious Clansman would be gagging.

The wind took his scent away. How well did Oud see? No point shouting—the pound of those heavy bodies as fronts thrust forward to drop to the ground, rears heaving up to thump in turn, would drown out his voice. Firing his blaster remained an option, but if they didn't stop before trampling him—

—they'd trample the helpless families behind him. That, the Human vowed, wasn't happening. Oud could talk.

Some, anyway. The intelligent ones. Minded. Makers. He pulled out his com, affixing it to his collar. One such Oud had rebuilt the device, complete with Cersi's common language in a form the sleepteach function had accepted. For all he knew, there was more in it, perhaps something to help him now. Worth a try.

Although, come to think of it, a Tikitik Thought Traveler had killed that particular Oud, it having tried to kill Sira, along with all remaining Clan.

New world, new problems. Morgan balanced on his toes, keeping his breathing steady. The pace of the Oud was deceptive; each thrust forward covered more than a body length. *Just another negotiation, chit,* he sent. *You know the drill.*

Understood. Then, almost lightly. *Make this work. I'd prefer not to drop them into the M'hir.* A chilling reminder those behind him weren't helpless at all.

Five Oud-lengths from his toes and fate, the herd dropped to its hundreds of feet and began to prance—he'd no other word for it—in place.

Morgan surveyed the towering wall of brown featureless lumps, feeling slightly ridiculous. None had heads; Oud were particularly inconvenient in that regard, the end moving forward being the head of the moment as far as he'd noticed, though the Maker Oud had shown a preference. Still, they'd stopped short of running him down. A promising start.

To speak first or—

The centermost pair of Oud began to fidget, bumping at their neighbors who bumped sideways and violently against theirs. Bumping became climbing, as those in the middle heaved themselves on those to either side, and those did the same—

Creating an opening, no, a corridor walled in struggling flesh that extended back through the herd. Down that corridor, toward Morgan, came a single Oud.

With a rider, a Tikitik, sitting astride.

Like recently old times, the Human decided. He'd have been more surprised not to find Tikitik here, if the Oud were.

Such cooperation, however, was new.

As the being's ungainly mount tiptoed closer, the four eyes set in the Tikitik's triangular head locked on him. Familiar yes, but like these Oud, different, too. The paired eyes—two large, two small—were borne on flexible cones, but the head was larger and carried on a down-curved neck half the length of Cersi's Tikitik, so it was held just below the being's shoulders rather than the midpoint of its concave chest. The tendrils that were lips and tongue were longer, white, and delicate, in this individual folded up to the sides like a mustache.

The Tikitik of Cersi wore, at most, a woven band from shoulder to hip. This one had a body-hugging jerkin of gray, accompanied by a black striped cloak over its shoulders and back. Its thin arms and legs were bare, with white, nasty-looking barbs lining their outer surface. The knobby skin matched the color of the Oud beneath it. No guarantee that was its true color, camouflage being a Tikitik trait.

Morgan kept still. The Oud rattled to a stop within reach, had he wanted to touch it, giving him a good look at its hide. Rather than part of the creature, it was a hood of tough supple fabric stapled to the lowest portion of each segment.

Had the Oud wanted to talk, it would have reared up to expose the cluster of appendages they used to create sound. Instead, it crouched, allowing its rider to dismount, then rose and moved sideways with a rapid flutter of feet to crouch again.

The Tikitik stepped forward without the grace Morgan remembered. Stiff from riding was a possibility. Nursing an injury or an older individual, just as likely. It waved a long-fingered hand as if to sweep the Human aside. "We have work to complete. This area is *sessened* to *nirsei-taden*. You must leave."

A small sample of the language, granted, but to his relief he understood most. "Hello," Morgan said, giving a short bow, his hands out and open. "My name is Jason Morgan."

The creature leaned forward, tendrils writhing. "What thing are you?"

Morgan bowed again. "New arrivals. We could use some help."

"'We.'" The head rose at a painful angle, the lesser eyes swiveling to aim past him. "More of you?"

He resisted the urge to let Sira know what was happening.

"One of me." Honesty, this early on, was safer. "The rest are Hoveny." A less safe choice, that word, but until they understood what "Om'ray" meant here, he wouldn't risk it or "Clan." Besides, they either were, or weren't.

"You must leave. Where are your machines?"

Bait, that question. It could see for itself they'd none. "We meant no trespass. We were left here," he told it. "Where is this?"

"Where we are to work." The head lowered slightly. This close, he could hear the meaty sound the cones made as they rotated to stare at him. "Jason Morgan." As if tasting the name. "What thing are you?"

"Human." The word wanted to stick in his throat. Why? He'd been alone most of his adult life—been the only one of his kind on a world more than once.

Just not the last.

A thought to ponder, ideally over an intoxicant, another time than now. "We need assistance. Shelter and supplies. Can you help us?"

An eye rolled back to consider the sullen line of Oud. "We must work." The eye came back to Morgan. "You and your Hoveny must leave."

Making this a chance to trade. "We will leave," Morgan offered, "if you help us."

Tendrils writhed as if tasting the options. Then, "I can take you to those in authority." Its barking laugh was all too familiar. "The Hoveny will not enjoy the journey."

Guessing the means, the Human had to agree. "Take us," he said before the creature could change its mind.

Sira, he sent. *I've found us a ride.*

"So how do I get on?"

Chapter 16

"**R**IDE THOSE THINGS? He can't be serious."

"I'd say he is," I replied, though I shared my cousin's incredulity. Seeing the line of giant Oud come to a peaceful halt had been a relief, however anxious the moments as Morgan negotiated with, yes, a Tikitik.

Who'd arrived on one of "those things," so it could be done. *Barac's not happy.*

Amusement. *He won't be alone. Keep everyone calm, Witchling. We don't want them spooking the Oud.*

As assignments went, I thought darkly, he'd taken the easier one. Calm? I'd do well if most of the silent crowd behind me didn't start screaming. *I'll do my best.*

Resolutely, I put my back to Morgan and what he was about to do. *These are not the Oud who harmed you,* I sent to them all. *These are*—monsters? Not reassuring—*of this world and have offered us their help.*

Those who could tear their eyes from what was happening, at a distance that no longer seemed far enough, stared at me in disbelief.

I kept going, shamelessly underscoring each word with a cheerful optimism I was far from feeling, reinforcing my sending with Power to drown out any other. *Our new allies will take us to the local authorities. This world is our beginning. Let us make this first en-counter a brave and mannerly one. Do not frighten them.* Last, but not least, the truth. *We've no choice and everything to gain. My Chosen will go first, to prove we'll be safe.*

Instead of turning, I watched Morgan's progress in the faces of those around me, knew when he approached the crouching Oud by the way eyes went round and hands sought hands. Guessed when he'd climbed aboard when mouths dropped open and there was a communal gasp.

Followed by a giggle, startling in the overall hush. I looked down to find Andi, who'd pushed forward to see past the adults. Her eyes shone with wonder. "Do I get to ride one, too?"

Only then did I let myself turn around.

The Oud herd was on the move, this time with two out in front, each with a rider. While I didn't need his wave to know which was my Human, I waved back, tentatively at first and then with enthusiasm.

Hands rose around me, as the Clan resolutely did the same.

The Tikitik's eyes tried to follow all of us at once, which disturbed me but not our Om'ray. If anything, they broadcast grim satisfaction, their universe finally behaving in known ways.

They shouldn't count on it. For now, I was mutely grateful for their courage, for M'hiray nerves were close to breaking. Not that any nerves were steady when it came to our mounts.

"Up you go."

I wrinkled my nose at Morgan, and it wasn't just the smell. "You're sure about this?" No need to whisper or send. This close, the Oud were noisy, their unseen appendages clicking and clacking so what towered beside me might have been a machine.

Except for the part where green fluid oozed from the wounds made by the metal staples holding its "cloak" in place. *They don't like the sun,* Aryl supplied, feeling her own satisfaction.

A sun yet to impress me. I squinted up. The clouds were memory, but the sun was dull and distant, producing a sky more mauve than blue. It could be seasonal, but the air was warm enough.

"Sira."

Right. Riding the monster. I gritted my teeth and gave a short nod. The Oud, helpfully, had crouched, if flattening its massive torso could be called crouching. "Face west, toward the hills. That should be the front," Morgan informed me as I stepped into his cupped hands.

Hands that heaved.

I flew up, landing face- and stomach-down on top of the Oud, a position difficult to improve, for the dusty, wrinkled Oud-cloak came complete with tiny hooks. My hair pulled itself loose with firm yanks, but I had to peel my clothing free, then try to move without being grabbed again.

Finally sitting, breathless but triumphant, I leaned over to smile at my Chosen, only to be met by a roll of blankets I didn't so much catch as fend from my face.

"Good! Wait there."

There being no other choice, I glowered down, meeting an unrepentant grin. Enjoying himself, my Human. "Do not," I warned him, "throw me your—"

Up came the pack. I lunged for it, managing to snag a strap without losing my grip on the roll or, the other option, falling off the other side. Although falling would have been difficult, given the width of the Oud's back and the avid little hooks, this did nothing to alter the fact I was sitting atop a giant Oud clutching whatever Morgan had brought to this planet, some of that being explosive.

He saluted. "I'll help the rest and then come back."

The cloak protesting with a sucking rip, I pried my legs free and crossed them, making myself comfortable. My perch made an excellent vantage point. The others had collected their belongings and were forming in lines to be tossed to the top of their mounts. As if to make certain we accepted our fate, the Oud who weren't crouched to receive a passenger formed fidgeting walls around us.

Except, I noticed, for where we'd landed. The pods had finished fragmenting, leaving behind a litter of black flakes. Surely no impediment to the hulking beasts, but they avoided them, encompassing that area within their circle. Morgan had collected some of the flakes, tucking them into his pack. While I'd no idea why, if my Chosen was anything, it was thorough.

I watched him, with Barac, work with the Tikitik to match riders to mounts. Fortunately, each broad back had room for several adults, so families could stay together. Those families still intact. Eighteen hadn't finished the journey with us, by Barac's grim tally. He believed they'd faltered and dissolved in the M'hir.

To become ghosts.

Ghosts they were, but the more I thought about what had happened, the less I believed so many could have lost their will and focus. After all, *Sona*'s conveyances had done the work for us. No, we were eighteen less because some*thing* had taken them from us, the same way it had taken Risa and Jorn.

I'd *heard* it.

A vibration passed along my Oud, though it remained still, as did the rest. I watched Degal and his Chosen Signy being helped up by Destin, joining Teris and Vael di Uruus. No surprise to see that faction stayed together, though I'd sympathy for Destin's Chosen, gentle Elnu, caught in that company.

The Sona and Tuana Om'ray simply walked up the sides of their beasts. Those who hadn't grown up in the canopy needed assistance. While some could have used Power to shift themselves or at least belongings to the top of the Oud, none would. Until we knew our place in this new world, exposing any Talent wasn't worth the risk, a caution shared by Om'ray and M'hiray alike.

There was another reason. On Cersi, there'd been Oud able to detect the use of a Talent. Their reaction would cause the M'hir to *ring* painfully, with that pain increasing with an individual's strength. This wasn't the time to test if the trait was found here, too.

Oud after Oud filled with passengers and what cargo they carried, until all were mounted but Morgan and the Tikitik.

The Tikitik swarmed up its Oud. My Human climbed less quickly, but just as surely, accepting my hand for a final pull to the top. "What now?" I asked.

"We hold on." Morgan wrapped his arm around me. "I've warned the rest."

It wasn't beyond my Chosen to make up an excuse for contact; my hair, ever-approving, tried to wind a tendril through his beard. Still, "Why—?"

The Tikitik let out a warbling cry and the crouched Oud erupted to their feet, passengers shouting in panic as they found themselves rising skyward. Before any did more than that, the Oud were underway.

Instead of the full body contortion that had brought them to us, those with riders ran on their hundreds of small feet. I could see those of the nearest Oud, blurred into a long rhythmic wave. If I closed my eyes, only the wind in my face told me we were moving.

I settled back against Morgan. "This is amazing."

He reclined on an elbow. "Isn't it?"

The Tikitik's Oud took the lead, aimed at the low hills, followed by our thirty-three, accelerating in unison till we passed over the flat ground at a remarkable pace. I shared the experience with Aryl, feeling rather smug. *What do you think?*

Stay watchful. I've ridden with Tikitik before. There's always a surprise.

One seemed unlikely—

Morgan sat up. "What are they doing?"

The Oud to either side of us were running at an angle to cut off ours. No, they all were. "Aryl's surprise," I guessed gloomily. Everyone was taking notice now, pulling up any dangling limbs and baggage as their Ouds prepared to collide.

And did, turning at the last instant to reduce the impact to a soft brush of cloak to cloak. Every Oud pressed itself firmly to its neighbor, until we were sitting on what might have been a massive oval carpet, albeit a dusty smelly one, floating over the world.

I could have reached out and touched Tle and the di Kessa'ats to our left; Morgan do the same with the di Licors to our right.

"Interesting." My Human didn't mean the closing of the Oud ranks. Our Tikitik was on its feet, hopping casually from Oud to Oud. It avoided those carrying the Om'ray armed with knives, making good speed as it tiptoed and hopped.

Heading for us.

The Tikitik squatted out of reach, its knees above its shoulders and head outstretched. It was smaller than Cersi's Tikitik and I thought Morgan was right: this one was old, for its kind.

"Hoveny, the Human says." Its large, rear eyes focused on me, the smaller anxiously turning on their cones. A three-fingered hand gestured to those around us. "I have never seen so many, so different, all sexed." One finger indicated my hair, presently writhing with dislike. "And this. How is this possible?"

Sexed? And what was wrong with my hair? Other than attitude. I pushed the sullen stuff back. "We aren't from here," I said gruffly. Could work. Tikitik on Cersi had been territorial, only Thought Travelers moving beyond a limited space.

The white tendrils of its mouth curled into a dissatisfied lump.

"You look different to us, too." Morgan produced his scanner, turning it so the display faced our "guest." "This is the Tikitik we know."

I tensed as the eyes riveted on the small screen, mouth tendrils outstretched. A thin barbed arm streaked forward as if to snatch the device, only to withdraw. Its demeanor altered; without knowing more of them, I couldn't tell if it was amused or wary. "A privilege," it said at last. "The Makers do not leave Tikitna—" a hand lifted skyward. "You are Far Travelers indeed."

Morgan glanced at me, gave a tiny nod. *Knows tech.*

Someone else had been listening. *'Tikitna?' It can't be coincidence, Sira, that name here, too.* I sensed Aryl's dismay. *This isn't just our home, but theirs.*

Could be worse, I assured her, thinking of the reptilian Scats, with their tendency to consume rivals. Thinking also of my Human, no longer the only non-Clan in the world. Would it help?

Regardless, manners were overdue. "Thank you for your assistance," I said, gesturing gratitude.

Eyes rotated to me. "We assist ourselves. This area is *sessened*. With you gone, we can do our work."

Morgan raised a curious brow. "What work is that?"

The Tikitik barked the laugh I remembered. "This land's skin is too delicate for the Hoveny's machines. We will ready it for planting."

Questions trembled on my lips: what it planted and for whom; about this world; most particularly what it had meant about our sexes, my hair, and what made us "so different." Could I trust this being's answers?

Was I ready for them?

My Human had a more pragmatic interest. "Where are we going?"

"The border of the Ribbon Lands." The Tikitik rose to its feet. "There will be authority. What kind I don't know, but you will no longer be in our way and we can do our work."

I decided not to thank it again.

$$\infty$$

I waited until the Tikitik squatted on its mount—having disrupted Oud-loads of Clan on its way back—before eyeing my Human warily. "'Authority,' it said. Is that wise?"

"No choice. If it was just you and I, yes, we'd keep low, scout the situation before attracting attention. As it is?" Morgan spun a finger. "No hiding this lot. Better we show up on our terms than have those in charge find us."

"So our plan's to hope for the best?" I grimaced.

"It does happen," with an easy complacency I didn't for an instant believe, especially since he'd the lightest of shields in place—a request for distance and privacy.

Plotting, he was. My Human left nothing to chance, "know your exits" being one of many lessons he'd taught me.

Another? Rest when you could, which went hand-in-hand with eat when you could, drink, wash, use an accommodation, and so forth. We were saving our rations till nightfall—however long that might take here—and washing? Out of the question. Of the containers and bags filled with water, few had made it into the pods.

Might not be a problem. After all, I'd tasted rain this morning. Hadn't turned so much as mauve.

My hair played with the wind of this new world, and I felt my mood lighten at last. "What should we call it? This planet."

Morgan laughed. "I'm sure it has a name, Witchling."

"Until we know it," I pointed out, "there's no reason we can't give it our own." I pulled a leg free of the cloak to face him. The wind played with his hair also, and the sun found russet in his beard. My Chosen gazed back at me, blue eyes full of emotion he wasn't sharing mind-to-mind. "You pick."

"Hope." His lips quirked at whatever he read from my expression. "Too much?"

"No," I said huskily. "Hope, it is."

Interlude

KEEPER EMELEN DIS knelt as if to pray; upon feeling the warmth of the soil, he did, under his breath. Others used instruments, demarcating the affected area with little green flags in the sod. He stifled the impulse to stop them; they cared, too. Here, in their lifetime, proof.

It wasn't only the lingering, unseasonal heat. He rose to his feet, examining the dark flakes on his palms and, yes, on both knees. Only one mode of travel left such remains, and it hadn't been used since the Fall.

"Well over a hundred, Keeper." Oncara Su shaded nes eyes. "The Oud riders must be those we seek. My regrets."

Emelen brushed aside nes apology. "The sect needs this evidence. Your decision to make all speed to the blessed landing site was the right one."

Room for the Twelve here, the land originally scoured flat and left sterile, but as memories faded and belief eroded, nature had returned. The presence of Field Oud meant the sacred plain was to be sliced and plowed. To grow tea, or some such. All it would take was water, and the tunnel to bring that through from the Ribbon Lands had been built. He'd done his utmost to slow its progress.

No longer a concern. "When the work here is complete, return me to the Sanctum."

Ne dared frown. "Should we not go from here to the project site? Shall we not be first to greet them?"

"Our role is not to put ourselves forward, Oncara," Emelen said sternly, "but to prepare for the Rebirth. If a new Founder has come, all must be told and everything put in place. There has been negligence. Neglect. No longer."

It was time. Cersi-So, he chanted to himself, well pleased. Cersi-So.

Chapter 17

A S IF MOCKING our choice of name, Hope's flat plain deceived, promising the hills long before the terrain finally lifted under the Ouds' scurrying feet. None too soon. The tiny hooks of the cloaks not only held clothing tight—and those wearing it—but soon produced a burning rash on any bare skin left in contact. My people endured without complaint, outwardly calm and determined.

They wearied, as did I, huddled together; a few tried to sleep.

The area appeared barren, other than the turf, but every so often great flocks came into view, their shadows flickering across the ground. They were made up of thousands of small birds—or their equivalent—wheeling and spinning, forming tight balls then rivers through the air. To our disappointment, the beautiful flocks didn't linger, busy heading north. If we were in that hemisphere, pleasing thought, this could be spring.

If we weren't? Morgan had shrugged.

So when another shadow crossed our path, I didn't pay attention until I saw the Om'ray rising to their feet, staring up. Doing the same, I glimpsed a dot, higher than the birds, heading east. *Someone's there,* Aryl informed me. *Someone like us.* A pause. *Like Om'ray.*

A distinction I hadn't heard from her before, Om'ray sensing the presence of M'hiray as instinctively as they did each other. *Do they sense you?*

I don't know.

Morgan had pulled out his lens. "Definitely a machine," he informed me. "Can't make out much else."

"Aryl says there's—" about to say Clan, I changed to "—Hoveny on board. The Om'ray sense them."

"Reassuring." Absently.

Well, yes, to have the first real proof we'd come to the right world—our world—but still. "It's not coming this way." I sat again, deflated.

"Doesn't mean we're not on scans—or those Hoveny didn't sense you in return." My Human remained standing, surveying what was ahead with the lens. "Huh."

I stood again. "What's 'huh?'"

He handed me the lens. "That."

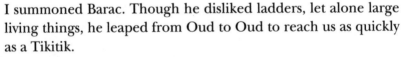

I summoned Barac. Though he disliked ladders, let alone large living things, he leaped from Oud to Oud to reach us as quickly as a Tikitik.

Ours appeared to be taking a nap.

Having arrived, my cousin frowned thoughtfully at the long stony rise ahead of us. "Doesn't look like much."

Morgan offered his lens. "Five degrees left."

I knew why my cousin stiffened. Through the lens, the hill jumped closer. While most of the rise was bare tumbled rock, my Human had found what had to be our destination: a narrow archway leading into the hill.

There was nothing natural about it. An assortment of wheeled vehicles bustled around the opening, some going inside, for the interior was brightly lit. A plume of gray dust rose behind the hill like a stain in the sky, and rubble stretched to either side of the arch. Most heartening, there were figures, with two arms and two legs. People.

"Think it's a mine?" Barac handed back the lens.

"Maybe." My Human tapped the Oud with his boot. "But if they put these to work above ground, why not below?"

Who cared? People, as far as I was concerned, promised all that went with them, from shelter to showers. Restaurants. My stomach growled, and I blurted, "It's civilization."

"Remember Norx, chit."

"I try not to." I scowled. The planet was the latest source of a key ingredient of ysa-smoke, the Trade Pact's most popular addiction and one Captain Morgan had used to explain my wearing a helmet my first time on Plexis. A stuffy, smelly helmet.

Barac raised an eyebrow. " 'Norx'? I don't know the name."

"A world uninhabited till the syndicates sent recruited miners to do their dirty work. Point being appearances can't be trusted. Until we know who we're dealing with, we should avoid unnecessary risks."

My cousin rolled his shoulders. "My turn—"

"No. It is not anyone's 'turn.' " Their identical expressions of dismay would have been amusing had I not been waiting for exactly this. "No more heroics. We do this together. Besides, we're a giant mass of Oud covered in people. If we can see them, they already see us." I paused then went on heavily, "We'll need the children."

"The—?" I'd shocked Barac. "For what?"

"A test." The corner of Morgan's mouth deepened as he nodded approval. "We put our children in plain sight. Prove we've families. How these strangers react will tell us what we need to know."

"No deceptions." I felt Aryl's silent agreement. "We show them who we are. Roll the dice." There was nothing to add; these two understood the odds. "Agreed?"

Barac bowed, offering the gesture of respect. "I'll spread the word."

"As will we," Morgan announced, bowing too. *Well, Witchling?*

If my cousin could jump along the backs of monsters— "You first," I dared him.

Interlude

OF ALL THE IMPOSSIBLE, implausible futures, jumping on Oud backs, while they ran, no less, was one he hadn't come close to imagining. An experience the First Scout planned to forget as soon as he was on the ground, along with how they'd arrived here in the first place.

Alive. That's what counted. Even if he never got that stink out of his clothing. Alive and with his Chosen.

Although he'd be happier once Ruti stopped being furious. "They'll come to no harm." Had he said that twice or three times?

Ruti sat on the back of an Oud, arms around a bundle, regarding him with as much warmth as she'd give a Scat. Her shields tightened, and her face creased with unfamiliar distrust. "What if these strangers are child-stealers? Did Sira think of that?"

"We can't hide them, Ruti." Jacqui tucked her hands under her arms to keep from rubbing the rash on both palms, pain tightening the corners of her mouth. "Just think. There could be parents—maybe a Birth Watcher—who'll see our children and want to help."

"Strangers won't help us." Ruti's chin trembled. "We need our families. That's where we belong. With our families."

"You've said that before." Jacqui gave Barac a meaningful look, as though he was supposed to hear something more in the words.

Words were hollow, empty things. He'd have *reached* for the Chooser's mind and demanded answers if not for Ruti. She'd locked away her thoughts, but not her mood. *Fear* was part of it. *Suspicion.*

There. A disquieting bone-deep *weariness.* Of course. She was exhausted, between the baby growing inside and caring for everyone else.

So where he might have pressed or argued, Barac chose to bow his head in acquiescence. "I'll make sure families are together and assign scouts, with weapons, to stay near each child. We'll keep them safe."

But Ruti hunched her shoulders and turned from him, and there was nothing he could do but go.

When had the acrid *taste* of change become normal?

Chapter 18

A S ENTRANCES WENT, ours would be memorable, not that we'd a choice.

We'd rearranged ourselves according to plan: families and children to the front of our island of Oud. The Tikitik watched for a moment, then resumed its nap, squatting with eyes almost closed. Just as well. I doubted it would appreciate seeing our armed scouts take their posts near those families.

I stood with Gurutz behind the sud Prendolats, to be close to Andi. Morgan had donned his pack and stood alone on the outermost Oud to my right. He was our most potent weapon. It made sense to leave him free to act.

My role? To ensure weapons of any kind weren't necessary.

The miners, or whatever they were, had indeed seen us coming. They'd moved their vehicles inside the tunnel, taking shelter there themselves. A few heads peered out. I empathized. It couldn't be pleasant having a massive clot of giant Oud run straight for you.

Hopefully, we'd stop first.

They'll stop, Aryl assured me. *Tikitik enjoy drama, but they don't risk themselves.*

What about us?

I don't know. This one lacks the arrogance of Cersi's. I suspect it will do as it said and be glad to leave us behind.

My assessment of the creature as well.

Andi twisted to smile up at me. Nik drew her daughter back on her lap, *disapproval* radiating like heat. Whatever trust the parents had in me, they trusted Ruti di Bowart more.

They were welcome to, so long as they cooperated with our plan. I'd greater concerns than the protests of a Chosen a quarter my age, even one I considered family, and kept my focus ahead as the Ouds continued their breakneck speed.

Establishing a rapport wasn't going to be easy when our origins were, to put it mildly, hard to explain. While we should be able to slip by without bringing up the Trade Pact or Assemblers, Cersi was another matter. *Sona* had transmitted and been heard. What it transmitted, we'd no idea, but Morgan cautioned there could be those on this world, or this system, fully aware of who and what we were.

What they'd think of us? Anyone's guess.

As was when our Ouds planned to stop. We were close enough to cast an ominous shadow over the vehicle parking area on the hill before the great body beneath me gave a promising shudder. I fought to keep balanced rather than put my unwelcome hand on Nik's shoulder, sharing the *relief* from all sides as a second collective shudder was followed by, at last, deceleration.

Suddenly, our island began to break apart! The Oud on the outer rim peeled away. Those in the midst of others struggled to be free, slamming impatiently into those too slow to move out of the way.

Ours joined in, throwing itself sideways into its neighbor, the result like an earthquake. I found myself staring into terrified faces, all of us toppling—I heard screams—

Chit!

Here. I clung to the sud Prendolats and they clung to me. We'd have to 'port. There was no other way—

<<*Death is the way.*>> Words *tasting* of ash. Words grinding deep inside, with impossible intimacy. How? Where had that—I froze amid all else, afraid I'd hear that hollow voice again—

<<*Come. Come now.*>> The world around me faded to *darkness*, opened on a balcony, beneath a sky I knew, with mountains—

And *she* was there—

Somehow, I wrenched free, terrified I'd recognize— "No!"

"Yes." Andi's sweet face appeared over her mother's shoulder. The child's peaceful smile was something from a nightmare. *Families should be together. You should go, Sira. You can.*

NO! I prepared to 'port all of us—to safety, not to that voice—

Hold! Morgan, a lifeline.

The Tikitik was standing on its mount. It let out a sharp wail and the Oud stopped where they were, then sank to the ground.

"Get down! Hurry!" I shouted, reinforcing that with Power. The gaps between the beasts would last only as long as they obeyed. The tiny hooks of their cloaks, once a help to stay in place, fought our desperate movements, tearing clothing and skin. "Get away from them!"

If I ran from anything else, that was something I wasn't prepared to admit even to myself.

Gurutz helped Nik with their belongings. I passed Andi to Josa, then dropped down myself. We gasped as one, half smothered by the reek. "Keep moving toward the others. Hurry." I watched them go, trusting the scout as much as the child's Talent, then turned, *reaching* with my own sense.

Anxiety. Fear. Nothing with clear direction. We were too close together, trapped in this maze of overheated flesh. The Hoveny could make of us what they chose, I thought bitterly. We had to get out first.

I can find them. Aryl, with confidence. *Let me use your eyes, Sira.*

So I did.

For the second time, I staggered into the fresh, cool air, this time following Gricel and her baby, her Chosen and son leading; a path found only because the Om'ray, including Aryl, were drawn by the growing concentration of our people.

Sira, hurry!

I swung back, only to find the opening gone, the Oud rising— moving! But the di Eathems weren't the only ones still trapped—

"Sira, no!" Arms like metal bands clamped around me.

YES! Aryl, with fury. *Hap and her Chosen—I can take us—*then, her mindvoice ragged with grief—*we're too late.*

My sense of her vanished, swamped by *darkness.* The M'hir bled everywhere, colored everything, filled with the dreadful howls of Watchers.

Witchling. The naming spread around and through me, bringing with it all that was sane and good and didn't belong in the M'hir. *Beloved. This way.*

This voice I followed without doubt or hesitation. Back, I permitted myself a heartbeat inside Morgan's arms, then gave the tiniest resistance. He let go, and I opened my eyes.

Reality wasn't an improvement. What had been the fronts of the giant Oud became their rears as the creatures humped away, leaving the groups gathered on either side to stare at one another through a cloud of dust.

Dust that settled over mangled husks and ownerless belongings. Whether the Tikitik had been careless or cruel, this ride had cost more than the di Annks. I didn't try to count. Didn't dare try to see who wasn't there but was no longer here—

Had they *heard* a voice, too?

I shook myself. We'd the living, our injured to care for—

"Company." Morgan, low and urgent. His hand dropped to his side, flexed.

Coughing dust, I looked toward the archway. Company, it was. Their vehicles barely stopped, people poured out, rushing toward us.

With blankets.

Some had small cases that implied medical supplies and others were empty-handed, but all ran to reach us, and all had faces shaped like ours, full of determined concern and kindness.

As an entrance, I thought numbly, leaning against Morgan, they couldn't have done better.

Interlude

GLANCES. An instant's distraction. The beard, maybe. Have to lose it if he wanted to blend, Morgan judged, though if this group represented the majority of Hoveny, it wouldn't be remotely enough. Oh, in the dark, maybe, but here he fit, strange as it was to think, best with M'hiray like Barac.

The Hoveny had hair, though none here had the thick tumble of opinion that marked the Clan Chosen, but what he did see was white. They'd more variety in skin tone, from midnight black to the translucence of the Vyna. For Vyna, beyond question, had been the control, the baseline, the real, if he'd call them that, Hoveny. He'd come up to the chin of the shortest here. Outmassed any, for they were slender. Two thumbs and four fingers per hand, though these had nails and were the same length as his. Clothing was similar, there being practicality in tough pants, boots, and jackets. Workers.

Could be a mine after all.

They knew he was different, Morgan thought, if not how or what it meant, but no one wasted time on him and he approved. Without invitation or greeting, the Hoveny flowed through the Clan like a wave, sweeping them up in a triage and evacuation procedure either regularly used—or well practiced.

Practice was his guess. The Human picked out the individual

in charge, a tall male, older than most, with devices in both ears and "Hope's" version of a noteplas in one hand. Confident, calm, but a little too intense for this not to be their first real emergency.

Their tech was sophisticated. Wheels instead of anti-grav on the vehicles, but that could be economics or some constraint of the work. The quiet engines contained nothing more mysterious than detectable powercells and the Hoveny med-kits could pass for those ubiquitous on Human worlds, other than being black with green bands. Up close, the sturdy clothes had no markings to imply rank or service. Civilians.

Perhaps.

Add the space capability implied by the Tikitik, and—too soon, but he'd dare think it— "Hope" was starting to look reassuringly familiar.

Palming his scanner, the Human set it to record. As with the Tikitik, the language was the one he'd learned, from Cersi, though the accent differed. These Hoveny clipped and shortened some words, added others, but nothing that hindered mutual understanding.

Kindness and competence lent their own. The wounded were being assessed, the most serious lifted on the flat backs of freight vehicles that moved off at once, slowly enough that those caring for them—and those concerned—could walk alongside. Just as well. They'd started with too few Healers.

They'd less now. Ahur hadn't reached the planet, Ghos had been killed by Oud, and elderly Eand was one of those carried off.

The survivors able to walk were to go in small personnel carriers, with paired bench seats, and those waiting their turn had clumped into groups. Tellingly so. He looked over at his Chosen, standing alone and at a small distance, and knew better than *reach* along their link.

Sira stood, her hands together, her hair straight, clothing dust-covered and stained with blood from a scrape along her jaw that promised a bruise beneath.

And was so much more. Ancient. Ageless. Powerful. He wasn't

the only one to feel it. She radiated strength, a strength that denied fear and insisted on peace. The Hoveny needed no introduction to grasp who led these people, and who protected them.

If they glanced at him? Morgan thought with grim pride.

They stared at her.

Chapter 19

I STOOD gazing out at the Hoveny and the Clan, living legacies of a shared past, and instead of satisfaction or wonder or anything else I'd hoped to feel, I was frozen with fear. At last I understood how Aryl could have put herself in that crystal. She'd feared what she saw our people becoming enough to reach from the past to stop it. It hadn't worked, not as she'd planned. The M'hiray had taken advantage of their Human hosts and paid the price. She'd arrived in time to save us from our folly.

Could I, here and now? For what I saw was the same dreadful potential for harm. What I knew? The cost.

I was aware of Morgan. He hovered—not that he'd use the word—nearby, offering comfort by his silent, understanding presence. Not that he was idle. I'd seen him unobtrusively adjust his scanner. By now, my Human likely already knew more than anyone else about our new "friends."

On the outside. The instinct to *reach* for like minds, to *compare* Power was hard to resist at a distance, impossible to deny if touch was offered. Our rescuers showed no restraint, handling the wounded, placing blankets over shoulders. It was as if they didn't comprehend—

Oh, but they didn't. I'd realized it almost at once. The Hoveny were Clan enough to be glowing, albeit dimly, in the M'hir, but I sensed no deep connection to one another, nothing like that pervading our minds. The Hoveny were *real* by Om'ray standards and possessed the rudiments of Power.

Yet, as far as I could tell, these individuals lacked the Talents to use it.

Making them weak. Defenseless.

I wouldn't be the only one to sense it. While the Prime Laws existed to protect such vulnerable minds, forbidding the stronger from entering to touch their thoughts, we'd those among us accustomed to doing far worse.

To Humans. The aliens they'd feared most and used. And where had that brought us?

They mustn't make the same mistake here.

They won't, Aryl sent grimly. *You won't let them.*

Whatever it takes, I agreed, feeling the vow take hold inside me. To safeguard our place among the Hoveny, as equals. Nothing less. Nothing more.

So as I stood, waiting for the questions sure to come, I watched the M'hiray.

To see who might threaten this world.

Gurutz was the first to approach me, his hurried gesture of respect little more than a flick of his fingers. "Your help, Keeper— Sira. There's a problem with the husks."

Morgan came alert. "I'll go."

"We both will." I shook off the stasis I'd been in, glad to have a purpose.

The M'hiray *pushed* the physical remnants of our lives into the M'hir. The Om'ray disposed of theirs even more simply—dropping them into a swamp, to be eaten, or leaving them out on the ground, to be eaten. Not an option for those of us who'd lived in cities.

Especially Human ones, where authorities tended to frown upon the eating of corpses. It was, as I recalled, a humanoid-specific prejudice; they'd no problem at all with beings who didn't look like them serving a grandparent for supper.

From what Gurutz could tell us as we walked to the knot of people around our husks, the Hoveny shared the Human view, insisting "something be done" with them.

Not, I sighed to myself, the inaugural topic I'd thought to discuss with our rediscovered kin. *Care to take this one?* I sent, willing to play the coward with my Chosen. Who was, I reminded myself, our negotiation specialist.

Deal.

Sona's blankets and bright coveralls lay strewn on the ground, along with soiled lengths of gauze and heavy coats. No knives or other objects of use; the Om'ray were efficient. There were bodies, too, some unrecognizable, others that might have been asleep. We'd lost eighteen M'hiray in the M'hir during our passage.

Twenty-one more, Om'ray and M'hiray, had died here. Only twelve husks remained, a disturbing discrepancy we wouldn't mention to the Hoveny. More had fled reality.

The mere thought tormented me. Had each heard a familiar voice? A loved one—now dead?

Had I?

I shuddered and Morgan's fingers brushed warm against my wrist. *Okay?*

I've something to tell you—The leader, at least of this group of rescuers, was walking toward us.

Offering his hand.

My Human didn't hesitate, stepping forward to grip it in his. The Hoveny looked down, turning their clasped hands. Counting digits at a guess. His eyes, pale and intelligent, widened briefly before he let go. "I am Pauvan Di," he said, his voice pleasantly deep. "We grieve with you."

"Thank you," Morgan replied, dipping his head. He'd been observing their ways, I realized. "Jason Morgan. This is Sira and Gurutz."

The Sona scout pointedly put his thumbs through his belt, but I didn't hesitate to offer my hand to the Hoveny, bending my head that slight bit, too. "We are all grateful," I said earnestly.

His skin to mine allowed a subtle exploration. I sensed *goodwill* and burning *curiosity*. There. Another presence. So they'd Chosen, or something like it.

The mind linked to his was stronger, as we measured Power, roughly equivalent to the average Human telepath. She, for I sensed that, too, saw what Pauvan saw. They'd be able to communicate.

Unfair to hide what I was, but this wasn't the time for revelation. In case either of the pair could sense emotion—consciously or not—I filled the outermost layer of my thoughts with *gratitude*, adding the *worry* and *grief* he'd expect. The truth—always the safer course. I reclaimed my hand.

"We would like to remove your—" the Hoveny's hesitation made me like him even more, "—your lost ones." He gestured toward a waiting transport, larger than the others and with an enclosed back.

Let me, chit. "We appreciate it," Morgan said, his tone somber. "How can we help?"

"We're strangers." Pauvan appeared to brace himself. "We shouldn't—strangers shouldn't handle the dead."

I felt Gurutz's *impatience*. From the look of those in the vicinity, the Hoveny had tried to make this point already and failed. The Clan, tired and upset, weren't about to volunteer to clean up after the Oud.

Morgan handed me his pack. "I'll do it."

Jason—

It's not the first time, Witchling. With quiet resolve. *Let's make it the last.*

I helped. Seeing what we were doing, Barac came, and Ruis, then a few others. The Hoveny proved willing to place the husks, if wrapped in blankets, in the transport. They did so with such respect and care, I might have been ashamed.

But these pieces of flesh weren't us and hadn't been. This was work, filthy and hard, and like Barac and the others, I did it not for the Hoveny sensibilities or for our dead, but for Morgan.

When we were done, the Hoveny gave us round flasks of water, pausing for a moment's silence before drinking themselves.

While the Clan watched.

And some of them judged.

There will be those who fall, Sira. Aryl's mind voice was almost stern. *There was nothing anyone could have done.*

Though I'd rinsed my mouth and drank, the acrid taste of dust, what it meant, lingered. *Tell Ruti.* One of the husks had belonged to Rasa. Since that dreadful discovery, Barac's Chosen had gathered the other children together, keeping them and their parents as far from me as possible.

I will not. If blaming you helps her function, so be it. Grimly. *You're strong enough to give her time.*

She's not the only one who blames me. Josa and Nik, the latter having yet to let go of their daughter's hand, stood pointedly with Degal.

And me. Morgan entered the conversation, his sending dark with grief. *I brought the Oud.*

You stopped them from running us down! Aryl's tone softened. *We've been here before. Do not regret what can't be changed.*

Listen to our daughter-to-be. I slipped my hand into Morgan's, sent *strength.* Not that my Human was in need, but to see something warm again in his eyes and know I'd put it there.

One of the Hoveny approached, dipping his head courteously. It was Pauvan Di. His face was drawn, sweat-dampened dust caught in the fine lines at the corners of his eyes and mouth. "If you'll come with me, please, Sira. Jason." He indicated the remaining vehicle.

I'd sent Tle di Parth first, with Destin, the pair being the most potent combination of Power and suspicion among us. The Chooser had agreed to stay connected; I'd felt nothing but her *attention* along our link, deep inside the M'hir.

We were the rearguard, in Morgan's parlance. Against what, I'd no idea and would be delighted not to discover. *Any problems?* I asked Tle.

We're fine. Waiting for you. The Chooser's tone for once had no bite to it. *Our hosts are courteous.*

Would there be Candidates for her among them? Our initial sample didn't bode well.

Morgan picked up his pack. "Lead on."

I climbed in and sat. The bench seat wasn't padded. That, and the lack of doors suggested the climate here was moderate—or would be hotter. The little bit of reasoning pleased me, even though I suspected my ever-capable Human had determined how to drive and rebuild the vehicle, as well as predict the weather for the coming—what did I call it here, months? The Om'ray used fists.

Months would do, I decided, till I knew better.

The driver sat in the middle of the front bench, Pauvan Di to her right. Or his right. She or he was one of the individuals here who, though adult, felt neither female nor male to my inner sense, doubtless the reason for the Tikitik's consternation over our being "all sexed." I needed new pronouns, as well as names for time.

Though tempted to lean forward and ask, I stayed put, not that I'd much choice, squeezed between the open side and Morgan's pack. He grinned at me over the top and pointed.

The archway, with its lit tunnel, was about to swallow us.

As we drove inside, I craned my neck, determined to observe everything I could. Not that I expected a tunnel to be all that informative, but at this point, anything about this place and people had to help.

The construction was new, based on the perfect brickwork lining the walls. The light fixtures were more haphazard, strung along ribbons of thick wire—primitive, or expedient. I could almost hear Morgan warning me against premature assumption. The wheels crunched on a road made of coarse gravel, dampened to keep down dust.

Our destination became clear before we'd gone far: another world.

An old one. Instead of smooth brick to either side, we drove between the rounded sides of buildings, as though entering a narrow street within a buried city. Making this tunnel an excavation and these buildings? *Aryl, what do you think?*

Hoveny Concentrix, she confirmed, seeing through my eyes. *These look like the structures the Oud freed from the mountain ridge, that Marcus and the others were so excited to find.*

The structures here hadn't been freed from the surrounding rock, but even this meager glimpse was enough to excite me. The architecture was unlike any I'd seen and stunningly beautiful, more art form than building. Throughout, the lights and wires were suspended from hooks in the rock overhead, or on poles, as if to protect the surfaces. *Marcus said they couldn't drill into the walls,* Aryl sent.

I passed that along to Morgan, who nodded, eyes bright with interest.

The "street" carried on, sometimes wider, often narrow and twisting. One long section shrank inward, threatening the sides of the Hoveny vehicle, but our driver drove through without slowing.

This hadn't happened three hundred years ago. I didn't know how long it took the surface of a planet to engulf what appeared to be an entire city—or how a city survived being buried like this, for that matter, so its streets and structures remained intact. Norval had succumbed to its own mass. The puzzle of the Hoveny Concentrix stared back at me, written in graceful lines and alien curves, no easier to comprehend than before.

When the tunnel opened again, widening into a bulb, I realized there were others looking for answers here. One building had been singled out for attention, the rock that must have encased it removed. Lights played upward, revealing the top to be a dome, rising to a central peak. Around the building's base were fabric-sided tents, some quite large, as well as a parking area presently filled with familiar vehicles.

As ours joined them, I could see beyond the tents. Dazzling beams of sunlight poured through an opening even larger than the one through which we'd entered. Through it, I glimpsed what interested me far more than the Hoveny relics.

A verdant, living landscape rose before my eyes, carpeted in farm fields crossed by glittering streams. The gravel road from the tunnel continued outside, becoming a walled ditch up the middle.

The vehicle came to rest. I climbed out, then gave Morgan's pack a helpful push in his direction.

Our people are here, Aryl, with relief.

I dared *reach,* keeping the searching tendril within the M'hir. Minds were tightly shielded, as I'd expected, emotions dampened. Sendings flickered along the bonds between Chosen. The impression I gained was a reassuring calm.

My Human shrugged on his pack, then raised an eyebrow at me. Situation update, that meant.

Improving, I decided, by the moment.

And found I could smile.

Interlude

HOME. Lemuel Dis wished ne'd thought to put in noseplugs. Planets stank, there was no way around it, and this one still smelled to ner of poverty, struggle, and despair.

Others holidayed dirtside. There was no accounting for taste.

Nor any acceptable delay. Ner absence would be remarked by the upcoming shift change, but not made public unless there was a system-wide emergency—

Say the sort brought about by knowledge of a ship from outside the system before context was established and the necessary controls in place. Ne didn't care to imagine the panic. Ne wouldn't permit it.

Hence the plunge straight from the moon, bringing those already exposed to the information: some of nes staff, the historian, and, of course, Thought Traveler.

To be delayed here.

Lemuel regarded the on-duty supervisor of Brightfall's SysCom with little favor. "Explain the problem, Nermein Dis. I ordered statements from every individual in contact with these visitors." A neutral word for the shocking appearance out of nothing by one hundred and fifty-seven living things who pinged as Hoveny on remote detectors.

Plus one who registered "unknown."

"I began the process at once, Director, but the Tikitik won't cooperate."

Little became none. The Cooperative relied on two principles: no species' law overruled another's, and every member had the right of access to their own kind, however annoying. Lemuel hesitated. Involve Thought Traveler, presently contained with the others, in this mess?

Might as well call in the major newscomms now and be done. Tikitik of its status didn't come to Brightfall. Nothing happened here to attract their infamous curiosity.

Until now.

Nes role, to see the system worked for all. This supervisor should have arranged to have himself declared—albeit temporarily—a Tikitik. Lemuel arranged nes face to show benevolent patience. "Have you obtained dispensation from my counterpart on Tikitna?"

Nermein's eyes widened. No, that meant. "May I have your authorization to do so, Director?"

Save ner from the planetborn, who considered everything beyond their skin of sky out of reach. "You have it." Lemuel waved to nes staff, who'd provide the codes.

Time wasn't on nes side or theirs. Several visitors had been killed, no doubt with blame to be laid and dealt with and protested. More pressing? There were others with the ability to detect the visitors and no guarantee their reactions would be palatable or safe. "Speed is of the essence." Lemuel Dis ordered. "Send the statement directly to me once you've obtained it. And, Nermein?"

"Yes, Director."

"I remind you this is a System matter, of the utmost sensitivity. Should news of it travel by unofficial channels to Brightfall's government or elsewhere, haisin will be charitably severed and everyone from this office relocated to an asteroid in the mining belt. A distant asteroid. For life. Am I clear?"

"Yes, Director." He gave a short, proper bow. "Rest assured we appreciate the seriousness of the situation. The background you requested." A data crystal changed hands from one of his staff to nes. "You'll find it's complete: profiles of site personnel; a summary of the research underway."

"'Research?'" Lemuel was almost startled; nes thoughts had moved to the next step: meeting those visitors. "I was told the site was a construction project." Specifically, another expansion into unsuitable land—it'd be the next generation of farmers who'd suffer for it, as far as ne was concerned. Brightfall's present government? Not known for its long view.

"A survey and record team, to be exact, Director. There's a *seesor* from Hilip present, with discretionary authority over the project's continuance. There are pre-Fall structures within the area to be flooded—of itself unremarkable—" it being impossible to dig anywhere on the planet without hitting one, "—but these are controversial. There's local resistance to their loss."

Coincidence? In Lemuel's experience, it was wise never to assume so. "Your summary will be useful, Nermein."

He'd a well-disciplined face, but ne caught a flash of gratification. "Your transport waits on the roof pad, Director." A final bow. "May I offer my personal wish for your success?"

Discipline and the ability to grasp ramifications. An individual to watch, perhaps groom; new staff for the Hub being hard to find. Lemuel inclined nes head, slightly. "I accept, Nermein Dis. Though at this point, I've no idea what 'success' will be."

Or if they'd be fortunate to survive it.

Chapter 20

IT DID the Hoveny a disservice to call the shelter they provided within their tunnel a tent. Temporary, maybe, but despite their woven appearance, the walls were solid to the touch, the ceiling featured inset lights and air circulation, and it boasted a cushioned floor. There was no obvious clue how they'd used this space before being inundated with Clan. Someone—likely several someones—had worked hard and fast to prep it for us.

We'd been lucky to find these people and be in their care.

Five cots with our wounded stood along one wall, each connected to a machine and tended by a Hoveny wearing a clear overcoat. Along another were rows of astonishingly pink inflated couches. The middle space held a selection of tables, chairs, and stools that looked to have been grabbed from a variety of sources. These were placed near a long counter loaded with white bins, half containing the round water flasks and the others filled with small clear bags of green crisps, with more Hoveny in brown standing by.

Their offerings sat neglected. My people stood without moving, carefully distant from any stranger, their grim faces streaked with dirt and blood, their belongings at their feet or still in their arms. They'd been betrayed too often, I realized, my heart aching.

I stepped away from Morgan, spreading my arms wide. "Our thanks to our gracious hosts," I said, my voice ringing through the silent room. Under the words, I sent: *I've found no harm in these people but I am watchful. Trust me, if not them. Rest. Recover. Accept help.*

SIRA! SIRA! My name was their acknowledgment, like a warm blanket around my shoulders, and even those I'd angered gave me weary smiles and nodded. My hair, enthused, rose around me—to the intense interest of the Hoveny—and I was mildly surprised the stuff didn't fly in front of my face.

Motion, all at once, as statues became people, going to the counter, others choosing a spot to leave their things.

Much as I wanted to join them, there were those I needed to see first.

"Med-cocoons," Morgan observed. "Close enough."

The *Silver Fox* had had such a device, essential in a ship with a sole inhabitant. I hadn't liked it then.

I didn't like these. A featureless opaque dome covered each cot, making it impossible to see who was whom. That wouldn't stop my inner sense. I went to touch the nearest—

One of the Hoveny caregivers deftly put herself in the way. "Please do not interfere with treatment."

"We won't," Morgan said with a pointed emphasis on the "we."

"Thank you. I am Aracel Dis, *edican* in charge." Aracel was the oldest Hoveny I'd seen so far, wrinkles softening the corners of her upswept eyes and along her lips. Her white hair was so tightly bound mine twitched in sympathy and this close, I could see the clear material she wore over her work clothes had a hood, presently rolled up, and extended to cover her hands. Tall, of course. Rather than step back, I craned my neck to look her in the eyes, finding compassion and no little curiosity.

Inadvertently, I *reached,* to find nothing there.

No. Not nothing. A perfect shield. Morgan's were impressive, but this? I dipped into the M'hir and *looked.*

There. Maybe. *Something* encased her mind in an impenetrable bubble, keeping out the M'hir, keeping out any questing thought. Proof the Hoveny might not be as vulnerable as I'd feared, but how was it possible? This wasn't like the implants used by Bowman and her constables. This *felt* innate.

And purposeful. Even for protection, how could anyone choose such terrible silence? I'd experienced it; that I hadn't gone mad, trapped within my own mind, had more to do with finding Morgan than strength.

Who was amused at my distress. *Most do quite well, Witchling,* he reminded me. Aloud, with the impeccable manners of a trader, "You have our gratitude, Aracel. I'm Jason. This is Sira. How are our injured?"

"It's too soon to say," the edican replied. "We've done all we can for them here." She gestured toward the cocoons as though apologizing. "They've been stabilized for transport."

Easy, chit, Morgan sent, forestalling my protest. *This isn't a medfacility. Evacuation's likely standard procedure and could save their lives.*

Two Om'ray: frail Eand and Destin's Chosen, Elnu. Three M'hiray: Kita di Teerac, Lakai sud Parth, and Vidya di Serona. Each a Chosen; worse, none were a pair. Ten lives at risk.

They were not leaving here like this—not alone. I managed to ask calmly, "Where will they go?"

"Landerslee. There's an excellent trauma center." Aracel's face softened. "Heart-kin mustn't be separated at such a time. Please have them identify themselves to me or any of us, Sira. We'll ensure they're kept together."

As though to the Hoveny 'heart-kin' meant Chosen—

And as though no one else here is able to sense the link between our pairs, from Aryl. *What sort of people are they?*

Private, I replied, wondering what else would prove different.

"May I treat this?" Aracel indicated the side of my face. I reached up, surprised by soreness and the feel of something sticky. My fingertips came away red.

I supposed I'd run a bit close to that flurry of Oud feet, though it had been that, or be plowed under its neighbor.

"I'll take care of her." Morgan answered before I could, the tiniest edge to his voice.

Neither of us was in a state to make important decisions. "Water first," I countered, forcing cheer into my voice. "And if that's food, Aracel?"

The edican smiled. "It's nourishment," she qualified. "I'm sure Alisi Di—Site Seesor—will arrange for something better for you all, and accommodations, before this arn's end."

Plans and time. Some of us lacked either. My gaze fell on the cocoons. "May I touch them? For—" The Hoveny might not have "luck," though Morgan had told me most species had some expression for chance improving their fortune. "—my own comfort."

Aracel inclined her head slightly.

So before I left the five, I did what little I could, sending *strength* through that meager contact. Most of all, letting those sleeping minds know they'd not been abandoned.

And wouldn't be.

"Not bad." Morgan put another of the green crisps into his mouth and crunched, an intent look on his face. He would, I'd learned, eat anything, anywhere. Though these he'd scanned first, blatantly employing his offworld tech in front of the Hoveny.

Who were still fascinated by my hair. I grabbed for a straying lock; it evaded me to investigate Morgan's upper shirt pocket. Again. The stuff had stamina, I'd give it that.

Blue eyes glanced my way. *Care to tell me what's bothering you, Witchling?*

"Other than those three?"

Our Council had reformed: Teris, Degal, and Nik. Absent was Odon, who'd elected to stay with Japel and guard their son. Noil nursed an arm the edicans had wrapped and secured with a sling; not coincidentally, Jacqui and Alet were circling, as far from each other as possible, but with equally avid interest. I'd no idea if his wounded state increased the unChosen's allure, or the Choosers reacted to the lack of alternatives in range, but whatever had quenched their desire for Choice had been left with *Sona* in space.

Confounding expectation, our most potent Chooser—and once outspoken member of Council—sat on a pink couch with Eand's Chosen, Moyla. Tle di Parth, the image of restraint and courtesy?

I didn't plan to ask. We'd a table, two chairs, and a moment's peace. "They've requested a meeting with Alisi." I dutifully nibbled a crisp. The things tasted pretty much as I imagined the bottom of a boot might taste—fried, of course.

"Let them." Morgan finished his drink. "Come here." He opened his med-kit, retrieved before he'd stowed his pack, and coat, under our table.

I turned the aching side of my face to him and found myself gazing at the doors through which we'd come. They remained open, affording an excellent view of the ancient building. "Who do you think lived there?"

"Someone who matters a great deal to our new friends." My Chosen applied a cool spray to my cheek and jaw, shooing my hair aside with his free hand.

"Are they?" I asked very quietly. "Friends?"

"So far. The rest depends on us." A tidy patch of medskin came next, from a scant and irreplaceable supply. "By that, I mean you. Hold still, chit."

I'd flinched. Who wouldn't? *You think I can control the Clan— stop them doing here what they did in the Trade Pact.*

I know you will. Punctuated by a daring kiss behind my ear. "There." Finished with his ministrations, Morgan pulled back, tucking away his kit. "Shouldn't scar." He pretended to frown at me. "You need a bath."

Who didn't? I stuck out my tongue.

Rewarded by a grin. "Charming." He leaned forward, face serious again. "Now, what's going on?"

I put my hand on the table between us. His covered it at once, warm, rough, and alive.

Through that contact, I shared the voice of the dead.

I'd shaken him to the core; I could see it and certainly felt it. Fair enough. Reliving that impossible voice had shaken me, too.

"Rael," Morgan said finally, his whisper hoarse and low. Much as I wanted to deny it, he knew my sister's mindvoice, too.

My sister, Rael di Sarc. Beautiful, powerful, proud. More than a sister. She'd been my heart-kin and truest friend in the years of my solitude, and afterward. Her final act had been to send me a desperate warning, for she and her Chosen had been betrayed by a Human she'd trusted.

A warning sent even as she'd dissolved, a ghost, to save those of us left from the same fate.

"It was Rael." Cold settled around my heart.

Your sister, as Enris has called to me. Aryl sounded every bit her age. *What is this, that uses love against us, and why? Where have we come that such things are even possible?*

"All good questions." Blue eyes glinted. "I've one. Say the others we've lost 'ported themselves into Andi's "boxes," or somehow followed ghosts into the M'hir. Then what?"

The only fact was their absence. "I can't sense them," I told him, "even as ghosts."

They're dead. You heard *the Watchers, Great-granddaughter.*

I'd *hear* them now, if I dared *listen.* I gave a weary nod, accepting the truth. "Aryl's right. Answering these voices is fatal." My fingertips dug into my thighs. Aware of those around us, I chose to send instead of whisper. *We're being hunted again. This time it isn't by strangers.* Though it was still, I thought bitterly, because of what we were. *Anyone who can 'port is in danger.*

Morgan's face was expressionless. "We'll warn them."

Of what? I shifted restlessly, my hair doing the same.

Just then, Jacqui passed our table, her face pale and intent. She'd my sympathy. It wasn't pleasant, or easy, fighting an instinct you knew could cause harm, yet promised so much.

It was almost tangible, that *snick* of familiarity. "It's as if we're unChosen, hearing a Chooser's Call." Almost as irresistible.

Traps need bait, Aryl supplied grimly.

How do we know this isn't our own doing? I countered, feeling Aryl's shock. *We've suffered—enough to make our minds unstable.*

What if this is our unconscious longing for those we've lost, one strong enough to manifest—

Or our common guilt, clamoring for death and justice, but that bleak thought I reserved for myself.

"It would explain why the voices are specific, but nothing else." My Human looked thoughtful, then shook his head. "I don't believe this is anything self-inflicted. Ruis assures me our people are recovering, and I've checked a few myself. Being away from the ship helped them all, despite—despite what happened. They've hope, Sira." His eyes softened. "We do."

"Then what's stealing it?" I found the warmth of his hand, wrapped my numb fingers through his. *What's after us now?*

His fingers squeezed, hard. "After how far we've come, chit, whatever this is, we'll stop it."

My reply wedged itself in my throat as a yellow-haired child ran through the room, laughing and carefree. Andi'd known I'd *heard* a voice. She'd known and urged me to follow, to be with family. How?

There's no harm in her, Aryl sent gruffly.

"There could be answers." *Morgan.*

Understood. Another, gentler squeeze, then my hand was alone and cold. I kept my eyes on Andi, aware my Chosen watched her, too.

He'd do what I'd asked of him. Would learn what Andi could tell us and if we were wrong and that sweet innocent face was a lie?

Morgan would act as I, being a coward, could not imagine. All I could do was hope he'd be able to forgive me.

Andi stopped, ducking behind the nearest adult before peering around. At what? I turned with the rest to face the entrance.

A Hoveny child stood in the doorway, no taller than Andi, perhaps as young. She wore a green dress with yellow frills along the bottom and at the neck, and her long white hair was tied atop her head with a dark green bow. An old but serviceable tool belt was wrapped twice around her small waist, and from it hung an array of digging tools sized to her hands. Her feet were in rugged boots, caked with dust, and a dusty fabric bag bulged at her hip, suspended from a band crossing from shoulder to hip.

Seeming oblivious to the presence—and attention—of so many strangers, the child walked in, heading straight for the nearest food bin. The Hoveny beside it smiled down at her; the rest didn't appear to notice. She'd the run of the place, that told me.

Interesting.

The child wasn't the only arrival. Pauvan Di appeared next, entering with two other Hoveny. The three went directly to where Teris and Degal held their court and, after a brief exchange, the Councilors rose to their feet and followed the Hoveny out. Nik remained seated.

Like a grim shadow, Destin stayed by Teris' shoulder but once at the door, the Sona First Scout glanced back to where her Chosen lay, encased. Her head turned, her eyes on mine. Ah. She'd felt what I'd done.

We'll watch Elnu, I sent, tight and private. *Keep those two safe.*

I felt her *surprise* before she dampened it. Had Destin expected me to ask her to spy on our self-appointed leaders?

No need. I'd gladly leave administration and our settlement details to those who'd enjoyed both and weren't worrying about the dead.

Unless Degal was tempted to make his points with Power rather than words, but I doubted it. Very few Clan were as fond of their own voice as Degal di Sawnda'at. He'd talk my father into retreat.

Meanwhile, the child, a bag of crisps in her hand, wandered the large room. Maybe she was curious about this rearrangement of a familiar place, for the people in it didn't appear to matter as much as the chairs and couches they used. She ignored the Hoveny and when she came to any of us, regardless if that person smiled and greeted her, or not, she paused to stare a disquieting moment as though noticing them for the first time.

Done, she would dip her head and move on without a word.

Mute?

Hunting, suggested Aryl.

My Human chuckled. "Someone's noticed."

Andi followed the Hoveny at a small distance, miming her every movement. Dre joined the game. Their playmate dead within hours, the husk barely cool—their lack of grief seemed incomprehensible, even for children, and I shivered.

Morgan reached across the table, capturing my hand, sending *love* and *encouragement* through our link. *There's an explanation and we'll find it, together. That's what we do.*

My hair flowed down to wrap his wrist. *Yes, it is.* I sent my own *trust* and *love* back to him.

All at once, I realized we weren't alone.

Interlude

SUCH A SERIOUS FACE, the Hoveny child, and Morgan resisted his first impulse to smile. "I'm Jason," he told her.

The irises of her eyes were multihued, like several of the Om'ray, with light purple predominant. They stared at him, the pupils dilated as though to drink him in. Before he could feel uncomfortable, she shifted her earnest regard to Sira.

Who stared back, a hint of pink developing along her cheekbones. "I'm Sira. What's your name?"

The child's white eyebrows dipped together. She reached down to bring up her bag, wriggling out of the shoulder strap so she could put the shapeless and decidedly filthy thing on the table.

The bag moved.

A black claw, no larger than the tip of Morgan's little finger, poked from under the flap and waved.

"What is it?" Sira breathed.

Another claw appeared beside the first, then a cluster of three. They fiddled at the fastening of the bag, clicking with what seemed impatience. The child watched, so they did, fascinated.

Andi and Dre came to stand nearby, peering with interest. Their parents followed. Barac and Ruti. Until they were surrounded by curious Clan.

Morgan spared a glance up. No Hoveny adults.

Finally, claws succeeded. The flap gave way.

And out rolled a ball.

A hard segmented ball, the size of his joined fists, its pale surface painted with, yes, those were flowers, the sort a young child would draw—recognizable, if unlike any he'd seen. A kindred spirit, the Human decided, letting himself smile.

Losing his smile as the ball quivered, then unrolled, for he'd seen this shape before. *Tension* flowed from those around him, who had as well.

The tiny Oud spun about, its hundreds of little clawed feet tinkling like rain on the table, then stopped, one end aimed at the Hoveny child. Her lips puckered, then she sighed and spoke. "Nes name is Tap Tap."

The claws drummed a complex pattern.

"It's not nes full name," she corrected. "You know I can't say all that." This to the creature.

Morgan heard a stifled laugh.

"Hello, Tap Tap." Sira leaned forward. A red-gold lock of hair slipped along her arm to lie on the table, curling itself at the tip. She gave it a frustrated look but didn't object.

The tiny Oud reversed, then turned to "face" Sira. It moved toward her, then back, then forward, stopping a little closer before scuttling back. In this indecisive manner, it came within touching distance of the tip of hair.

And stopped.

A pet? Sira sent.

It spun in place, feet moving too quickly to make out, then stopped.

"I doubt it," Morgan said, carefully aloud.

The lock of hair slowly uncurled, a few strands brushing over the creature. "Oh," Sira exclaimed, pulling back.

The "oh" hadn't been alarmed or offended. Morgan stilled the motion of his wrist before the knife came free.

The tiny Oud lifted its front end, pulling up until almost erect. Exposed, its undersides were the typical Oud paired line of black specialized appendages, complete with the talking cluster near what they'd consider its "head," whatever that concept meant to the creature, only these appendages were miniaturized and delicately beautiful, like the inside of an antique clockwork he'd seen for sale on Plexis.

Appendages that began to move, producing clear, if faint, words. "Tap Tap, best is."

The Hoveny child rolled her eyes. "I told you."

"Milly Su, best is."

A smile, at last, on that too-serious face. "Thank you." Milly turned to Dre and Andi. "See? Ne's my best friend." Loftily. "I don't need any more."

"Milly, manners."

She inclined her head. "Sorry." A mumble.

Creating smiles. The innocent exchange had relaxed the adults on all sides, and Morgan didn't for an instant believe it an accident. Whatever they were dealing with, the Oud was definitely no pet.

Sira realized it, too. She leaned toward it again, offering her hand this time, palm up. "My name is Sira. I mean no harm."

It dropped to all feet and rushed with a cheerful clatter to climb on to her palm, coming erect again. "I am Tap Tap."

His Chosen bravely raised her hand, bringing the creature to eye level. "Where are we?"

Tiny appendages fussed, flowing up and down, then, one word.

"Home."

Challenge, assessment, or welcome? Sira's gray eyes lifted to his—no question, she'd know the options—then lowered. "We're glad to hear that. It's been a long and difficult journey."

"You are Sira Di." The Oud twisted, aiming the underside of its upper body at Morgan. "Jason Di. Heart-kin."

He felt the *tension* return. The creature had some Power, that was clear; Oud of any size who did were dangerous.

But Sira smiled as the Oud twisted back to her. "We are Chosen and Joined for life. You sense it, Tap Tap."

"I hear haisin. His, yours, theirs, nes, hers, all. Good. Better. Yours, best is. Home, yes yes." A pause, as if it considered what to say, then, "Founder, you, Sira Di."

The child gasped and covered her mouth with both hands, her rainbow eyes round as she stared at Sira.

And Morgan wasn't the least surprised to see a group of Hoveny adults heading their way.

Chapter 21

A SETUP. I eyed the Oud, which had, as far as I could tell, no eyes at all, and wondered if it was worth asking if the creature had summoned the Hoveny, or if our hosts had added surveillance to this room as part of our welcome.

Didn't matter. They'd neatly discovered what we'd thought we had to keep secret: that we'd greater Power—haisin, as the little being called it. So much for my worry about the vulnerability of weaker minds. You think I'd have learned from the Drapsk. Technology—or the right help—was more than a match for our avowed Talent.

"What is a 'Founder?'" I asked Tap Tap. It had better not be like a Keeper, or I was going to protest, loudly. For what good it would do. If I were wise, I'd cultivate a certain fatalism when it came to our new "home" and my place in it.

Appendages fluttered. "Here is where the Founder lived, the first, the best was. Yes yes yes."

"Is claimed to have lived. That's up to our Seesor, Tap Tap." Pauvan was among those Hoveny who'd arrived, the Clan making an aisle for them to approach our table.

The tiny Oud dropped down on my hand and wrist, as if to prove it would say nothing more.

Its clawed feet prickled, though less than the hooklike fabric of the cloaks of the giant version. I couldn't say if it were cold or warm—and neither "it" or "he" was right. What had Milly used? "Nes?" My hair was fascinated with it, locks tumbling over my shoulders to reach but not quite touch again.

When the stuff had met the Oud, there'd been a not-unpleasant tingle, followed by a confused burst of images and words. Shocking, but I hadn't been alarmed, for with the tangle came *hope*.

The rest was a message, still sorting itself into sense within my mind. The images were colorless and skewed; the words lumped together as though overheard or recorded. They'd gained a sequence: a pillar twin to *Sona*'s access portal, surrounded by stone and shadow; *Confirmation request. Identification: Cersi-So;* a streak of light across darkness, perhaps a night sky; again the pillar; *the gate to futures past.*

With a final image, not least: a city of buildings like the ones here, gleaming in the sun.

I'd shared the message with Morgan and Aryl. He was intrigued; my great-grandmother perturbed by the *feel* of Oud and wary. Their reactions encompassed my own. The ship's transmission had been received, that much was clear. But a gate?

Pauvan inclined his head. "The Seesor would like to meet with you, Sira Di."

Tap Tap spun about and flowed from my hand, diving end first back into the fabric bag. I rose to my feet, eager for some answers.

Morgan rose, too, his intention plain.

The Hoveny glanced at him, then to me. "With you only, Sira Di," he emphasized. "You and Jason Di will remain in communication. I give my personal oath we will not interfere with your haisin."

Implying they could interfere—unless it was a bluff. Even if true, I refused to believe they knew the extent of our capabilities. As for my Human's? So far, the pack under the table hadn't seemed to interest them. Their mistake.

Of course, they could know exactly what was in it and not care. That'd be disturbing.

"I'll come," I said, fingers moving in the signal for "remain here." Usually one Morgan sent me, the occasional negotiation being outside my—

What mattered was he stay: to watch our people; to find a way to question Andi. Not to mention our wounded. I looked meaningfully toward the cots. What we could do if a transport came to move them I didn't know, but if Morgan had to go along?

I'd follow.

A barely perceptible nod relieved those concerns. Not happy, my Chosen, but he understood.

"This way, please."

Milly reached for the bag. Instead of picking it up, she pushed it toward me. "You're to carry ner."

There being no polite way to refuse, I picked up the bag of Oud, tucking it in the crook of my elbow. Aryl retreated to the limit of my awareness; being the more cautious of us. My hair, of course, took advantage of proximity to drape itself over the bag.

"My mother's hair can move," Milly informed me, "but she doesn't let it. When I'm old, I won't let mine move either."

My hair gave a shiver. Take that, I thought at it, not that it ever listened.

Pauvan led, and I followed with the Oud and child, the remaining Hoveny falling in behind as escort. I brushed fingers with the Clan I passed, offering *reassurance* with the Power I no longer bothered to hide.

Each time, feeling the strange little Oud quiver.

Interlude

"WHERE ARE THEY TAKING SIRA?"

As if anyone could take his cousin anywhere she didn't want to go. More telling, Barac judged, was the Human's willingness to stay behind. Still, Ruti's concern was a good sign—the first in too long. "To see Alisi, the person in charge. Maybe," he dared a small smile, "she's had enough of Degal."

There, a tiny dimple. "Good luck with that."

Encouraged, the Clansman edged closer. What he'd hoped to be a subtle move was broadcast by a dismaying squeak heard by at least five others, not to mention a sag and bounce from the ridiculous inflated couch.

But the dimple deepened, and Ruti leaned his way. Barac's relief lasted as long as it took her small palm to plant firmly on his chest, holding him where he was. "We need to talk."

He composed himself. *Anything, Beloved.*

She settled, hands together on her lap, then said as if it were the most ordinary request possible, "I want to go home."

Had he heard right? Barac ventured carefully, "We'll have homes soon—"

"Not here," with a disarming chuckle. "Home, Barac. Our home. We'll visit Acranam, of course, but then we'll need to get back to Plexis—Huido's counting on me to be his new chef and you'll be wonderful as host."

Instinct kept him still and quiet, when what Barac wanted to do was grab hold and shake sense from her. No, better to send, now, for Jacqui, their Birth Watcher. No, Ruis—Morgan—

Ruti's dark lovely eyes searched his, her hair twining up his arm. "I'm not mad or delusional," she told him quietly. "I'm aware, as I've never been. We don't belong here. We have a home. We have so many people who love us." Her full bottom lip trembled. "So many I thought I'd lost forever. And you. Don't you want to be with your brother again? Your mother—?"

"They're dead," he said, his voice strange to his own ears.

Her gentle smile was betrayal. "That doesn't matter anymore."

Barac found himself on his feet, gasping for breath. Before anyone could react, he dropped to his knees before his Chosen. "Ruti—" *Don't. Please don't* listen. *The dead are gone. The past. We have to think of the future. Our daughter.*

"Oh," a sigh. "I'm sorry, Barac. I thought you were ready." She bent to press her lips against his forehead. *We won't go without you, I promise.*

Barac buried his face between Ruti's soft full breasts, and didn't ask where.

In case she told him.

Chapter 22

WE DIDN'T GO FAR, walking past the parked vehicles to enter the other large "tent." Walls divided the interior, creating a central corridor, with panels hung from metal rails across the openings to rooms. Some were rolled aside, allowing light and sound to spill into the hall; others closed. Milly skipped ahead to slide open a panel and disappear inside.

"This way, Sira Di," Pauvan put his hand on the panel closest him, the first in the tent, and rolled it aside. "Alisi, our visitor is here." He gestured for me to enter, closing the panel behind me.

I'd expected to join the three who'd already been summoned. Instead, I found myself in a small office, its walls lined with open bins of rock bits and the floor cluttered with larger ones so I had to tiptoe between them to the empty stool.

A female Hoveny sat on another, her back to me as she examined something on a table through a large lens. She raised an absent hand in the universal "give me a moment" signal, so I took my seat and waited.

Her white hair was confined in a series of snug black bands, but I hadn't needed the clue. I'd been exploring with my inner sense since entering the tent, finding the bond between this Hoveny and Pauvan, along with a second, stronger, to Milly. This was the child's mother.

And the leader here, Site Seesor Alisi Di, the one whose Power I'd sensed earlier.

Like the others, she wore a brown padded jacket, but hers was snug at waist and reinforced with heavier material across the shoulders. The jacket sleeves ended just below her elbows, her slender wrists covered by tight cuffs that either were part of another garment beneath, or protective bands. Brown pants completed an outfit designed for hard use, tucked into black boots with the tops rolled down. One boot was propped on a convenient rock sample. She'd a device strapped to one leg and another to her arm.

In contrast, I and most of the Clan wore torn, now-flimsy seeming ship's coveralls and slippers. I decided to ask the Hoveny if they'd clothing to spare; a request to leave until I knew why I sat here, with a bag of Oud.

I rested the bag on my lap, unopened. Tap Tap could come out if it chose—I wasn't inviting it to the meeting.

With a satisfied murmur, Alisi turned off the light she'd been using and turned on her stool to face me.

She had her daughter's rainbow eyes, though her irises were more yellow than mauve, giving them a glow. Unlike the other Hoveny I'd seen, her cheeks and chin were round, both liberally covered with tan freckles, as was her broad forehead and short nose.

She folded her hands neatly, as though to prevent them moving without permission, her features composed. Like my Human, I decided, showing only what he wanted. If the Hoveny governed their faces, odds were they read facial expressions the Clan, reliant on their inner sense, would miss.

"Greetings, Sira Di. My name is Alisi Di," she said in a surprisingly low voice, nodding her head in their version of a bow. "I'm the seesor appointed to this project." She stood and held out her hand. "Welcome."

I rose to take it in mine, shifting the bag under one arm. "We're glad to be here. Thank you for your help."

She had a warm, strong grip and, like most of the other Hoveny, no shields. I felt *curiosity* and *goodwill.*

Along with a significant and recent *frustration*. While her thoughts were too deep to reach without an effort I wouldn't make, I could make an educated guess. Degal and Teris.

Acting on instinct, I lowered my own shields, just enough to let something of me pass to her. *Gratitude. Determination.* Above all, *hope.*

Alisi's fingers tightened before letting go, the hint of a smile warming her face. "Welcome, Sira," she repeated. "Please, sit."

I settled the bag back on my lap; her gaze touched on it, then returned to me. "Your leaders were unwilling to answer my questions, though not to make demands."

"Degal and Teris are concerned for our future," I replied, choosing diplomacy. I'd knock their heads together later. "I apologize if they offended you, Alisi Di, but it's been a difficult journey. Many of my people are fearful of strangers."

"And we are strange to you, aren't we?" Her expression lightened. "There's no need to apologize, Sira. I've put your leaders with my staff, who are making lists I'm sure will prove useful. That is not my role here and now, nor yours."

The bag squirmed. I wanted to do the same, but held still. "And that is?"

"A seesor judges the validity of claims brought before them. Before you arrived, I was investigating one concerning the building you saw when you arrived, a claim that, if true, would not only halt construction of this irrigation tunnel, but begin a major research project. I was studying these." Alisi lifted her hand, indicating the rocks. "I now have a new claim to judge, one of import not only to this small part of Brightfall, but the entire System Cooperative."

The world beneath my feet had a name—a name and was part of something bigger—which was enough to make my heart pound wildly in my chest, were it not for the rest, which made it want to stop.

"You mean us."

"I mean you, Sira Di, and the claim made by my colleague in front of witnesses."

"That I'm a 'Founder?'" We'd appeared out of thin air on her landscape, arrived bleeding on her doorstep after riding giant Oud, and one word from Tap Tap was more important? I'd no problem looking shocked. I was. "I don't even know what that is."

"Then you're alone." Alisi's face lost expression, becoming guarded. "We know what you are. The edicans analyzed your wounded during their treatment—at my order. Hoveny, yes, but without contact with those like us for generations. Together with the rare traits common among you, the lack of neuters, your speech, and where you arrived?" Her hand rose. "I am in no doubt. The Twelve left this system. You are their descendants, returned home. To this I, Alisi Di, Seesor, set my seal."

Rote, those words; I'd a feeling they were spoken for other ears than mine.

We'd assumed—naïvely, it seemed—our origin would be the hard part to explain. I wished I believed her calm acceptance was a good thing. "We're from a planet called Cersi," I said. "We hope we've come home. We need to have come home, Alisi Di. My people are battered. Exhausted. I want to tell them they're safe."

Her eyes flickered at "Cersi," then narrowed. "They are safe," with reassuring firmness. "I've sent for those who can arrange housing and whatever else you may need. The calamity with the Field Oud will be investigated, I promise. Bringing me back to you."

And this Founder claim of the Oud. "What do you think I am?" I asked cautiously.

"A demonstration, if you'll indulge me." Alisi swung around on her stool, grabbed a small rock at seeming random, then spun back to hand it to me. "Tell me what you see."

I took it gingerly. "A rock." Another twitch on my lap. I shrugged. "It looks like the rest here and outside." I went to give it back to her.

"Look without your eyes. With your haisin."

At a rock? I'd half-expected the seesor to produce a Hoveny artifact and ask me to connect it to the null-grid. Hadn't that been the point of Cersi—of all this?

They may not know. It's easier to hide an intention than starships, chit. Morgan, following my thoughts. *If Cersi's experiment was kept secret . . .*

He left me to imagine the consequences. I tried not to, well aware of groups who did in secret what wouldn't be allowed otherwise, seeking gain at the expense of others. What we'd hoped would be our currency here? It could taint us instead.

We need to learn all we can.

Good advice.

"Sira?"

Look at a rock. Seemed harmless enough. I closed my eyes and opened my awareness to the M'hir.

I wasn't alone. Though weaker, Alisi had *presence* here, her light faint but steady, yet bound only to her family.

Brighter—crimson. Another light *darted* past, as strange as it was a surprise. *Tap Tap?*

Here here! Good good. Sira—Sira BEST IS!

Wonderful. I focused on the rock, or rather the feel of *solid* between my hands, expecting nothing.

Finding a door.

Interlude

BETWEEN—*cracked*—and a flaw appeared in AllThereIs. Too small to see.

Too vast to ignore.

The Watchers *stirred,* alarmed. Sped forth in answer. Defend. Defy!

The one closest was already there. She refined her *attention.* Drew herself closer—closer.

Saw the flaw defined by *light.*

Tasted *surprise.* Experienced *awareness.*

Grasped—

Identity.

—and paused.

Chapter 23

I'D DROPPED the bag and thrown the rock before I realized I was in motion, scrabbling across the floor on my hands and knees. The bag spilled a ball of Oud that kept rolling.

I forced myself to stop. "What was that?" If my voice was hoarse and shook, well, I think I deserved it. What I'd seen in the M'hir—

What had seen me—

Sira?!

I'll tell you later, I promised, sending *reassurance* to Aryl as well. Later being when I wasn't on the floor and terrified. Had that blur—had I seen a Watcher?

Unfair! *Hearing* the things was enough for a lifetime.

"I don't know what it is, Sira. I'd hoped you'd know." Alisi retrieved the rock, putting it back on its shelf, and nudged Tap Tap from under the table with a toe. "Here. Easy." She helped me stand. Once we were both convinced I could, she guided me back to my stool.

The stool tried to tip. I planted both feet firmly on the floor. "I've never experienced anything like that before." And fervently hoped never to again.

Nor have I, Great-granddaughter. Be wary.

"I'm sorry it was unpleasant, Sira." Alisi sat, hands in her lap, a wistful look on her face. "I'll admit I'm grateful you experienced something. I can tell it's not just rock. That it has a connection elsewhere. But I haven't the haisin to learn more—and I've been afraid to speak of it, even to my heart-kin. There's a myth about the rock that buries our past. A dreadful one."

Morgan valued local legend and myth, gathering such stories wherever we stopped to trade. They told, he'd assert, more about a species than all the datacubes he could buy.

I wasn't at all sure I wanted to hear one about that rock, but he was *listening,* as was Aryl. It'd be his first from this new world; the notion pleased me. "What's the myth?"

Alisi moved her hand as though wiping something away, the first such gesture I'd seen them use. "What matters is you, Sira, and that you were able to see something of its secrets. I must explain about the Founder, first—how much do you know of our past? About the Concentrix?"

Not enough, I thought, by far. "Only that the Concentrix included vast numbers of systems and species as well as the Hoveny." The positive. In that much, I continued, "And it ended—abruptly. I don't know why."

"To this arn, 'why' remains a mystery, Sira, though anyone you ask has their favorite theory." Her eyes clouded. "How it ended— that we do know. The Fall, we call it, when what our ancestors had built and shared across their empire stopped working. All at once, everywhere. Because their power source—what we'd given to our partners, freely—was gone."

The null-grid. We'd been right. I felt a pang of sympathy for those earnest researchers—past, present, and future—poring over Hoveny relics for an answer they weren't equipped to find. "And the Founder?"

"The Hoveny who discovered the null-grid and trained others to harness it. Ne died after the Fall, driven mad by guilt. Before the end, the Founder destroyed nes notes, telling nes staff the dead were calling ner home."

A Hoveny, the null-grid, now the dead. I went cold. *Morgan—*

I heard. We need more, chit. What happened to the rest of the Hoveny who used the null-grid? Those not in this system?

I didn't want to know. What I wanted counted as much as a single Retian egg in the swamp.

"What about the rest?" I said aloud, feeling my way. "What did they do after the Fall?"

"We're taught," and oh, the delicate emphasis on the word, "our ancestors everywhere buried their useless cities along with the technology that failed us, as they did here, on Brightfall. To reclaim their worlds. To forget. Those outside our home system? We're taught they made new, better lives for themselves where they were, but few believe. There's been no communication with Hoveny from outside this system since the Fall. Until you."

Because there were no Hoveny outside this system, I thought sadly, other than the Clan.

No need to tell them what they already know, Witchling, Morgan sent, his mindvoice gentle.

Even if these Hoveny comprehended they—we, I corrected—were the last of our kind, they were no closer to understanding why, I decided, than the researchers of the First or the Trade Pact.

A soft click drew my attention from the past to the floor. Unrolled, Tap Tap stood between us, dwarfed by the rocks around it. "Taught a lie. Bad."

Alisi frowned at it. "It's the prevailing theory. We've few reliable records during the Fall itself—there was chaos."

The tiny creature scurried up a pointed rock, swaying as it rose to speak. "'And the land shamed by the Hoveny became as Night Water and all sank within it.' After, rock. No more Hoveny works. No more empire. No more Hoveny. True yes?"

If this was the myth Alisi meant, it was a terrible one indeed.

Sira. "Night Water" could be the M'hir.

Aryl could be right; the wording was as good a description as any I'd heard. Had the null-grid somehow escaped the Hoveny's devices, engulfing what was around it before returning where it belonged?

Had that happened to *Sona?*

If I could have thought of an excuse, I'd have fled this room of unreliable rocks and too-eloquent Oud.

"Excuse our Oud-Key, Sira. Ne quotes scripture from our neighbors—a fringe sect—" Alisi paused, tilting her head as she studied the creature. "—yet ne does nothing without reason." Almost to herself, "The Sect of the Rebirth is one of those who brought forth the claim that this building once housed the Founder, a claim I know you support." Her voice became stern. "Tap Tap, I ask now as Seesor. What does the sect have to do with your claim that Sira Di is a Founder?"

I felt a *trill,* as though tiny claws strummed the M'hir like an instrument. "The sect can test the truth. Who is Founder. They can prove yes. Prove no. Better. Best is."

Was this what I'd been waiting for? A chance to show this world our value, by reconnecting the null-grid to a device? What else might it do—the possibilities were breathtaking. But first. "You're one of them," I stated. The message. The image of a pillar. "You received our ship's transmission."

"Not the only ones to hear Cersi-So." Tap Tap gave a twist and leaped from the rock to the floor, spinning in agitation before rising to speak. "Not the only ones to come here. Sira should go to sect. Now. Best is."

"Why?" Alisi demanded. "What's going on?"

The tiny being went still, only its speaking appendages in motion. "Not all want another Founder. Those who do, not all want the same."

Interlude

WHATEVER NEW ODDITY Sira had encountered in the M'hir, Morgan judged, had to wait on the rest. Once she'd regained her composure, she'd pushed him, gently, from her surface thoughts, newly cautious of Tap Tap.

Who'd turned out to be a living sensor called an Oud-Key, and part of a Hoveny religious sect. Fascinating. Brightfall. The System Cooperative. Sects, governments, justice systems, secrets. Their new home promised to be as complicated as any segment of the Trade Pact, the Human thought with growing satisfaction. Complicated allowed for adjustment and change. Complicated, in his experience, meant opportunity.

If you survived the stage where you hadn't a clue and decisions had to be made based on fragments of information, none of it guaranteed to be reliable or complete. Had a great deal in common with flying a starship made of used parts, that did.

He'd done both. Would do this. Sira had found an excellent resource in the Seesor, Alisi Di.

Morgan had an idea where to find one of his own.

"What's the play?" Barac kept his back to their quarry.

Pauvan Di had returned after taking Sira to her meeting with his heart-kin. Information of value. Also of value, he was responsible for the care of the new arrivals, by assignment or choice.

The others went to him. He was the only one Morgan had seen giving orders or suggestions.

And the Human liked him. He liked several of the Hoveny. Instinctive, that snap judgment. Potentially misleading, given these weren't his species—

Such judgments hadn't failed him yet. "I'll get him alone. You keep watch in here. Make sure no one follows us."

The Clansman nodded. He glanced at the rows of cocoons. "Their Healers aren't happy. Did you notice?"

"Hard to miss," Morgan agreed. Aracel Dis had received a messenger. Afterward, she and the other edicans had clustered, talking in low voices, then she'd sent one to stand by the door. That edican had leaped at Pauvan the moment he'd arrived, drawing him over to converse, heatedly, with the rest.

Another reason to talk to him. "We don't know how remote this area may be. Transport might be more of an issue than they'd like. Keep me posted, if you see anything change."

"How do I tell? I *taste* it all the time." Flat, almost lifeless. "Don't you?"

No, but if the Clansman did, it was family. Morgan gripped Barac's wrist, hiding the contact with his body. *Tell me.*

Ruti. With an undertone of *despair* so dark the Human hurried to block it from his Chosen. *What you just told me, about the dead, about them—something using them—trying to lure us to our deaths. It's happening to her. Morgan, she has so many dead.*

Gods, no.

Jason, what's wrong?

So much for the effort. *Ruti's hearing the dead.*

And if he'd been afraid before, it was nothing to the *anguish* and *FEAR* that seared along their link—

—before Sira locked it away to protect him. *We can't lose them,* with utter calm.

Knowing they could. *We'll do whatever it takes,* he vowed, feeling his Chosen's *agreement* as she withdrew.

Morgan looked at Barac. *Has Ruti tried to leave?*

We'd be dead if she had. The Clansman turned his wrist. Morgan released him. *She promised not to go without me,* grim and full of pain. *Morgan, we have to keep her away from Andi. The things that child says—believes—it's making Ruti worse.* "I don't blame the child," the First Scout said aloud. "She doesn't understand."

Or understood too well, Morgan thought. "Andi's with her parents at the moment." He'd shamelessly made up a story about Hoveny culture and foreign children; Nik and Josa, already anxious, had been willing to sit on their daughter if necessary.

Unfortunately, they weren't willing to have him question the child. Yet.

In the meantime, if all else failed, well, he'd tranks in his pack; no solution, but if it saved lives—especially these— "Barac?"

The other grimaced. "If you say we should have taken our chances with the Assemblers, I'll have to hit you."

"I'd let you." He met the other's troubled gaze, held it. "Trust your Chosen. Tell Ruti what I've told you, that these voices are like the lights of Nightsfire: bait in a trap. Tell her she's the only one who can keep you and your baby safe. It's up to her to protect her family."

"Why that's—" Almost a smile. "Sly as a Scat, you are," Barac said with sincere affection. "I should warn my cousin."

"She knows." Morgan clapped the other on a shoulder, uncaring what Hoveny or Clan thought of such a Human gesture. "We've a shiny new planet, Barac. It's time we stopped looking back."

The view ahead being the one they could change.

"Human."

"'Hu-man.' Human." Pauvan had a contagious smile. "And this?" He stroked his own smooth chin, raising a brow.

"A beard." Morgan dug his fingers in, gave the stuff a tug. "Adult Human males grow facial hair; our females don't." No point mentioning how quirks of style occasionally put beards on feminine faces—or any body part. He had the opening he'd been after since they'd come outside. "Your turn. The Hoveny. He, she, and—?" A suggestive tap near the comlink resting on the vehicle roof.

The Hoveny was a tech specialist, judging by the sparkle in his eyes when Morgan had offered him a chance to see some "alien" versions. No fool, either. When the Human had suggested they step outside, Pauvan had assigned one of his fellows to stay by the door. Perhaps to signal if something went awry inside.

Perhaps to come to his aid if this stranger proved dangerous. Morgan approved of caution—especially in someone who might be a friend.

Wasn't yet.

His pack, weathered as it was by hard use and time, had several virtues: scan-proof—at least by routine Trade Pact tech; waterproof—he'd used it on Karolus to make a river crossing. Tough—buried for safekeeping, it had rebuffed the efforts of a narbear to rip it open, though he'd had to track the creature to its den to retrieve his property.

Best of all, the pack could be opened in a variety of ways, each without revealing the others, or what he wasn't prepared to share. Anyone who managed to slice it open?

Well, if they didn't do it in a vacuum, or wearing protection, he was hardly responsible for what they'd release from the lining.

He'd shown Pauvan his bioscanner and lens, drawing those from pockets in his vest. His coat was in the pack where it mightn't be noticed. The comlink and ensuing vocabulary game had come next.

White eyebrows climbed. "So it's true? No neuter among these people, despite their being Hoveny?"

Human gender, despite what some aliens thought, was a spectrum. Someone had made very sure it wasn't among the Om'ray, and so the Clan, a design intended to produce breeding pairs. Hindsight, Morgan reminded himself, wasn't what he needed. "Not to my knowledge," he said, picking his words with care. "Not to theirs." Sometimes you gave a little. "You aren't what we expected." And asked, without asking.

"You surprise us, too," came the answer. "It's not my place to question you, Jason Di, but I am curious how you arrived without any warning from the Hub, the System Comm—they oversee all travel within the system."

Fair enough. "My guess is we surprised them, too," Morgan said easily. "Our ship was programmed to bring us here but didn't land. We dropped to the surface in lifepods that disintegrated soon after. I salvaged these." He brought out the glove, tapping pod flakes into his palm where they gleamed like dark glass, and held out his hand. "You're welcome to analyze them."

Pauvan gave them a hungry look, but repeated, "It's not my place. Keep them safe."

Interesting. Morgan nodded, replacing the samples and tucking away the glove. Time to push. "So someone's coming to take charge of us. That's why our wounded are still here."

"I cannot say."

He'd take that as a yes.

The Hoveny controlled their expressions; some more effectively than others, all better than any Clan. Didn't matter. They'd each their giveaways: a flicker of the eyelid, tightening of a lip, a shift in body posture. The Human could read faces far more alien than these and, unlike his Chosen, he'd no compunction using his Talent to sniff out any emotions their hosts let slip.

Whomever was coming made Pauvan Di anxious. No, it was more than that. What Morgan sensed was frustrated, almost righteous, anger. Pauvan didn't approve of those coming to take over—and felt powerless to do anything about it.

Not good. Still, it told him he'd been right about this Hoveny. The Human smiled and held out his hand. "Whatever happens next, we've you to thank for our rescue."

Pauvan gripped it, *relief* flowing across the contact. "And I am grateful to meet you, Jason Morgan Di. Human with a beard. Who else can say that, on Brightfall?"

He laughed. "You're the first." Morgan waved at his comlink. "Those neuter pronouns?"

The Hoveny bent over the device, enunciating carefully: "She, he, *ne*. Her, him, *ner*. Hers, his, *nes*." He straightened. "Use the neuter if you're in doubt. It's a compliment."

"Most appreciated." Morgan put the 'link in his pocket.

Leaning against the side of the vehicle, Pauvan pulled a small flask from his tunic. "In honor of new words for us both."

Tipping his head back, he squeezed a stream of amber liquid into his open mouth. He swallowed and smacked his lips before handing the flask to the Human.

Morgan took a sniff of the smoky stuff, eyebrows rising in appreciation. "Much as I'd like to join you," he said ruefully, returning the flask, "different biology. Another time—when I've learned what's safe for me." He leaned companionably next to the other. Sunlight filled the tunnel entrance, stroking shadow along the curves of the ancient Hoveny building. The breeze brought the tantalizing scent of growing things and soil. If he'd thought for an instant their hosts would allow it, he'd have walked outside.

With Sira.

"Another time. For now, this is for you, Jason Di." The Hoveny squeezed another drink for himself, with a relish the Human envied, then put away the flask. "What else should I tell you?" A moment's pause. "We're born with gender or without. Either can have heart-kin; some are solitary, by choice or lack of haisin. You will hear 'dis' as part of their names. Di, for one heart-kin. Din, more than one. Su, those who have yet to find such a connection."

How Hoveny had evolved, a revelation of their true nature with, Morgan thought, dishearteningly few points of correspondence to present-day Clan. What about Choosers, driven by the Power-of-Choice clinging to them in the M'hir? Not only those pacing the tent, but those who'd grow up with that same instinct?

One hurdle at a time, Morgan told himself.

"We're given private names at birth." Pauvan chuckled. "Very long and complicated names, Jason, and no one bothers with them other than in government records, though some attempt to sing them at special occasions. Normally, we use the shortest unique plus our avowed status. I am Pauvanal when my cousin Pauvanor visits; we are both Pauvan when apart." A sideways look. "Which brings me to the extra names your people gave us. Teerac. Parth. Uruus. Sawnda'at. Why?"

He'd bite. "What do you mean?"

"Those aren't names. Not here. Not for people. Excuse me if I'm too curious," the Hoveny added quickly. "But anyone with an interest in history would notice."

Morgan went still. "If they aren't names, what are they?"

"Worlds. Worlds within the Concentrix, before the Fall."

The past lived here, ripping its claws into the Clan and what they were. The Human kept his face set to neutral interest; inwardly, his mind raced. Understandable, that Cersi's experiment would have needed a way to identify founding pairs, to permit lineage to be followed and traced.

But to use lost worlds? It reeked of hubris—and ambition. The more he learned of those behind all this, the less he liked.

"Those are the only names they have," he said bluntly. "I'd be grateful if you kept this between us, until I can tell them the source. They've arrived with so little. It'll be—" devastating, to both Om'ray and M'hiray. He settled for, "—hard, to lose what they thought they knew of their family history."

"It's not my place to ask what happened, Jason Di." Pauvan paused, then went on in an earnest tone. "The edicans can test for heritage; we've such records back to the Fall. Your people will find family here. And heart-kin."

He couldn't promise that family would be willing or interested in such strange new members. Still, the overture was another kindness from this Hoveny, who'd shown sincere concern for the Clan.

That meant something, to his Human sensibilities. Maybe it would to Clan; maybe not. But he'd a stake in this new relationship, too, and Morgan could feel it going wrong. They were being too cautious, parading the Clan as returned Hoveny, with quaint accents and meaningless names. They weren't the same, and those differences either came out now, among well-intended individuals, or later.

Which could be disaster.

He faced Pauvan, weighing where to start.

"Such a face," the Hoveny said, sounding amused. "Are you sure?" He shook the flask suggestively.

Sure? He was. "There are things I have to tell you, too, and one is urgent. What's arrived on your doorstep are the descendants of Hoveny selected for their Power—their haisin. Their memories were altered and biology changed, making them perfect breeding stock. They were left on Cersi as an experiment."

Pauvan looked dumbfounded. "What? I—I don't understand—the Twelve left Brightfall to find other civilizations. To restore the Concentrix."

"A lie. The Twelve went to Cersi. One ship made it back, with us. You have proof," Morgan pointed at the tent. "The Oud measured us. I'm sure it told you the Clan have more haisin than any Hoveny and believe me, they know how to use it in ways you can't imagine. They have no neuter, only male and female. Before they can mature, their females must form a permanent bond—"

The Hoveny drew himself up. Thrust a hand between them, making a sharp wiping motion. Not for discussion, that said.

Too bad. "—A bond with a male, their Chosen." Morgan touched the side of his head. "As Sira Joined with me. We aren't heart-kin, my friend. We are one for life and will die together."

"Only a mother and child may have such a bond." Red stained Pauvan's cheekbones and his hand flashed again. "Between adults is unacceptable! Dangerous to both—rightly discouraged! Don't say this to anyone else."

The protest felt personal. "You know how it feels to be Chosen, don't you? Sira said your link with Alisi was—"

A hand shot out, gripped his arm. "Do not speak of this," in an urgent whisper. "I beg—"

The sun went out.

Lights snapped on to compensate, unseen engines giving a deep whine.

Pauvan looked over Morgan's head, his eyes widening. "We must go back inside, with the others." The grip became a pull. "They're here."

Morgan glanced over his shoulder. The tunnel entrance was now blocked by a transport as similar to the vehicles around him as a starship was to a groundcar. Its massive rear door dropped open with a clank that echoed in the tunnel.

"Then we're out of time." Morgan pressed his free hand to the other's forehead.

And entered Pauvan's mind.

Chapter 24

A LISI SURGED to her feet. "What's he doing?!"

Being reckless? Not that either of the pair had the ability to touch Morgan's thoughts or mind, but, like Aryl, I reserved judgment about the Oud-Key. "Morgan has things to say to your Chosen," I used the word to shock her into paying attention.

It worked, though her nostrils flared and there was emotion aplenty on her face now. "And this is how? By forcing himself into Pauvan's mind?"

"Morgan's decided to trust you. Someone's come for us. From what you've just told me—both of you—that may not be a good thing."

Nor was the news about Ruti—I pushed it back to simmer with the rest of my nightmares. No one was going to die today. Not if I could help it.

"You arrive on our world, you abide by our rules," Alisi said frigidly. "What's coming is authority, System authority, and what happens next is up to them, not us and not you."

Such appalling innocence. I could snatch her memories of any place she'd been and 'port there. Could seize control of her mind—have her say or do whatever was to our benefit. Could—

My hair whipped around my shoulders, and I watched the Hoveny's scorn turn to something else.

Fear.

Sira. Have a care.

Great-grandmother. I clenched my fists, fought for control, and was startled by a light drumming on my ankle. I looked down at the Oud.

"This is not why you've come, Founder."

"No," I agreed, and sighed. "Sit, Alisi." My hair subsided, ends moving in slow, sullen waves. I was no happier, but Alisi wasn't an enemy.

She could be a friend.

"Morgan's sharing who and what we are with your Chosen," I said, fully aware of one side of that forced conversation. "That information is yours, too. Digest it, quickly. We don't have much time."

Alisi remained standing, her hands together as if to deny me, but I sensed the inner concentration signifying her *reach* to her Chosen, Pauvan. I waited.

Her face remained set, but emotions flooded from her in waves: *Revulsion. Horror. Indignation.*

Curiosity.

Finally, as her eyes refocused on me, *astonishment.* "You." With awe.

Morgan—

I only told them what they needed to know, chit. Unrepentant, that was.

We'd talk later.

I didn't doubt his decision: before we asked for help, they needed to know about Cersi and the experiment. My ever-cautious Chosen had provided enough, I hoped, to enlist this pair on our side. "You know what we are," I began, though I continued to wonder myself. Were we heroes, returning home with treasure?

Or monsters, carrying our dead.

"I know what your Morgan cared to tell us." Alisi's gaze sharpened. "You want us to believe the null-grid has something to do with haisin."

"It does! It does. The sect knows," Tap Tap insisted, limbs

churning. "Sira must go to them. You, Seesor, must go. Prove my claim. Brightfall will have Founder, best is! Brightfall again Hoveny Prime. Best best best!"

We'd moments, if lucky, before those who'd arrived in a machine able to impress even Morgan took charge. No question they'd move us. We'd lose what we'd found here. I looked at Alisi. "This is your world. What do you want?"

"Ne is clever," she admitted. "A seesor's right to assess information pertinent to a claim supersedes all others. No matter who the government has sent, I can insist you be tested by the sect. As Seesor, my responsibility is to the truth." Rainbow eyes studied me. "It is not my place to withhold it."

"You think others might?" We'd no markers yet, no guides other than these Hoveny. And one Oud.

A shoulder rose and fell. "I don't know why they would. If you are a Founder, it will be remarkable, stunning news, certain to arouse controversy as much as excitement. But Brightfall won't change all at once. How can it? Restoring the null-grid as a power source only matters if there's something to use it—and there's precious little left pre-Fall. Scholars and collectors compete for intact pieces. I assume the sect has some."

As did we. Morgan's foresight never ceased to amaze me.

What's the plan, chit?

An instant before, I'd felt how easy it might be to go over that line, to push these people in a direction of my choosing, for my reasons. *Up to them,* I told my Chosen. As it must be. Feeling Aryl's *agreement,* I stood. "We are in your hands, Seesor Alisi Di."

The tiny Oud dropped to its myriad feet and began to dance in dizzying circles.

Alisi came close to smiling. "Come with me, Sira, quickly."

I followed her from her office, Tap Tap speeding ahead. Instead of leaving the tent, we turned left, going to the door the child had picked. I'd an instant to realize we'd entered their personal quarters before Alisi threw open a cupboard. "If I'm taking you to the Sanctum, you'll need clothes."

I was shorter than Alisi; wider at breast and hip. A belt helped the roomy pants stay put; fortunately, the hems rolled. The under shirt felt like being hugged by a Carasian but the tuniclike jacket, Alisi's, fit as though made for me. I put my well-traveled bracelet over the cuff and admired my new boots: Milly's. My toes hardly bent at all.

Hopefully, there'd be no long walks ahead. As for Milly, she didn't appear to notice either boots or my presence. When we'd arrived, she'd been sitting on the floor, staring into a tank empty except for a few nondescript pebbles the size of my thumbtip. She hadn't budged. Tap Tap crouched beside her, occasionally touching a limb to the glass as though making sure it was intact.

"Your communicator," Alisi told me. The device slipped into a holster strapped to my left thigh. "I can show you how to use it later. Not that you need it, Sira Di." She winked at me conspiratorially. While it was nice to see we'd winking in common, the reason disturbed me.

Were those with enough "haisin" to speak mind-to-mind so rare in her life? A question—and potential problem—for much later.

"I know how." Milly looked up. "I can show Sira."

"There's no time, my sweet. Finish what you're doing."

I couldn't help myself. "What are you doing, Milly?" But she'd resumed staring into the tank and didn't answer.

"Our daughter exposes Tap Tap's progeny to her haisin," Alisi explained, her pride evident. "It is quite an honor, for one so young. Don't forget to feed them."

The child held up a small box and shook it. The ensuing high-pitched squeaks made me sorry I'd asked, especially when the little pebbles began rolling toward the glass of their own volition.

"For Tap Tap." Alisi dumped out the contents of a leather satchel and handed it to me. "Hurry."

Having seen its offspring, I balked. "Why?"

The tiny Oud rose, fluttering limbs at me. "I'm Oud-Key! Best is!"

As if that was a reason to carry it with me. I looked at Alisi.

She pointed to the bag. "Ne is drawn to greatest haisin. They won't believe you could be the Founder without ner."

"Milly, exceptional," Tap Tap proclaimed with what seemed touching delicacy, then and louder, "Sira, better. Best is."

Save me from aliens. I took the bag, putting my head through the shoulder strap, then knelt, holding the flap open. "Don't make me regret this."

Tap Tap zipped inside before I could change my mind. I noticed "ne" made no promises.

Alisi changed, too, putting on a white knee-length, high-collared coat, the fabric stiff with white embroidery. There, any similarity to a Clan, or Om'ray Council robe ended, for complex symbols in black and red spilled over the shoulders and back. Noticing my attention, she laid her palm over the symbols. "These are my designations, marking me as Tikitik and Oud, as well as Hoveny. A seesor must hear from all, and speak to all."

The proclamation would have sounded more imposing if this particular seesor wasn't broadcasting *anxiety* to the point where I'd tightened my shields, but to Alisi's credit, none of her feelings showed.

Waiting at the door, chit. These new folks aren't the patient sort.

I passed that along. Alisi pressed her lips together, then held out her hand. With contact, came *words*—faint, as though shouted across a distance, but clear. *The haisin that binds can be severed, Sira, even ours. Do not give them cause.*

Between heart-kin, I told myself. Between the feeble bonds I'd felt among these people, threads to the mighty rivers coursing the M'hir between Clan Chosen and even those binding all Clan together.

Yet, even as I stared at Alisi in disbelief, something rose in me I wanted to deny but couldn't. A terrible hope. If the Hoveny could sever a Joining, should Ruti fall? We could save Barac.

Right behind that thought, the truth. My cousin wouldn't want to live, not alone.

Who would?

Morgan's "waiting at the door" hadn't prepared me to step into the midst of six tall, silent Hoveny in shiny red armor. Alisi Di ignored them and kept walking, so I took her cue and did the same. Without a word, the six Hoveny formed around us and kept pace.

It didn't feel like a welcome. Might have been the weapons—the large weapons—they carried. I'd used enough creative approximations in the past to recognize what could put significant holes in things. Pointy ends. Nasty little sights and dials. Huido would have loved these.

Then again, in my new clothes, maybe they'd take me for a member of Alisi's staff. On the short side, admittedly, and there was the hair, but it was behaving. I'd a feeling it didn't like weapons any more than I did.

I peered between elbows and bodies, rewarded by glimpses of the monstrous craft that had brought our escort and more. Most of the end facing into the tunnel had opened, like a great mouth. Inside was darkness.

Conserving power, maybe. Concealing resources—likely. If that was our ride to wherever we went next, I told myself, I wanted proof of proper facilities. This looked like a low-class freighter.

Or a warship.

Freighter.

Dithering kept me from worrying about anything else, so I was honestly startled when we reached the tent full of Clan and our escort peeled away to remain outside.

Morgan stood near the door, between two of the armored strangers. His pack wasn't on his back or in sight. He might have had time to hide it. Or they'd taken it. Neither of us risked a sending, but I saw his index finger draw a small circle.

He wanted me to take notes? I frowned at him. He raised a judgmental eyebrow at me, then repeated the gesture.

Meaning I should know this—oh. <u>One to watch.</u>

Not helpful. It didn't tell me who to watch and the room that had offered us such a cheerful expanse was now claustrophobic, its open space consumed by strangers. My people, well aware of a new threat, had taken refuge on couches, stools, and chairs.

Silence greeted me—outward silence. Having noticed me, my people expressed themselves with such force I missed a step, struck by a barrage of sendings: *Who are they? What do they want? Are we safe? Where are they taking us?* Words overlapped, rode each other. *Trust/Who/What/Them/Danger!* Beneath, understandable *fear.*

Less explicable, an overwhelming *weariness.* Not of the body, but of the mind, as though everyone here was burdened.

Safely in Alisi's shadow, I sent back: *I'm here. Peace. Patience. We'll have answers soon. A place. Rest.*

Then, because I was afraid: *Stay with me. Please. Don't leave. No matter who calls you.*

It was then I spotted the Tikitik.

Interlude

A THOUGHT TRAVELER. Of course they'd be here, too.
This Tikitik was closer to the Cersi variety, tall and black and formidable. It wore a red-and-black robe that flowed around its thin body and the bands of cloth on its wrists bore the familiar symbol. Round metal beads hung from gold threads along those bands, giving a disarming tinkle of bells with every movement of its long clawed hands.

Not that anything was disarming about the creature. Its four eyes were in ceaseless motion, and it kept what seemed a wary distance from both the Clan and the other new arrivals: Hoveny of a different ilk.

Security. Guards. Soldiers. Dressed for combat and unpleasantly suspicious. They'd taken his gear, going straight for his pack—handling it with a respect that told him they knew what it contained—then asked in no-argument tones for his vest.

Morgan had nodded politely and cooperated. If they thought him disarmed, they were welcome to that opinion.

If they thought the Clan cowed and harmless, they were welcome to that, too. He'd felt Sira's *wince* at the bedlam greeting her. Saw how those seated visibly relaxed at her calming response. Unreasonable, how they leaned on her, but they weren't wrong to trust her strength.

Though Sira would, he promised himself, be reviewing their hand signals.

The new arrivals had been smart, he granted, entering in such numbers they'd daunted even the Om'ray scouts, going straight to the physical threats and dealing with each without fuss or intrusive search. Barac was without his force blade. The Om'ray had lost their knives. They'd taken the packs of the M'hiray scientists as well as any loose belongings, so this wasn't just caution. Someone here was after information.

And that someone stood by the cots, talking to the senior edican, making the rest wait on nes pleasure. The neuter—his guess—was ordinary height, for a Hoveny, with shoulder-length straight hair, white, matched by pale skin and eyes. Ne was dressed in a well-cut beige business suit that could have come off a rack on Plexis. The boots, though. Those were, he'd bet on it, designed for use where gravity could fail. Meaning no time to change before coming down here, but enough clout to bring a small army. A decision-maker.

Even the Thought Traveler kept an eye bent in ner direction.

One to watch, he'd signaled his Chosen.

Morgan didn't need the *taste* of change to be sure of that.

Chapter 25

"**M**Y NAME is Lemuel Dis. SysComPrime for the System Cooperative. Director will suffice. Or Lemuel."

My Human was right, as usual. Lemuel was neuter, though how he'd guessed was a mystery and how I knew? I ascribed my certainty to some Hoveny instinct, at last of use, for ne could pass for a mature unChosen or older Chooser, nes features and build little different from mine in the latter state.

What mattered was the "dis" attached to nes name, denoting a solitary life and secured thoughts. Like Aracel's, the Director's mind was locked away. If ne had Power—haisin—and wanted to use it, there'd have to be a door. Somehow, I didn't expect any vulnerability.

"Sira Di," I replied, inclining my head politely as ne hadn't done. I looked over nes shoulder. "Thought Traveler." I ignored Aryl's grumble.

Its head bobbed up, mouth cilia flexing. "Sira. Hoveny, however unique your—appearance." Lemuel gave it a look. The Tiki-tik spread its arms, bells chiming. "I offer confirmation, Director."

"Thank you," ne said flatly, turning back to me. "I'm sure my esteemed colleague would also confirm that this—" nes hand lifted toward Morgan, then dropped, "—is proof of a ship come from outside our system, without notice or permission."

My hair writhed over my shoulders. "'This,'" I countered, "is Captain Jason Morgan and my Chosen."

The writhing hair probably made more of an impact than my snarl, but Lemuel stared at me, then finally inclined nes head. "I meant no disrespect, Sira. The arrival of a new intelligent species after so long is a marvel." Even tone, no change in expression. Either ne had a different opinion or was by far the best Hoveny we'd encountered at concealing emotion. "Welcome, Captain Jason Morgan, to the System Cooperative."

Not Brightfall. Notice, chit?

I did. Lemuel wasn't local authority. What had ne said? "Sys-ComPrime." We faced the equivalent of a Trade Pact Board Member, I judged. Or higher.

Morgan bent in a full graceful bow, rising to offer Lemuel his hand. Raising the stakes, that was. Acknowledge me as an equal—

Or show everyone here you don't.

Ne took my Human's hand without hesitation, the grip long enough to make the point aliens didn't bother ner, then let go.

My turn. I stayed as I was, making my own point.

With a glance at me, Alisi Di stepped forward, holding out her hand. "I am Alisi Di—"

Lemuel accepted the hand, inclining nes head more deeply than for Morgan. "Seesor Alisi. We've been briefed on your litigation here."

That "we" drew a hitherto silent Hoveny male to our small group, assembled near a table in the center of the room. Like the Thought Traveler, he kept his hands together. He inclined his head to Alisi, giving Morgan a nervous look.

Avoiding me altogether. "Koleor Su, Historian. My field is—"

"Sit," Lemuel interrupted, taking one of five waiting chairs at the table.

Thought Traveler removed its chair, instead squatting in that space. Its head cleared the table, cilia courteously withdrawn.

Sitting together around a table implied negotiation, or its potential. That didn't alleviate risk, and I wasn't surprised to see Morgan ease into the seat beside the Tikitik to put himself between us. I was still close enough to Thought Traveler to catch a whiff of spice, the not-unpleasant scent of its kind, and to see how its cilia waved in my Human's direction, presumably catching his scent, too. Or whatever it did.

The historian looked grateful to be excluded, a feeling I suspected Teris and Degal shared, given the company. Lemuel's armored staff formed a wide loose circle around us, enabling the Clan around us to observe, if they didn't mind leaning one way or the other.

More than sufficient force if we decided to, what, leap on top of them? I added excessive caution to the list. Morgan had been right. Lemuel was one to watch.

Though it was Lemuel's meeting, Alisi spoke first. "Director, Thought Traveler. I act now as seesor in a new claim."

"Is this new claim pertinent?"

"It concerns Sira Di."

"Ah. Let me guess. The claim that all of our visitors are from another world?" Lemuel rocked back, steepling nes fingers together. Two bore wide, plain rings; if this were the Trade Pact, they'd contain devices to record, track, or send an alarm. "Or the claim," ne continued, "to be descended from those who left this one in the Twelve lost starships?"

Thought Traveler's head jutted over the table, cilia writhing. Tasting, I thought with discomfort. The thing was a living bioscanner. The head pulled back. "Both are true. I so testify."

If Lemuel was annoyed by the interruption, ne gave no sign. Unless, I winced, ne'd planned to have the Tikitik assess us all along. *So much for secrecy.* I felt Morgan's grim *agreement.*

"In that case," Lemuel went on, "is there another of which I—we're—uninformed, Seesor Alisi? Or may I continue."

"We are not the only ones here, Director," Thought Traveler announced, eyes locked on me. For an instant, I thought it meant Aryl and tensed.

The satchel bounced against my hip. I fumbled at the clasp, the flap coming up on its own as the Oud swarmed out and onto the table with a drum of little legs. It assumed its speaking stance in front of me, facing outward so I had the better view of Milly's floral art.

"I am Tap Tap."

Thought Traveler barked its laugh. Lemuel bent nes head. "Your reputation is known to me, Oud-Key Prime."

"Prime?"

A tiny appendage waved at Morgan. Fair warning, I judged it, and didn't respond.

"Yours I know, Director Lemuel. Quick. Right. Capable. Best choice is."

"I am gratified."

I couldn't tell if that was sarcasm at being flattered, or if the tiny being was as important as it now seemed.

"Mine the claim." Tap Tap dropped, spun in place, then rose. "I claim Sira Di to be Founder."

The historian gasped. Armor creaked as someone shifted.

The Tikitik might have been made of stone, all eyes aimed at the Oud.

Lemuel looked to Alisi. "Seesor, have you accepted this claim for scrutiny?"

"I have." The Hoveny lifted her head, her eyes flashing with determination. "Further, to expedite this claim's settlement—for the sake of these people, Director, who need urgent care, and in respect for your time—I require Sira Di leave immediately to undergo testing."

Lemuel rocked forward again, palms flat on the table. "By whom?"

"The Sect of the Rebirth. The nearest Sanctum has been notified."

A fingertip found the back of my hand under the table. *Care to explain, Witchling?*

Later, I promised. Presuming I'd figured it out myself by then.

"I see." Lemuel turned to nes historian. "In your expert opinion, Koleor. Is the Founder folly or fact?"

"Nes work remains—"

"Let me clarify. It's been over a thousand solar orbits since the Fall and this fabled individual's death. Generations replete with legends and myths about who knows how many others, most no more than self-serving air." Lemuel held out a cupped hand, tipped it. "What proof exists there wasn't a group of brilliant minds behind the null-grid—how do we know the Hoveny invented it at all, and not, say, our esteemed Oud or Tikitik partners?" Nes hand flattened on the table.

Before the beleaguered historian could open his mouth, Tap Tap rushed across the table to confront Lemuel. "Oud not the Founder. Tikitik not. Haisin from Hoveny essential. Wasting time. Badbadbad." It dropped down with a thump that would have caught nes fingertips in its sharp little claws had the Director not snatched them clear.

A bell chimed. "I assure you the Founder did exist and was assuredly Hoveny," Thought Traveler said, eyes swiveling to aim at me.

"Tikitna refused null-grid technology," Lemuel said, nes tone a warning.

One the Tikitik chose to ignore. "Wisely so," it almost purred. "Nevertheless, we were and are aware. The Makers of that era were intrigued enough to make inquiries. Then, as now, we value variation."

They'd been involved in Cersi's experiment.

Had they been behind it? "You know what we are," I challenged.

Another languid wave, another tinkling of bells, then Thought Traveler uttered one terrible word.

"Made."

Interlude

"CERSI-VY." Emelen Dis thrust a trembling finger skyward, adding the next with each naming. "Cersi-Ray. Cersi-So. Cersi-Gro. Cersi-Ne. Cersi-Tua. Cersi-Ye. Cersi-Pa. Cersi-Am. Cersi-Nor. Cersi-Xro. Cersi-Fa." Until he stood, the digits of both hands outstretched to the Heavens, his shoulders burning as he held the pose with all the passion in his soul.

He took a deep reverent breath and slowly lowered his arms. Closing his eyes, he drew his clenched fists to rest over his heart. Last but never least. "Cersi-Vy."

Tension drained from him. Not the traditional time for the Invocation, this, but the news had shaken him to his core. The familiar, Blessed names restored his purpose.

His duty.

Emelen opened his eyes. Gerasim Su knelt in the doorway, her young face shining with trust. A trust deserved, he reminded himself, for was he not the Keeper? This very orlas, his foresight in urging his brightest disciple to seek a position of responsibility had been rewarded. "No one will interfere with our work," he assured his helper, waving her to her feet. Nermein's warning had come in time. The Director of the Hub nerself was on Brightfall.

With the summons just come? He could ask for no better

witness. The Blessed Ancestors had arranged it; he'd no doubts. None.

"I must prepare. Do you have any questions, child? Your task is vital."

"I know what to do. I will not fail," she vowed, inclining her head. "The call will be sent, Keeper, in your name."

A call that would propagate itself, as planned. "Good. I will leave at once."

She struggled not to frown. "Surely you'll wait for the others, Keeper."

"There's no time. No time." Emelen brushed at his vestment. The youngling rushed forward, helping straighten the robe. He took hold of her small chin and formed his lips into a benevolent smile. "The Rebirth, Gerasim. In our lifetimes. Think of that."

Tears swelled in her eyes. "May it be so, Keeper," she whispered.

And if she trembled?

Why, so did he, and all should.

For when this day was done—

The world would change.

Chapter 26

"MADE."

The M'hir *heaved* as those listening on every side reacted to the word. Tap Tap spun frantically, then froze.

I ignored everything but Thought Traveler. "How, exactly?"

Sira. From Aryl, with concern. *Do you want to do this now, here?*

Then where? When? I replied. Morgan sat, still and intent. He understood. Hadn't he taught me this? That you didn't back away, not when what you had to have was this close. The Tikitik tried to play me against the others, for reasons of its own. Or entertainment.

I'd learned from the best. "How?" I repeated, leaning forward. "Or don't you know?"

An eye sought Lemuel, but ne remained silent.

"You're here to see how we turned out." My hair, for once cooperative, slipped over my shoulders and coiled in front of me. The eye joined its fellows in staring at it. "Why not boast? You make living things into whatever you need. Fair, don't you think, to tell us how we started?" I sat back. "If you know." Lacing my tone with doubt. "You're no Maker."

The smaller eyes rotated up to regard me. "What value has that knowledge to you? How does it matter now, Sira Di, if our Makers learned the Hoveny Founder had an extra sense, an ability new to any life we'd encountered? How does it matter if these—" a claw-tipped finger pointed at Tap Tap, "—possess the same gift? Innate. Potent. Above all, pliable. How does it matter—" third time, with the ringing of bells as the Tikitik reclaimed its hand, "—if our Makers decided in their magnanimity to grant this gift to those who left on the Twelve?"

I could hear the ragged breathing of everyone in the room. A baby's hiccup. My own heart, thudding in my chest.

"It matters. What were you promised in return?" Morgan asked, taking his turn, able to be as cool and calm as if we discussed a trade—

And not the insertion of Oud genes into my ancestors, willing or not.

The Tikitik replied, "The satisfying of a curiosity."

They don't lie, Aryl said, her mindvoice faint and anguished. *Sira, what* are *we?*

This isn't the truth. Not all of it. Not enough.

My Human knew it. "Curiosity about what?"

"I've no time for this," Lemuel snapped.

Thought Traveler barked its laugh. "And here it is: the wisdom of those who care not for the past nor learn from it. Time as fleeting. Time as currency. While Tikitik live in the now and set in motion eternities. We are willing to wait generations for a worthy answer." The creature stood. "It will be my greatest honor to prepare Tikitna for this one."

The Director rose as well. "I demand you explain yourself, by my authority as SysComPrime."

Cilia wriggled. "Ah, but I've told you all I choose, my good Director, and need answer to no authority as you well know. Besides, you'll see for yourselves soon."

A clawtip, filed smooth and civilized, pointed at me. "We made you. The consequence shall be enlightening."

"GO!" Tap Tap spun, then rose. "GO. Stupid. Bad is!"

"We made you, too," Thought Traveler finished smugly and stalked away.

Lemuel Dis stood motionless, staring after the Tikitik as it was escorted by three of nes staff from the tent.

I took advantage of the pause to send an urgently needed *reassurance* to my waiting, anxious people, adding a plea for patience. Tap Tap's reaction was muted, a restless click, its "head" swaying as though it sought direction in that *other* space. I was reminded suddenly of the Drapsk, whose feathered antennae somehow did the same. Those and other species had a connection to the M'hir. Was ours any less natural? It seemed so.

The Thought Traveler spoke of consequence, Aryl warned. *We must be vigilant.*

She worried. Morgan smiled at me, warmth in his sending. *Well done, chit. You had our friend squirming.*

Not how I recalled the past few moments, but I managed to smile back. *We did.*

Always. Aloud. "Here we go."

The Director took nes seat. "With respect to Tikitik beliefs," ne said without preamble, voice pitched to carry, "they are not pertinent, nor will I act on the basis of its unsupported testimony on any point. Until I'm satisfied these people," a wave to the surrounding, grim-faced Clan "are not simply in the employ of this—"

"Human," Morgan supplied, ever helpful.

"'Human,' I will not support this test, Seesor. He brought weapons of alien design. Had in his possession pre-Fall artifacts, of inestimable value. From this Cersi, as claimed? How much more likely these were stolen with their help from this world and," Lemuel warmed to nes topic, "for all I know, from this very site! Everyone here could be in collusion. With the exception of the Oud-Key Prime, of course."

Tap Tap fluttered.

"But—the null-grid," the historian protested, his face pale. "The Twelve couldn't return without it. And how these people just appeared—they must have arrived in pre-Fall travel globes. The null-grid is the only explanation—"

"Far from it. They could have used some Human technology unknown to us."

The Director was halfway to convincing me, and I knew the truth.

Alisi Di surged to her feet, the embroidery on her coat glittering in the room light, throwing the dark symbols into vivid relief. "You've had access to every record at this site. We are innocent and we are not fools, Director, to be taken in as you suggest. Sira's people came to us injured and in need and we have helped them." Her face might have been made of ice. "Your continued suspicion delays the urgent care several of them require. As Seesor, it is my responsibility, not yours, to confirm or refute a claim given to me. I insist you respect my authority here."

"Then deal with mine first," Lemuel countered, looking up at Alisi. "I claim we've one visitor here, an alien who made his way into our System without detection or permission, to commit criminal acts. Unless you've proof otherwise, I'm taking everyone here into custody for questioning on the Hub."

"If that's what you need, Director?" Morgan's lips curved up at the corners. "Allow me."

Oh, I knew that smile—the one meaning those on the other side of the table had run as far as he planned to let them—and did my utmost not to show anything.

So when my Human showed his hands, then reached—slowly—inside his shirt, I felt a thrill of anticipation—not that I knew what was coming, but he'd a knack for surprises.

He produced a small package, peeling off the metallic film I knew he used to conceal items from scans. There. The Speaker's Pendant dangled from his fingers, like a leaf caught on a chain. My pendant. If Thought Traveler had sensed it through the film, I'd seen no evidence of it. Just as well.

Morgan dared wink at me as he handed the thing to Alisi, not Lemuel.

It was the latter who spoke. "What's that?"

"Something made on this world by those who sent starships full of Hoveny—and Oud and Tikitik—to Cersi. Something then used on Cersi until we brought it back here. Analyze it. You'll have your proof."

"Tikitik, stupid, bad is. Oud bargain to travel in space. Ships confined, finite." Tap Tap spun, showing off its flowers. "Tikitik Makers helped create new form, better is. We do well. Thrive. Next, try to make Oud Founder. Bad bad. Tikitik stupid. Not make Sira-Oud. Not make Hoveny-Oud." A flurry of tiny taps. "Only good thing Tikitik, made Oud-Key by accident, better, best is!"

Not in my opinion, Aryl sent, fading back.

The creature was adept in the M'hir, I thought wryly, dipping within it, able to sense Power moving through and assess it in others. Not, as yet, with Clan-like control or Talent. Unless I counted being a spy. *Do you* hear *me, Tap Tap?* I sent at it.

I saw it twitch, appendages moving furiously, then stop. "Did something, Sira. What?"

Looks tasty to me, from Morgan, along with an image of prawlies, which had more than a passing resemblance to the Oud, sizzling in a pan.

Tap Tap oriented to Morgan. "Did something, Jason. What?"

If our little friend heard *that,* my Chosen sent with *amusement, I'm never playing* Stars and Comets *with it.*

The three of us were in one of what Lemuel called "passenger accommodations." The room had a gray metal floor, walls, and ceiling. I'd paced it: three strides by two. There was a long bench on the outer wall which I supposed could be a bed if you added a mattress. Above that, a wide locked cabinet or closet. Lighting came from a recessed fixture protected by wire. If there'd been a door, it'd be a prison cell.

Or troop carrier. Morgan had made himself comfortable in a corner of the bench, one foot up, arms around a knee. I sat, when I sat, at the other end to leave space for the tiny Oud, who scurried back and forth between us as if too excited to be still. Or anxious.

Or, like me, still processing what Thought Traveler had said and what it implied. Genetic modification was commonplace med-tech for several species in the Trade Pact, including, Morgan assured me, the teeming masses of humanity. Others, for their own reasons, either practiced or outlawed it. Cross-species tinkering was frowned upon—which only made it expensive. That by the Tikitik Makers? Something else entirely. My skin crawled when I thought of it, not that it changed a thing.

The Director had acted quickly; I gave ner credit for that. While one of nes staff went with Alisi and the pendant, Lemuel had invited us to board the transport.

For the most part, the Clan were relieved. It was progress, after all. The shelter Pauvan and the others had supplied, however welcome at first, was a temporary solution; those who gave the armored guards wary looks were mollified when those guards helped carry blanket rolls and returned packs.

Morgan's hadn't been returned, nor any weapons, but I wouldn't have returned those either.

My people were nearby, in rooms like ours. There were three levels of them, each with accommodations, connected by a narrow lift we were free to use and a large one we were not, requiring a key. In the same way, while we waited, we were welcome to move within the areas set aside for us.

And nowhere else.

Our wounded, accompanied as promised by their "heart-kin" as well as Aracel Dis, one other edican, and our Healer, Holl di Licor, were in a larger room at the front of the second level. I'd been to see it. It was nothing more than a cargo hold, with power couplings for the cocoons.

The reality was we were all cargo, currently the property of Lemuel Dis, the SysComPrime, whom I suspected had swept in to have us in nes possession before any mere planet-bound authority could arrive.

Fortunately, Alisi Di had been truthful: her right as seesor superseded any other, in orbit or on the ground. If the pendant, and whatever traces clung to it, proved its origin and travels, Lemuel's transport would take us to the nearby town, where the Sect of the Rebirth had its Sanctum, and I'd be tested.

If not, our destination was nes space station and a tribunal to decide if Morgan was an antiquities thief from another part of the universe and we, his accomplices. Ironically, all true, depending how you looked at it, and certainly not how we'd hoped to enter this society. His plan was to let it play out. My part would be to keep the Clan on the space station while it did.

To stop them following the dead.

How's Aryl?

Avoiding Tap Tap. So well, I could believe I was alone in my body if it weren't for the other's small, rapid heartbeat and an emphatic spot in my mind labeled *don't bother me.*

Morgan nodded, returning his attention to the Oud. "You're saying all three species decided to make a new Hoveny Founder."

"All Sect members, yes yes. Needed knowledge for the Rebirth. Needed more. Hoveny, most, afraid to look outside system, want to forget past. Past, best is."

I raised an eyebrow at this. "What's wrong with the present?"

"Not room," the Oud replied promptly. "System puts air around rocks," with drum of disgust. "Bad is. Too little food, Brightfall, not room. Bad is. Need empire. New neighbors. Space! Best is!"

Reminding me of Cersi and another ambitious Oud.

"Seesor comes soon," it finished.

I hoped so. Tap Tap wasn't the only one twitching; it just did it more effectively. My Human, of course, might have been relaxing in our cabin on the *Fox*. Our cabin—

Our lives there.

Longing filled me, irrational.

Impossible.

Then, for an unfathomable moment, I *saw* our cabin . . .

. . . The 'fresher door was closed. Painted stems festooned with leaves and buds curled and wove over tile and wall. Flowers burst beside the ceiling lights. The table-desk was out, our bed neatly made—I'd only to step forward . . .

. . . I wasn't alone. A voice filled me. <<That's it. Come home, Sira. Take that step . . . >>

"—Cersi wasn't necessary." Morgan's voice snapped me back to here and now. I clung to the sound, not trying to understand.

That voice again. Deep, hollow. Everywhere. Nowhere at all. It couldn't be my sister's. It wasn't Rael—she wasn't this.

Better she be gone and dead, than this.

I focused on my Chosen with everything I had.

"The original Founder was born here, among the Hoveny, but the ones we've met so far don't have that kind of Power." Morgan frowned. "Why add Oud genes? What are we missing?"

Don't ask, I thought, then wondered why. Surely my Chosen had good reason. The aftereffects of that voice, I told myself.

But Tap Tap was no happier. It backed into the wall, curling on itself. Not quite a ball, but defensive.

Morgan got off the bench and squatted in front of the Oud. "Oud-Key Prime, answer me. After the Fall, did the surviving Hoveny turn against those with great haisin?"

It explained Alisi's concerns about revealing her Power, little though it was. I held my breath.

Slowly, Tap Tap unrolled, just enough to expose the cluster of speaking appendages. The others stuck out at odd angles, as if to fend off danger. "No, Jason Di. The Best disappeared with the null-grid. 'And those who heard the dead cry out, did weep for joy and join them.' "

Cold filled me. Wrapping my arms around myself didn't help.

A quiver passed from segment to segment. "Sect Tikitik say Hoveny with good haisin became too rare after, became almost none. Bad is. Oud-Keys nurture, better is, but Hoveny today problem. Many/some think too much haisin bad is."

If too much had led to the Power-of-Choice and to me? To dead who didn't die but corrupted the M'hir, luring us into boxes shaped like love—

I found my voice. "That's why you're here, with Milly."

A limb bent to touch a painted flower. "Lovely Milly. Yes yes. Nurture. Too few, are."

Morgan's eyes met mine, a warning in his. *This isn't just a test, Witchling. This is about the future of the Hoveny. About turning toward Power or away from it. That could be the Tikitik's "consequence."*

If they turn away—if this was another world where the Clan were labeled a threat, another place we couldn't belong, until all we had were boxes—*we lose our chance at a home.* Something vile exploded through me, like rot, full of disappointment and fear. *They MADE us,* I sent, uncaring that he winced. That the Oud fled, leaping to the floor and out of the room. *We're what they wanted! They should be grateful!*

My Human closed his eyes, pinching the top of his nose between finger and thumb. Holding back what he'd say as if I'd mixed up a cargo code on the *Fox* and he wanted me to figure it out for myself.

I had figured it out. All of it. *THIS IS ALL WE HAVE,* I shouted at him.

Could he not understand?

If I have to tear a place for us from this world, WHO'S TO STOP ME?! Silence. He didn't look at me. Wouldn't. My Chosen.

Say something!

What, Great-granddaughter? Before I could be relieved to *hear* Aryl at last, she struck. *That you'd fall and take us with you? FOOL!!* With stinging disappointment. *We met Humans and took the wrong path out of fear. We've the chance to do better here, with these people. Do not waste my sacrifice. My Chosen. My beloved Enris.*

Sira. Her mind voice altered, suddenly so gentle, so full of *love,* I gasped. *Despair destroys. Courage. Hope. Those can save us.*

Aryl was right. In every way, she was right. What had I been thinking? What had I—a bitter sob escaped my lips.

Blue eyes shot open and Morgan put his hand on my knee, that pressure the only stable point in a universe that fought me like the M'hir. I stared down at him. When had those fine lines etched themselves beside his blue eyes? When had the bones of his cheeks come closer to the surface? How—

A lock of hair came around my waist, winding around his thumb, and I felt something cold slide down my cheek even as I warmed inside. "I'm sorry."

His lips quirked. "For giving me another headache, or for sounding like your father?"

I was off the bench and on my knees before he finished, my arms around him in a fierce grip. I buried my face in his shirt. "Everything," I mumbled. "All of it."

Denial, quick and implacable. A whisper in my ear, "You'll find the right way, Witchling. You always do. I trust you. So do the people who've followed you this far. The Hoveny," a prickly kiss, "will figure it out soon enough."

I love you.

That's because you have good taste. Light the words and tone, but the M'hir boiled between us and I could have lost myself in my Chosen—

"Sira."

I worked myself free of Morgan, my hair, as always, last and reluctant to relinquish its grip, and stood to face Alisi, my Human rising with me.

She'd the ball of Oud under one arm. With her free hand, she held out the pendant, now in a small transparent sack. "I, Seesor Alisi Di, declare Sira Di and those with her have come from the world of Cersi, are descended from those who left Brightfall on the Twelve, and have returned to us now with the Human, Jason Di.

"By my authority, we proceed at once to the test of the claim brought forth by Tap Tap, Oud-Key Prime, that Sira Di is a Founder."

Well, I thought, here we go.

Interlude

HER SMALL HAND was cold in his, refused to warm no matter if he rubbed it gently or not. Her hair hung dull and limp down her back, and Barac would have given anything if Ruti had asked after the children, or argued, or—

Did anything but sit, her brows knit in a frown, her eyes locked on what he couldn't see. "Ruti," he tried again. "Do you hear that? Feel it? We're underway. Look out the window." He'd thought it a cupboard, but once the transport had begun to move, the panel covering it had rolled to one side. "There are little creeks. Fields." A green lush feast for the eyes, after the sere landscape of the Oud. "Won't you look?" *Dearest,* he tried again.

Her mind was closed. He'd taught her to intensify her shields; he hadn't, the Clansman sighed, thought she'd use them to keep him out.

"If you'd *listen,* you'd understand." The child stood in the opening, her gray-green gaze earnest, her voice sweet.

His hand reached for his force blade, but they'd taken it. "Get away," he said harshly.

"Ruti doesn't belong here. She stays for you. It's very hard. You should *listen*—"

"Stop!" He jerked to his feet, ready to—

Ruti's hand stirred in his, held tight. "It's all right, Andi," she whispered. "Everything will be all right. You go and play, sweetling."

Barac sank down beside his Chosen, gathered her unresisting form in his arms, and closed his eyes, breathing in the scent of her hair. "Don't leave me. Don't. Please don't. You promised."

"I promised," Ruti agreed, distant and calm. "I'll wait for you."

Then he *heard* it.

A hollow voice, tasting of ash and death.

<<*I'm here, little brother.*>>

Chapter 27

I PRESSED my nose to the window, trying to see everything at once. A low ridge bordering a wide expanse. Fields, criss-crossed by streams that sparkled in the sunlight. Turning so my cheek was against the window, I could make out where the ridge bent like a hook, squared buildings pressed into its slope and clustered along the top, while curved roads connected the ridge to a neat array of smaller buildings on the flat. Smoke curled thin from chimneys. Colorful bits waved in the air. Flags? Laundry, I told myself hopefully, that being a peaceful, ordinary thing. "What's it called, Alisi? That town?"

"Goesen. We can't see its Sanctum from here, but you will once they send you down."

"The transport's not landing?" In Morgan's sternest "captain" tone. I turned around.

Alisi held up one hand. "At the Keeper's request, only Sira—"

His face darkened. "No."

"Morgan—"

We don't separate in unknown territory.

They can't separate us, I reminded him, strengthening our connection until our hearts beat in synchrony. Or would have, if mine hadn't been racing. I tried. "We'd prefer to stay together, Alisi."

"Emelen Dis was adamant, Sira," she said, her rainbow eyes gentle. "No one else may be on the ground, or the test result could be corrupted. The transport will hover overhead, providing a clear view. The Director's staff will doubtless monitor and record everything, but so will I. If you want to end the proceedings at any time, Sira, simply say so. We'll hear you."

End a responsibility I neither sought nor desired. Avoid being the cause, as Morgan feared, of fundamental change among the Hoveny. Tempting.

"If I do?"

Tap Tap rose. "If you stop the test, you fail the test. Fail the test, bad is."

Nothing was ever easy. I frowned at the Oud. "Explain 'bad is.'"

"Sect waits for generations. Now hears 'Cersi-So.' Knows you used null-grid to return. Won't stop if Sira fail." Appendages moved in undulating waves, then settled, clasped together. "Others have haisin, too. Tle Su, better, maybe best is. Others."

They'll test the Clan till they find one willing to make their device work. It won't take long.

I nodded. Morgan was right. *Sona* had shown us how to pull in a thread from the M'hir and secure it. Anyone could.

I could name at least twenty who would, especially if they thought they'd gain an advantage on this world.

My Human raised his head. "We're descending."

I went back to the window. Our destination wasn't the town at all, but one of the square fields. As we sank down, I made out rows of dark green plants with sharp, yellow-edged leaves, their tips overlapping. A fence ran around the edges, too low to appear enough to keep out grazers, though the gate was substantial, a panel of wood attached by chain to a stubby pair of stone columns.

There were other such gates in view. I thought it odd their columns were coated in brown moss.

Until Morgan, beside me, murmured a satisfied, "Hello."

And I realized where I'd last seen a column just like these.

On a starship.

His name was Emelen Dis, his title Keeper of the Sanctum of the Sect of the Rebirth, and he looked, I decided, like a being about to step off a cliff. Which might have been because we were standing at the back edge of the transport, its massive rear door having retracted to allow the Keeper's aircar to nip neatly inside, looking over a drop that would break most of our bones.

That wasn't it, I thought. Emelen had forgotten his surroundings the instant he'd laid eyes on me and hadn't looked away since. I did my best not to mind.

Lemuel Dis was there, with six of ner armored staff and a bevy of techs with equipment. Our M'hiray scientists would do well here, given any chance at all. I resolved that instant to ask Alisi and maybe the historian about opportunities.

After the test.

"As Seesor," Alisi said formally, "I ask the Sect of the Rebirth to test the claim that this individual," she gestured me to come forward, "is a Founder. Keeper Emelen Dis, I present Sira Di."

He swept his hands out and back in the Clan gesture of respectful greeting between peers.

My response was automatic, adding the twist and elevation of one hand to signal my greater Power, then I stopped, struck by realization. What we'd thought mannerisms common to Om'ray and M'hiray?

Were from this sect. Those who'd volunteered to go to Cersi had remembered this much of their former lives—or been allowed to remember—and passed it down to us.

Us. I put my hands safely at my sides. Using these gestures here proclaimed us part of a religious order we hadn't known existed at breakfast. Using our full names, for Morgan had told me the truth? If we weren't mocked, we'd be pitied.

Not to mention the Oud in our blood.

The past consumed what we thought we were—what would be left by the end?

"I trust this test of yours won't take long, Keeper," Lemuel's tone was neutral. "We've injured on board that need care this arn."

"It will be, Director. Sira?" With a bow, Emelen indicated his aircar. "The controls are preset. You need only descend to the appropriate spot and 'Embrace the Heavens.'"

"Pardon?"

"I ask yours." With, yes, the gesture of apology even a M'hiray child knew how to make. "A lifetime of euphemism and prayer— it's difficult for me to speak plainly. But I must. Engage the null-grid is, I believe, the correct terminology." He appeared charmingly flustered.

Appearances could deceive. Emelen Dis had us waiting on his whim, including a high-ranking offworld official as well as a see-sor. Add to that list Tap Tap, the Oud-Key Prime, who'd scurried around and in and out of the Keeper's aircar with blinding speed as though confirming it was free of stowaways, and a Human—an alien given not a second glance.

But not unremarked. A mutual interest. I saw how Morgan kept his eye on Emelen Dis; he'd palmed his scanner—which I'd assumed was in his pack—to pay even closer attention. If I had to guess, my Human suspected the Hoveny carried something in-side his conveniently voluminous robe.

They want me to pull the null-grid into some device, I sent, tight and private. *It's what we expected.*

Maybe. A flash of blue eyes. *No assumptions, chit. Not today.*

Emelen beckoned. "If you please, Sira. We'll see any result from here."

"Very well." As they were waiting for me to enter the aircar, I did. Awkwardly. The machine came complete with ornate side-rails to step over, which was fine, except the seat was covered in a tapestrylike fabric clearly not intended for my boot. I lurched forward, losing my balance—

A hand had my arm, steadying me. Morgan, moving before any-one else could think to, betraying his speed to save my dignity. A speed and focus that wouldn't go unnoticed, especially by those assigned to guard Lemuel. They wouldn't underestimate him now.

So they shouldn't. My hair lifted, and I grinned at my captain. "See you in a bit."

There'd been a few times in my life when I'd been plopped in a strange aircar and taken someplace. Such things happened when you'd Scats and Recruiters and your own kind after you.

I was pleasantly surprised to find Emelen's machine had better manners. After floating smoothly out into the sunshine, it sank with a businesslike hum to the field below, no faster than a lift, and came to rest with a polite thump.

A breeze cooled my cheeks, and I was glad of Alisi's jacket. Around me, plants swayed, their leaftips clattering like teeth; those pressed beneath the aircar perfumed the air with a suggestion of, yes, beer. Beer left on the floor overnight, to be exact. Rather welcoming.

I climbed out, snagging Alisi's empty satchel on the hand rail, and almost fell on the beer plants.

Miss me already?

I looked up at the transport and waved. *Should have left this behind.*

Show me, Aryl asked.

Turning slowly, I surveyed my surroundings. I stood in the middle of a slender valley, green from edge to edge. The valley and bordering hills flowed in tandem from side to side, explaining the name "Ribbon Lands." Presumably there were more valleys like this, beyond those hills. Goesen was in the distance, its buildings stone, with tiled roofs. Trees—or what passed here as trees—showed between. I spotted a homely line of pants blowing in the breeze and smiled to myself.

I could live here, Aryl agreed.

First things first.

From Morgan, *Sira, look up.*

I raised my eyes, startled to see transports approaching from all sides. "Who's that?" I shouted.

A voice from the aircar. "The Sect gathers, Sira Di."

Lemuel wasn't informed. Ne isn't happy, chit. Nor is Alisi.

Makes it unanimous. I could see my people lining the windows of our flying machine and sensed their unsettled *attention.*

At least this time I'd decent clothing. I straightened the jacket with an annoyed tug. Emelen could have provided a table with a nice, small, inoffensive Hoveny device waiting. Something I could activate that would give off a light or signal and be done. But no.

The audience said it all. This was to be a spectacle. Here. In this field.

The transports slowed to hover at a respectful distance. The designs and sizes varied, implying a mix of personal craft and commercial, some large and others less so, in common only that they were jammed with people, at windows or leaning on railings. No Tikitik that I could see, nor Oud, but the latter would be impossible to spot if they were as tiny as Tap Tap.

Who'd put me in this mess. I didn't plan to forget that.

Hundreds of spectators. Could be thousands. The hum, buzz, and growl of their machines was distracting. No, more than thousands. This was a technological society. Whatever I did, fail or succeed, would be known across this world, and throughout the entire system.

Imagining Thought Traveler as one of my observers, I took a moment to glare up, hair slapping my shoulders.

Don't let it go to your head, chit. My Chosen, deliberately amused. *Fame's fickle.*

Sticking out my tongue seemed the logical response.

To it, then. I slogged my way through rows of beer plants, the soil between them a cloying mud, so I was grateful for Milly's too-small boots. Not far to the gate.

To the columns, I corrected. The one on the right was my height, the other shorter. The gate they supported yawned open, the end of its worn and crooked panel stuck in mud, the chains and ropes used as crude hinges still in place. The stone had been scraped, not washed, presumably in preparation for this test. There were strands of moss still clinging to the dark, almost black-green surface, a surface I discovered to be covered in thick slime. Lovely. I pulled my fingers away, decided against wiping them on Alisi's gifts, and shook my hand vigorously in the air instead.

Stalling.

Caution is a virtue, I replied haughtily, feeling Aryl's assent. Their steadfast presence wrapped me in comfort.

Comfort I needed. I studied the columns. Size, shape, outward appearance: all disturbingly similar to the pillar the ship had called its access interface and had been the Om'ray's Maker. A device capable of altering minds and signaling through space wasn't to be taken lightly. No telling what this pair did, if they were a pair at all.

I moved to stand between them, raising my arms slowly. With a preparatory grimace, I pressed my palms to the cold, slick stone and took a steadying breath. Easy to imagine everyone else in the valley doing the same.

Well, I thought, here's something you can't all do.

And opened my awareness to the M'hir.

Interlude

FROM HERE, to Morgan, the fields might have been designs on a carpet, the transports paint on a canvas sky, and the distant town blocks discarded by a child. Only Sira had dimension. Only she commanded the eye.

And more. Through their link, he shared the instant she opened to the M'hir.

The next, the barrier she threw up to protect him from it. Morgan's jaw clenched. He'd known she would. It made it no easier to bear. Reduced to vision, he leaned out, one hand gripping the metal frame.

Emelen Dis moved to stand beside him. "I'm told you are her heart-kin. You must be proud."

Morgan didn't take his eyes from Sira. "And you're wearing armor under your robe. Expecting trouble?"

"None of us knows what to expect," with candor. "We follow the Blessed Instructions, passed down from the Fall."

Save them from zealots. "So nothing may happen," he started to say, then stared.

For something was.

Blue light, like that dripped from the pod shards, flickered along the columns. More blue limned Sira's body and glowed along her outstretched arms. Morgan watched, mouth going dry, as her glorious hair rose in a cloud, red-gold edged in blue.

Then, the world screamed.

Chapter 28

BLUE LIGHT TRACED LINES. Glowing dots chased one another. The familiar signs of a Hoveny machine waking up seemed—premature. All I'd done so far was be aware of the M'hir.

Oh, well. Using *Sona*'s technique, I *grabbed* with what weren't hands and pulled some of the *darkness* closer.

Blue appeared on my arms. That was new.

My hair crackled with energy. The locks I could see had a blue glow to them. Also new.

Enough to pass this test?

I doubted it. I *grabbed* again. Pulled more, and harder.

And more than the M'hir came.

<<*Don't do this. Come home.*>> Rael's voice.

<< *Sira, dear. You don't belong there. Come home.*>> Gods, that was—that was Enora.

<<*Daughter, end this. Come home!*>>

Mother? More and more voices. Some soft and familiar. Some loud and strange. I reeled, buffeted from within, staying up only because I couldn't free my hands from the pillars.

On some level, I heard Aryl weep, call out names I didn't know: *Seru!Bern!Worin!*

I had to stop them, stop all of this!

I *grabbed* more and more *darkness,* poured it out like madness and grief.

The world screamed in answer.

Interlude

WHAT HAD BEEN rock was hard no longer.
  What had been buried, rose to take breath.
Gleaming blue.

What had waited did so no longer.
  What had slept beneath a crater pushed through, cracking seals and spilling atmosphere.
  Gleaming blue.

While in AllThereIs, Watchers shrieked in despair and fought to hold in their universe with hands that shredded and burned—
  Only one dared plunge Between.

Chapter 29

I WAS—
Where I couldn't be.

Not the most useful thought, since I was. But—how? I ran my hands along the stone rail, looked out over mountains I knew, and had no idea what I was doing home.

This wasn't home.

Well, then.

As if I'd 'ported with no effort at all, I was elsewhere. I walked along the corridor of the *Silver Fox,* drawn by the aroma of fresh sombay to the galley.

Where I couldn't be.

I stood still. The corridor, perversely, didn't. I found myself going through the galley door—and there wasn't a galley, there wasn't a *Fox,* this was a trick—

STOP THIS.

Darkness surrounded me. I'd thought I'd seen all the moods of the M'hir. This—this was like nothing I'd experienced before.

Because this wasn't the M'hir. This was—absence. Of anything.

Making a point, was it? Whatever it was. I had to believe there was an "it." Something to talk to—something to—what could I say?

"Hello?"

After a lifetime . . . or was it a heartbeat?

Light.

Light that coalesced into a figure, moving toward me without walking, or drawing me forward. It was annoyingly difficult to tell which.

Suddenly, the figure was close enough to touch—not that I'd a body at the moment. I'd checked that.

I was.

I just wasn't, at the same time.

Promising, to be bodiless. Either that or terrifying.

Promising it was, I told myself firmly. I'd wandered in a dream-state before now. Hadn't been quite like this, but—

<<Pay attention.>>

Hollow, that voice. Or was it rich and full?

Death and ashes. Or was it vibrant? Alive?

Confusing, everything not being one or the other, but I wasn't about to be chastised by a luminous non-thing in my own dream. "I am paying attention. Where am I?"

<<Between.>>

Unhelpful. "Where's that?"

<<Where we are.>>

Another tack, then. "Who are you?" Polite that was, not to ask "what."

The face appeared. Grew solid. A Clanswoman, Chosen by the net around her black hair, with wide gray eyes and—

Aryl *gasped* inside me. *Mother!*

The strong brow furrowed in lifelike puzzlement, a neat trick. There was nothing like life in that face.

Say rather, that memory of a face.

<<*I have been Taisal di Sarc. Sira must listen. She must come home.*>>

"I'm not going—" But I was somewhere else already, wasn't I? "I'll listen." If anything here could make sense, I was willing.

The details of the face shifted, became that of someone else. A stranger. Elderly, with a high forehead and hooked nose. <<*All-ThereIs bleeds again. It must stop!*>>

Arms that weren't flesh *grabbed* me.

And pulled!

Interlude

THE HOVENY were frozen: in shock, or horror, didn't matter. There was no time to try and get sense from any of them, let alone demand they land the transport or take him down in anything smaller. Morgan tore through the hangar, searching for rope or cable, his mind already sending an urgent summons. *Barac!*

Faced with what Sira had just done? He'd take the bet a Clan popping from thin air wouldn't be noticed. Not that he cared.

He had to get down there—

Barac appeared, stepping forward without hesitation to put a hand on Morgan's arm. No need to tell him where to go . . .

. . . Morgan sank to his knees in what had been a field, grateful it was no farther—the softened land could have sucked them both down. He squinted to see, coughing with Barac as dust filled their lungs. Heavy stuff, settling quickly.

Sira knelt between the pillars, her hands at her sides. Her hair hung straight and her eyes were shut and she was smothered in colorless dust.

The blue was gone. From her. From the pillars.

Not from the world.

As they struggled toward her, Morgan couldn't stop staring at what now filled the valley beyond. A building—a Hoveny

Concentrix building—stood touching the sky. Dust flowed down its curved sides like water. More boiled along the base.

The building dwarfed those in the tunnel. Dwarfed any he'd heard had been discovered in the Trade Pact. He'd watched with the rest, appalled as it thrust up through the ground, setting off quakes that stripped tiles from the town and toppled trees.

At rest, the structure was pristine, as though newly built.

Alive. That, too. Blue chased along edges and gleamed from windows. The uppermost openings shone with white light, hinting at inner chambers.

His boot stuck, and Barac helped pull him free. "Sira did that?" The Clansman's voice shook.

"And more." The Human had been there as the report came in, the Hoveny relaying it close to hysteria. "There's another on the moon."

Barac looked up, as if he could see it. "How?"

"The null-grid must connect them." He'd ponder the implications of that later. No casualties here, unless some hearts had failed among those watching. The moon—there'd been construction workers, researchers. Didn't sound good.

Change. The *taste* of it boiled in his mind. This wasn't over.

They reached Sira to find the blue wasn't completely gone. It ran over the soil and caught on bits of dying plant in fits and flashes, impossible not to step on, so Morgan didn't try.

"Are you sure you should—"

Morgan ignored the rest. He put an arm around Sira's shoulders, the other behind her knees, and lifted, cradling her against him. Her head lolled back; unconscious, not that he'd needed to confirm it. Their link remained strong, but her mind—was elsewhere. He gazed down helplessly.

"Morgan!" When he looked up, the Clansman gentled his tone. "Jason. Where do you want to go?"

They'd no choice. "Emelen Dis." Who "hadn't" known what to expect.

What other lies had he told?

Sira first. "Up there," the Human said, staring up at the transport. "Where we can care for her."

Chapter 30

I'D DONNED A SPACESUIT and gone outside the *Fox*. Where I was now felt similar: weightless, drifting, queasy.

A line, of sorts, kept me in place. Normally, I wouldn't have thought being tied to a stranger—more accurately, a face and perhaps arms—could be a good thing. Here, where nothing extended in all directions, and none?

Having come far enough <<*Between*>> to have shape and form of my own, I'd have held on to him if I'd hands.

I'd gained a torso and head, yes. With a neck and eyes, since I could bend the former to use the latter to see the rest. I supposed the head was a guess on my part.

<<*Pay attention.*>>

<<*I'm trying to.*>> My voice! It sounded like his now. <<*What have you done to me?*>>

<<*Nothing. We approach AllThereIs. If you were whole, you'd be more than this.*>>

More here, I thought grimly, meant less there—assuming I'd a body left on Brightfall.

Morgan was not—NOT—going to be happy. His first stop: Emelen, getting answers—no, he'd be with me, the part of me still there. Worried.

Then he'd go after Emelen.

Unless I'd failed the test and this was the result. Being stuck here for good.

<<*Pay attention.*>>

<<*You keep saying that. I am!*>>

His face appeared, hooked nose to mine. <<*Not to what I say. To AllThereIs!*>>

Not "all there is" but one word: "AllThereIs." A name? A state of mind? A—before he could say it again, I spoke, or voiced, or whatever this was that sent words flying into nothing. <<*I know. Pay attention.*>>

How? To what? Was it literal? I stared over his nose into his eyes, hunting details. Paying attention.

Lashes, long and dark. Spots on the eyelids. The eyes themselves, dark-pupiled, gray—no, green, a green brightening with notice. Myriad lines—wrinkles. From squinting, not so much age. He wasn't as old as I'd thought.

I drew back, or he did. Black hair, streaked with white. Bushy eyebrows. The high brow I'd seen before, narrow shoulders I hadn't. Behind those shoulders—

It was as if Morgan painted a scene while I watched, each stroke multicolored and textured. A wall took shape, then shelves. The shelves filled with containers, grew labels. Beside the shelves, draperies, dark blue, beside them a door, arched at the top.

All at once, I was out of nothing and into a room as real as any I'd ever seen.

Nor was I alone. A Hoveny male, with a now-familiar face, sat at ease in a well-stuffed chair, his legs crossed. He put aside what looked like a clipboard, as if I'd disturbed him in the midst of work.

He gazed around the room, smiling. "Better than I'd expected, Sira. Well done."

I staggered back, having grown legs and feet, and dropped, more than sat, into a chair like his. "Who are you?"

His smile disappeared. "The first to make a terrible mistake." He bent his head. "I am the Founder."

"So you're one of them." I was too disappointed to be tactful. "Dead."

The smile came back. "Not exactly."

I felt it important to establish some rules. "I know I'm dreaming."

The Founder finished pouring a dark steamy liquid into two cups and handed me one. "In a sense, so am I." He took a sip, looking around the room. "I haven't brought myself here for a very long time."

I'd never been here, making the concept of dreaming slippery at best. "Why now?"

His eyes rested on me. "A Watcher thought you'd listen. Is that true?"

A Watcher. So I'd finally met one in the—what wasn't flesh. It—she had named herself Taisal, Aryl's mother, my great-great-grandmother.

Aryl?! She hadn't come here with me, I realized, feeling bereft. Wherever here was. No, she hadn't been *pulled* here by the Founder. "Between," he'd called it. Feeling clever, I asked, "We're in the M'hir, aren't we?"

Then knew I wasn't, for as I spoke, the room was consumed by that familiar *roiling darkness,* and to my horror, I felt myself *dissolving—*

<<*PAY ATTENTION!*>>

The room. The Founder. As if he were a locate, I concentrated . . .

. . . and was back. "Sorry," I mumbled.

The Founder seemed unperturbed. "Those of NothingReal who can *touch* Between have their names for it. M'hir isn't one I've heard. A gift. Thank you. Now. Will you listen?"

"Yes." I took a sip, only to find nothing in my mouth.

"Pay attention," he suggested, drinking his with pleasure.

I stared into the cup. The color was right for sombay. If it were sombay, it would—I could smell that heady aroma. After a cautious sniff, I lifted the cup and sipped again.

My mouth filled with my favorite morning drink, at the temperature I liked best, with the hint of sweet I'd sneak in as an indulgence. I swallowed eagerly and took another mouthful before the stuff could change.

The Founder raised his cup, tasted. His eyebrows shot up. "I like this. What do you call it?"

Dream rules, I told myself. "Sombay."

He nodded as though committing the name to memory. "Another gift, for which I thank you." The cup vanished. "Your time here, like this, is limited, Sira. The Watcher who brought you expends her strength to make it possible. That—" he pointed to my arm, "—will warn us when you must go."

I looked down. For some reason, I was wearing my spacer coveralls, their blue faded but at least clean. On my wrist was a band of white light. Small flecks of dark green were floating up to its surface; those that met, merged, dimming the light. "How—?" Didn't matter. "I'm listening."

"It isn't me you must hear. This will be difficult for you. Those who leave NothingReal and come Between—"

"Who die," I interrupted, determined to be clear on that point. As for his calling my reality, "NothingReal?" That name fit here much better, but I'd no inclination to argue.

"If you wish. Those who die there, arrive here. But you, Sira, are an anomaly. You remain in NothingReal. You visit here. You can pass no farther on your own. I've agreed to guide you, on one condition."

"That I listen." I looked him in the eyes. "I promise."

All at once, I wasn't sitting with a cup, but standing with the Founder, his hand in mine.

And we weren't in a room.

But in space.

Space. I use the word, but this isn't part of any universe I know, or only now I see it.

Stars burn and planets spin around them, matter dances and energy swirls, moving the fabric of everything—of AllThereIs—in a song defining existence itself.

There are singers both infinitesimal and infinite. Themes. I hear some: Love. Imagination. Hope. Remembrance. Laughter. Others are mysterious and fascinate. All are part of the song; all create it. To pay attention to any strand is to add my voice—

I have none, here.

I hear my silence spread like grief, silencing others. Protectors notice, slip toward me through the fabric like gathering clouds. They howl instead of sing, howls growing loud and louder till they deafen all else. Howls I've heard before, but didn't hear at all.

For they aren't names, but they were.

And it isn't rage, but triumph.

I listen. I listen and I understand at last the dreadful truth and wonderful the Watchers tried to tell us. Tell me.

Changespice.

We don't dissolve in the M'hir. We step Between, guided by the howls of the Watchers, to be welcomed, here.

For we are the Stolen.

And this is our home.

Interlude

HE TRACKED MUD across the deck and along the corridor. People stepped aside, pressed their backs to the walls. Some covered their eyes, others their mouths, but so long as they got out of his way, Morgan didn't care.

Sira's head rode his shoulder, her hair falling limp over his arm. He could feel her breathing, sense the slow steady beat of her heart. She might have slept in his arms, but he knew better. Her mind was empty.

It wasn't Lost, not if he could walk and breathe and be so afraid every muscle threatened to spasm. *Taking a trip without me, chit?*

Barac stepped around him, leading the way into the first of the bare cabins assigned to the Clan. Whomever may have been there vanished before the Human stepped through the door.

Morgan sat on the bench, still holding his Chosen, and looked up at the Clansman. "They did this." His voice was a stranger's, so he put his cheek against Sira's dust-caked hair and closed his eyes.

Take the ship.

∞

He eased Sira to the bench—to be sure he was free to move, should the need arise—but held her tight. The trouble with the Clan was their tendency to vanish.

He expected the Hoveny to notice that very soon.

"Hom Morgan?"

All that showed in the doorway was an eye peering through a mess of golden hair and a smidge of round cheek. "Hello, Andi," he said gently.

The rest of the child appeared, a hand and arm still outside as if she held on to the wall. "I stayed to check on the baby." The little Birth Watcher leaned in. She frowned in disapproval. "Sira's all dirty."

"Come in." He hadn't heard from Aryl. Hadn't thought of her, was the guilty truth. He *reached* quickly, finding a daunting void.

Andi entered the room, her palm trailing with a squeak around the doorframe. Instead of walking straight to Sira, she continued around the room, fingers on the wall.

As though it was important to hold on. Her face was pale and unhappy, her clothes disheveled. Morgan focused on her. "What's wrong?"

"The dead aren't being nice anymore." Matter-of-fact. "I don't *hear* them as much if I touch something." A pause. "Can't be a person. If I touch a person, they get louder, and they're too loud already." She bent to bring her hand to the edge of the bench and continued to approach.

"What do the dead say?" A question he'd never imagined asking, not seriously, but after watching buildings push through the ground?

"'We're bleeding! We're bleeding!'" She grimaced. "They aren't, you know. I can see them and they're in their boxes and fine. They're just being mean. They don't like what Sira did."

Shields tight, Morgan controlled his features to hide dismay and kept his voice calm. "Could the dead hurt Sira?"

Andi gave him a too-wise look. "Why do you think she's

sleeping so much?" She moved her free hand over Sira's abdomen, eyes partly closed in concentration.

Uttering a cry, she scrambled away, both hands outstretched. "Go away. I won't come by myself. Stop shouting at me!"

"Andi, what—"

He was talking to air.

Chapter 31

HOME. Great flocks whirled through space like rivers of sparkling gems. One streamed close, then split around me, and I floated amid reflections of interest/curiosity/amusement. Not birds, though they flew.

Singers.

Who were—what we were, I judged, weeping jewels of joy. Or should be. Would be, again. The distinction seemed pointless here.

<<*Pay attention.*>>

I moved, or AllThereIs shifted; regardless, I found myself elsewhere.

Vines of *darkness* formed around me, cloaking and calm. Fruit clung to them, or so my overloaded mind insisted, being globes of star-flecked black, varied in size. Vessels, I thought, or like enough. Not here, like me. Belonging, as I didn't yet, for these—sang.

<<*They are caught in their memories of NothingReal. They will linger Between until they remember who they are and choose to be free.*>>

Andi's "boxes."

Curious, I spotted one swelling and wished myself nearer, to see for myself, to know what to expect.

Contrarily, I moved, or AllThereIs shifted, and I was elsewhere.

Darker here. The vines were thick and writhing. They clung to what I was, stifling, pushing me. I fell against fruit that hung loose and shriveled, and heard no song at all.

They had to be empty. If there was mercy, they were empty.

I couldn't stay here. I couldn't—<<*SAVE ME!*>>

The universe shrank to a dot and a breath and I found myself back in a room. Or, rather, standing on a balcony. It wasn't mine but the Founder's, sliding like a drawer from the smooth curve of a windowed wall to overhang a vague-ish garden without plants, merely a blur of riotous color with a floral scent.

Perhaps, I thought desperately, he hadn't paid attention to it.

There was a railing and I clung to it, grateful to have hands again. "What did I see? What are we?" I turned my head to stare at him. "What are you?"

"You know." He swept a hand downward at himself. "This is but memory—my memory—from NothingReal. I left it behind, but for now it's convenient, with you still as you are."

"As I am . . . ?"

He looked more impatient than kind. "You know," he repeated. "Others from AllThereIs can leave it safely. But if we venture Between? If we come too close to NothingReal?" He pointed at my abdomen. "We can be taken."

I pressed my hands over the life within me. Taken into a Hoveny unborn, he meant. Our wombs were partly in the M'hir; our bonds to our children went through that other space, so very close to AllThereIs. "What happens then?"

"We exist in bodies that aren't ours, until we die and shed them. From being caught to being freed, we live as those around us and know nothing more."

As he'd been, I realized. "And when you died?"

"The body dies," he said gently. "The Stolen return Between, bringing with them what was, in NothingReal. You saw what happens next."

The fruit. Andi's boxes. Inside one was Enris, in the home he'd wanted with Aryl. In another, my father, in his workshop. Each and every one clinging to a memory—existing there—before letting go to become who they really were.

Or, I thought suddenly, thinking of those shriveled globes, never letting go at all. "My life—our lives. Are they so terrible?"

"No," with a sad smile. "But Stolen were rare, once. Each brought ideas—gifts of new experience—and some viewed it as an adventure, eluding the Watchers to try and be caught. Then, suddenly, there were strangers able to move within the boundary of Between. Close and irresistible. The Watchers did their best to keep us safe, but more were Stolen than ever."

The M'hiray. "The Hoveny and Tikitik bred the Clan," I said grimly. "You saw us 'port."

"The greater the Power, the harder to resist. Do you understand now, what you are?"

I put my hands beside his. Held on to what he remembered as solid. I'd the Clan view of this body as a husk, my mind what was *real*—but those, I discovered now, were words and empty. "Stolen." It could be worse, I thought. I'd die one day, but "not exactly." To become, again, part of AllThereIs, to sing its song with all those I'd loved—

Save one.

The one I loved most.

Jason and I were in the prime of life, for our kinds. We could share full rich lives till the end, or die at any moment, those lives being what they were. Together. That was the comfort of being Chosen.

To continue, alone? I felt sick.

"Sira, listen. You aren't here for this. You must save the innocent." The Founder stared out, seeing what only he could see. "While Stolen, I believed I'd a rare gift, one I was proud to use to help my people and share across the known universe. But in releasing that energy source, I opened the first breach."

Of course. The vibrant energy of the null-grid had nothing to do with the M'hir's—Between's—seething *dark*. "The null-grid draws from AllThereIs, doesn't it?" I felt a twinge, thinking of the song. The life there.

"Yes." Heavily. "Watchers threw themselves into the wound—the first one—all of them—to slow the bleeding. Others tried to flee, but what touches AllThereIs touches all and all began to fade. Because of me. Because I'd given the untold billions of NothingReal the means to drain and steal—I couldn't imagine the consequence." He faded, too; I could see the railing through him, the building.

"What consequence?"

"The Great Ones defended themselves."

I heard words. What I felt—was indescribable. I knew them, now. In AllThereIs, they'd appeared as stars and planets, galaxies of them, their grand, complex dance creating so much more: a home for life. My kind. Others.

AllThereIs. The Great Ones listened to its communal song. Were part of it. Of me. Immutable, permanent.

They were part of that other, oddly distant universe, too, for I'd met Great Ones before and hadn't known it. White, the world of the Rugherans. Drapskii, latest home of those dear little balls of trouble.

"What did they do?" I whispered.

Faint—far away. "You came to listen. Will you?"

About to protest I was listening, intently—moreover, listening to what I'd prefer not to, most of it frankly terrifying—I realized the sky was now the dull russet of sunset. We weren't on a balcony over forgotten flowers, but riding up the side of the Drapsk stadium in a bowlcar full of fragrant petals.

And I was alone. Relieved, I picked up a handful of petals. The band of light on my wrist was three-quarters dark green, flecks floating into place like destiny. That meant . . .

<<*Pay attention!*>>

Time was running out, if it was time at all. I should be with the Founder. I had to find him. Hear him.

The balcony reformed. I turned to face him.

"You asked what the Great Ones did." Where his eyes had been, stars wheeled through space; as he spoke, I heard their song. "Listen well, Sira. Before sealing the breaches, they entered them. They followed to everything that used what bled from

AllThereIs and buried it, leaving a trace of Between to lock them in time as well as place.

"That would have been enough, but flesh and building are the same to them. The Great Ones followed to every Hoveny, anywhere, who'd *touched* AllThereIs and wiped them from existence. Those here called desperately to those they'd lost, their Stolen—to me—to summon us home. Only then did the Great Ones stop, satisfied they'd ended the threat."

A threat alive again. A threat I'd recreated. I made a wordless sound.

"The Great Ones will end this one," as though I'd spoken. "They understand neither mercy nor restraint. We've tried calling home the Stolen who listen. Now you—what you've done? I've been sent to you, because the Watcher said only you can stop this." The Founder seized my hands, pulled them forward. The band was dark green save for a tiny point of light, like a star. "This isn't just about us and AllThereIs. Sira, I've remembered the Hoveny. The Tikitik and Oud. No more innocents of Nothing-Real should pay for my mistake—for ours. You can save them. Listen, Sira."

And I did, I tried with all my might, but his voice was growing fainter, my arms impossibly long.

"The Great Ones will only stop when AllThereIs is whole again. Bring the Stolen home, Sira. Bring them all—"

Interlude

WHEN THE MAGNIFICENT BUILDING punched through the ground, Emelen Dis had wet himself. There was no shame in a body's weakness, faced with such a demonstration of the Divine.

He'd been, however, grateful the armor Oncara imposed on him was absorbent.

"The tunnel's fine," Alisi Di was reporting to someone behind him. "Milly didn't notice the tremor, but I've ordered an evacuation."

"Sira Founder, best is!"

Ah, the Oud-Key. Hard as it was to take his eyes from what was happening below, Emelen collected himself and turned, giving the expected dip of his head. "I believe the Seesor has her evidence."

Alisi gave him a haggard, angry look. "This isn't evidence, Keeper Emelen, but disaster. There are casualties in Goesen—"

"More on Raynthe." Lemuel joined them. "I've received a report—" Nes hand gestured disbelief. "Another of these structures erupted through the Twelve installation, taking out the construction crews and their air locks above. No survivors—yet—rescue's heading there." Ne gazed at Emelen, face set and grim. "If I find you knew any of this would happen—"

"I did not. We—speaking for the sect—did not." The moon? His hands wanted to tremble. "The pillars were believed to—are null-grid conduits. We'd hoped for a display like the one on the access portal. Detectable energy. Something to show—" he faltered.

"—the world," Lemuel finished in a dreadful voice. "You've managed that. I want the valley cleared of spectators, now. I want the Founder taken into custody and kept as far as possible from any more of these conduits."

"She's gone!" Lemuel had staff keeping watch out the open back of the transport. One turned, a stunned look on her face. "Director. It's—I don't know how—Two figures appeared near Sira. One picked her up. They've vanished!"

"People don't vanish." Ne looked around. "Where's Morgan?"

"I don't know—he was here, then there—we were watching—See for yourself, Director. They aren't there now."

Emelen followed Lemuel to the opening, hesitated before looking down himself. It was true. The pillars stood, their blue fading, and there were marks in the soft ground. Footprints. Nothing else, as far as the eye could see. He looked at Alisi.

Who bent to regard the Oud. "Did you know they could do this?"

Appendages waved in agitation. "No no. Bad, this. Bad bad."

"I agree." Lemuel stepped away from the opening and raised her voice. "Check on the rest of Sira's lot. NOW!"

Chapter 32

I WAS—

In the empty corridor of the Hoveny transport, open doors on both sides, and for an instant believed I was done with strangeness and AllThereIs. Back in what I'd thought the real universe but was NothingReal.

Making it the Hoveny's reality, not mine. Not to keep.

Until I tried to take a step. My feet, in their too-tight boots, were embedded in the spongy flooring. It didn't hurt.

It was inconvenient. How was I to reach my people if I couldn't go to them?

"Call them to you, Sira."

I swiveled my head. Beside me stood a Clanswoman, her age worn as lightly as gauze. White hair cloaked her shoulders, moving to a breeze I couldn't feel, and her lean body was clothed in a simple blue dress, belted at the waist. A longknife and hook hung from that belt and her feet, in sandals laced up her bare calves, floated above the deck.

I'd have known her strong lovely face anywhere. "Great-grandmother. What are you doing here?"

Aryl didn't smile. "I'm here for the same reason you are. To restore the Stolen to their rightful place. To bring our people home."

Making us the ghosts now, I supposed. For some reason, that didn't bother me as much as it should. I suspected I was in denial or shock, but that wasn't what mattered. "Do you know how? I didn't," I chose to complain, "get instructions."

"Call their names." A new voice.

Yet one I'd heard, once before. Enris. He came up beside Aryl, his arm going around her waist, hers around his. A lock of willful hair slipped around his neck, and he growled happily in his throat, bending to give her an enthused kiss.

Chosen did that. They were Joined, again. I didn't need to reach to feel their link, it glowed in their faces, and I would have been thrilled for them both—but for one very personal problem. "Are you dead, then?"

They separated, smiling into each other's eyes, before turning to me. "We've waited this long without hope," Aryl said gently. "We can wait a little longer, having it. I promise I'll stay with you, Sira, and be born, if that's what you ask of me."

She made no promise to stay after that, nor would I have expected her to—everything, I thought with a pang, was turned around. Here was danger and imprisonment. There? Freedom. Family. Be born to NothingReal?

I'd never ask it of her.

"We will guide them, Sira," Enris told me, his voice deep in my bones. "It's time to come home. Call them."

I couldn't smile.

Not because there wasn't joy; the universe—both of them— rang with it. Not because this wasn't right; it was. By going home, to AllThereIs, the Clan would save so much more than themselves, sealing a wound that should never have existed, wiping away generations of grief.

What was the loss of one against all that—

I spoke the first name, feeling it leave me like the start of a melody.

"Tle di Parth."

—everything.

They answered. One at a time, Chosen as pairs, the Clan appeared in the corridor, walking toward me. They'd been housed across three decks, but bodies weren't what came. These were their true selves, freed of flesh. To each, I offered the palm of my right hand, which wasn't flesh either, but how was I to know the rules of this?

Through each fleeting touch, I sent my *certainty*. This, I told each, was the end of our flight from death. Here would be the beginning of life.

Then I showed them the way.

Some smiled and laughed, seeing me there, and didn't wait, disappearing as though my presence granted them permission to follow their own unheard voices. I supposed it did. I'd asked so much of them, until now, to stay for me. It was time they did what was right for them.

And go.

The M'hiray scientists came together, gesturing respect to Aryl, their faces shining. Andi laughed and pulled her parents to hurry, dashing from them to run into Aryl's arms, then mine. "We'll see you soon," she whispered, with a child's innocent joy.

I'd no doubt of that.

Ruis took my hand without smiling, sending *strength*. She knew.

Others were afraid. Distrustful. Suspicious. Most still came to me, slowly. I shared with them what I'd experienced in AllThereIs, what we were, what they would be again. Most of all, I let them listen, for the song had come with me.

And the Watchers. I felt them hovering, protective and intense. Enris was one. I recognized others. The Stolen, reborn, choosing to be guides to those they'd loved. All along, they'd brought home those who'd dissolved in the M'hir.

We'd been wrong to fear them.

Now? I feared what else would be watching. How long would the Great Ones wait? Did time flow in AllThereIs as it did Between as it did—wherever here was? Or did they count the new arrivals as they budded like fruit—

Pointless. I'd a chance to do for Brightfall's innocents what the Founder hadn't. Save them.

I'd take it. The Clan must leave.

And did. Going as they'd come, one at a time, Chosen in pairs. However long each lingered Between, in memory of this life, they'd find their way back to AllThereIs, there to sing with those they'd thought lost and with all those they'd forgotten, who never had.

Until eight remained, and me. I didn't need to *reach* to know why. Fear held Degal and Signy here. Ambition, Teris and so Vael. Duty bound Destin, which was no surprise; Elnu, though injured and in pain, wouldn't go without her.

"Nor I, without Barac," Ruti said firmly. She'd come to the corridor, standing aside to watch the children go.

Barac. He refused to hear, or couldn't. My heart ached for him.

You've done all you can from here, Great-granddaughter. It's time.

I was—

Where I should be, was my first thought, in Morgan's arms. Filthy, was my second, as hair shivered itself clean, creating a ridiculous cloud of—

"Sira!" Morgan grabbed me, was shaking me, or he was shaking. Whichever way it was, he was upset, I could feel it along our link.

It's all right, I sent back, with *love* and *reassurance.*

Knowing it wasn't.

Interlude

TAKE THE SHIP . . . take the ship . . . every step Barac took down the corridor beat to Morgan's order; every panting breath filled him with glorious fury. They'd no revenge on the Assemblers. No justice from the Blues and Grays and all who'd betrayed the Clan—

At last, he could make things right again. His fingers twitched. Recover their weapons, that first and quickly. Might not even need to take over Hoveny minds—but he'd do it and gladly.

The first room he'd passed was empty. Why was the next? And the next? There should be Clan here. Barac broke into a run, looking from side to side. Glimpses of the giant Hoveny structure flashed at him through windows to his right; the hill and sky beyond full of other craft to his left. Neither mattered. Where was everyone?

Where are you?

No one answered.

He reached the end of the corridor and 'ported to the level below, to the room where he'd sat with Ruti before Morgan's summons.

She looked up with her wonderful smile, her dark eyes bright, hair like a cloud, and for a heartbeat, he believed the nightmare over. "Barac! I'm so glad you've come. I promised to wait but can't you *hear*? Sira's called your name. It's time to go."

Sira—among the dead? A ghost?

Barac spun on his heel and ran blindly. "Take the ship," he panted. "Take the ship." Solve everything. Put them in control—at last—

More empty rooms, half shadowed by the past, half threatened by the present. Gear abandoned. Foolish blankets. Useless clothes. His breathing became gasps, became ragged sobs.

Barac, my Chosen. Beloved. Come back. Everything's possible. Please stop and come back. Listen!

He tried to block her voice, push aside the waves of *love* and *longing* she sent him. He'd orders.

"Take the ship."

His lips pulled back from his teeth.

If he had to do it alone, he would.

Chapter 33

IOPENED my left hand, unsurprised I'd clenched it, even less surprised to find the palm held a coin of brown dust unlike that coating most of me and my Chosen. I tipped my hand slightly, watching how it slipped along, staying together.

I concentrated, returning the speck to the M'hir, close as I dared to where it had been flower petals and memory, and looked at my Human.

Who was having some difficulty hiding his glee.

"You told my cousin to 'take the ship.'" Considering what I'd been through and learned, I shouldn't have been taken aback, but was. Maybe it was perspective. "I thought we were working with the Hoveny. What did I miss?"

Lifting an arm behind his head, Morgan rapped his knuckles on the window. "This, for starters."

Hands on his shoulders, I pulled myself up to see outside. "Oh, dear."

"There's another on the moon."

I eased down again. I'd been inside such a building. The Founder's memory of it, at least, though it had felt real enough at the time.

The Founder. The Great Ones. The wonderful—and

terrible—things I'd heard flooded through me with a vengeance, and it was all I could do to breathe.

"You can take us to Barac," he continued, getting to his feet. "Don't worry. They've seen us 'port."

As if that was even remotely a concern. I sat, looking up at my Chosen, memorizing his face. I knew it, beard or no. Knew the shape of him. The taste. The warmth and real and—

Morgan sank to his knees in front of me. "What's this?" He searched my face, brushed hair from my cheeks, hair that turned and curled and held his wrist.

I'd fallen into the blue of his eyes so many times before—had never thought there'd be a last. You didn't, that was all. Self-protection, that blindness, because looking into them now, I couldn't imagine taking that step—not for the Hoveny, not for anything.

Tell me.

If I did, I'd never smile again.

Interlude

BAD? The Oud-Key had a gift for understatement. Lemuel went to what passed for a bridge on the clunky transport, taking reports from ner second as they walked, gleaning more through the feed in her other ear. Fear and outrage. Excitement and curiosity. They'd spiral into hysteria, either way, disrupting travel, communications, commerce. Ne sighed to nerself. Not a situation to leave to underlings. In no sense.

Ne'd a functioning pre-Fall structure. Two, if the one on Raynthe was airtight. Possession didn't equate to ownership, by System law. It did equate to responsibility. Ne'd been here and involved.

Making it nes mess to sort.

Susibou Di acknowledged nes arrival with a curt, "Director," keeping her eyes on the console of the sophisticated detector they'd brought from the station. "Issued your warn-off to the civilians. They haven't budged. Permission to ram them."

Susibou joked when others wouldn't dare; Lemuel wasn't sure the tech was joking this time. "Not yet. There'll be government officials on some of them—who knows who else. Any news from Raynthe?"

"The advance team's taken a flyover. They don't expect survivors."

Whatever Sira had started seemed to have stopped with her—disappearance. This could be the last of it.

Or the start. Lemuel preferred pessimism as a working platform. "Where are we on this—vanishing?"

Susibou swung her head around to glower, hair beads tinkling on her shoulders. "It's not my equipment."

"I didn't say it was. Did you record it?"

Another tech interrupted. "Director, Morgan's back on board, with Sira. They—" he swallowed and went on calmly. "They appeared in the passenger section with the one called Barac."

A cloaking device, with some form of personal flightgear? There'd be time for answers once the situation was contained. "Send—"

"I believe we can help."

"Excuse me, Director. They say it's urgent they see you," her second explained. Five figures stood in the door to the bridge, surrounded by staff.

Lemuel recognized three, dismissing the rest as unimportant: Degal Di, with an unknown female, presumably his heart-kin; Teris Di, with an unknown male, presumably hers. The pair claimed to represent the rest. Completing the group, Destin Di, who belonged in the cargo hold with her wounded heart-kin. A simple guard, weaponless, but nes own protection stiffened, alert to potential threat.

The only threat from these three was distraction while ne dealt with crisis. "Take them back to their quarters and keep them—"

Degal disappeared.

Then reappeared by one of the techs, who let out a shriek.

He held out his hands placatingly. "A harmless demonstration, Director, of our value. Sira isn't the only one with something to offer."

"We're all Founders," Teris stated. "We can do what she did."

These people smiled freely; Lemuel put one on nes face. "Come in. Tell me more."

"Director." Susibou had been crouched over her console. She turned, her face stricken. "They're gone."

"If you mean the rest of the Clan, the fools listened to her," Teris sneered. "We don't need them."

"That's not what I mean."

∞

The Great Ones slowed. Stopped.

Then *REACHED*!

Watchers tumbled. What lived was shunted aside, the dance abandoned, the song distorted as the fabric of space itself folded and stretched.

Like arms, what *reached*. Like gaping mouths. Holes they might have been, or hands. Whatever they were, they coursed along the channels of what bled AllThereIs to consume what they found.

Withdrawing, they sealed the wounds behind them, tossing into the *seething dark* what didn't belong.

But they didn't move.

So nothing did.

Waiting.

Chapter 34

MY THIGH STARTED RINGING.

As I stared down at it in confused offense, Morgan didn't hesitate, freeing the Hoveny communicator from its holster. He stabbed buttons until the ring stopped, then threw the device against a wall with such violence it broke in two. When he looked down at me, my heart wanted to stop. "Tell me!"

Before I could utter a word, he took me by the shoulders and pulled me to my feet, and I knew that dangerous expression.

I just hadn't been the one facing it before. "You know, Jason," I said softly. "You *taste* it. The change coming."

A sharp move of his head, side to side. Rejection, not of me, but of what instinct warned him I meant. I'd never fooled him.

I couldn't imagine trying. "I'm not from here. The Clan aren't."

His eyes glittered. "Brightfall? Then we—"

"This reality." I licked my lips. "Yours."

His grip tightened. There'd be bruises. There already were, on my heart, if not flesh. "Explain."

"I've been somewhere else. Learned the truth." Like pulling medplas, I decided. "It turns out I'm a noncorporeal life form trapped in this body."

My Human gave a tiny nod, lips in a grim line. Keep going, that meant. Or he humored insanity.

So long as he listened.

So long as we'd time.

"I'm not supposed be here," I told him. "None of us, the Clan, are. We come by—by accident, entering Hoveny unborn as Aryl entered mine. We don't remember our other life. We live here, these bodies us—until we die."

When he didn't say anything, I frowned. "I'm not making this up."

Morgan's face lost that deadly focus. "I've seen you in the M'hir, Witchling." His lips quirked. "It's not hard to believe that's what you really are."

He thought he understood. That nothing had changed. I swallowed and went on. "I've learned that the Founder was one of us, with Power like mine. He made a breach into that other reality—ours—to bring its energy here. He didn't know better, Jason, but what he started caused such harm, they—the entities of that reality—had to defend themselves. That's what happened to the Concentrix. Why it stopped. Why the Hoveny almost went extinct."

His gaze sharpened. "You believe that could happen here."

Never slow, my Human. "Yes. When I reconnected the null-grid, I opened a new breach. Everyone's in danger until it's closed."

"It hasn't yet," he said grimly. "There are still lights in the building you—pulled up."

"The breach will be closed." Of that I'd no doubt.

"That's not all of it, chit." His hands slipped from my shoulders to my arms. He searched my face. *What haven't you told me?*

"This can't happen again. They—the entities are instinctive. They'll seek out whatever might reach them again and destroy it. They don't comprehend life as we know it. They could—they could obliterate this system." Beneath the words, I shared my utter *conviction.* "Time's running out."

Morgan braced himself, gave a determined nod. "So what do we—" he began, then stopped. He stared down at me.

When he spoke again, it was a horrified whisper. "What have you done?"

"What I had to," I replied evenly. "The existence of the Clan in this reality is a threat—"

"They're your people—"

"They deserved to go home."

His mouth worked without sound, a flood of *anguish* filling our link. *They're gone? Our friends. Our family. Without telling me— without—*

I'd caused this: his pain, his loss. "I couldn't tell you. There was no time. The voices tried to keep us from getting here, from harm, but I was" beyond irony, "too strong for them. I had to do it, before it's too late. Return the Clan where they belong. Where they'll be—" Singers. Where they'll fly through space and dance with planets. "—happy," I finished. "What's done, is done, Jason."

<< *You saved them, my sister.* >> Rael's voice, no longer a thing of dread, but of promise.

A measure of my Human, that he straightened, his jaw working, and then bowed his head. Accepting. "Barac? Ruti."

"They're still here." That much, I thought with a pang, for now.

As I am, Human. Aryl, sure and sharp. *We've work to do, and—*

The room suddenly darkened. As one, Morgan and I turned to stare out the window.

Where there'd been sky and a building was now obscured by plumes of rising dust. Lumps began striking the window. Some stuck. Mud, I realized, watching the thick stuff slide over the transparency. Harder lumps—stone.

The Great Ones. We were out of time. "It's starting," I said, numb inside.

"We have to get to the bridge." Morgan shook me. "Sira. We need to know what's happening!"

I'd failed. We were scattered. The world was ending—

He crushed me against him, his mouth on mine, the kiss half passion, half desperation. *Witchling. We aren't done. Not yet!*

I had to find the rest of us. Mine was the greater Power. I needed—*Aryl.*

Yes. Here they are.

Our minds linked. I *reached,* finding Barac, finding Ruti, finding Degal di Sawnda'at and the others, *knowing* where to start.

And how to end this.

I concentrated . . .

. . . it wasn't a proper bridge, but this wasn't a starship. We were lucky Lemuel's guards hadn't shot us. Or unlucky, dire thought, for wasn't that a way to be done?

But the guards were preoccupied, staring, with everyone else, at a single tech, a female Hoveny with beads in her hair, hunched over a piece of apparatus. "—confirmed," she was saying.

"What is?" Morgan demanded.

Lemuel straightened and turned. "You tell me." Nes eyes went to me, cold and hard. "Tell me how the Sanctum in Goesen can be stripped bare from the inside. Tell me how buildings are pulled from underground like splinters, leaving the land above them to collapse." Ne took a step toward me. "Tell me, Founder, how a moon and everyone living on it disappear, all in the blink of an eye. Was this your doing?"

A moon? It wasn't hostility. It was terror and I shared it. If the Great Ones could do this— "I was the cause," I told ner. "What powers the null-grid is alive. It's defending itself, as it did before."

"The Fall! It's the Fall again."

I didn't catch who said it, busy watching comprehension fill Lemuel's face. "Can you stop it?"

"No, but I can end it. That's why I'm here." I looked at Destin. "It's time to go home."

Her scarred face relaxed into a smile. "Elnu's been waiting." Sona's First Scout dropped her knives to the deck, gave a graceful bow—

And disappeared.

I turned to Teris and Degal. The latter drew himself up proudly, Signy sheltering behind him. "You're wrong, Sira, as you've been from the start," he declared in his Councilor's tone, eyes glazed with emotion. "Your father knew the truth. The Clan were meant to be gods. Now, we will—"

Without hesitation, I dropped Degal di Sawnda'at into the M'hir, knowing his Chosen would follow.

Let him rule his own little box.

"So that's it?" Teris' dark eyes glistened with tears. "You've intended our destruction all along, Sira Morgan. You and your Human. I've known it since you came—"

"Hush." Her Chosen, Vael, stirred. "Have you not *heard* our little one call? We can hold her again, beloved." He smiled at me. *What do we do?*

Listen to your daughter, I told him. *Enter the M'hir. She'll be your guide.*

He nodded, taking Teris' hand in his. As the pair vanished, her despairing "Nooo!" echoed in the room.

A room full of stunned Hoveny. A legend, I'd no doubt, was in the making.

I bowed to Lemuel Dis. What could I say? What should I?

Then, I knew. "What binds us together," for Morgan was beside me, "is the better part of us all. Mother and child. Family. Heart-kin. Love. Friendship."

The Founder, remembering his fondness for the Oud and even the meddling Tikitik.

Rael, calling to me.

Enris, staying close to Aryl the only way he could.

Taisal, above all, who'd refused to free herself from the past, to help us now.

"Today, Director, that's saved you from extinction. Cherish it." Without looking, I held out my hand to Morgan, felt him take it in a firm grip. *Barac's with Ruti.* "You will not see us again."

"Wait." Lemuel looked at my Human. "I don't pretend to understand all of this—or most—" with an exasperation that made me appreciate the Director even more, "—but I know you're not one of them. You're welcome to stay, Jason. I'll find you a place, anywhere in the system."

They had starships—

Morgan's fingers tightened around mine. "I've made my choice."

Not if I'd any say in it.

"Well enough." Expression filled Lemuel's so-controlled features. It was respect. "Farewell."

Interlude

THEY FLINCHED from him; why, he didn't know. Ran, when they could, leaving inconveniently locked doors behind. It was maddening and Barac shouted after the Hoveny, using words you couldn't help but learn in any shipcity in the Trade Pact.

Words they wouldn't know. Even that satisfaction was missing. Everything was missing.

Everyone was gone. Almost everyone. To make things worse, it wasn't Ruti in his head now but—

<<Brother, come home.>>

He cursed Kurr, too, for dying in the first place, for not staying properly dead, for haunting him now, when he'd a mission. Take the ship.

In a way, he had. At least these lower decks, now abandoned. Not what the redoubtable Human would expect, but a start.

<<Brother, please. Let this go. Come home with your Chosen. Your daughter—>>

Barac slammed his forehead against a wall. Once. Again. Anything to get that foul evil thing out of his mind. He'd a duty. "A duty," he muttered, sliding limp to the floor.

"Gods, Morgan, what's he done?" Hands touched him, lifted him.

Strength followed, raw and familiar. "I'm on a mission," Barac said, very clearly.

"We're done here." And it was the Human's living voice that convinced the Clansman to open his eyes and look.

"Sira?"

She was here, and alive, which was a good thing. Dirty, but they all were.

But she was different. Older. Unsmiling.

Barac *tasted* change. He climbed to his feet with Morgan's help, then staggered, his hand going to his abused forehead. "What's going on?"

The Human did the strangest thing. Twisting a button from his shirt, he tossed it up, flickering white over white, then caught it in a fist. "Tracker," he explained. "Can't leave my pack here to cause more trouble. Then?" He looked at Sira, his face open and vulnerable.

But she was looking at the floor and didn't see.

Chapter 35

WE SAT together in Barac and Ruti's pitiful cabin. I'd have 'ported us anywhere with an open sky, if I could.

Brightfall was a ruin. Better here, than that.

Morgan had his trusty pack. He took out the Hoveny artifacts and sent them into the M'hir himself, while Ruti exclaimed over Barac's bruised head and held her Chosen close.

This wasn't how—or where I'd imagined our farewell. Not that I'd imagined one at all.

Ruti's dark eyes met mine. "Sira—"

She wanted to warn me against delay. That the Great Ones didn't know mercy or patience. That no delay would make this easier.

I nodded. "You can go."

Barac looked up. "No."

The corner of my Human's lips quirked up. "This place you belong. It sounds perfect."

It wasn't. It couldn't have him.

My cousin shook his head. "It's not that." Wonder crossed his face. "Now that I'm *listening*, I can't understand why I was so afraid. This is right. For us." The wonder left, replaced by concern. "But what about you?" A frown. "What about you both?"

Be strong, Aryl sent.

I tried, swallowing hard. "Morgan can stay here—"

NO. Flat and implacable.

You'll die if you follow me.

We'd come to our feet. My hair lashed my shoulders. His eyes were pits of despair. *Then I die. I won't live without you.*

You'd make me live without you? "I can't let you die."

Morgan shook his head. "It's what happens, chit, at least to beings like me. Think what you're asking. Even if the Hoveny can sever—even if, how long would I last, half of myself, alone here?"

"I know what I'm asking." Ruti and Barac stood. I felt Aryl's presence. Sensed their *agreement.* What we planned—was it possible? I refused to allow doubt.

I took Morgan's hand, rubbed my thumb over calluses I knew better than my own. On impulse, I pulled the bracelet from my arm and pushed it on his. "Not here," I said, uncaring that my voice shook. "We're going to send you home."

You're my home.

Stubborn as always. Precious as—Tears ran down my face, but I wasn't alone in that. "Do this for me, Jason. Let me go, knowing what we've had together. Let me go, knowing you'll live. Promise. As you love me."

Unfair.

As I love you.

He coughed. Gave a pained shrug. "Should never have taught you to be a trader, chit."

You have taught me all I've needed to know, or be.

I took Morgan in my arms and he took me. We'd no need of the Hoveny. *Aryl, a last gift, if you please.*

My hair flowed around us, soft and warm. And as our hearts beat together, as our lips met, I accepted the knowledge of my great-grandmother, who'd taken this dreadful road before me, and *cut.*

Through *love.* Through layers of Power and desires and dreams. Through to the bottom of what I was and we'd been.

Until I was alone . . . alone . . . ALONE.

Before the grief overwhelmed me, I stepped back.

Morgan shouldered his pack, getting ready to go. He

looked—how could he look the same? But that was good, I told myself as I bled inside. That was—

Then I saw his face.

Now! Aryl gave it a *snap.*

With that, the others poured their lives into me, holding back nothing, for this was our agreement: if we were to dissolve in the M'hir, these bodies to die?

We'd use our strength, all we had, first.

I formed the locate, looked into blue anguished eyes, and concentrated . . .

—Barac and Ruti fell away . . . going home . . .

—Aryl spun into the *darkness,* finding Enris . . .

—heedless of anything but Morgan, I spent myself. Lost, fraying apart, the final moment I had of that life . . .

—held his voice.

Forget me, Witchling.

Forget us.

Let go and live.

Interlude

"**U**P TO ME," Lemuel Dis stated, raising nes glass to the dour shadow that was the Tikitik Thought Traveler, "you'd be up on charges of endangering the system."

"Bah." The insufferable creature gestured disdain, bells tinkling. "The system survived."

"Despite us. Despite me." Emelen Dis held his glass with both hands. The fourth in the Director's private office, Koleor Su, sat hunched in a corner, scribbling notes. The former Keeper glanced at him. "What you write, historian? Who will understand it, once we're gone? Who will remember this?"

Those being evacuated from Brightfall, a birthplace now unlivable. Those beginning the rehabilitation of Hilip, Yont, and Oger, for gaping wounds marked where those worlds had had their buried ruins, too. Coordinated through the Hub, of course. Ne needed more staff, critically.

Tomorrow. Lemuel shrugged. "Maybe it's better to forget," ne mused. "When we rebuilt after the Fall, we couldn't move without stepping on the past, one too many wanted back again. Now we've a fresh start."

"There's no such thing." Thought Traveler barked its laugh. "We are our past, Director. Every cell of your body holds it."

Emelen put down his glass. "You can change that. Change us. Make us—"

"Better?" The Tikitik's eyes bent to stare at Lemuel. "Is this a formal request, Director? How delightful."

They would, too. For all ne knew, the Makers of Tikitna were planning their next "question" to ask of the Hoveny and the Oud, willing to wait generations for the answer.

Not this time. Ne leaned back, swirling the amber liquid in nes glass, and smiled. Cherish the bonds between, Sira'd said. As dis, most assumed Lemuel had none of nes own. Far from it.

Being SysComPrime meant having bonds to everyone— everything—that orbited this star.

And protecting them. "Your kind will be too busy, Thought Traveler," ne said, experiencing a rush of freedom as ne let ner- self chuckle. "I've authorized the reversion of Tikitna to the Oud."

Aghast silence.

"Just need to pack," Lemuel assured it. "The Oud are willing to reshape their world. We'll supply transport."

The Tikitik rose to its feet. "And where shall we live?" it roared.

Smiling felt good. "There's an empty world suited to your skills." So did losing that smile to glare. "Or you're welcome to leave the system."

They wouldn't. Together, as the Cooperative, they were more than any of their species alone. The Tikitik, no less than the Oud, were harmless if occupied. As were the Hoveny.

And this time?

Ne'd be watching.

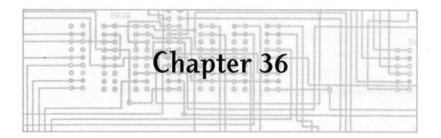

Chapter 36

Morgan

J ASON MORGAN set down his pack, ordering on the lights. He was vaguely surprised they worked.

Even more surprised he was alive. The M'hir hadn't been a beach, with waves. It had been a river, wild and infuriated. He might have been part of why.

A river that carried him here, nonetheless. A river of light, illuminated by Power. By love. That, too.

Sira. He'd seen it, felt it, the moment she'd flared like a sun—then gone dark.

Where she belonged was cold and empty. He'd never be warm again.

As you love me. She'd made him promise, Morgan thought wearily. To live, for her sake, when he wouldn't for his own.

Together, they'd given him a chance. Barac's idea, at a guess, sending him here. Ettler's Planet. His hideaway—inside the hangar, to be exact, redolent of oil and sand. No one would find him here.

Good. He didn't want to be found. Not yet. Maybe never. He hadn't decided.

What he did want was simple. Why not? "Should be some beer," he said aloud.

Something rattled in a shadowed corner of the hangar.

The Human twisted his wrist, felt the small handle hit his palm, and threw in one swift motion.

The knife clattered against the something and fell harmlessly to the floor, the sound immediately dwarfed by louder rattles and clangs as part of the shadow heaved and rose.

Dozens of black eyes caught the light, dust and sand sliding to the floor.

"There's no beer," Huido Maarmatoo'kk informed him, waving the stub where a great claw had been. "I got thirsty waiting for you." His eyes bent this way and that. "Where's Sira?"

"Sira's where she belongs. Happy."

Then, Morgan folded without grace to the floor, buried his head in his arms, and wept.

Interlude

PAUVAN DI slipped his arm around the other half of his heart, tipping his head to touch hers. "We'll be docking soon."

He felt Alisi's smile, as he felt her *strength* and *resolve*. "That's good. Isn't it, sweetling?"

Milly didn't look up from her tank of Oud. "I thought we were going home. You promised. I want my room and my things."

A room and things—and home—dropped into one of the thousands of craters scarring Yont and the other Hoveny worlds.

Among the casualties—Alisi stiffened, fighting *grief*.

Understanding, sharing it, Pauvan let her go. He went to sit on the floor by their daughter. Pebbles in the tank edged his way, ever-hopeful. "Not yet. We'll live on a station for now."

Milly looked sideways at him, lower lip caught between her teeth, then pulled the little trowel from her belt. "Will there be an excavation?"

"Not—for a while." When there was, he thought with determination, it wouldn't be to find the past, but to recover from it.

"Milly not bored. Milly has Tap Tap! Best is!" The Oud-Key spun in a dizzying circle until nes ends touched and ne toppled on nes side.

The display made the child giggle, as usual.

The strangers had brought their children. He could see their faces when he tried to sleep. Pauvan sighed. "They came with such hope. Wanted what we have: home. Family."

Alisi laid her hand on his shoulder. "It's very sad," she agreed.

"Why? Andi isn't sad."

Her parents exchanged puzzled looks. "Milly, Andi's gone," her mother explained gently, "with all her people."

"No, she isn't. I *hear* her." The child went back to staring into the tank. The pebbles of Oud rolled into a line in front of her.

Tap Tap stood nearby. "Milly *hear* others?"

A careless shrug. "When I want. They're all busy, busy. Happy busy."

The little Oud dropped, tiptoed closer, then rose again. "And Sira? Best is? *Hear* Sira?"

Pauvan held his breath, felt Alisi's hand tighten.

Another shrug.

"No."

Epilogue

THE 'FRESHER CLEANED ME of dust and debris. I stepped over the clothes I'd dropped on the floor, too tired to fuss with them.

Foam ran down my spine. I reached around, feeling a soggy mass. How odd. My hair dried itself. Didn't it?

The cabin was as it should be. Leaves and flowers covered every possible space. One section was unfinished, and I wondered what it would become. They were always a surprise, his paintings.

His—

I sat on the bed, running my hand over the blanket. I didn't need one, usually.

He—

Forget me, Witchling.

"Morgan."

But he wasn't in here. He wasn't with me. How odd. Why?

I went to the door, cued it to open.

It stayed shut. It stayed shut because he wasn't on the other side. The way the com wouldn't fill with his voice.

The way my mind was now empty of his.

Forget us.

I sat on the bed, running my hand over the blanket.

Let go and live.
"Never."

The Great Ones moved in their endless dance, AllThereIs bending and flowing and forever part of it, while singers flew and sang.

The Watcher waited.

Not her duty, this vigil. Nor was she alone in it.

The buds of Between shone and grew, those within them closer and closer to coming home. To becoming what they had been, again. Eager loved ones flew past and around, singing their anticipation.

Some shriveled, hanging loose. A warning those within would take longer to be free, caught in a dream of their own making. No matter. They'd loved ones, too, here.

None were her concern.

This was, for it was . . . new.

A single bud, armored in *darkness* that *boiled* and *hissed* and would allow no approach. Violent flashes of light illuminated it without touching, revealing something—someone—inside.

The Watcher waited.

She feared in vain.

The Clan

M'HIRAY

Ahur sud Vendan, Chosen of Sennis, Healer

Andi sud Prendolat, child, Birth Watcher

Arla di Licor, brother of Asdny, Looker

Aryl di Sarc, once Chosen of Enris, great-grandmother of Sira, inhabits her unborn

Asdny di Licor, brother of Arla

Barac di Bowart, Chosen of Ruti, former First Scout, cousin of Sira

Celyn sud Lorimar, Chosen of Kele

Cha sud Kessa'at, Chosen of Deni, died on Cersi

Degal di Sawnda'at, Chosen of Signy, *Sona* Council Member

Deni sud Kessa'at, Chosen of Cha, died on Cersi

Elba sud Parth, Chosen of Lakai

Enris di Sarc, Chosen of Aryl, great-grandfather of Sira, died on Stonerim III

Ermu sud Friesnen, Chosen of Oseden

Holl di Licor, Chosen of Leesems, mother of Arla and Asdny, scientist, Healer

Inva di Lorimar, Chosen of Bryk, Council Member

Illis sud Friesnen, child

Jacqui di Mendolar, Chooser, Birth Watcher

Jarad di Sarc, father of Sira, died on Garatis 17

Jorn di Annk, Chosen of Risa, father of Noson, Healer Apprentice to Ahur

Josa sud Prendolat, Chosen of Nik, father of Andi, scientist

Kele sud Lorimar, Chosen of Celyn

Kita di Teerac, Chosen of Vinar

Lakai sud Parth, Chosen of Elba

Lees di Annk, Chosen of Susi, father of Rasa

Leesems di Licor, Chosen of Holl, father of Arla and Asdny, scientist

Luek di Kessa'at, Chosen of Nyso

Nik sud Prendolat, Chosen of Josa, mother of Andi, *Sona* Council Member, scientist

Noson di Annk, child, son of Risa and Jorn

Nyso di Kessa'at, Chosen of Luek, (went by Gersle Nape as Human)

Oseden sud Friesnen, Chosen of Ermu

Ped di Serona, Chosen of Vidya

Pirisi di Mendolar, Chosen of Ru

Rasa di Annk, child, son of Susi and Lees, friend of Andi

Rael di Sarc, sister of Sira, died on Deneb

Risa di Annk, Chosen of Jorn, mother of Noson

Ru di Mendolar, Chosen of Pirisi

Ruti di Bowart, Chosen of Barac, formerly of Acranam

Sennis sud Vendan, Chosen of Ahur

Signy di Sawnda'at, Chosen of Degal

Sira di Sarc (Sira Morgan), Chosen of Jason Morgan, former Speaker, *Sona* Keeper

Susi di Annk, Chosen of Lees, mother of Rasa

Tle di Parth, Chooser, *Sona* Council Member

Vidya di Serona, Chosen of Ped

Vinar di Teerac, Chosen of Kita

OM'RAY

Alet di Uruus, Chooser, Tuana Clan

Charo di Nemat, Chosen of Ruis, Rayna Clan

Dama di Lorimar, sister of Tal, Tuana Clan

Destin di Anel, Chosen, former First Scout, Sona Clan

Dre di Eathem, child, son of Gricel and Oluk, brother of Yanti, friend of Andi, Amna Clan

Eand di Yode, Chosen of Moyla, former Council Member, Healer, Sona Clan

Ecra di Annk, Chosen of Hap, Rayna Clan

Elnu di Anel, Chosen of Destin, Sona Clan

Eloe di Serona, unChosen, Tuana Clan

Ghos di Eathem, Chosen of Worra, father of Gricel, *Sona* Council Member, Healer, Amna Clan

Gricel di Eathem, daughter of Worra and Ghos, mother of Dre and Yanti, Amna Clan

Gurutz di Ulse, Chosen of Merr, Scout, Sona Clan

Hap di Annk, Chosen of Ecra, *Sona* Council Member, Rayna Clan

Japel di Rihma'at, Chosen of Odon, mother of Noil, Sona Clan

Klor di Edut, Chosen of Nyala, Sona Clan

Kunthea di Mendolar, Chosen of Nockal, *Sona* Council Member, Tuana Clan

Merr di Ulse, Chosen of Gurutz, Sona Clan

Moyla di Yode, Chosen of Eand, former Council Member, Sona Clan

Nockal di Mendolar, Chosen of Kunthea, Adept, Tuana Clan

Noil di Rihma'at, unChosen, son of Odon, Sona Clan

Nyala di Edut, Chosen, former Council Member, Sona Clan

Odon di Rihma'at, Chosen of Japel, father of Noil, *Sona* Council Member, Sona Clan

Oluk di Eathem, Chosen of Gricel, father of Dre and Yanti, Amna Clan

Ruis di Nemat, Chosen of Charo, former Keeper, Healer, Rayna Clan

Taisal di Sarc, mother of Aryl, Speaker Yena Clan, died on Cersi

Tal di Lorimar, brother of Dama, Tuana Clan

Tekla di Yode, Chosen of Ures, Sona scout, died on Cersi

Teris di Uruus, Chosen of Vael, *Sona* Council Member, Sona Clan

Ures di Yode, Chosen of Tekla, died on Cersi

Vael di Uruus, Chosen of Teris, Sona Clan

Worra di Eathem, Chosen of Ghos, mother of Gricel, Amna Clan

Yanti di Eatham, daughter of Gricel and Oluk, sister of Dre, born on *Sona*

HOVENY

Alisi Di, Heart-kin of Pauvan, mother of Milly, Seesor

Aracel Dis, edican

Emelen Dis, Goesen's Sanctum Keeper, Sect of the Rebirth

Gerasim Su, Emelen's helper

Koleor Su, Historian

Lemuel Dis, Director, SysComPrime, Hub

Milly Su, daughter of Alisi and Pauvan

Nermein Dis, Senior Tech, Brightfall Comm

Oncara Su, Emelen's pilot

Pauvan Di, Heart-kin of Alisi, father of Milly

Sorina Din, Head of Reclamation, Raynthe (moon)

Susibou Di, Lemuel's scantech

OTHER SPECIES

Jason Morgan, Human, Chosen of Sira

TapTap, Oud, Oud-Key Prime

Thought Traveler, Tikitik